When the Tiger Kills

Vanessa Prelatte

H & S Underveq, LLC

This is a work of fiction. Names, characters, corporations, institutions, organizations, events or locales in this novel are either the product of the author's imagination or, if real, used fictitiously. Any resemblance to actual persons (living or dead) is entirely coincidental.

When the Tiger Kills
by
Vanessa Prelatte

For information address:

H & S Underveq, LLC
1525 Park Manor Blvd., STE 295
Pittsburgh, PA 15205

When the tiger kills, the jackal profits.
(Afghan proverb)

Prologue

The young man exploded out of the driver's side of the red SUV like a tornado just beginning to hit its rope stage, throwing off sparks of energy in all directions as he shot around the hood toward the passenger side of the vehicle. But it was the girl who emerged next that riveted the spectator. Tall but slender, swathed almost from head to foot in a long black leather coat, she tossed her head as she exited the vehicle, throwing over her shoulder a shower of long blond hair so light it glinted like platinum in the autumn sunlight. Smiling, she linked her hand with the boy's as they sprinted into the store.

The watcher smiled too. He called himself Michelangelo, and he had just found the latest incarnation of his ice goddess.

Chapter 1

"I hated the little creep, but I didn't want him dead. It wouldn't have suited me at all, Officer."

Dawn Cimarron briefly considered reminding the witness that her proper title was *Detective*, but decided it wasn't worth the extra effort. She had been up since two in the morning, ever since she had received the call that had summoned her to Lewellen Memorial Park, where Cullen Torrense, Gwen Mallinder's late, and – based on her reaction to his death – apparently unlamented stepbrother, had been found lying dead under a cluster of aspen trees. Lying there clad in his silver jacket, he had reminded Dawn of a huge, elongated Idaho potato, wrapped in foil and ready for the oven. A shower of golden leaves had rained down from above and lay like pats of butter on the body, almost obscuring from view the handle of the lethal switchblade that protruded from his ribcage.

After finishing with the crime scene and breaking the news to the next of kin, Dawn and her partner were now interviewing friends and family members of the deceased. Gwen Mallinder, the stepsister, was turning out to be a fount of information, despite her strained relationship with the victim.

Gwen's hair, a fire engine red with inky black tips, was cropped in a sleek cap that framed her small, gamine face. A gold nose stud, a diamond eyebrow ring, and some sort of weird, geometric tattoo that wound up the left side of her neck made her a dramatic contrast to Dawn, who wore no jewelry but her wedding ring, used minimal make-up, and had her dark brown hair tied up in a knot on the back of her head. It wasn't the most flattering look for her, but that was okay. She didn't want to look like a beauty queen when she was on the job. She wanted to look like a cop.

Within a few moments of meeting Gwen, Dawn had gotten the distinct impression that Ms. Mallinder had little use for her fellow women, and that she would rather focus her attention on the other half of the team – namely, her good looking partner, Sergeant Rafe Melbourne.

"Oh?" Dawn responded to Gwen's comment in a carefully neutral tone of voice. "If you hated him so badly, why wouldn't you want him dead?"

Gwen eyed her scornfully. "Well now, that's easy. I wanted him alive and kicking so that he could go on torturing his ghastly mother and suck all the life out of the witch. Incidentally, how did she take it when you told her that Cullen is dead?"

"She fainted."

Gwen brightened up at the news. "Really? Did she hurt herself when she fell, I hope?"

"No. She's fine, but we had to call a doctor to treat her when she regained consciousness. She became so hysterical that she had to be sedated."

"Sounds like Monieque. She's the original drama queen. Anything for attention. And her son? Well, here's what I have to say about him: Good riddance to bad garbage."

"You don't believe in mincing any words, do you?" said Rafe.

"Why should I? I know you don't seriously suspect me; if you did, you'd have hauled my ass downtown for this interview."

She was wrong about that, he reflected. Probably came from watching too many cop shows on TV. But it wouldn't do to let her in on that. So Rafe decided to string her along.

"Got me there," he said. "So tell me all about your baby brother. Why did you hate him so much?"

"Stepbrother! He was my stepbrother, not my brother!"

"Sorry," Rafe said patiently. "Why did you hate your *stepbrother* so much?"

Gwen leaned back and took a drag on her cigarette before she answered. "Because he was a monster, that's why. And his mother is the Frankenstein who created him."

She settled herself back in her chair before continuing. "My mother died when I was twelve. A year later, my father met Monieque. Before even a week had passed, she had moved in on us, and brought her obscene little offspring with her. Cullen was eleven at the time. Within a month, she had convinced my dad to marry her. And things started going wrong from then on."

Gwen stared off into space, as if trying to connect with the ghost of her younger self. "We lived in a nice house with three bedrooms. There was the master bedroom, another nice, big bedroom, which was mine, and a smaller bedroom that Cullen moved into. And right from the get-go, he started whining. 'Why do I have to sleep in the little bedroom? Why can't I have the bigger one?'" As far as Monieque was concerned, what Cullen wanted, Cullen got. At night I'd hear her working on my dad. 'Don't you think that it would be nice if Gwen learned to share a little more? She's had that bedroom for thirteen years. It's selfish of her to expect to have it always. Why don't we let the children take turns? One of them gets the big room for a year, then they swap. Don't you think that would be the fair way to handle things?'"

Gwen hitched a pillow a little more comfortably behind her back before continuing. "One day a few months later, I came home to find that Cullen had moved into my room. All of my things had been tossed into the little bedroom. And there was Cullen, giving me that sly little grin of his and crooning, *'told you I'd get my way, told you I'd get my way,'* the nasty little turd!

A tear slid down Gwen's eye and her voice caught as she went on, "I played right into his hands, of course. I grabbed him and tried to force him out of my room. I'd dragged him as far as the doorway when I saw my dad and Monieque come in through the back door. Suddenly, he dropped down hard on the floor and started bawling his head off, screaming that I had hit him, knocked him to the ground, and tried to wrench his arm off. Monieque knocked me aside and started shrieking, 'What have you done to my baby? What have you done to my baby?' Meanwhile, my dad had this shocked expression on his face and was looking at me as if he didn't even know me."

The tears were trickling down her face now, leaving sooty black tracks as her mascara began to run. "That was just a preview of the hell that I had to live in for the next few years. What I wanted didn't seem to matter anymore; it was all about Cullen. I've never met anyone else so determined to have his own way. And his mother? She was hell-bent on enabling him."

A smile of malicious satisfaction crossed Gwen's face. "But you know the old expression, 'What goes around, comes around'? Well, I'm happy to say that it all came back to bite Monieque in the butt. As Cullen grew older, he became totally unmanageable. Lying, cheating, skipping school, shoplifting – that's what he started with. Then he graduated on to alcohol and drugs. Of course, Monieque tried to shield him from the consequences. She covered for him, lied for him. And then he started stealing from her. Finally, she tried to rein him in. She waited until Dad was out of town on business, and then she confronted him. Cullen just rolled his eyes and walked out on her. Right after that was the first time he got arrested for possession, but she got him a good lawyer who made sure that all Cullen had to do was go through a drug counseling program. Monieque thought that he was cured when he finished it, but he was arrested again not long after. Sure enough, all they did was send him back to counseling. After that, Monieque tried to restrict his activities, keep him from getting into any more trouble. But he responded by screaming that he didn't have to listen to her and telling her to shut up. Up until then he'd never been anything but apologetic and charming to Monieque, so I could see that she was totally shocked when Cullen started to defy her. However, beyond yelling at him and sending him to his room, she didn't discipline him or impose any other sort of consequences at all, so naturally he just kept getting worse. He was always sneaking off at night, getting into more trouble. When my dad tried to intervene, Monieque would go off on him, telling him that Cullen was *her* child, and Dad had no right to interfere."

With a savage motion, Gwen stabbed out her cigarette in the ashtray on the coffee table. "One night a little over two years ago, my dad was driving home from work. I'd talked to him on the phone just before he left. He'd finally had enough, he said. He was going to divorce Monieque. If she got some of his property and savings in the divorce, that was fine. He just wanted her and Cullen out of his life. I was so happy. I waited and waited, but he never made it home. His car went off the road on a bad corner, flipped over, and crashed into some trees. He was killed immediately."

Rafe had been listening patiently, but now he interjected, "When did you last see Cullen?"

But Gwen apparently wasn't ready to go back to the subject of Cullen yet. Getting up out of her chair and pacing the room restlessly, she picked up her story where she had left off. "I moved out right after the funeral. I was eighteen by then, just about ready to go off to college. We found out that Dad had changed his will shortly before he died. Originally, Monieque had persuaded him to leave everything to her.

But he changed it so that I got half of his estate, and he also made me the sole beneficiary of his life insurance policy. It was a hefty amount, too. I thought Monieque was going to have a stroke when she found out! Anyway, there was more than enough for me to move out, get my own place. I haven't seen much of either of them for a long time, which is fine with me. I ran into someone from the old neighborhood last spring, though, and she told me that Cullen had recently been arrested again. This time the judge gave him a choice: go to jail, or check into a residential rehab facility. Monieque hit the roof because the rehab facility was horribly expensive, and when Cullen was released, she refused to have him back in the house." Gwen stopped her pacing, shrugged her shoulders, and sat down again. "I thought that maybe being away from Mommy would do him some good, but I doubted it." Finally, she answered Rafe's question. "Not long before I ran into the neighbor, I saw Cullen while I was running in the park. When I saw him, I turned and went back the way I came. The last thing I wanted to do was to have any sort of conversation with Cullen."

"Was anybody with him when you saw him in the park?"

Gwen frowned for a minute, as if she was searching her memory, then she said, "Yeah. He was with a guy who used to come over to the house a lot – kid called J.B."

"Do you know J.B.'s real name?"

Gwen frowned. "His first name is really weird. Jabez? Jabo? No - Jago. That's it. I think his last name is Bolt."

"What were Cullen and J.B. doing?"

"What they were always doing, I suppose - drugs. Cullen had started out just smoking weed, but as he got older, he developed himself a nice little cocaine habit. J.B. was his supplier. Like I told you – that's why Cullen started stealing: to pay for the drugs."

"What about girlfriends?" Dawn interposed.

"Cullen was too in love with himself to have time for anyone else. He never had any girls over to the house, as far as I know."

Rafe caught Dawn's eye and rose from his seat. "Thank you, Ms. Mallinder. We appreciate your willingness to help."

Gwen Mallinder crossed the length of the room to take the hand that Rafe held out to her. "You're welcome, Sergeant. If I can be of any … assistance in the future, please let me know."

On their way out to the car, Dawn commented, "Didn't have any trouble remembering *your* title, did she?"

Rafe grinned and responded, "You're just jealous."

"Jealous? Oh, please – get real." She was tempted to add *Raphael*, but decided that the provocation hadn't been enough to justify calling him by his despised first name. And despite the teasing, they were both perfectly well aware that their own relationship went back too far and verged too close to being family for there ever to be even a remote chance of a romantic relationship between them. She knew, however, that his rugged good looks were extremely attractive to most of the other members of her sex. Rafe was not handsome in the classic sense, but his muscular build, strong, rough-hewn features, black hair, and cobalt-blue eyes had their own type of appeal. The end result was that it was a rare female witness who could resist opening up if Rafe decided to flash his mega-watt smile and pour on the charm.

"Getting back to the subject of the rude Ms. Mallinder, I think that her experience with her stepmother has left her with some definite trust issues when it comes to women. Did you believe her, Rafe?"

"About wishing Cullen was still alive so that he could go on torturing his mother? Maybe. Seems to blame the mother for the situation more than Cullen himself. No, I don't think that Gwen had anything to do with her stepbrother's murder. I'm putting my money on Cullen's buddy, J.B."

Men were so stupid. At least, that was what Lee was thinking as she strolled down the path from the campsite she and Will had set up. They had been eating food straight out of a can, and she had commented that her roommate had called Jason a pig once when she had caught him doing that. Well, the mention of her ex's name had been enough to make Will blow up. Okay, she had been thoughtless to bring Jason's name up, but after all, they were sooooo over. She hadn't seen or even thought about him for months. And now, here was Will, going all ballistic on her just because she'd happened to mention Jason's name.

As she turned the corner, she caught sight of the artist sitting at his easel. He was sitting at the very edge of the cliff, dabbing oil onto a canvas as he worked on a landscape of the river valley below. As she'd done when she'd first encountered him a little earlier in the day, she sidled up behind him and perused his work. It was good – really good. She'd considered asking him if she could buy it when he finished it, but she was afraid to ask, in case it was outrageously expensive. He was working on the background now, catching the treetops far below, all but the evergreens vivid in shades of orange and yellow and red, now that autumn was at its peak. Without looking up from his work, the artist asked, "What do you think?"

"It's wonderful, Michael." He'd laughed when he'd seen her reaction to his real name – Michelangelo. "Call me Michael," he'd said.

After cleaning his paintbrush, he commented, "I'm about ready for a break." He reached into the cooler beside him, pulled out a beer, and unscrewed the top. Taking a long pull, he pronounced, "Ah, that was good." With a gesture of good manners that Lee appreciated, he asked politely, "Want one?" At her nod, he reached back into his cooler, pulled out another bottle, twisted off the cap, and handed it to her with a smile. She thanked him and was taking her first sip just as Will, the scowl on his face signaling trouble, stormed down the path toward them.

Questioning Jago Bolt was not going to be easy, Dawn mused as she drove home that evening. No one had answered when she and Rafe had knocked on the door of his apartment, and they had discovered from a neighbor that J.B. had left early that morning for the airport in order to catch a flight to Florida. Since it was already near end of shift, and they had been up since the wee hours of the morning, they decided to head over to Dawn's house and take a dinner break before tackling the paperwork on the Cullen Torrense case.

A glance in her rear view mirror showed Dawn that Rafe was right behind her, sticking to her rear bumper like an industrial grade swatch of flypaper even through the worst of the traffic. As for the others who were tailing her – they were being discreet tonight. She'd had barely a glimpse of them as she maneuvered through the heavy rush hour traffic.

She smiled a little as she remembered the house she had lived in before she married Ty. A modest one-storey house in a working class neighborhood, it had been only a fifteen-minute drive from work. She didn't regret the decision to relocate to the other side of town after her marriage, though. She needed to keep a distance between the two sides of her life. Most of her fellow cops had no problem with the change in her circumstances after she married Ty. There were a few, however, who couldn't resist making snide comments about it, possibly motivated by jealousy. Or maybe something else. Her father-in-law, Sloan Lewellen, had made more than one enemy as he had built a string of family-owned companies into the entity now known as The Lewellen Group, one of the largest conglomerates in the country.

A few more blocks to go: then she was turning into the gated community where she and Ty had built their home. She nodded to the guard on duty, then made a few more turns until she turned into a cul de sac, and the graceful house swam into sight. Achieving that graceful look had not been easy, but it had been worth it. Looking at the house from the outside, no one would ever guess that it was actually two houses – identical in every way – structurally, if not aesthetically.

Ty had wanted to pay for the entire cost of constructing the house, but she had insisted on paying half. She had barely touched the settlement money she'd been awarded from a wrongful death lawsuit her aunt had filed on her behalf after the tragedy that had robbed her of her parents and her siblings. It had been sitting in a trust fund for years. When she'd told her husband that she planned on dipping into it so that she could meet her half of the expenses for building the house, he had tried to talk her out of it at first. He'd inherited a mind-boggling amount of money when his grandfather had passed away a few years before, so he hadn't seen any reason for her to tap her trust fund at all. She had been adamant, however, and in the end he had given in. She'd been happy to let him deal with the builders and the other contractors, though. He'd offered them all sorts of incentives and bonuses for quick results, so the house had gone up in record time. They were both more than satisfied with the end result.

Pulling into the driveway and parking in the garage on the right, she got out and walked back to meet Rafe so that they could walk in through the front door together. As she unlocked the door, she could hear a combination of barking and whining that told her that she stood in peril of being pounced upon momentarily.

Rafe joined her in the foyer. Inside, there were two inner doors, and Dawn proceeded to open the one on the left. A blur of movement resolved itself into a tan and white cocker spaniel, which launched itself upon her, licking her enthusiastically.

"Okay, Traitor, okay. Gee, didn't anyone pay any attention to you all day?"

"I still can't believe you named your dog *Traitor*."

Dawn cast a scornful glance at Rafe. "You already know the story. She was supposed to be *my* dog. I'm the one who rescued her, took her in, gave her a home. So you'd think she'd be grateful, right? But no – she took one look at Ty, and it was *looove* at first sight. Now she barely even acknowledges me when he's around." Dawn narrowed her eyes suspiciously at the dog. "Why are you so happy to see me? I know he's home – he texted me just a few minutes ago."

Mrs. Tilner, the cook/housekeeper that she and Ty employed, arrived on the scene just then and answered the question. "Your father-in-law arrived early. He brought the baby with him. She went down for a short nap, but they spent most of the afternoon playing with her. And she's still afraid of dogs, so Traitor has been either outside or stuck back in the kitchen with me for hours."

Dawn gave the dog a few pats before nudging its paws off her legs, taking its jaw into her hand, and commenting, "So that's why you're so attentive suddenly. Got banished again, didn't you? Serves you right." Traitor just wagged her stump of a tail in response.

"Where are they?" Dawn inquired.

"Upstairs. The baby just woke up from her nap. They both went up to get her."

Turning to Rafe, Mrs. Tilner said, "You look hungry. I made appetizers. You want some?"

Dawn waved Rafe ahead of her into the kitchen. "You go ahead. I'm going to run upstairs for a few minutes." She heard a noise from Ty's den as she made her way to the stairs. Looking in, she saw that the baby monitor, equipped with both video and audio, was still on. There stood her husband, Tyrell Lewellen, all six feet two of him, holding a toddler in his arms. He must have just picked up his little half-sister from the crib they had set up for her in one of the spare rooms, because Dawn could see the baby's small fists knuckling her eyes as she strove to drive the sleep out of them. Ty's voice on the monitor was crystal clear, as if he were standing right there in the room with her as he kept up a running monologue, the only possible form of communication with a small fry who had only recently celebrated her first birthday.

"Hey, don't look at me like that," Ty was saying. "I'm the one who saved you from being named *Angharad*, remember? Or *Iseult* – that was the second choice. *Tegwen* was in the running there too for a while. Yes, ma'am, when Dad was throwing around names like that just after you were born, I piled the guilt on the old man for the name he'd saddled me with until he gave you a nice, pronounceable name like *Echo*. Even if it does sound like we both just stepped out of the pages of a Louis L'Amour novel, it's better than what it could have been. Do you know that he was actually thinking of naming me *Aneirin* at one point when he was going through one of his 'Let's remember our Welsh heritage' stages? Can you imagine going through basic training with a name like that?"

"I don't imagine that she can – or ever will," Sloan Lewellen remarked as he strolled into view. Besides, I've never understood why you object so much to your name. Has a certain ring to it, don't you think, Echo?"

Ty put his ear close to the baby's lips and nodded a few times. "What's that?

Uh-huh, Uh-huh... Echo thinks it's bad enough that you named me *Tyrell*, without sticking *Kilkenny* in the middle of it."

His father just grinned and held out his arms. "Hand her over, son." Tyrell complied, and Echo was soon cradled in the arms of her father. "I thought I heard Dawn and Rafe come in," Sloan commented.

"Yeah, me too. Time to go down and see what Mrs. Tilner has made us for dinner, Echo. Not that you'll be getting any of it – not until you grow some more teeth, kid. It's baby food, baby food, and more baby food until then."

In the kitchen, Rafe popped a stuffed mushroom into his mouth and savored the taste. Hearing a noise, he turned just as Sloan and Tyrell Lewellen walked into the kitchen together. It was obvious at first glance that the two men were related; they had the same brown hair, strong jaw, and hazel eyes. But there the similarities ended. At six foot four, Sloan weighed in at 195 pounds. Barrel-chested and imposing, he emitted a powerful and rather intimidating aura, only partially diminished by the fact that he was holding a tiny baby in his arms. He wore his hair closely cropped, and the flecks of gray that were liberally sprinkled throughout its length were quite absent from his son's head of hair, which was slightly longer and had a tendency to stick up on the crown of his head, due to a stubborn and almost untamable cowlick.

Tyrell, who at six foot two was a couple of inches shorter than his father, was also much leaner at 167 pounds. In fact, when the two of them were together, it was not unusual for people to form the mistaken notion that Tyrell was not nearly as formidable as his powerful father. Appearances were deceiving, however. Ty might lack his father's bulk, but he was whipcord tough and roped with solid muscle. The training he had received in the martial arts and his years of experience in the military also gave him an edge. In fact, as Rafe had discovered as he grew to know father and son better, Ty was actually the far more dangerous of the two.

There was nothing dangerous about him now, however, as he smiled at his housekeeper and inquired, "What's for dinner, Mrs. T?"

"Beef Wellington, roasted red potatoes, some lightly seasoned asparagus, and a nice fresh salad." With a conspiratorial glance at Tyrell, "I made a double fudge chocolate cake for dessert. We can have ice cream with it."

Ty's face lit up with pure delight. "Mrs. T, you're the best. The ultimate. The…"

Whatever further accolades Ty was planning to add were interrupted by the entrance of Dawn, clad now in black jeans that hugged her long legs and a bright crimson sweater that complemented her dark brown hair, now set free and worn loose around her shoulders.

Rafe watched as Dawn kissed her husband, embraced her father-in-law, and commented on how much Echo had grown since she had last seen the baby. In his own private mental catalog, he counted one of his blessings in life the ease with which Dawn's husband and family had accepted him as one of their own. Ty had been a little guarded at first, until he had realized the truth – that Rafe was no threat to his relationship with Dawn. Since then, he had treated Rafe as if he were Dawn's older brother, which, in fact, Rafe guessed was pretty close to the truth.

They sat down to dinner, enjoying the good food and each other's company. Sloan entertained them with stories of the projects he was currently working on. The conversation would soon have grown boring had another man been talking about his latest business dealings, but Sloan invested them with the sort of wit and charm that stood him in good stead and had made him so successful in his business. Success, he maintained, had more to do with charming people into cooperating with your ideas than with facts and figures and numbers. Those were important, of course, and had to be correct, but if you couldn't sell your ideas to others, you were doomed to failure. The Lewellen Group had thrived under his leadership, grossing billions in revenue each year, and remaining relatively invulnerable to market fluctuations or recessions.

After the last piece of chocolate cake had been consumed, Rafe and Dawn excused themselves and took their coffee over to the alternate dining room on the other side of the house. The reports and other paperwork on the Cullen Torrense murder and the other open cases they were working on needed to be dealt with. Some of it couldn't wait until morning.

Sloan and Ty, meanwhile, took Echo downstairs. After arranging her in a playpen and providing her with her favorite toys, they decided that a game of pool was in order.

"You still planning on coming to the board meeting next week?" Sloan asked as he prepared to break.

"I promised, didn't I? As long as you keep your promise, I'll keep mine."

"What promise?"

"The one about living forever."

Sloan took aim at the five ball. "I'll try. But let's face it, son. One day you may have to take the helm of The Lewellen Group."

"People are living longer these days, you know. You take care of yourself, you could live to be a hundred and six."

As the five ball swished into the pocket, Sloan commented, "It was different when you were in the Air Force. You were following a career path that didn't leave you any time to be involved in the business. I understood that. But now that you've retired from the service, it's important to consider the future, and what role your holdings in The Lewellen Group will play in that future. You already own 25 percent of the company, Ty. Your grandfather saw to that. When I go, you'll have another 30 percent. That's a controlling interest, son. I know that the business world doesn't exert the same kind of pull on you as it does on me. You might never want to sit in the big chair yourself. But you need to understand how everything works in order to be prepared to choose the right person to succeed me, when the time comes."

He missed a shot at the ten ball, and Ty took over.

"Three ball in the side pocket." As he prepared to take the shot, Ty said, "I still think you're going to outlive me."

"Why?"

"Only the good die young, Dad."

Father and son were equally skilled, and the resulting match was therefore close, but Sloan prevailed and beat Ty by the slimmest of margins.

As he was bundling Echo up to take her home, Sloan commented to Ty, "What's wrong with Dawn?"

"What do y' mean, 'What's wrong with Dawn?' Nothing's wrong."

"She never asks to hold the baby. Doesn't she like kids?"

"Of course she likes kids. Come on, Dad, don't make an issue out of this!"

After his father had left, Ty wandered upstairs to check on Dawn. He entered the bedroom that she had decorated in shades of gold and white and turquoise, with occasional splashes of vivid red. He stood by the bed, picking up a framed photograph from the nightstand and gazing down at it pensively. It showed a happy family group. The father, big and blond, with a wide and generous mouth, his arm flung around the mother, petite and dark. Standing in front of them a boy of ten, his arms folded, pure mischief gazing out of his dark eyes. Next to him, Dawn at eleven years old, holding the last member of her slaughtered family, a tow-haired baby who, from a distance, could pass as Echo's twin sister.

Setting the photograph back down on the nightstand, Ty headed out of the bedroom and down to Dawn's kitchen, then crossed over into the dining room. Case notes and other paperwork were scattered all over the table, but there was no sign of Dawn or Rafe. He wandered on through the adjoining rooms and finally found Dawn stretched out on the couch in the living room. She opened one eye when he entered.

"Rafe go home?"

He got only a sleepy nod in reply.

"You planning on sleeping down here?"

She yawned and sat up slowly. "I was just going to lie down for a minute. I couldn't face the stairs."

"You ready to go up now?"

"Yeah. I guess so. Just give me a hand up."

Ty pulled her up off the couch and placed a companionable arm around her. Dawn leaned her head on his shoulder as they made their way to the stairs together. "I never got a chance to ask," she said sleepily. "How did the doctor's appointment go today?"

"Pretty good, actually. Doc says that he'd place my recovery rate at 97%, which is pretty good, considering that right after the accident they were telling me I might have to use a cane to get around for the rest of my life."

"What about the pain?"

He shrugged. "It's not been a problem lately."

She absorbed that, then said, "Ty? Was your father giving you grief again about why I don't interact very much with Echo?"

He hesitated for just a fraction of a second before answering. "Yeah, a little. I told him not to make a big deal about it."

"I just can't seem to deal with it. Maybe when she grows out of babyhood, it will be different. But right now, the resemblance is just so strong..."

"Don't worry about it."

"I try not to, but I don't want it to become an issue between you and your father. It's my problem, and I need to learn how to handle it. Maybe I'll bring it up with Nolan and Sylvia next time we see them."

"If you want to, fine. But don't worry about it. Seriously. I can handle Dad."

"Okay. Right now, the only thing I want to worry about is catching up on my sleep. It's been a long day. And tomorrow looks like it's shaping up to be just as busy. Lately, it seems like Rafe and I barely have the time to scratch the surface on one case before we get the call to take on another one."

He'd been mad before, but now Will was seething. He didn't like this Michael. The guy gave him the creeps. And he didn't like the way Lee was looking at the guy, stars in her eyes, just because the guy was an "artist". He didn't even like the guy's beer, for crying out loud. Give him a lager any day, not this pale, light crap. He didn't like to drink when he was on a camping trip anyway, so he'd taken only a few polite sips before surreptitiously pouring out most of the beer behind the rock he was sitting on while the guy's back was turned. And Lee – what was wrong with Lee, anyway? You'd think she'd had half a dozen beers instead of one, the way she was stumbling around and giggling like a silly little girl. Disgustedly, he set his beer bottle down, just as Lee crumpled to the ground. At Michael's move toward her, he jumped up, growling, "I'll take care of her." But he wasn't that steady on his own feet now. What was wrong with him? As he stood there, trying to clear his head, Michael moved in, landing a kick straight into his gut.

Chapter 2

Dale Thrushton was not a happy man. He usually enjoyed his job as park ranger, but he'd taken up the profession to spend time in the great outdoors, not to roust a bunch of good for nothing college kids out of the main camping area, where they'd been wrecking whatever they could get their hands on and tormenting families with young children throughout the previous night. By the time he'd set everything to rights and gotten back home, it was almost nine a.m. The shattering fight he'd had with his wife when she'd awakened him after he'd only had a couple of hours of sleep, insisting that he take his turn and watch the kids while she ran next door for coffee with a neighbor, had just been the last straw. She didn't seem to get it, what sleep deprivation could do to a man. He'd grabbed his car keys and stormed out. When he was angry, nothing calmed him like driving. He'd chosen this part of the park because, despite the narrow roads and hairpins turns, the scenery was breathtaking.

As he rounded a bend, a patch of red caught his eye through the trees. A tent. Someone was doing primitive camping way up here, and he wondered whether they had bothered to register with the park office. Sometimes people didn't, because the penalties for not doing so were ridiculously light. The park land had been willed to the city as part of a trust set up by a man named Tucker Borstall. Old Borstall was a descendant of the first settlers of Mountpelier, and he had hated big government, taxes, and regulation of any kind. As a result, he had stipulated in his bequest that the maximum fine that could be charged someone who camped on the land without permission was twenty dollars. So it wasn't surprising that many campers just went directly to their campsites without bothering with the formality of registering.

Dale parked his jeep and got out, with the intention of making sure that the campers had secured their food properly. Attacks by mountain lions and bears in this part of the state were rare, but not unheard of, and improperly storing food was one of the best ways of attracting them. When he reached the tent, however, no one was there. That made him uneasy, though he couldn't have told anyone why. For some reason, he walked to the cliff edge and looked down. Nothing. He was relieved. Then, just as he turned to go, something caught his eye downstream to the left. Another patch of red. Walking a little farther downhill so that he could see it more clearly, Dale pulled out his binoculars and focused. There. He saw the body – red sweater, blue jeans, sneakers. Running quickly back to his car, he radioed for help. Then he grabbed his emergency kit and began to don his climbing gear.

Dawn was already at her desk, working on her computer, when Rafe walked into the bullpen a few minutes before the start of shift. He got himself some coffee from the break room before strolling over to her desk. Looking over her shoulder, he was surprised to see her studying intently a photograph of Monieque Torrense. Something about her expression made Rafe exclaim, "You've got to be kidding. You're seriously taking a look at the mother for this one? Why? I told you, the missing Mr. Jago Bolt is our man. Unless you buy that it's a coincidence that he just happened to jump on a plane for Florida within hours after the murder."

Dawn swiveled around in her chair to face him. "I know, I know. But there's something off about her, Rafe. You know how she just crumpled and fainted when we went over and broke the news about Cullen to her? There was something about it that just didn't feel right to me."

Rafe looked skeptical. "It's hardly surprising that she fainted when we told her that her son was dead. I've seen it happen time and time again when I've had to notify next of kin. You've seen it yourself on more than one occasion. Remember when we had to notify Rochelle Brandtner's parents that their daughter had been killed? Her mother fainted dead away."

Dawn inclined her head thoughtfully. "I remember. I also remember Jaclyn Aultmore."

"Who's Jaclyn Aultmore?"

"A girl I went to high school with. Any time there was a test scheduled that she wasn't prepared for, she faked a faint. She'd just be walking along when suddenly, down she'd go. Her parents would come and pick her up, take her to the doctors. They did all sorts of tests on her, but never found anything. Some of us knew what she was up to, but we never said anything, because she was popular enough to make life hell for anyone who ratted her out. Anyway, when Monieque Torrense fainted, it triggered something in the back of my mind. Couldn't put my finger on it at first, but then this morning I finally got it - she reminded me of Jaclyn. The way she went down, it was kind of graceful, you know? Jaclyn used to do it that way too."

Rafe frowned and considered for a moment, then nodded in agreement. "Okay. Your instincts are usually good about things like this. We'll take a hard look at Monieque Torrense. Meanwhile, what about the physical evidence? Did we get anything back from the lab?"

"Not yet, but I just got off the phone with Ramón. He promised to have the results to us by the end of the day, at the latest."

Though his face betrayed nothing, Rafe was grinning to himself in his head. Ever since Dawn had helped Ramón Ouray's wife get a job in the accounting department at Sloan Lewellen's downtown headquarters, the chief lab tech had been far more accommodating than he had been before. And when it came to closing cases, getting the lab results quickly was key. However, since Dawn was sensitive about exploiting her connection with her father-in-law, he contented himself by merely saying, "That's good news. Maybe the results will be in by the time we get finished testifying in the Brandtner case."

"Yeah, I was thinking the same thing." Glancing at the clock on the wall, Dawn said, "We might as well head over to the courthouse. The ADA wants to go over our testimony with us one last time before we go on the stand."

After Dawn had finished giving her testimony, she headed out of the courthouse. She was hopeful that the jury wouldn't take too long to find Allyn Brandtner, the defendant, guilty. Brandtner, the married father of two, had called 911 six months previously, claiming that he had come home late from work to find his wife, Rochelle, bludgeoned and beaten to death in their bedroom. The kids, fortunately, had been spending a week at their grandparents' house. After questioning Brandtner, Dawn and Rafe had discovered that his story contained enough holes to drive a truck through. He had lawyered up quickly after that, but forensic evidence and an alibi that just didn't hold water had been enough to get an indictment for second degree murder. Dawn was confident that the evidence was overwhelming enough to secure a conviction.

Rafe had finished his testimony much earlier and had gone to the morgue in order to be present for the autopsy of Cullen Torrense. They had agreed to meet back at headquarters once she finished her own testimony. Therefore, she was surprised to see her partner walking up the courthouse steps toward her as she exited the building.

"What's up?"

"Quite a few things. Walk with me, and I'll fill you in." On the way to the nearby parking garage, Rafe began, "First, there were no surprises at the autopsy. Cause of death was just as it appeared at the scene. Second, the fingerprint analysis came back on the knife that was used to kill Cullen. Handle had been wiped, but the perp didn't do a thorough enough job. Ramón found a partial at the point where the handle meets the blade. When he went looking for a match, guess what he found? Print belongs to Cullen's good buddy, Jago Bolt."

"Well, well, well. What a surprise."

"Yeah. The lieutenant is working with the DA's office to get an arrest warrant. Hopefully, it won't take too long for the Florida cops to run him to earth. If we get lucky and he waives extradition, we could have him back here in a couple of days."

"Anything else come back from the lab?"

"Not yet. Still waiting on the hair and fiber analysis."

"You said that there were a number of things going on. Anything else?"

"Yeah. Hold onto your hat, partner - we just caught another case. Call came in right after I got back from the morgue. Attempted murder. Young man, late teens or early twenties, badly injured. Apparently, someone pushed him off a cliff and left him for dead. We need to get out to the scene. Let's take your car; it's more comfortable."

Dawn was not surprised to see her husband standing among the members of the search and rescue team when she and Rafe arrived at the crime scene. A career-ending injury may have caused Ty to opt for early retirement from the regular Air Force, but he had joined the Civil Air Patrol, its civilian auxiliary, as soon as he was pronounced sufficiently recovered to fly again. And providing emergency services such as assisting in search and rescue operations was number one on the list of CAP's three fundamental missions. In addition, CAP's services were increasingly being sought by various government agencies, including local law enforcement.

Mark and David, two members of Ty's team, were carefully transporting the victim to the top as Dawn and Rafe approached the cliff side. Ty nodded to them, but kept his attention focused on his team. Three patrol officers and a man dressed in the garb of a park ranger were also closely following the actions of the rescue team. After making sure that the scene was properly secured, Rafe hailed one of the patrol officers, Addar "Snake" Jordan, who walked briskly over to them.

"Hey, Jordan, what have we got here?"

"Park ranger over there – Dale Thrushton's his name – called it in. He spotted the kid, climbed down, and discovered that he was still breathing. He did what he could for the kid while he waited for the search and rescue guys. Kid kept drifting in and out of consciousness, and Thrushton got enough out of him to confirm that it wasn't an accident."

The ranger had walked over to the trio in the meantime and arrived in time to hear the last part of Jordan's statement. Nodding to the others, Thrushton picked up the story. "He was only conscious for a brief time. I kept asking him, 'What's your name, son? How did this happen?' He never told me his name. He just kept repeating, 'Pushed me. Tried to kill me. But it's Lee he's after. You have to find Lee.'"

Their attention was distracted as the search and rescue team crested the top of the cliff with the unconscious victim. Paramedics quickly took over, placing the young man gently on a gurney, checking his vital signs, and administering emergency treatment. Dawn and Rafe were able to talk to them briefly before the paramedics loaded the victim onto the waiting helicopter, but they were unable to glean any additional information. The victim was still out of it, and unlikely to regain consciousness anytime soon. Rafe, after looking at the victim's hands, ordered them to be bagged and requested that the hospital personnel follow proper procedures regarding his clothes. Anything else would have to wait for a more propitious time. After everything had been secured, they watched as the rescue helicopter, with Ty at the controls, took off for the hospital.

The helicopter Ty was currently flying was his own, one of two he had purchased for the use of the team, outfitted with all of the latest technology available for search and rescue missions. Although CAP maintained its own corporate fleet, there had been no squadron in Mountpelier before Ty had formed one, so, like many other members of the Civil Air Patrol, he regularly made his own aircraft available for missions mounted by the local CAP squadron.

After the helicopter had left, Dawn and Rafe made their way to the tent that had presumably been occupied by the victim, since the crime scene techs had just finished photographing and processing it for evidence. It was a small sports dome tent, about 7x7 at the base, that looked like it could sleep two or three people comfortably. A double sleeping bag occupied the center of the tent. To one side lay a portable catalytic heater; on the other side, a rechargeable battery lantern, a first aid kit, and a green backpack stamped with the logo *Mountpelier University*.

Rafe focused on the backpack first. "Only one backpack." He rifled through the contents quickly. "No wallet. No ID. Extra pair of socks, underwear, T-shirt, sweat shirt. All male. But only enough for one. Double sleeping bag says two."

Dawn nodded. "The other one was probably this 'Lee' the victim kept taking about. Lee can be either a male or a female name. A couple of college kids, probably, taking a long weekend alone. And they must have had a vehicle. No way that they hiked up here carrying all this stuff."

A voice calling Rafe's name drew them outside the tent once again. Walsh, one of the crime scene techs, was waiting for them.

"We've found something near the point where we believe the victim was pushed over." He led them to a spot where a clump of bushes grew. "Found a tube of green oil paint in there. And see these puncture marks here? Given the oil paint and the placement of the marks, I'm guessing that someone had an easel set up here, and quite recently too. And over here?" He led the way to a rock nearby. "We found a beer bottle set down beside the rock. There was another one lying on its side over there." He gestured to a spot a few feet away. "But the interesting thing? Someone poured out the contents of most of a beer behind this rock. See that indentation in the rock? The beer gathered there in a little pool. We were able to bag a good amount of it for analysis."

"That it?"

"Uh-uh. Come on over here." He led the way behind a small grove of nearby trees. "See that?" he said, pointing down. "Ground's too hard here to leave any usable impressions, but it's just disturbed enough so you can tell that someone had a vehicle parked here recently. Big one too. Maybe a pickup truck. And look at this." Like a magician pulling a rabbit out of his hat, Walsh pulled out an evidence bag and waved it under their noses. Rafe caught a glimpse of something sparkly inside. "What do ya think of that?"

Rafe squinted. "What exactly is it?"

"It's a jaw clip," Dawn responded.

"A what clip?"

"A type of women's hair clip. A pretty fancy one at that," Dawn commented, taking a closer look at the hair ornament as it sparkled in the sunlight. "Not the sort of clip you would usually take on an ordinary camping trip. Unless it was also a big, hot date." She met Rafe's eyes. "I'd be willing to bet that we've just found the first trace of 'Lee'. Girlfriend, probably."

Rafe pondered for a minute. "That was good work, Walsh. Did you already send a sample of that spilled beer you bagged to the lab?"

"Not yet. We were waiting so that we could send all the evidence in together."

"I'm going to have one of the patrol officers take the beer sample in right away. I've got a funny feeling about it..."

"You think it might have been drugged?" Dawn interposed.

Rafe nodded slowly. "The victim – He's a big kid. Wouldn't have been easy to take down. Drug him first, you've got a big advantage."

"Except he didn't drink all of the beer."

"Yeah. He might have put up more of a fight than the perp bargained for."

Dawn frowned as her phone signaled just then. "It's Ty. Let me go and take this. He might have some news from the hospital." She moved a little distance away just as Walsh returned to update Rafe.

"I sent Gomez in with the sample and called the lab. Told them to put a rush on it. They griped a little and complained about their backlog, but that's just routine for them. They'll come through for us in the end." He frowned as he noticed Dawn on the phone a few yards away. "How is she managing to get reception on her cell phone here? This part of the park is a dead zone for cell reception."

"She has a Satphone. No problem getting reception anywhere if you have one of those."

"Oh, well, that explains it. We have a couple of them, but they're older and much bulkier. That one looks just like a cell phone. Maybe we can get one or two of those put into the budget for next year."

He thought for a moment, then said, "Sergeant... about the missing car. Do you think she could have taken it? The girlfriend?"

"Still trying to play detective, Walsh?"

"C'mon, Sarge. We've known each other a long time. You know I'll keep my mouth shut. Won't say anything to anybody, especially the media. Humor me."

Rafe rolled his eyes heavenward. "I don't know why I put up with you, Walsh. Probably because of the entertainment value. It's way too early to be speculating like this. But – just to humor you: suppose 'Lee' was the victim's girlfriend, and she got away while the perp was trying to take the boyfriend out. If she'd made it to the car, she would have jumped in and tried to get away immediately. She wouldn't have gone into the tent first and grabbed all her things. Besides, if the beer was drugged? She'd have been in no shape to run, let alone drive a car."

"You think the perp planned it all. He had it all set up in advance."

"Maybe. It's early days yet, but it's starting to lean that way."

"Ty says that the victim is in surgery." They both focused their attention on Dawn as she rejoined them. "He talked to the paramedics who treated him and some of the other personnel at the hospital. The victim is in bad shape. Head injuries. Shock, hypothermia. On top of that, he's got a dislocated shoulder, a broken leg, and a couple of cracked ribs. But get this: kid had bruises all over him that are inconsistent with the fall. And you were right about the damage to his fists, Rafe. According to one of Ty's sources, it looks like he had been in a hell of a fight."

Rafe turned back to Walsh. "We need as much information as possible, and as quickly as possible, from all the evidence you've collected. How long before you're done with the scene?"

"We're almost finished now and ready to take it all back to the lab."

"Okay. Keep us posted."

As Walsh walked away, Rafe began to walk along the cliff, staring at the valley below. "The car's the key. Find the car, run the tags, we identify the victim. Find out who his girlfriend is. Prints from the beer bottle might tell us, but only if they're in the system. Once we identify them, start interviewing family, friends. When and where were they last seen? Trace their movements. Perp may have stalked them. Knew they were planning to go camping this weekend, knew where to find them. Find a witness who noticed someone taking an unhealthy interest in the pair of them. But first, the car. We need to find that car. Problem is, it's a big park. Where to start?"

Dawn replied, "It's not going to be easy. Remember the Chandra Levy case? They searched Rock Creek Park over and over looking for her, but her remains weren't found until a year later. And that park was minuscule compared to this one. On top of that, I talked to Thrushton again after I spoke with Ty. He says that they're way short-handed right now. Two of the park rangers are out with the flu, another is in the hospital recovering from emergency surgery, and a fourth left yesterday to attend his father's funeral in Phoenix. The search and rescue team will bring in the dogs and set up a search grid, but if the perp put the girl in a vehicle, the dogs won't be able to do much. And the victim's car? It could be anywhere."

"We could ask your Uncle Pete for help," Rafe reflected. "He may be retired, but after forty years as a park ranger, he knows this park better than anyone else alive. Ask him to put himself in the perp's shoes. What's the most logical place to hide a car?"

Dawn considered the idea. "It'd take about twenty-five minutes to get to the house from here. I could have Ty refuel and meet us there with the helicopter. We take Uncle Pete up with us, we have a better shot of finding the car quickly. Yeah, it's a good idea, all right. I'll call ahead to let them know we're coming – and why."

They had to consult with the remaining patrol officers and crime scene people before they could leave the scene, so it was actually more than forty-five minutes later before they approached the large ranch house currently occupied by Pete and Mattie Nevo. The wooden frame house stood in the middle of a meadow hollowed out in a bowl on the side of a mountain. A line of trees marched down a slope to the left and rear. A rustic split rail fence enclosed the ranch house. The facade of the dwelling sported an A-Frame roof at the center portion and spread out into two wings on either side. A stone chimney graced the left-hand side of the structure. Directly under the gable formed by the A-Frame stood the front door, with a plaque to the side bearing the name *Cimarron*. However, Dawn betrayed no emotion as she walked up and knocked on the door of her childhood home. Rafe noticed, however, that she kept her gaze focused straight ahead, not looking at the breathtaking scenery. Especially not toward the far edge of the meadow, where the land dropped away sharply and where, he knew, a stream flowed below.

The woman who answered the door would never have been described as pretty. Her face was too strong for that. Dark, piercing eyes dominated a broad face with a strong, square jaw. Rich, short chestnut hair softened the effect a little. Then the wide mouth broke into a huge smile, giving the strong face enormous warmth. Before uttering a single word, she reached out and enfolded them both in a huge embrace.

"Come in, come in! Pete's waiting for you by the fire. You go on and join him while I go make us some coffee. I'll slap together some toasted ham and cheese sandwiches for us too."

"I don't think we'll have the time, Aunt Mattie," Dawn began.

"Of course there's time. Tyrell's not here yet, is he? And you've got to eat sometime. Why not now?"

Dawn exchanged a look with Rafe, and then, with a sigh, followed Mattie into the kitchen. Rafe, in the meantime, walked down the hall and into an enormous living room, where he found Pete Nevo comfortably ensconced before the fireplace.

The scowl on Pete's craggy face may have intimidated some, but Rafe was wise to the act, and knew that underneath his fierce exterior, Pete had a heart as soft as marshmallow cream.

"You don't come around to visit nearly often enough," Pete growled in his gravelly voice.

"Haven't you been reading the papers? Crime rate is way up. Dawn and I barely have a chance to catch our breaths nowadays, let alone pay calls on grumpy old men."

"Who are you calling old? I could still take you down if I had a mind to, Rafe Melbourne."

"Out of the room for sixty seconds, and they're already starting a pissing contest," Mattie commented. Can't you give it a rest, even for a minute?"

Her husband grinned at her. "Mattie, my one and only love, engaging in pissing contests is as natural as breathing to us. You wouldn't want the men in your life to be unnatural, would you?"

"I'm not even going to dignify that remark with a reply. Why don't you make yourself useful and take that tray from Dawn? You can set it down on the coffee table."

They settled down to eat the sandwiches and drink some of Mattie's excellent coffee. Rafe's mind was elsewhere, though. Dawn's face may have been carefully composed, but her eyes kept straying to the object on the wall next to the fireplace. A measuring stick had been set up there, and it was obvious that at some time in the past, a couple of proud parents had kept careful track of their children's progression in height as the years went by. Three names were marked off at intervals, with dates scrawled beside each one. *Dawn. Josiah. Marina.*

Despite her pretense at impassivity, Rafe knew that Dawn's thoughts, like his, were back in the past. Nearly sixteen years ago now, but as fresh in his memory as if it had been yesterday.

He'd been much younger then, a rookie just out of the academy, and Pete and Mattie had not even met yet, let alone gotten married. He wouldn't even have been at the scene, except for the fact that he'd been out having dinner with his Uncle Nick when the call came in.

He'd walked into the park ranger's office with Nick and spotted the girl right away. Pete, though a stranger to her at that point in time, was stationed protectively by her side. She was filthy, shivering, and soaked to her skin. Huge dark eyes stared blankly into space, shock deep within them. As Nick strode toward her, she shrank back in her chair, and Pete moved to stand in front of her. Nick flashed his badge and introduced himself quickly: "Detective Nick Melbourne. You get anything else out of her?"

"No. Only what I reported on the phone. At first, she kept repeating over and over, 'They killed my brother, they killed Josiah; he's dead.' But for the last half-hour, she's just sat there. Can't get a word out of her."

Nick sidestepped neatly around Pete so that he could crouch in front of the girl.

"What's your name, honey?"

The terrified eyes took in first him, then Rafe, standing behind a little to the left of his uncle. Seeing her eyes fasten on Rafe, Nick sought to reassure her. "That's my nephew, Rafe. My name's Nick. What's yours, little girl?"

That got a response. "I'm not a little girl. I'm twelve years old. Why did you bring your nephew with you?"

"Because he's a policeman, just like me."

"You're not wearing a uniform. Neither is he."

"I'm a detective. We generally don't wear uniforms. And Rafe – well, he usually wears a uniform, but he's off duty right now."

Still her eyes were on Rafe. Nick sensed that a connection had somehow been made, so he motioned to Rafe to move forward a little. Rafe got down on one knee so that he was at eye-level with the girl.

"Would you let me see your uniform sometime?"

"Sure thing. But first we need to know your name, and what happened to you."

After a brief hesitation she whispered, "Dawn. My name is Dawn."

After a little prodding, she'd told him her last name, and where she lived. She'd told them enough to have Nick call for back-up, and when it arrived, they'd sped out to the Cimarron ranch. He would never forget the sight that greeted them. Not just her brother, but her entire family destroyed, wiped out...

A throbbing, humming noise like that of a thousand bees descending on a field full of clover called Rafe back to the present. Mattie cocked her head toward the door and announced, "Tyrell's here."

As one, they moved toward the big picture window, just in time to see Ty set the sleek black helicopter down in the middle of the meadow.

Dawn, Pete, and Rafe scrambled into their coats, said goodbye to Mattie, and headed toward the waiting helicopter. Climbing aboard and getting themselves strapped in and settled was a work of mere moments. Then the big bird was aloft again, with Pete up front next to Ty, and Dawn and Rafe seated behind them. All three of them had their binoculars out, scanning the terrain below, looking for any sign of the missing vehicle. Pete had already picked out some spots he thought they should check out, but it was unlikely that they would be able to canvass all of them before the light failed.

As the sun started to descend slowly toward the horizon, they finally had to change course and head back. Three of the areas that Pete had pinpointed had been thoroughly scanned, without any positive results. As Ty set the helicopter down once again in the meadow next to the ranch house, Dawn noticed that her car was not parked where she had left it. Giving Ty the laser eye, she inquired, "Okay, Mr. Highhanded Busybody: What happened to my car?"

"Being a far-thinking person and in the interest of saving the police from wasting valuable time, when I got the call to meet you here I arranged for someone to come out and drive your car back to town. Anything to help out the boys and girls in blue, you know." When he noticed her reaction, he said, "You know, you roll your eyes entirely too much, Dawn. It's probably bad for you. I'm going to look it up on the Internet when we get home."

Dawn stopped herself from grinding her teeth with great effort and preserved a dignified silence as Ty took the bird up again and headed toward Nyetimber, the airfield where he'd established his local headquarters for the private charter company he had founded, Lewellen Air.

Just as Ty set the helicopter down at Nyetimber, Rafe's cell phone signaled an incoming call. Checking the caller ID, he commented, "Well, well. It's Gwen Mallinder. Wonder what the world's most acrimonious step-sister has to say?"

While Rafe walked a few steps away to take the call, Dawn turned to Ty. Feeling that he deserved some payback for not consulting her before arranging to have her car picked up, she informed him, "I'm going to have to use your car. Rafe and I need to put in a few more hours tonight. Looks like something is breaking on another case we're working on."

"The Torrense case? The kid who was found stabbed in the park?"

Dawn nodded. "That's the one." As Rafe walked back in their direction, she could tell that whatever Gwen Mallinder had told him was hot. So she held out her hand for Ty's car keys and said goodbye, knowing that the fact that he'd have to make other arrangements to get home wouldn't inconvenience him one little bit. What a pity.

Once they were seated in the car, she turned to Rafe and said, "So give. What did Gwen Mallinder have to say?"

"You're going to love this one. Turns out that Gwen got a letter today – from Cullen."

"From Cullen?"

"Uh-huh. And from the postmark, it looks like he mailed it just before he was murdered."

Chapter 3

Michael examined the cuts and bruises on his body, tuning out the pain by forcing himself to look at them from an artistic point of view. After that first kick, instead of collapsing like an accordion the way he should have, the boy had fought back like a rabid wolf. Michael had the cuts and bruises to prove it. If the boy's balance hadn't been compromised, Michael doubted he'd have been able to take him down. In the end, his timing thrown off by the drugged beer, the boy had aimed a punch at him that he'd been able to sidestep, then land a blow that caused the boy to stumble back to the very edge of the drop-off. His arms had flailed wildly as he attempted to recover his equilibrium, but his efforts had been to no avail as he lost the battle with gravity and plummeted over the cliff.

Why hadn't the drugged beer worked this time? It had worked on the girl. She had been dazed, almost unconscious when he had turned to check on her. The boy should have been out of it as well, allowing Michael to search the pockets of his jeans for the car keys before helping him over the edge. He'd had a bad moment when he realized that the keys might have gone over the cliff with the boy. If he hadn't found them in the pocket of a parka back at the tent, his carefully laid plans would have been ruined. But he had found them, so he'd been able to proceed as planned. Another sign that the goddess was with him.

At first, he'd thought about sending the car over the cliff right then and there, after he'd removed all of the girl's belongings from the tent. But then he realized that it would be too suspicious. Sooner or later the authorities were going to identify the boy, and his friends, no doubt, would inform the cops that the girlfriend had been along on the camping trip. If the police then found the boy and the car, but not the girl, they'd automatically suspect foul play. If the car were missing as well, however, there were all sorts of other possibilities. The two of them could have had a fight, for example, and she'd taken off in the car. It was too bad that she'd had an accident and had then gotten lost trying to reach help on foot.

It was the most likely scenario, and to give credence to it, he'd removed all of the girl's possessions from the tent and placed them in the SUV. After carefully removing the batteries, he'd taken all the electronic devices with him too. From what he'd read, it was possible to trace their signals as long as they were powered up and active.

He'd chosen the spot for the boy's SUV well. A bad curve with a copse of trees below. With any luck, they wouldn't find it until spring.

Before he'd left the campsite, he'd taken his dirt bike out of his pickup truck and tossed it into the back of the SUV. Once he'd found the spot where he intended to crash the SUV, he'd removed the bike and then sent the vehicle over the edge. Then he'd ridden the dirt bike back to the campsite. A quick look in the back of the truck had assured him that the girl, whom he'd taken the precaution of tying up, was still unconscious. After that, it had been easy. He'd simply driven out of the park and made his way to the house that he had rented in advance.

He'd had a bad moment this morning, though, when he'd heard on the news that the boy had survived. A few minutes' reflection had been all that was necessary to calm himself, however. The boy was in a coma. He wouldn't be able to tell them anything. Besides, there was nothing to tie him to the artist named Michael. He'd been careful to change his appearance, after all. On top of that, they hadn't identified the boy yet, and there had been no mention that he'd been accompanied by his girlfriend. Michael could afford to wait for a little while and see how everything played out. It would be a pity to have so little time to spend with this latest incarnation of the goddess. Only after the appointed time of preparation had passed was he wont to release her spirit and fuse her mortal body completely with winter's frosty embrace. However, he was a realist. Sometimes hard choices had to be made. He might have to cut down the period of preparation this time...

Only a second after Dawn and Rafe had knocked on her door, Gwen Mallinder opened it to let them in, saying impatiently, "I thought you'd never get here!" Thrusting out a piece of paper toward Rafe, she said, "Read that!"

"Just a minute, Ms. Mallinder," Rafe said. "Let's all sit down first."

Gwen waved them impatiently into chairs in the living room and waited while Rafe pulled on a pair of gloves. Only then did he accept the letter. Holding it where both he and Dawn could see it, Rafe read Cullen Torrense's last communication to his stepsister:

Dear Gwen,

I'm writing this letter to you because I know you won't open any emails or read any texts that I send you. So I figured hey – you don't have to put your name on an envelope sent by regular mail – just the return address. Since I was pretty sure you wouldn't recognize the return address of the apartment I'm living in now, I decided to give it a shot. If you're reading this, I guess it worked, huh?

You're probably wondering why I'm bothering to get in touch with you at all. Well, I've got a couple of reasons. First, I wanted to apologize to you. After I got busted the last time, the judge ordered me into rehab. I've been in rehab before and I always just went through the motions, but this was a residential program, and it was different. There was a therapist there I really connected with. He convinced me to do one of those twelve-step programs, and I'm sober now for the first time in years. To make a long story short, I've reached the step where you have to make amends to people you've wronged in the past. Since I've realized that I was a selfish, spoiled brat who made life miserable for you the whole time that we lived together, I wanted to let you know that I'm sorry. I know this is probably a big surprise to you, but I've changed some since you last saw me. After your dad died and you moved out, I got a taste of what it was like for you. My mom was really angry when she found out that your dad had changed his will and his insurance beneficiary before he died, and with you two gone, she took everything out on me. Big surprise for me, but maybe not for you, I guess.

Anyway, the second reason I'm writing is actually more important. I guess I started thinking about contacting you after I went over to the house last week to try to mend things with my mom. You heard she kicked me out, right? Well, when I showed up on her doorstep, she was talking to Mrs. Lillipinner across the street. As soon as she saw me, she raced across the street, threw her arms around me, and started crying and hugging me at the same time. So I was thinking that everything was going to be fine. But it all changed once we got inside the house and nobody was watching. She told me that she didn't know why I had bothered to come back, unless it was for money, and I wasn't getting another penny out of her. Then she started ranting and raving that I was nothing but a disappointment to her, and she wished I'd never been born. She told me that she'd met someone while I was in rehab. In fact, she was getting married again, and her fiancé had a wonderful son whom I couldn't hold a candle to, so she didn't want me around anymore, especially when they were there. Finally, she told me to get out and never come back.

Well, needless to say, that shocked me. But it scared me, too, and here's why. When my dad died, he left me some money. It's all tied up in a trust fund, and I can't touch it for a couple of years – not until I'm 21. Anyway, one day, not long before she kicked me out, I was going through my mom's desk. (I won't lie to you – I was looking to see if I could find some money. You can probably guess why.) I didn't find any money, but I did find something else that surprised me. I found a copy of the trust with a note clipped to it. The note was in my mom's handwriting, and it said "Find out what happens if C. dies before he's 21." Well, that made me feel a little uneasy, but I was arrested for possession not long after, and I had other things on my mind for a while. Lately, though, I started thinking about it again. I told you that my mom was furious when she found out that your dad had taken her off as the beneficiary of his life insurance policy and put you on instead. She was counting on that money, Gwen. She raged for weeks, talked to lawyers, schemed and schemed for a way that she could cut you out and get that money. I'd never been afraid of her before, but she really started to scare me. And then one night when she'd had a little too much to drink, she said that you got the double indemnity only because of her efforts, and you didn't deserve it. When I questioned her about it, she told me to shut up. But she'd gotten me curious, and when I started to think back, I remembered something else.

I was at home that whole week, right before your dad was killed, remember? I was suspended from school because of the stink bomb incident. Well, I never told anyone this, but a few days before the accident, right after you left for school one morning and your dad was out watering the garden, I saw my mom doing something under the hood of his car. My grandpa – my mom's dad, was a mechanic, and Mom knows a lot more about cars than you'd think. Well, after she finished what she was doing and shut the hood, she saw me standing there watching her, and boy did she get mad! She told me not to tell your dad that I saw her even touching his car, because that car was his baby, and he'd be really angry at her. Then she sent me to my room. But I sneaked down again later after your dad drove off to work. She was in the garage again. She scrubbed the garage floor with some sort of industrial strength cleaner and then hosed it off. She did that every day that week, Gwen, always after you'd left for school and your dad went to work. I'd never seen her do such a thing before, and I never saw her do it again afterward, either. So I got to thinking: What if she did something to the car, something that caused the accident that killed your dad? What if she did it so she could collect on the life insurance?

And another thing. I talked to my dad's lawyer, and he says that if I die before I'm 21, my mom gets the money in the trust fund. That got me to thinking – what if she's planning to get rid of me too?

So I was wondering if maybe I should go to the police. Would you go with me? With my record, they probably wouldn't believe me, but if you go along they might take me more seriously. Anyway, I thought you would want to know, if not for my sake, then for your dad's. Please get in touch with me. And again, I'm sorry.

                                                                Cullen

PS I think she might have killed my dad too.

When they had finished reading the letter, Gwen demanded, "Well, what are you going to do about it? That bitch killed both Cullen and my dad! I want her arrested, and I want it now!"

Rafe looked at her steadily. "Ms. Mallinder, I think that investigating the possibility that your stepmother is responsible for Cullen's murder, as well as for your dad's death and that of Cullen's own father, is worth exploring. However, the contents of this letter aren't enough for us to get an arrest warrant."

"But you do believe it, right? I was afraid you wouldn't – the part about Cullen, at least – what with Monieque being such a doting mother and all."

"We are investigating multiple avenues with regard to Cullen's murder, Ms. Mallinder. We have not eliminated anyone as a suspect yet, including Cullen's mother. The statements contained in this letter appear to be credible, and we will be following up on them, including Cullen's allegations regarding the deaths of your father and his. You have my word on that. In the meantime, it would be wise for you to have no communication with your stepmother. Don't confront her. Let us do the investigating. We'll be thorough, I promise you. If there's anything to Cullen's suspicions, we'll do our best to uncover the evidence. Only hard, solid evidence that we can take to the DA will get us an arrest warrant."

Gwen looked straight into his eyes for a moment, then nodded. "Okay. I won't do anything on my own, unless I discover that you're just stringing me along and sitting on your asses doing nothing. In that case, I'll do whatever is necessary to get some action – go to the press, whatever. I want revenge. I want to watch that bitch fry in the electric chair for what she did to my father!"

Rafe thought about telling her that capital punishment in Colorado was carried out by lethal injection, but decided that now was not the time.

Gwen got up from her chair and started pacing the room restlessly. Taking some deep breaths in an attempt to rein in her emotions, she said presently, "You know, it never occurred to me that she had anything to do with my dad's death. I thought it was just an accident."

"Did the police determine the cause of the accident?"

"I don't know. If I ever saw the police report, I don't remember what it said. I guess I was in shock. I do know that they determined that it was an accidental death. I mean, he hadn't been drinking or anything." She paused for a minute, frowning in concentration. "My dad – he'd bought and restored one of those old classic muscle cars – a 1971 Plymouth Barracuda. I think it suffered some sort of mechanical failure, but I'm not sure exactly what. I don't know much about cars."

"What about Cullen's father? What do you know about his death?"

"Not much. Neither he nor Monieque ever mentioned the cause of his death, and I'll confess that I wasn't a bit curious about it." She pondered for a moment, then added, "You know, Cullen had an aunt he kept in touch with. She was his dad's sister. Her name is Ellanor Torrense. Monieque hated her, so at first I was a little surprised when she actually let Cullen go and visit her sometimes, but later I figured out why she was being so unusually accommodating. Ellanor Torrense is loaded. Monieque was probably angling for her to leave her and Cullen a nice chunk of change in her will."

"Can you tell us how to get in touch with her?"

"I don't have her contact information, but if she's not here already, she's on her way. She's not the kind that would miss the funeral. It shouldn't be hard to locate her. She'd know more about how Cullen's father died." After a short pause, she said, "I'll keep my mouth shut about the letter to everyone else, but I need to show it to Cullen's aunt. She has a right to know."

"Agreed. When we find out where she's staying, we'll give you a call, set up a meeting. It's too late to do much tonight, but we'll make it a priority tomorrow. I promise you that." He rose to his feet. "Thank you, Ms. Mallinder. We'll arrange for a meeting with Cullen's aunt as soon as possible. We'll also look at the police report on your father's accident and speak to the lead investigator on the case. In the meantime, sit tight and wait to hear from us. We'll be in touch."

Once they were back in the car, Rafe commented, "Looks like your instincts were right on the money, D.C."

Dawn suppressed a smile at the mode of address he'd used. From long habit, Rafe usually called her by her given name when they were alone. However, he referred to her by her initials when they were around other police officers. It was the norm established by Nick Melbourne when she had joined the force. She could still picture Nick when he'd dropped her off for her first day at the police academy saying, "You're going to need a nickname. Otherwise, some joker around here is going start calling you 'Cim' or 'Cimmy' or some other sissified variation of your last name, and we can't have that. So let's go with D.C. You got any objection to that?"

She hadn't, of course. Nick was her inspiration, her mentor. She'd have gone along with just about anything he'd suggested back then. And although nowadays Rafe sometimes called her by her nickname even when they were alone, she understood that his use of her initials on this particular occasion was a sort of compliment, an acknowledgment of her skills as a detective.

Knowing that he wouldn't want her to make a big deal about it, however, she didn't comment on it, merely responding, "The contents of the letter sure seem to confirm that Monieque Torrense may be something other than the grief-stricken mother she appears to be on the surface. I'll be interested in finding out if there's a connection between her and Jago Bolt. And the reports on Gwen's father and Cullen's dad might make for some mighty interesting reading."

"Yeah, but that's for another day. You know what Nick used to say: 'A tired cop is more likely to end up as a dead cop.'" Let's put it away for the night, get some sleep, and pick it up in the morning."

Once she had dropped Rafe off at his place, she made her way home. Ty was still up, but taking Rafe's words to heart, she said good-night and went straight up to bed. As she lay there poised just at the edge of consciousness, the image of the ranch and the memories associated with it rose to the top of her mind. Then, as she went over the edge into slumber, the memories melted into dreams, and dreams transitioned into nightmares...

The child was running as fast as her little legs could carry her, but she was not even three years old yet, and the bear was gaining on her, getting closer and closer as the seconds ticked by. Soon, very soon, it would be upon her.

Dawn stood on the far side of a stream, watching as a twelve-year-old phantom of herself desperately raced into the water. She had to get across before the bear caught up with the child, snatch her up and get the baby to safety. But as she reached the middle of the stream, she got stuck. Looking down, she saw long, black weeds twined around her legs, holding her back. She had to free herself from them before she could get to the other side of the stream and rescue her sister. Impatiently, she bent down and grasped a handful of the weeds, trying to tear them loose and free her legs. But instead of weeds, she was holding hair in her hands, clumps of long black hair that was just like her own. She looked down again into the flowing water, refusing to believe her eyes at first. And then she recognized what she was looking at, and she heard herself, as if from a great distance away, give a long keening wail of anguish..

Heart pounding, sweat pouring down her back, Dawn pulled herself out the depths of the dream. She reached for Ty, but her groping hand found nothing but empty space. A little shakily, she raised herself to a sitting position, unfolded her legs over the side of the bed, turned on the light, and picked up the photograph that sat on her nightstand. Slowly, she traced their faces, her mother's and Marina's. This is how she wanted to remember them, laughing and happy on a carefree summer day.

Forcing the nightmare out of her head, she placed the photograph back on the nightstand, stood up, and crossed into the adjoining bedroom, where Ty was sprawled out exactly in the middle of an ocean-sized bed. She pulled back the covers and slipped in with him, cuddling close, seeking his warmth like a frozen woman. At the first touch of her body, Ty immediately awakened.

"Nightmare?" he said. A sound of assent from Dawn.

"Bear again?" Another murmur of assent.

Ty put on his best official voice: "No bears in here, ma'am. Just us horny, lecherous, aggressive military types, that's all."

He got a poke in the ribs for that one, but he heard the laugh she tried to suppress, and felt some of the tension drain out of her.

Later, after he could tell that she slept again – which was a small miracle in itself, since she usually slept better when she was alone in her own bed - he rolled onto his back and propped his head on his hands, musing on all the steps that had led them to this point on the thorny path of marriage.

Getting her to marry him – that had been easy. Getting her to agree to *remain* married to him - now that had been difficult - almost as difficult as a military op. And they would never have gotten married in the first place, if it hadn't been for the wild streak that lay buried beneath Dawn's cool surface, a wild streak that she indulged in only in the company of a select group of people she absolutely trusted.

He'd been surprised that day when she'd asked him to fly her to Vegas. Dawn and Vegas? Not exactly a combination that he would have put together. But he had complied eagerly, gotten the best accommodations at one of the top hotels, and joined her in a nonstop excursion of drinking, dancing, and gambling. Finally, she'd turned to him and said, "That's it. I'm busted. No more gambling. So what do you want to do now?"

He hadn't gotten the reputation for being the quickest-thinking pilot in the Air Force for nothing.

"How about getting married?"

She'd blinked at him, nodded once or twice, and replied, "Great idea. Let's go do it."

It was Vegas. It was so easy.

The next day they had scarcely made it out of bed, and the sharp edges of time had been blurred as they reveled in a sexual marathon that had precluded anything even resembling rational thinking. The following day, however, it had been a different story. Dawn had shaken him awake and told him in a voice verging upon panic that she hadn't been thinking clearly for the last couple of days, and she was having second thoughts. In short, she wanted a divorce, and she wanted it now.

Knowing that her past history had made her wary of forging long-lasting attachments that held within them even the remote possibility of loss, he had been expecting something of the sort, so she had not caught him unprepared. He'd had his campaign all mapped out in advance, and he had never engaged an opponent in battle with more finesse than he used that day to persuade her into giving the marriage a chance. He'd zeroed in on her as he listened patiently to her explanation of why she wanted to dissolve the union: according to her, the whole thing was doomed to failure because they had rushed into it and never talked about all the important marriage things - things like finances and kids, future goals and mutual compatibility. Then he'd gotten around her by doing the one thing he usually avoided like the plague: he'd talked about his feelings. How he'd never felt this way about anyone before, ever in his life. How he was sure she felt the same way about him. Some people never found that. Why throw it away without giving it a try? When he saw that she was weakening, he went for the green light. As soon as they got back to Mountpelier, he'd promised, they'd contact a marriage counselor and discuss all the things couples were supposed to discuss when they were considering marriage. If, after a year, they found that they weren't compatible enough to remain married, he'd give her a divorce. That had done it. Admitting that she loved him too much just to walk away, she'd agreed to give it a try.

Secretly, he'd been hoping he could avoid going through with the marriage counseling bit. He realized he'd been way too optimistic after they'd returned home and moved in together. Within weeks, it became obvious that they needed help. Serious help.

Fortunately, they had found the right couple to counsel them. Sylvia and Nolan Drizedale had been a godsend, helping them thread their way through the minefields of their first year of marriage. Advising them to build the duplex had been one of their strokes of genius. Both he and Dawn had been pretty set in their own ways. With the duplex, he was free to do what he wanted on his side, and she on hers. It was working. But even if it hadn't, he would have found another way. Because there was no way he was ever letting go of Dawn Cimarron. Not after everything that they had been through together.

Still, just in the interest of fairness, when their first anniversary rolled around, he'd reminded Dawn that he had promised her to give her a divorce if things didn't work out. He'd been gratified at her startled look. She'd totally forgotten about it, which was just fine with him.

"There's no way I'm ever going to divorce you," she'd told him flatly. "You're stuck with me, Tyrell Lewellen."

Since she'd put it that way, he'd persuaded her to have a second ceremony, this time with some family and friends in attendance, and renew their vows. She'd agreed, telling him that it was a good idea, since she could barely remember the first ceremony. So they'd done it, and this time they had pledged to spend the rest of their lives together. Always and forever, they'd promised, and it was a small miracle that, given her commitment issues, he'd been able to get Dawn to say it in front of witnesses. There was no going back now, he'd thought with relief. Keeping promises was just as important to her as it was to him.

He turned his head to look at her again as she slept beside him. In the moonlight that was streaming in from the window, he could just make out her features. They were composed and peaceful, so he was hopeful that there would be no more nightmares tonight. Easing his arm from under her head, he used the discipline he had acquired from years in the military to clear his mind so that he could drift back to sleep. He needed to be fresh and alert when they resumed the search in the morning.

The sound of the alarm screaming viciously in her ear pulled Dawn out of the welcome depths of unconsciousness. Of Ty there was no sign, but that was not unusual. He generally woke up as hungry as a horse and just pulled on a pair of jeans and a sweat shirt before bounding down to his kitchen to begin getting out whatever he needed to make breakfast. No matter what time he got up, though, Mrs. Tilner would make her appearance before he had finished shutting the first cupboard. Breakfast 'a la Tilner would follow, an enormous spread. Dawn, whose stomach took longer to wake up than the rest of her, always showered and dressed before joining him and breakfasting on a far smaller repast of coffee and toast, all the while marveling at how her husband could tuck away so much food and still remain as lean and sleek as a panther.

She wandered through the connecting door to her own bedroom and grabbed a warm terrycloth robe in a shade of rich burgundy out of the closet. After studying her wardrobe thoughtfully, she proceeded to pull out a pair of chocolate brown slacks to start with. If they got lucky and spotted the car, she wanted something that wouldn't show stains easily. A pair of sturdy boots followed. A forest green sweater and a jacket in the same chocolate brown as the slacks followed. Satisfied, Dawn walked into the bathroom, hung her robe up on the hook, and climbed into the shower. Reveling in the hot, pulsating spray, she smiled when she recalled the pitiful trickle that had passed for a shower when she had been a child growing up on the ranch. Any time she and Josiah had complained, Mom had pointed out the advantages of the set up. It was the ultimate in time efficiency, she'd insisted. They wouldn't be tempted to linger in the shower, so they'd have more time to play. Josiah would just roll his eyes. Josiah...

With a conscious effort, Dawn forced her mind back to the present. She finished up her shower expeditiously, got dressed, and went down to her own kitchen. Ty, upon discovering that she preferred to make her own coffee, had gifted her with a state-of-the-art coffee maker; so in a matter of minutes, coffee cup in hand, she was on her way through the connecting door to the twin kitchen of the duplex.

It was omelets today, she noted as she crossed to the breakfast nook where Ty was seated. Omelets and hash browns, fat little sausages, orange juice and English muffins. As she seated herself at the table, Mrs. Tilner appeared magically at her side with a plate of toast in one hand and a jar of peanut butter in the other. Dawn smiled her thanks and watched as the housekeeper made a discreet exit into her own quarters at the back of the house. After a rocky start, she and Mrs. T. had learned to respect each other and make their relationship work. It hadn't been easy, considering that the hiring of Mrs. Tilner had provoked the first serious fight she and Ty had had as a married couple.

Ty had met Mrs. Tilner at a veterans center where they both volunteered. He discovered that she was a widow who had lost her only son, a marine who had been deployed to Afghanistan and killed in combat there, and that she constantly struggled to make ends meet. She always brought marvelous food and cookies to the center, though, and one day shortly after he and Dawn had been married, he had impulsively offered her a job, without talking to Dawn first. The resulting fight had been epic in proportions, and it had prompted them to go through with the idea of marriage counseling. Dawn smiled, remembering how she had held Ty to his promise to seek out marriage counseling at the first sign of any marital problems, one of her conditions before she'd agreed to give the marriage a shot, instead of seeking a quick divorce after their drunken Las Vegas wedding.

"What are you smiling about?"

"None of your business. Are we still set to leave by nine?"

Ty nodded. "I'll need to get there early, do the preflight check. You want to come with me, or take your own car and come over later?"

Dawn checked the time. "It's not even six-thirty yet. I'll catch up on some paperwork and meet you there."

"Okay. It'll take me just a few minutes to get ready – then I'm out of here." He leaned over to give her a quick kiss. "See you in a few."

Rafe was already there and waiting when she pulled into the parking lot outside the hangar at Nyetimber shortly before nine o'clock. He was also dressed in dark clothes and boots, and the huge grin plastered on his face told her that something was up.

"Did you hear the latest news?"

"No, but obviously you did. Are you going to tell me, or do I have to play twenty questions first?"

"This news is too good to waste any time playing guessing games. I heard it from Wynicki, just after I got home last night. The Minotaur has gotten a promotion."

Lieutenant Wesley Collander, christened "The Minotaur" by Rafe (because, Rafe insisted, he was 'half-man, half-bullshit') was universally detested throughout the Mountpelier Police Department. A big, beefy man with a gut so large that it looked like he'd swallowed a tire from a monster truck, Collander liked to strut around and talk big, but when the going got tough, he folded like a house of cards in the middle of a hurricane. His meteoric rise to the rank of Lieutenant was propelled not by any significant contribution to police work, but by the fact that he was the son-in-law of the former chief of police. When his father-in-law had resigned (or been fired, according to rumor), cops throughout Mountpelier had crossed their fingers and prayed that Collander would soon be booted out as well.

"He got promoted? How is that good news?"

"Because he isn't going to be directly in the chain of command anymore. Even though his title was "Special Liaison to the Chief of Police", he's actually been acting as a sort of assistant chief the last few years. But now his father-in-law is out, and Chief Wirthing wants his own people around him. So to deal with the Minotaur, he's created a new division called "The Special Unit for Crime Prevention." Collander has just been promoted to Captain in charge of the Unit. And D.C.? It's a one-man unit. He has a secretary, but nobody assigned to work under him. It's brilliant. A bullshit job with a bullshit title. The Minotaur's horns have just been sawn off."

"Yeah, but don't forget: even without any horns, a bull can still trample you to death."

At a hail from Ty, they walked over to the waiting chopper and boarded. After stopping to pick up Pete, they continued their search for the elusive missing car. The first two sites they checked were wash-outs, and Dawn had to fight against the frustration that was ballooning inside her gut and force herself to concentrate. Every minute that went by without any clues to help them locate the missing girl they knew only as "Lee" made her prospects for survival more and more bleak. At the third site, however, Pete saw something that prompted him to ask Ty to circle back for another look. Ty dropped the helicopter so low during this second pass over the search target that Dawn could swear they were almost skimming the tops of a line of tall evergreens that sloped down the incline leading to the bottom of a ravine.

"There's something down there!"

At Pete's excited statement, Ty looked for a place to land, finally settling for a narrow strip of grass next to the road at the top of the ravine. Scrambling out of the helicopter, Dawn and Rafe let Pete take the lead in blazing a trail down the slope toward a clump of trees. Branches tore at Dawn's clothes, but she paid no attention to that. For she could see it too now – a patch of red peeking out from amidst all of that green.

Chapter 4

Lee sat up on the cot slowly, relieved that this time her surroundings didn't dance before her eyes. She'd surfaced from the drugged sleep a few times before, but the dizzy spells had prevented her from getting up and examining her prison.

From the looks of things, she was in a basement of some kind. The cinder block walls had been painted a soothing shade of pale blue, but it was still obviously a cellar. To her left, she could see a furnace, a water heater, and a couple of stationary tubs. To her right, a closed door that perhaps led to a storage area of some kind. And directly in front of her, a wall covered with sketches. All of them of the same person. Her own face stared back at her, captured time after time in pencil and in ink. An easel sat to one side, with a stool in front of it and an artist's palette sitting on a small table set beside it. She recognized it at once as Michael's. She had only the vaguest memory of being brought to this place, but she remembered clearly the horrifying moments just before she had lost consciousness for the first time. She'd seen Will, clearly drugged as she herself had been, but holding his own at first in a desperate fight with Michael. She'd tried to get up then, do something to help Will, but her body had felt like lead, and her heavy limbs refused to respond to her mind's commands. Then the terrible moment when Will had lost his balance and disappeared over the edge of the cliff. She'd tried once again to take some kind of action, but she'd been too weak even to scream, let alone move.

Then Michael had come, picked her up, and put her in the back of his truck. Her next memory was of waking up here, wherever this was. A wave of desolation threatened to paralyze her, but she shook it off and rose, determined to at least find out where the door on the right led. *She could make it that far, despite the shackle clamped around her right ankle - the chain was long enough.*

To her relief, she discovered that the door led to a small powder room. After making use of the toilet, she studied the sink area. A bar of soap, a small tube of toothpaste, and a toothbrush in a holder lay there, along with a couple of hairbrushes. To her left was a towel rack, which held a couple of face towels and a washcloth.

Dampening the washcloth, she used it to wash her face thoroughly. Then she brushed her teeth, thankful to get the nasty taste left over from the drug out of her mouth. After that, she used one of the hairbrushes to smooth out her tangled hair. Feeling marginally better, she made her way back to the cot and sat back down. Despite the presence of the furnace, there was little heat in the basement. She was still dressed in her tank top and her jeans, but of her coat and boots there was no sign. Picking up the blanket from the bottom of the cot, she wrapped it around her shoulders. Then she buried her head in her hands, trying to determine what to do next. She was still thinking things over and considering her limited options when she heard the sound of a door opening above, followed by the sound of footsteps pattering down the stairs leading to the basement.

While the crime scene techs processed what they were pretty sure was the attempted murder victim's vehicle, Dawn did some multitasking. First she called the lab to find out if there were any results yet on the poured-out beer discovered at the campsite, and then she made a few calls regarding the Torrense case. After spending some time on the phone, she disconnected and waited for Rafe, who was running the red SUV's plates, to finish up his conversation with the DMV. Raising her eyebrows, she looked at him inquiringly.

"You first," Rafe responded. "What did you find out?"

"The lab report on the beer came in. It was definitely drugged. And I was able to connect with Cullen's aunt, Ellanor Torrense. She flew in from Arizona this morning and checked into the Mountpelier Arms. I've tentatively arranged for us to meet with both her and Gwen Mallinder at one o'clock this afternoon. I figured we should be finished up here and on our way back by then. I also contacted the officer who investigated the accident that killed Gwen's father. He's agreed to meet with us after he goes off shift. He's bringing a copy of the accident report with him."

"Good. Now it's my turn. According to the DMV, the vehicle is registered to Willoughby Preisinger. I've got his address. If Preisinger is our male victim, we can talk to his family, his friends, his roommates – find out everything they know about his girlfriend."

One of the techs signaled them just then, indicating that his team had finished with the SUV, so Dawn and Rafe approached the vehicle and studied the evidence that had been retrieved from the car's interior. A man's parka and another backpack, this one filled with women's clothing. In the trunk, a large cooler filled with food and bottles of water, a camping stove, some junk food. And in the glove compartment, the most important find – a man's leather wallet.

"Willoughby Preisinger," Rafe confirmed with satisfaction as he came across the driver's license that had been discovered within. The photograph on the license was clearly that of their male victim. Rafe whistled when he came across another photograph that the techs had found tucked in the wallet. "Look at this," he said, passing the photograph to Dawn, who studied it intently. It showed the victim seated in what was obviously a photo booth, a girl with long, silver-blonde hair at his side. On the back, someone had written: *Will and Lee – Manitou Springs – September 20.*

Passing the photograph back, Dawn said, "Okay. Now we know what she looks like, but we still don't know her last name. They didn't find a cell phone, like we were hoping they would, so there's no contact list for us to check."

"We'd better get a move on it, get to the address listed, and start the friends and family route."

Dawn checked the time. "It'll be close to two by the time we get back to the airport. The Mountpelier Arms isn't that far from Nyetimber. We could reschedule the appointment with Ellanor Torrense and Gwen Mallinder and head directly to Will's address, then circle back later and meet them after we're finished there. The problem is, Will's place is all the way on the other side of town. Going there and then back will take a lot of extra time."

Rafe considered. "Let's leave the one o'clock appointment as it is. After we've spent some time on the Torrense case, we can pick up where we left off on this one."

Ellanor Torrense answered the door right away when they knocked. After they'd identified themselves, she said, "Come in. Gwen's already here, and she's shown me the letter. I wish I could say that I'm surprised, but I'm not. Once I'd gotten over the initial shock, I realized that I should never have underestimated the evil that horrible woman my brother married was capable of."

They moved into the sitting room of the suite. Gwen Mallinder sat on one of the chairs, gripping the arms of the chair so hard that her nails were digging into the soft leather. Since Cullen's aunt took the other chair, Rafe and Dawn seated themselves on the sofa.

"Ms. Torrense," Rafe began, "we're sorry for your loss. Gwen tells me that you were quite close to your nephew."

Ellanor Torrense nodded. "Cullen was all I had left of my brother. I loved him, even though I was not blind to his faults and failings. For most of those, however, I place the blame on his mother. She was the worst possible influence on him. When he was with me, he was an entirely different boy – at least when he was young. A most pleasant companion, in fact." Her voice faltered and she cleared her throat. "Excuse me. I swore to myself that I would not lose my composure. I'm sure you have some questions for me. Please proceed."

"Thank you, Ms. Torrense. We need to get some information from you, first about your nephew, then about the circumstances of your brother's death. Now, can you tell me when you last spoke to Cullen?"

Ellanor sighed. "I hadn't seen or spoken to Cullen in over a year. Although we were quite close when he was a boy, everything changed between us as he grew older. I blame that on his drug use. After he was arrested the first time and finished the drug counseling program, I was hopeful that it would make a difference. I contacted Cullen and invited him to spend some time with me in Arizona that summer, thinking that getting him away from his former associates would be good for him. Everything went well at first. Then one day I came home after spending the afternoon with some friends and found a note from Cullen, thanking me for my hospitality and stating that his mother needed him, so he'd had to leave and return to Mountpelier. I was hurt that he hadn't waited to say goodbye in person, but I soon discovered that that was not the worst of it. It turns out that Cullen had used the time while I was out to search my house and find information that made it possible for him to access one of my bank accounts. He withdrew the maximum amount allowed for a twenty-four-hour period. Ten thousand dollars. My beloved nephew stole ten thousand dollars from me."

Her voice cracked, and she seemed to find it difficult to go on. "Excuse me. I need to get myself a glass of water."

"I'll get it for you," Gwen said, leaping to her feet and crossing over to the adjoining kitchenette. Taking a bottle of water out of the refrigerator, she proceeded to open cabinets until she found some glasses. She filled one of the glasses with some water and hurried back to Ellanor, who accepted the glass and drank gratefully. "Thank you, my dear. Perhaps you'd like a glass yourself? And what about you two?" she said, indicating Dawn and Rafe. When they both declined, Gwen poured out a glass of water for herself and returned to her seat. Then Ellanor continued her story.

"I could have pressed charges, of course, but I decided not to. Instead, I came here to Mountpelier. I waited until I knew his mother would not be home, and then I went to the house and confronted Cullen. He broke down and cried, said he was sorry, he didn't know what had come over him, he'd never do it again. I responded that he wouldn't have a chance to do it again, because I was breaking off all contact with him. He begged me to change my mind, give him another chance, but I was adamant. I told him that until I had evidence that he was serious about getting clean and staying clean, I wanted no more to do with him. He promised he would do anything, go into counseling, anything. I responded that receiving drug counseling had not worked the first time, and I was doubtful that going through a similar program would have any better results a second time. I told him that he needed to make some radical changes in his life. Find some sort of residential rehab program that worked, get clean and stay clean. Then he needed to get a job and start paying back the money he stole from me. Only then would I consent to see him again." She paused for a moment. "It was the right decision, but it doesn't make it any easier. Now he's dead and gone, and I'll never see him again. And if Monieque had anything to do with his death, I'll see to it that she is prosecuted to the fullest extent of the law."

"Did you have any suspicions, any at all, before you read the letter that Cullen sent to Gwen?"

"No, none at all. Of course, I've known for years that Monieque is totally selfish and quite incapable of loving anyone but herself; however, much as I dislike her, until I read the letter, it didn't occur to me that she would go so far as to commit murder. In addition, it always seemed to me that she thought of Cullen as an extension of herself, and it was the farthest thing from my mind that she would ever want to be rid of him. Now, of course, I see how naive it was of me, to think that there were any limits to Monieque's selfishness. As I told you, I was not surprised when I read that letter. Shocked, yes. But surprised? Given what I know about her, I immediately knew she was capable of it. So I was not surprised, no."

"What about your brother, Ms. Torrense? What can you tell us about his death?"

"My brother died while he and Monieque were away visiting some old friends in Monieque's hometown. The cause of his death is listed as severe acute pancreatitis. Since he had suffered from mild pancreatitis for years, and was in the hospital receiving what I believed to be competent treatment at the time, I did not suspect that his death was due to anything but natural causes. No autopsy was performed on my brother's body, which relieved me at the time. However, Gwen and I did a little research on the Internet just before you arrived. It turns out that certain poisons can mimic or even induce severe acute pancreatitis. Given that, I intend to get in touch with my attorneys and begin the necessary steps to have my brother's body exhumed for an autopsy." Seeing Dawn and Rafe exchange glances, she demanded, "Is there some sort of problem?"

Rafe replied, "Ms. Torrense, in most states it requires a court order to have a body exhumed. If the purpose of the exhumation is merely for reburial in another place, getting such an order is generally not a problem. However, it's usually much more difficult to get a court order if the purpose for exhumation is to have an autopsy done. The court usually demands substantial evidence that such a step is warranted before granting such an order."

"Why? He was my brother. After he died, we brought his body back home to be buried in our family plot. I own title to that plot. Some doubt has arisen concerning the true cause of his death. Why would a judge not allow me to exhume my brother for an autopsy?"

"Ms. Torrense, an autopsy is a very invasive procedure. Most judges hesitate to consent to disturbing the dead in such a way except for very serious reasons. That you own title to the plot is helpful, but without proof of some kind, I doubt that you could get an exhumation order at this point. Remember, all we have right now are our own suspicions and the line in Cullen's letter where he asserts that he thinks his mother may have killed his father. That isn't proof. Speak to your attorney, by all means, but don't be surprised if he or she advises you against acting at this time."

"I see. This is most unsettling. So you advise me to wait?"

"Yes. Give us a few more days, at least. We don't want to tip Monieque off that we're even looking in her direction. If we can dig up some evidence that she was somehow involved in Cullen's murder and in the circumstances leading up to the death of Gwen's father, it will give you more ammunition to use when you petition for an exhumation order. Tell me, can you think of any reason why Monieque would have wanted to do away with your brother? Was there any monetary benefit, for example?"

"I've been thinking about that. She did not inherit what I considered at the time to be a substantial amount after my brother's death. But I was looking at it from my own perspective, which I realize now was a mistake. I received a considerable amount in a divorce settlement when my husband and I decided to part ways. Millions, in fact. What Monieque received seemed paltry in comparison to what I walked away with. I realize now that my vision was clouded by such comparisons. So in answer to your question, yes, Monieque did benefit from my brother's death. First, she was the beneficiary of a one hundred fifty thousand dollar life insurance policy. There was also a nice amount set aside in savings, and she was able to cash out my brother's retirement account as well. I don't know the figures for those, but I'm sure you can find out. As for the house, since they had quite a bit of equity in it and she was later able to sell it at a profit, she made out there as well. And as a widow with a dependent child, she got social security benefits on top of all that. In fact, once you put it all together, which I never stopped to do until just now, I wouldn't be surprised to find that Monieque profited by almost a million dollars as a result of my brother's death."

"Okay, Ms. Torrense. Now, I know that this might be difficult for you, but can you tell me about their relationship? Any indication that there was trouble between Monieque and your brother?"

"Well, she and my brother were having a rough time about a year prior to his death, and for a while, he talked about divorcing her. They seemed to have patched things up, however, and appeared to be quite happy again at the time of his death."

Rafe glanced over at Dawn, who shook her head almost imperceptibly. "Thank you, Ms. Torrense." Turning to Gwen, he said, "Ms. Mallinder, we haven't forgotten about your father. We've made arrangements to speak to the officer who investigated his accident, and we are going to take another look at the accident report. We'll keep digging into all three deaths, and we'll get back to you as soon as possible. Please be patient."

After rising and shaking hands all around, they left the hotel and got back into the car. On the way to Will Preisinger's apartment, Dawn commented, "Sounds like Monieque did better as a widow than she would have as a divorcee."

"I was just thinking the same thing. A lot of food for thought, but nothing solid yet. All that could change in an instant, though, once we get Jago Bolt back in town and into interview. Now, if we can just get as much information out of Will's family and friends, we should know Lee's identity shortly."

Standing in Will's apartment about an hour later, however, Rafe had to admit that he had been a little too sanguine in his expectations. Will Preisinger apparently preferred to keep his personal life private. A call to his widowed mother had netted them no leads. Will didn't like to talk about his romantic relationships, she'd stated. She knew nothing about whom he had been seeing lately.

Mrs. Preisinger hadn't been inclined to talk much, and was off the phone in a hurry, stating that she was going to jump into her car immediately and drive as fast as she could to Mountpelier to get to her injured son's side. Since she lived in the city of Grand Junction in western Colorado, it would take her several hours to get to Mountpelier. In the meantime, they had been let inside Will's apartment by his roommate, Carl Brassner, a good-looking boy who reminded Rafe of a poster his father had once owned of a young Lou Gehrig.

"Will isn't much of a talker, you know? We get along and everything, but we hang out with different groups of friends," Carl stated. "Will runs track and spends a lot of time with his teammates. He's also way serious about his studies. Got some brains, Will does. He's pre-med, taking all those hard math and science courses and shit. Has a sweet schedule, though. Classes only Monday through Thursday. He's usually finished by noon on Thursday. No Friday classes. He spends a lot of time studying on campus in the library, though. Needs to keep his grades up. It's not easy to get into medical school, you know."

"What about weekends?" Dawn asked.

Carl paused to take a sip from the bottle of soda he was holding before replying. "Like I said, Will usually spends a lot of time studying, even on weekends. But sometimes he takes a break, throws his camping stuff into his car, and disappears for a while. He just takes off, you know? He doesn't go into the details. Just, 'See you Sunday night,' and he's gone. Hey, what hospital is he in? I should probably get down there, be there when his mother gets in. She's okay, you know? Sends us care packages regularly. Always asks to talk to me when she calls to check in on Will."

"Who are Will's closest friends on the track team?" Dawn inquired.

"Uh, that'd be Jupe Dunsinger and Hunt Farolle. But they're not here this weekend. Will mentioned that they were going fishing someplace up in Idaho."

"Do you know where they'll be staying?"

"No, but you can reach them on their cells."

"Can you give us their numbers?"

"No, but Will should have them saved on his phone."

"Unfortunately, Will's phone wasn't found on him or among his belongings."

"No shit? That's weird. Will always has his phone with him. What about his iPad? You could probably find some email addresses."

Dawn glanced at Rafe. There had been no sign of an iPad, either in the tent or in the car. Meanwhile, Carl was getting impatient.

"Look, I've got to get going. I don't want Mrs. Preisinger to get there and find out that Will's all alone. Even if he isn't conscious, somebody ought to be with him."

"Mind if we stick around and look through Will's things? We might find something that will tell us more about the girl who was with him – Lee."

"No problem. Look around all you want."

A thorough search of the apartment, however, turned up nothing useful. In Will's room they found numerous textbooks and notebooks, sports equipment and clothing, but nothing much of a personal nature. The walls were decorated with posters of sports figures and cars, but there were no photographs, no letters. Everything of that nature, Dawn and Rafe concluded, must be on the missing cell phone and iPad.

"When Mrs. Preisinger gets here, we can find out if she knows how to reach Jupe Dunsinger and Hunt Farolle. The University might be able to help us there too," Dawn commented.

"Getting around privacy laws will be a bitch, but we'll get a warrant if we have to. But it's not going to be easy, with all the offices closed for the weekend. What about high school buddies? Maybe Will's more forthcoming with them about his relationships than he is with his roommate. Mrs. Preisinger could help us there, maybe give us some names of his old friends from high school."

"I've been thinking, Rafe... the perp would have had to stalk them, follow them around, to know where they'd be this weekend. This was not a crime of opportunity. How did he target them? Where did he see them?"

"Good point." Rafe looked around the apartment one last time. "You know, if Will hadn't fought back, if he hadn't survived and let Dale Thrushton know he was pushed, if he hadn't told him about Lee, what would have happened? Everyone would have assumed it was an accident. Nothing to suggest that anyone else was with him. No indications of a missing girl, so everything would have been less urgent. Looking for the car wouldn't have been as much of a priority. Weeks or months might have gone by before it was found. And what would the accident investigators have thought when they found the car, found Lee's things? Maybe that the two of them had had a fight, and she grabbed her things and took off in the car. That Will got drunk, maybe, went for a walk, got too close to the drop-off, and stumbled over the edge. Meanwhile, the girl's so upset from the fight that she isn't driving carefully and crashes the car. Afterward, she can't just call 911. There's a huge hole in the cell phone coverage for that area, remember. Park rangers have to use their radios to stay in touch. You had to use the Satphone to get in touch with Pete and Mattie. So what does the girl do? Gets out of the wrecked car and starts to walk. Might be dazed, hurt in the accident. Gets lost in the woods. That's what we were all supposed to think. It'd spin out in the media as a tragic, unfortunate accident. Dead boy, lost girl. That's how it would have been. No reason to call in Homicide."

They'd been on the way out to the car as Rafe speculated. Suddenly, Dawn stopped, stock still.

"What?" Rafe said.

"Something just occurred to me. Last year, at about this same time of year, I went up to visit my friend Desiree, remember?"

"The one who lives up in Michigan? I remember. What about it?"

"Well, there was a big story all over the news while I was there - about a couple of teenagers who went missing while they were hiking in the Porcupine Mountains. A few days later, they found the boy, dead, at the foot of a cliff. Accident, they figured. But Rafe? They never found the girl. They kept looking for her, showed her picture over and over again on the news. And here's the thing: from what I remember, she was a dead ringer for the girl in the photograph. Lee."

"You think we could have a serial killer on the loose." Lieutenant Westbrooke's voice stayed cool and even, but Rafe could hear the disquiet underneath. The lieutenant had been on the point of leaving for a briefing with the Chief when they'd walked into her office, so she hadn't asked them to sit down. Standing six feet tall in her stocking feet, Lieutenant Westbrooke was the offspring of a Polynesian mother and African American father. Her first name was Moetua, but she was known to her friends and colleagues as "Moe." When they were alone, Rafe, who had partnered with her on more than one occasion when they were both still in uniform, still addressed her by her nickname. Not when there were others present, though. Then it was "Lieutenant" or "LT."

Rafe met her eyes steadily as he responded to her statement. "It's beginning to look that way, LT. The cops who investigated the incident in Michigan were skeptical too, but they sent us a copy of the case file, and we're convinced that there are too many similarities between the two cases for it to be a coincidence." He placed a photograph on her desk. "That's Tamara Norti, the missing girl from Michigan. And here's the photograph of our missing girl – Lee."

After scanning the photographs for a minute or two, the lieutenant looked up at Rafe and said, "I see what you mean. The two of them could be sisters, the resemblance is so strong,"

Rafe nodded. "We began a search for like crimes. Turned up this one." A third photograph was placed next to the other two. "Crystal Rogar, a student at the University of Alaska in Fairbanks. She and her boyfriend went missing in the Chena River Recreational Area in early October of 2011. Neither of them has ever been seen again. Not quite as strong a resemblance as the other two, but still, same body type, same long, white-blond hair."

"Have you contacted the local police?"

Rafe nodded. "Again, the cops from the Missing Persons Unit who handled the case were skeptical about what we had to say. We haven't received the case file yet, but they've promised to send it."

"What's your next step?"

This time it was Dawn who replied. "We'll keep searching for like crimes, try to see if there's any sort of pattern. Meanwhile, we've been talking about how the perp stalks and selects his victims. So far, besides the resemblance between the girls, an interest in the outdoors seems to be a prominent connection. So we talked to Will's roommate again, asked him some questions, and he remembered that Will had mentioned that he was low on fuel for his camping stove, and he needed to stop and buy some more before he left town. We thought we'd canvass the local stores that sell camping supplies. Show the photos of Will and Lee around, see if they visited any of the stores recently. Find out if anyone noticed a man nearby taking too much of an interest in them. Also, we'd like to have a guard posted outside the entrance to Intensive Care at the hospital. Will can identify the perp. He may want to try to finish what he started."

Lieutenant Westbrooke nodded. "I'll see to it. In the meantime, if you're right, you're going to need some help. I'll free up Prentiss and Noritaki. They can help you run down some of the leads. But I want to emphasize something." She paused for a moment. "Right now, all we have is an attempted homicide and a possible kidnapping. The idea of a serial killer is pure supposition at this point. Keep a lid on it. The last thing we need is for the media to get a whiff of this. They'll go after it like a pack of jackals. I've scheduled a press conference for this afternoon. At that time, I'll be releasing Will's name. They already know that a young man was found unconscious at the foot of a cliff yesterday. I don't plan on announcing that he regained consciousness briefly or make any mention of the fact that there was someone called 'Lee' with him. Nor do I intend to announce the fact that we've found the car, or what we found inside."

"Lieutenant?"

"You have a problem, Cimarron?"

"Maybe we should mention that there is a missing girl, release the photo of Will and Lee. Somebody out there might recognize her. We could identify her that much more quickly."

"After reading your initial report, I considered that angle, Detective. Yes, it would probably help us to identify the girl sooner. However, it would also alert the perp to the fact that we know about her, that we're looking for her. If he thinks that we've bought the fact that what happened to Will was an accident, and we emphasize that Will is in a coma, with a poor chance of recovery, it might buy the girl a little more time, if she's still alive. He might cut his losses, kill her, and disappear if he suspects we're looking for her... and him." She paused for another minute, but there was no argument from either Dawn or Rafe. "That's it, then. Let's get to it. Keep me posted."

Since it was on the way, they decided to swing by the hospital first. They found Carl Brassner in the Intensive Care waiting area. Mrs. Preisinger was in with Will when they arrived, but joined them in the waiting area when she learned that the detectives who were investigating the attack on Will wanted to speak to her.

As soon as she saw them, she came rushing up to Dawn and Rafe. "Do you have any news? Any information about who did this to my boy?"

"We're following all available leads ma'am," Rafe responded. "How's Will doing, Mrs. Preisinger?"

"He's still in a coma. The doctors don't know when he'll come out of it. They say it's a miracle that he survived at all, considering the distance he fell. The rescue squad that brought him up told me they found indications that he was able to grab on to something about half way down – a little shelf that was projecting out the side of the cliff – and hold on with one hand for a few seconds. It was enough to break the fall, slow down the speed of his descent. They think that's how he dislocated his shoulder... I've been sitting with him as often as they'll let me." Her voice broke and she blinked back tears, cleared her throat. "He's so still. I've never seen him this still, even in his sleep. I used to call him my little perpetual motion machine..."

"Mrs. Preisinger..."

"Call me Naomi. We're going to see a lot of each other, until the monster who attacked my son is caught and punished." She paused for a moment, and seemed to recollect herself. "You told me on the phone that Will wasn't alone, that there was a girl with him, and that she is missing. Have you found her?"

Dawn replied, "Not yet. We can't tell you much while the investigation is ongoing, Naomi. But anything you can think of that might assist us in identifying the girl would be a big help. So far, all we have is her first name – Lee."

Naomi shook her head. "Like I told you on the phone, Will doesn't talk much about his romantic relationships." She smiled. "The first I knew about his high school girlfriend, Jackie, was when he asked her to the Junior Prom. Turned out they'd been seeing each other for over a year by that time. Will is a very... private person. I try to respect his privacy."

"Would Jackie have any idea about who Will is seeing now?"

The smile faded from Naomi's face. She shook her head. "No. She broke up with Will in the middle of their senior year. Will didn't say much about it, but I know he was hurt. He doesn't keep in touch with Jackie."

"What about his other friends from high school? Does he keep in touch with any of them?"

Naomi considered. "He still keeps up with most of them. The only one I think he'd confide in, however, is Sam Lathmore. They've been friends since kindergarten. Sam might know."

"Do you know how to get in touch with Sam?"

"Yes. I called him as soon as I heard about Will. He's away at school right now – Towson University, in Baltimore. He wanted to jump on a plane right away and come out here, but I persuaded him to wait until I have more news."

"Can you give us Sam's phone number?"

"I can do better than that. I can get him on the phone for you right now. He's expecting a call from me, anyway."

If he'd been the type to tear his hair with frustration, Rafe reflected, he'd have pulled every last hair out of his head by now. The phone call to Sam Lathmore had been fruitless. Yes, he'd known that Will had been seeing a girl called Lee, but that's all he knew. Will had never mentioned her last name. Or anything else about her.

"Time's running out for her. And we don't even have her full name. She might as well be a ghost."

Privately, Dawn couldn't help agreeing. Nevertheless, she kept her tone neutral as she said, "We're doing everything we can. Sooner or later, we're bound to turn up something. The lieutenant promised that she'd try to push through a warrant for the names of all female students with a first name that resembles 'Lee' who are currently attending Mountpelier U. Once we get the names, we'll run them down. Find out if any of them are missing."

"She might not go to the University. Then we're back at square one."

"We've had so much bad luck, we're due for a break. Maybe someone at one of the sporting goods stores will remember seeing the two of them."

They struck out at the first two stores they visited. At the third store, however, it was a different story. The clerk's eyes lit up with recognition as soon as they showed him the photograph.

"Yeah, I saw those two. Couple of days ago. Remember it because of the girl. She was really something, you know? Pretty enough to be a model."

"Think back," Rafe encouraged. "What day was it, exactly?"

"Thursday, I think. Yeah, it was Thursday. They came in around one o'clock. I'd just come back from lunch. This kid," he pointed to Will, "was wearing a Mountpelier University sweatshirt, and we got to talking about college sports. My cousin's girl, she plays on the women's basketball team at the U. There was a game that night. I asked the kid if he and his girl were going to the game, but he said no, they were leaving on a camping trip. Just came in to pick up some more fuel for their camping stove."

"Did you notice anyone else hanging around? Anyone who seemed to be interested in this particular couple?"

"No. That time of day on a Thursday isn't exactly busy. I think they were the only customers I waited on for quite a while."

"Thanks for your time. If you think of anything else, would you give us a call? We'd sure appreciate it." Rafe passed his card to the clerk; then they headed out the door.

"Okay. Suppose the perp followed them here. Didn't go into the store because he didn't want to be noticed. Where would he have watched and waited for them?"

Dawn glanced around the street. "I'd opt for that one." Rafe followed the direction of her pointing finger. It was some sort of coffee-house/bakery type deal, with bay windows on either side of the door that jutted out into the street. "He could go in, order himself some coffee, and sit at one of those tables in the window until Will and Lee came out. Then all he had to do was pick up his coffee and follow them."

They crossed the street and entered the shop. It seemed that the gods of good fortune had finally decided to smile upon them, for after ordering coffee, identifying themselves, and explaining what they were looking for, the waitress immediately said, "Oh, yeah. There's this creep who's been coming in the last few weeks. Not one of my regulars. Somebody new. He comes in and spends hours here, doing little drawings on a sketchpad. They always seem to be of customers going in and out of the stores across the street."

Dawn could hardly contain her excitement. "Why do you call him a creep?"

"I don't know. He's real polite, tries to be charming as all get out. But there's something behind his eyes... And he wears a wig. Now mind you, he's a young man. Why would he want to wear a dirty blond wig?"

"You're sure it was a wig?"

She shrugged. "Yeah. I know when a guy is wearing a rug. My dad wore one. Couldn't bear it when he lost his hair. I always thought he looked ridiculous in that wig, but I never told him."

"Do you remember when he first started coming in?"

"Sure, back at the beginning of the month. He was in here every day until Thursday. But he didn't show up yesterday, or today."

"On Thursday? Was he here all day?"

"No, he came in the morning and sat there until just after lunch. Then he suddenly picked up his sketchpad and raced out the door. Left his coffee behind, too. I've never known him to do that before."

Rafe looked at her name tag and put his most charming smile on his face. "Barbara, what you saw may have an important bearing on a case we're working on. Would you be willing to come down to headquarters and work with a police artist? We'd really like to have a sketch of this man."

Barbara's eyes went wide with alarm. "Police headquarters! Am I in some kind of trouble?"

"No, not at all. In fact, you'd be doing us a great service."

Barbara still looked doubtful. "I get off in about an hour. I guess I could come down then."

"Great! I'll meet you there. If for any reason I'm detained, give this card to the sergeant on duty." Scribbling a note on the back of his business card, Rafe handed it to Barbara. "He'll arrange for you to get to the right place." He turned another million megawatt smile on her, and Dawn thought that the girl was going to melt right before her eyes. She had no doubt that Barbara would keep the appointment, if only for a chance to catch sight of the handsome and fascinating Sergeant Melbourne again.

As they made their way back to headquarters, Dawn said, "Rafe? We were talking about patterns before. In two of the cases, the one here and the one in Michigan, the male victim ended up at the bottom of a cliff. I think that killing the male that way is as important to him as snatching the female. In fact... what if killing the male is symbolic in some way? What if there was some figure in his life, a camper, an outdoors man, that he is symbolically killing, over and over again? If we're right, and he's done this before – in Michigan, in Alaska – he might not necessarily be following the couple first. All he'd have to do would be to stake out the sporting goods stores, waiting for the right type to walk in. It would explain a lot."

Rafe pondered. "You could be on to something. But where does the girl fit in?"

Dawn replied, "It could be like Bundy. Rejection by his college girlfriend is apparently what set him off on his killing spree. What if something similar happened to our man? Take that trauma, add it to an earlier one involving some sort of father figure, maybe – and he could literally be killing two birds with one stone."

She broke off and checked her phone briefly. It didn't take her long to read the text that had just been sent to her.

"Tyrell?" Rafe inquired.

Dawn nodded. "Maeve's flying in from New Orleans. He wants to know if I can carve out some time to meet them at Fredo's for dinner."

"You should do it."

Dawn gave him a look. "Are you sure? We're on a roll here. I thought we could order in, start a search for rental properties in the area. I mean, he gets around, right? He's not local. He needs a place to take the girls once he abducts them. I'm thinking a house, not an apartment. With an attached garage, so that he can just lift them out of his truck and walk them in with no one the wiser."

Rafe considered. "Yeah, that's the next step. But first we need Devlin to sit down with sweet little Barbara and come up with a sketch of our suspect. Once we have that, we can start tracking down real estate agents who deal in rental properties. I'll meet with Barbara, take her up to Devlin, and get the process started. You go ahead and spend some time with your husband and your mother-in-law. Unless something has changed, and you're trying to avoid Maeve?"

The denial came swiftly: "No! Of course not. You know how I feel about Maeve. When it comes to mothers-in-law, I got cut the luckiest break in the world."

"Then go meet her for dinner. Besides, Fredo's is only across the street. If something breaks, you can get away and be back in a matter of minutes."

"Okay. But I want to meet with Officer Taylor before I leave. He's bringing up the accident file on Gwen's dad. That should take no more than an hour. I guess I could take a little time after that for dinner."

"Is Ty flying Maeve in himself?"

"No, he sent Jack to pick her up. She's due to arrive in just a few minutes."

Ty walked out of his own office and headed for Cal Skornac's domain, with the pleasing intention of dumping a mountain of paperwork on his right-hand-man's shoulders. As he passed the front desk, he heard Diana, Cal's oldest daughter, cooing soothingly to a prospective customer on the phone. Ty grinned. Cal himself, while a financial and logistical genius, had the tact and patience of a bull elephant in rut, so it had been a stroke of genius to hire his daughter, a bright and charming senior in high school, to help out in the office on weekends. Monday through Friday, his regular receptionist, Millicent Duras, served as a buffer between Cal and the customers, as well as with the rest of the staff at Lewellen Air. Milly, a no-nonsense woman with the emotional hide of a rhinoceros, was impervious to Cal's gruffness and frequent storms of bad temper. As for Diana – she was totally immune. However he might behave to the rest of the world, Cal was the soul of gentleness when it came to his girls.

Giving a thumbs up to Diana, who smiled radiantly at him in return, Ty passed on and entered Cal's office. As usual, he was stunned by the sheer volume of paperwork that occupied Cal's desk. Yet he knew from experience that Cal knew exactly what was in each pile and could retrieve any document necessary with lightning speed. Cal looked up as Ty sauntered in, the almost perpetual scowl of concentration on his face smoothing out when he saw who had entered. He was only a little over average in height, but stocky and solid in build. His square face was dominated by a pair of piercing hazel eyes, which looked out over an aquiline nose and a jaw as pugnacious and hard as concrete.

"Here I am drowning in paperwork, so naturally the big boss decides to stroll in and toss some more at me. I don't know why I put up with this shit."

"It's because you're so good at your job, Cal. You know the reward for hard work? You just keep getting more and more of it."

The smile that creased Cal's face was unexpectedly charming. "Toss it down, then. I'll get to it when I can. Anything urgent?"

"Nothing that can't wait 'til Monday. When are you going to pack it up and head on home?"

Glancing at his watch, Cal winced. "Ouch. It had better be soon. I promised Tess that I'd get both Diana and myself home in time for dinner tonight. Then we're heading out to the high school. Ben has a game tonight."

"How's our future Heisman Trophy winner doing?"

"Pretty damn good. Team's 9 and 0. If they win tonight, they'll have a lock on home field advantage for the play-offs. Just pray that Ben's shoulder holds out. He got banged up pretty bad last week."

"Major Ty?"

Ty turned toward the doorway at the sound of Diana's voice. Although Cal himself invariably used his given name when speaking to Ty, Cal insisted that his children address the boss by his proper rank. Even though Ty was no longer in the Air Force, he still maintained the rank of major in the Civil Air Patrol, in accordance with its policy of advancing retired members of the Armed Forces to the CAP grade equivalent of their rank upon joining the civilian auxiliary.

"What's up, Diana?"

"Jack just called in. He'll be landing any minute now."

"Okay. Thanks for letting me know. I appreciate it. Hey, how's everything going at school?"

"Great! Senior year is the best!" Turning to her father, she said, "Dad, I just got a text from Mom. She wants to know when we're leaving before she picks up the twins so that she can coordinate dinner."

Ty watched, fascinated, as Cal positively beamed at his daughter. Only Diana and her younger sister, Jolene, could put that special smile on Cal's face.

"Well, I should be able to wrap things up here shortly. Tell your mother that we'll be leaving in about ten minutes. That should give her plenty of time to pick up Adam and Zack."

"Okay, Dad." She angled her head at Ty and said, "Are you coming to the game on Thursday? We're playing our biggest rival."

"I'll pencil it in."

"Awesome! I'll be looking forward to it."

After Diana had waltzed out the door, Cal said, "Thanks. She always enjoys looking up into the stands and seeing you there. Makes her feel special, the boss coming to watch her and all."

"I like softball. It's fun to watch her, besides. She's got the moves."

Cal chuckled. "Takes after her mother. Tess was a star on both her high school softball and basketball teams. Paid off too. Put herself through college on a basketball scholarship."

"Football game tonight, softball game on Thursday. Sounds like you have a full plate, Cal. Give my regards to Tess, and good luck to Ben. Gotta get going. If I'm going to be in time to greet my mother, I'd better hustle."

Sometimes it paid to have a shopaholic for a mother, Ty reflected as he waited for the door of the plane carrying her to open so that Maeve Lewellen could descend. When she had called him that morning, the first words out of her mouth had been, "Ty, darling, I've found the most beautiful present for you to give to Dawn for her birthday. Send one of your planes and that gorgeous hunk of a blond pilot to come and get me at once."

The blond hunk of a pilot in question, Jack, hurried around to help Maeve descend. Ty watched her as she murmured her thanks to Jack and made her way toward him. In her late fifties, Maeve was still beautiful, her honey-blonde hair just skimming her shoulders, her deep blue eyes gazing out on the world from a sculptured face that barely showed a wrinkle. When people first met her, they often made the mistake of dismissing Maeve as an airhead, but Ty knew that Maeve deliberately cultivated her dumb blonde persona as a strategy to get people to underestimate her. She got away with murder that way.

When she reached him, he enfolded her in a bear hug. At 5'5", she'd always been dwarfed both by her tall husband and by her son.

Slender and petite, at only 120 pounds, she had an air of charming fragility about her.

As soon as Maeve disengaged herself, Ty said, "So, where's the present?"

Maeve turned eyes wide with astonishment upon him and responded, "Of course I didn't actually *buy* it, Ty. I'm just going to take you to the store where I found it so that *you* can get it. You have to buy it yourself."

"Why?"

Maeve rolled her eyes. "Because it's your wife's birthday present, Ty. You have to be able to look into your wife's eyes and answer her truthfully when she says, 'Oh, it's beautiful, Ty. Wherever did you find it?'"

"You could have bought it yourself and then just told me where you found it," Ty pointed out.

"She'd know. You're just going to have to trust me on this."

This particular excursion into the shopping arena was relatively painless, Ty considered as he helped his mother back into his car, parked in a space fortuitously close to Alexandres, the high-end jewelry store Maeve favored in the heart of Mountpelier's shopping district. Since Maeve had already viewed the items in question online and called Alexandre himself, an old friend, to have him set them aside for her, they had managed to get in and out of the store in record time. Now he had his purchase tucked away just in time for Dawn's birthday. His mother had been right. The ruby and diamond necklace with matching earrings was perfect for Dawn.

As they pulled away from the curb and headed toward Fredo's, Maeve glanced back and watched with approval as a gray sedan pulled out behind them, tailing them from a discreet distance. Ty had originally balked at being shadowed by Lewellen Security, but she had insisted. Dealing with one kidnapping attempt on her only son had been enough, she'd told Ty. She wasn't sure she could live through another one. As she studied his profile next to her, she felt the familiar surge of fierce love for him that she'd felt from the moment he was born. She remembered holding him in her arms that first time, Sloan at her side, weak with relief that it was all over, and they had a healthy son. That reminded her...

69

"I talked to your father this morning. He's joining us for dinner tonight."

"That's fine by me. Dad's always in the mood for some good Italian food." Ty kept his voice cool and matter-of-fact as he replied. Deep in his heart, however, he felt a stab of relief and joy at this sign of thawing in his parents' somewhat frosty relationship.

Dawn walked in through the bar entrance to Fredo's, nodding at several off-duty cops she recognized on her way through the bar to the private dining room. Because of its location across the street from Police Headquarters, Fredo's had always been a cop bar. Fredo himself had built a successful business by offering a combination of reasonably priced drinks and fabulous food. The rising fuel costs of the last few years, however, had caused his operating costs to skyrocket. Unwilling to skimp on quality, Fredo had sunk deeper and deeper into debt. The business had been in real trouble. Then, shortly after Dawn's marriage to Ty, Sloan Lewellen had taken an interest in the place. He'd bought a half interest in the business, giving it a welcome shot in the arm. Able to buy supplies in bulk at the discount price offered to businesses under the umbrella of The Lewellen Group, the business had rebounded. Sloan had also bought the building next door, enabling Fredo to expand his bar and restaurant, and to add a private dining room and a banquet facility as well. Fredo still presided over the bar, and his wife, Rosa, still ran the kitchen with an iron hand, so everyone was happy. Especially Sloan, who recognized the value of making sure that his son and daughter-in-law had a convenient place to eat on those occasions when Dawn got tied up on a case. The office space above the private dining room and banquet facility could be put to good use as well.

Leaning against the fireplace mantle at the far end of the private dining room, Tyrell and Sloan were arguing about the Mountpelier University football team's chances of making it to the semifinals. Maeve, seated in a comfortable armchair to the left of the fireplace, was sipping a glass of white wine and nodding occasionally, pretending to follow along with the conversation. A look of pure relief crossed her face when she saw who was standing in the doorway.

"Dawn!" With the grace of a ballerina, Maeve arose and crossed the room, embracing her daughter-in-law warmly. "Come over to the fire. I ordered us some hors d'oeuvres to start with. Have some bruschetta, or the prosciutto cups. There's some marvelous antipasti as well." As

Maeve waved toward the tray on the coffee table set before the fire, a sparkling trail of light seemed to leap and dance from her left hand.

"New ring, Maeve?"

Pleased that Dawn had noticed, Maeve held out her hand. A deep purple stone set in an intricate Greek key design winked as she turned her hand back and forth.

"Isn't it gorgeous? I picked it up when I was in Greece last month."

"You were in Greece last month?" said Sloan, catching the last part of the conversation.

Maeve inclined her head. "Cruising the Greek Isles was on my bucket-list. Daphne Bartelli went with me, and Julian Notler came along as a sort of a guide. He spent a year studying in Greece, so he knows where everything is and understands the language."

"Who's Julian Notler?"

"Oh, he's an artist I met at a gallery in the French Quarter last summer. He's a sculptor, actually, so whenever we visited a museum or one of the archaeological sites, he could tell us all about the artifacts. We stayed in Athens for a few days before we set sail, visited all of the major museums, and toured the Acropolis. We all enjoyed it so much that we're planning to return in the spring. We want to spend some time at Delphi, see *The Charioteer*. On the way there, we're going to stop at Thermopylae and see the spot where Leonidas and his 300 Spartans held off the entire Persian army. Then Julian is taking us up to some of the quaint mountain villages in the Pelion region, way off the beaten track. He says that sometimes it's good to get away, avoid some of the more touristy spots."

Nibbling on a piece of bruschetta, Dawn asked, "How did you like the food?"

"I liked it a lot, but Italian will always be my favorite. Speaking of which, I think that dinner is about to be served."

Rosa herself, along with several of her daughters, bustled in and ceremoniously placed the entrees on the table. Ty had ordered Dawn's favorite for her, and she made an appreciative sound as she ladled up a spoonful of Rosa's famous cioppino, savoring the taste of the clams and shrimp and scallops swimming in a spicy tomato-based stock.

Over dinner, the conversation touched upon a variety of subjects – Maeve's fledgling interior decorating business, Ty's plans for expanding Lewellen Air, and Sloan's ambition to make Mountpelier's annual Winter Festival one of the top tourist attractions in the state.

"Adding the ice-sculpting competition last year boosted our numbers up considerably from previous years," Sloan commented. "Our market research projects that attendance over the next five years could double, and that kind of tourist boom will add millions to our local economy."

Turning to his ex-wife, he said, "You ought to come down and spend a couple of weeks this year, Maeve. It's pretty impressive. You'd like it."

Ty added some encouragement of his own. "I like the ice village the best. You have to see it to believe it, Mom. Whole mansions sculpted out of ice. Dad and the other members of the planning committee have some lights rigged up in such a way that it looks like a string of diamond palaces."

Maeve responded, "It's a thought. I haven't had much of a chance to spend time with my son or daughter-in-law lately."

Just then, Dawn's cell phone beeped. Seeing that it was Rafe, she rose from the table as she said, "Excuse me. I'm afraid I have to take this." She moved a discreet distance away and studied the text from her partner: *You're going to want to get over here. Prentiss and Noritaki just found another one.*

Chapter 5

"You're awake – good! Did you sleep well?"

Lee couldn't think at first how to respond to Michael's greeting. Whatever she had expected him to say, it wasn't that. It was crazy - he was acting as if she were a guest that he'd invited for an overnight, not a victim whom he'd drugged and kidnapped and chained to a wall. But years of living with an alcoholic who liked to spend most of her time in a fantasy world had taught Lee that the worst thing to do with people who were unbalanced was to argue with them. So she decided to play along with him, try to gauge what was the best way to handle the situation.

"I slept well, thank you. And you? How did you sleep, Michael?"

"Like a baby. Are you hungry, Vanadis?"

Vanadis? Lee picked her words carefully. "I'm a little confused, Michael. I've always been told that my name is Lee."

"That's only a part of you – the mortal part. Vanadis is the other facet of your identity, the immortal aspect of your being. I recognized that as soon as I saw you for the first time. Together, we're going to bring Vanadis to the surface and release her. Only then will you be truly happy, truly free."

In that moment, she realized a couple of things with startling clarity:

First, he was planning on killing her. There was no use in pretending otherwise; she could see it in his eyes.

And second, there was no sense in trying to reason with him, because he was absolutely freaking crazy.

"They disappeared on Mount Mansfield, near Stowe, Vermont, in November of 2010." Rafe pointed at a picture of the missing teenagers on his computer as Dawn looked over his shoulder at the screen. "No trace of them at first. Then, just this past summer, a few bones were found scattered by a stream. Turns out they belonged to him," Rafe's finger stabbed the image of a boy who sported a scruffy beard and was raising a mug about the size of the Empire State Building. A pair of skis stood propped in the snow at his left. His head was turned to the right, where a girl wearing a bright blue ski jacket gazed adoringly into his eyes. Pale blonde hair peeked out under a ski cap in the same shade of vibrant blue as her jacket.

"And the girl?" Dawn glanced at the names mentioned in the caption below the photo. "Alissa Gordena?"

"Nothing. Family posted a $50,000 reward for any information on her whereabouts, living or dead, but still - zip."

"There's only a vague facial resemblance to the others, but still – the pale blonde hair, and the fact that she and her boyfriend went missing at approximately the same time of year as the others. Yeah, I'd say that there's a connection. Did you tell the lieutenant?"

Rafe nodded. "She thinks it's intriguing and worth following up, but she's still not convinced that we're dealing with a serial killer."

Dawn gave a low mutter of frustration.

"I know," Rafe said sympathetically. "My gut is telling me that the guy who took Lee is also responsible for the others. Tamara Norti. Crystal Rogar. And now," jerking his head toward the screen, "Alissa Gordena. Find the link between them, and we're that much closer to finding Lee."

"How's it going with the sketch Devlin is working on with our witness?"

"Slowly. Barbara's initial description was pretty broad, but when I left them, Dev was already coaxing more details out of her." Rafe took a sip of coffee and continued, "I'm glad that I'm not a forensic artist. I don't have the patience for it."

Dawn walked over to the coffee station and poured herself a cup. "The link – it's there, somewhere, Rafe. In the case files."

"Yeah. You want to tackle them? I've been working on the reports. I can have them finished up in another half-hour or so." Rafe yawned, shook his head, and continued, "Tomorrow, we can start contacting the local real estate agencies that deal in rental properties. Show them the sketch, ask them if they've rented a property to anyone who even remotely resembles our guy within the last month or two. Maybe we'll get lucky."

Sloan Lewellen wasn't even thinking about getting lucky that night. He and Ty had dropped Maeve off at her hotel after dinner; then they'd driven back to his house to watch the Alabama/Nebraska game – always a good match-up. Ty had then departed, and Sloan made his way upstairs to check on Echo. His cousin Lotti greeted him with a finger to her lips as he entered the sitting room that connected with Echo's bedroom.

"We need to keep our voices down. She's been fussy all evening. I think she's got a tooth coming in," Lotti said.

"I'll just sneak in quietly and look in on her then." At Lotti's raised eyebrows, Sloan said, "I won't wake her, I promise. It's just that I haven't managed to spend any time at all with her today. I need to see her, if only for a minute."

As Sloan disappeared through the doorway of Echo's room, Lotti reflected that it was unusual for Sloan not to have spent any time with his daughter. She tried not to pry into his personal affairs, but she couldn't help wondering if the fact that Maeve was in town had anything to do with it.

True to his word, Sloan reentered the room only a moment later. He seemed inclined to linger, so Lotti said, "How about some hot chocolate? I was just about to make some for myself."

"Sure. Sounds like a great idea, Lotti. You need any help?"

"I think I can manage. You just sit down and relax, Sloan."

It had been a good idea on his part to hire his first cousin's daughter to take care of Echo, Sloan reflected as he waited for Lotti to return with the hot chocolate. She loved Echo, and she'd needed a safe place to stay while she recovered from what her bastard of an ex-husband had put her through.

When Lotti returned carrying a tray with a pot of hot chocolate, a couple of mugs, some spoons, and a bowl of miniature marshmallows, Sloan jumped up and helped her get everything settled on a low table near his elbow. He waved her away as she made a move as if to wait upon him, taking care of pouring out the hot chocolate and handing a cup to her before he served himself.

Lotti accepted the mug gratefully and sipped on the hot chocolate while Sloan added some marshmallows to his own cup. She'd always marveled at how someone as rich and powerful as Sloan Lewellen could still be so sensitive to the needs of others. Even though she worked for him, he always took care not to treat her like a servant.

"How did dinner go?" she asked cautiously.

"Fine, fine. Dawn managed to get away and join us for about an hour. She's been tied up with a new case." He paused for a moment and then added, "Maeve looked well."

Since he'd brought up his ex-wife's name himself, Lotti commented, "I'm glad to hear it. How does she like New Orleans?"

"We didn't talk much about New Orleans. She did mention that she took a vacation to Greece about a month ago."

"Alone?"

"No, Daphne Bartelli went with her, and some character named Julian Notler. They're going back there in the spring, Maeve says."

Since Sloan's tone warned her that he was less than pleased with the inclusion of the unknown Mr. Notler in Maeve's vacation plans, Lotti was careful to keep her tone neutral as she replied, "That sounds nice. Would you like another cup of hot chocolate?"

Sloan took a final gulp out of his mug. "No, I'd better not. I'm going to turn in, Lotti." He stood up and leaned down to kiss her on the cheek. "I don't have any commitments tomorrow. How about you and me and Echo just hang out together?"

"Sounds like a good plan. See you in the morning, Sloan."

As she cleared away the dishes and took them into the small adjoining kitchenette to load them into the dishwasher, Lotti mulled over her latest conversation with her cousin. She'd worked for him for almost a year now, and he was as open and easy with her as he'd always been, but she noticed that there was one topic that he never discussed: Echo's mother – Renea Lewellen.

Sloan didn't like to talk about Renea, but that didn't mean he never thought about her. In fact, as he stood in front of the mirror in the bathroom of the suite he'd installed just across from the nursery, she was front and foremost in his mind. Renea had been his Waterloo, his one great mistake. By the time he'd finished with her, he'd sunk so low in his own estimation that he'd begun privately thinking of himself as "Sloan Lewellen: Dumb-ass doofus who thinks with his dick instead of his brain."

He'd never seen it coming. Oh, he and Maeve had experienced some problems in their relationship over the years, especially after Maeve had endured a string of miscarriages, followed by an emergency hysterectomy, but he thought they'd weathered them all. In fact, he'd been so secure in his love for Maeve, and hers for him, that he'd scoffed at the idea of falling for someone else. When it had happened, no one had been more shocked than he. But when he'd first seen Renea, the administrative assistant of a business associate with whom he was working out a merger, he felt like someone had sucker-punched him right in the gut. With her long, tousled reddish-gold hair tumbling down her back, she had looked at him out of emerald green eyes and held out her hand to him, her full, pouty lips curving into a smile.

After that first meeting, he'd found excuses to see a lot more of her, as they worked through the details of the merger together. At night, she haunted his dreams. And Maeve had been gone so much, working on establishing her own business in New Orleans. They'd had a big fight about that one. Why couldn't she open an interior decorating business here in Mountpelier, or at least in some other city nearby in Colorado? But she'd been insistent. She wanted this business to be all her own, she'd said - something she could be proud of. If she opened a business locally, she would never be sure if people were hiring her for her own sake or simply because she was Sloan Lewellen's wife.

After a few months, he'd realized that he was in trouble; he couldn't get Renea out of his mind, and he could scarcely control himself when she was around. Desperately, he'd flown to New Orleans and confronted Maeve, telling her that she needed to put aside this nonsense of starting her own business and come home with him where she belonged. During the fight that followed, he'd admitted that he was attracted to somebody else. That was one of the reasons he needed his wife with him – to anchor him once again. Maeve had really hit the roof then. She'd accused him of just making it all up, of using this as an excuse to sabotage her efforts to build her own business, independent of him and of The Lewellen Group. He'd stormed out after that. When he'd returned to Mountpelier, he'd contacted his lawyers and filed for a formal separation.

He'd expected Maeve to respond by hopping on a plane to Colorado and hightailing it home. Instead, she had filed for divorce. He had called her bluff and told his lawyers to start the necessary proceedings. When a week had passed and she still hadn't come home to try to work things out between them, he had called Renea and asked her out on a date. They'd gotten married six months later, as soon as the divorce decree was final.

When he was in high school, he'd watched, fascinated, as his chemistry teacher had burned a piece of magnesium in a controlled experiment. It had burned white-hot, with an incredibly intense light – but only briefly. Within seconds, there was nothing left. Everything had been consumed. That's what his marriage to Renea had been like. Now she was gone, and with any luck, he'd never have to see her again. After he'd caught her cheating on him just a few months after Echo's birth, he'd filed for divorce. According to the terms of their pre-nup, she was entitled to nothing from him, so she had been happy to grant him full custody of Echo in return for a generous financial settlement. The last he'd heard of her, she was in Venice, hanging out with some Italian nobleman and playing with the beautiful people. As long as she stayed away from Echo and him, that was fine with Sloan.

He finished up in the bathroom, turned the light out, and crossed over to his bed. He fell asleep thinking not of Renea, but of Maeve, and planning the next move in his campaign to bridge the gulf between them. The business proposal he had pitched to her when he'd called her that morning might help...

Rafe decided to call it a night a little before midnight. Prentiss and Noritaki had left at about ten, and he'd persuaded Dawn to go home shortly afterward. "Fresh eyes," he'd told her. "We need to look at it again in the morning with fresh eyes."

Dawn had reluctantly agreed. She'd been poring over the case files for hours, trying to find that one link that would help them crack the case. Meanwhile, he'd spoken to Will's mother again. She'd finally reached Will's friends, Jupe Dunsinger and Hunt Farolle, but they'd known only slightly more than Will's other friends had. He'd mentioned that he'd been seeing a girl named Lee, but true to form, he'd been close-mouthed about the relationship. They still didn't have a last name. Naomi Preisinger had gleaned some precious bits of information from the pair, however, and one of those pieces of information rendered it unnecessary for them to get a warrant for any names from Mountpelier

University: Lee wasn't a student there. Will had mentioned that she worked in some sort of fancy salon. She was working as a hair stylist, he'd said, and was trying to save up enough money to begin attending college next year. And she had a roommate named Maya.

Will himself was holding his own, his mother said. His vital signs were better, and that was encouraging. Rafe had given her his cell phone number and asked that she call him at any time, day or night, if Will showed signs of regaining consciousness.

Meanwhile, things were progressing nicely on the Torrense case. Shortly after Dawn had left to go over to Fredo's, he had heard from the police in a town called Reallto City, not far from Jacksonville, Florida. Jago Bolt had made life easier on them all by getting himself arrested earlier in the day on a charge of drunk and disorderly. A routine check by the arresting officer had led to the discovery that there was an outstanding warrant for his arrest on murder charges in Colorado.

After consulting with a public defender, Bolt had waived extradition, so the wheels were in motion to get him on a plane back to Mountpelier as soon as all the necessary paperwork had been filed. It didn't get much better than that.

After hanging up with the Florida cops, Rafe had discovered that J.B.'s plane ticket to Florida had been paid for by credit card. However, the name on the credit card was not Jago Bolt; it was Monieque Torrense. Yep, it was going to be mighty interesting to sit down and have a chat with Mr. Bolt when he arrived back in town.

Rafe shut his computer down, grabbed his jacket, and walked over to Jordan, the officer who had been first on scene the previous morning. Jordan had wandered in at the end of his shift and volunteered to put in some extra time on the case. He felt a personal connection to the case, he'd said. He had a younger sister who was just beginning her first year of college. Couldn't imagine what it would have felt like if she were the one who was missing.

"C'mon, kid. Time to pack it in and call it a night."

Jordan looked up, his eyes still bright and alert, which was pretty impressive, considering the hours that he'd put in that day. "Okay, Sergeant. Let me just save this file, then I'm on my way." His fingers moved expertly over the keys; then he rolled back his chair and stood up.

"Uh, Sergeant Melbourne? Do you have a moment? There's something I need to talk to you about."

Rafe, who had turned away, looked back over his shoulder at the officer. "Can it wait 'til tomorrow? I'm pretty beat."

"Uh... tonight would probably be better. It won't take long, Sergeant. I promise."

Sighing, Rafe changed direction and led the way into the break room, Jordan close behind him. A refrigerator stood on the wall to the right, with a long counter running down the remaining part of the wall. A coffee maker sat on the counter, along with a small microwave. A water cooler sat in one corner, and at right angles to the far wall, two small blue tables had been shoved together to make one longer table, with five metal chairs surrounding it.

Pulling out a chair from the table, Rafe said, "How's your grandfather, Jordan? He miss being on the job?"

"Can't say that he does, sir. He loves retirement. And my grandmother loves the fact that he's able to keep regular hours instead of being liable to be called upon to go out on a case at any hour of the day or night. They're on a trip now – went to visit some relatives in Israel. They just sent me a picture of my grandma putting a prayer slip into one of the cracks in the Wailing Wall. Probably praying for me to find a nice Jewish girl and get married. She's been after me for years to settle down and give her some great-grandchildren." He paused for a minute, cleared his throat, passed a hand through his wavy black hair nervously.

Rafe waited a moment, then said, "What's on your mind, Jordan?"

"Well, sir, you know that I live across town, don't you?"

Rafe didn't know, but he nodded anyway. "What's that got to do with anything?"

"Sometimes I see Detective Cimarron in her car when I'm heading home. She lives across town too, you know? Best way to beat the traffic if you're going that way is to take the Boulevard to the East End Bypass and then cut across Kennedy Avenue to Lexington Way. Well, a few times recently, I noticed that this gray car always seemed to be behind her."

"What about it?" Rafe said cautiously. "You're behind her on a regular basis too. Probably hundreds of people take that same route home every day."

"Yeah, but I don't make it a point to keep her car in sight. This car does. It looked to me like they were tailing her, sir. And there's something about the two guys inside. I just got a feeling, you know? So I ran the tags."

Uh-oh, Rafe thought. He waited expectantly.

"That car, sir, the gray car? It's registered to the Lewellen Group."

Now the fat was in the fire. "So you were concerned that maybe her husband or his family are having Detective Cimarron followed?"

Jordan nodded. "Yes, sir. I don't know Cimarron very well, how things are between her and her husband. But I think she should know that she's being followed. I just don't know how to tell her. So I decided to talk to you instead, ask you how to handle it."

Rafe took a moment to contemplate the situation. Then he asked, "Just how much *do* you know about Detective Cimarron and her husband, Jordan?"

"What most everyone else around here knows. That Tyrell Lewellen is Sloan Lewellen's son. That he moved back to town a couple of years ago to recuperate from the injuries he sustained in an accident that caused him to take early retirement from the Air Force. That some local yahoos decided that the best way to get rich quick was to kidnap him and hold up his old man for a hefty ransom. But Cimarron stumbled upon the whole set-up by chance while she was off-duty, helped Lewellen to escape, and brought down the kidnappers. They got married not long afterward."

Rafe nodded. "What you don't know is how the kidnapping affected Ty Lewellen's parents. Sloan Lewellen handled everything stoically, but Maeve Lewellen – the mother – it practically destroyed her. She was beside herself, hysterical, until it was all over and her son returned safely. And she blamed Sloan for not protecting her son better."

Rafe got up out of the chair and poured himself a glass of water before he continued. "Sloan Lewellen has his own security detail; it's been providing protection for him and his family for years. During his son's time in the Air Force, his protection detail was dropped, for obvious reasons. And Ty, who never considered himself to be a prime target for kidnappers, refused to have the protection reinstated after he retired and moved back to Mountpelier. He reasoned that after all those years in the military, he could take care of himself. He's been trained in self defense, and he's proficient with any number of weapons. Unfortunately, he didn't reckon on the fact that none of that would do him any good if he was unconscious. The guys who kidnapped him managed to slip him a drug, and that was that. Next thing he knew, he was bound and locked up in a cabin in the middle of nowhere."

Crumpling the paper cup he had been drinking out of and tossing it into the waste paper basket, Rafe continued, "After it was all over, Sloan made sure that his son was once again placed under the protection of Lewellen Security. Detective Cimarron was aware of all of this. What neither she nor her husband realized at first, however, was that Sloan Lewellen had arranged for a team from Lewellen Security to keep *her* under surveillance as well after her marriage to Ty. Of course, she spotted them almost immediately. Why they thought that a trained cop wouldn't pick up on the fact that she was being followed is beyond me. She was angry, of course, and confronted her father-in-law at once, demanding that he put a stop to it. He just picked up the phone and called Ty's mother. Have you ever met Maeve Lewellen, Jordan?"

"Can't say that I have, sir."

"Well, suffice it to say that she has no equal when it comes to the power of persuasion. The long and short of it is that Cimarron, for her mother-in-law's peace of mind, agreed not to interfere with the arrangements that Sloan had made with Lewellen Security, as long as they keep in the background and are discreet about it. But you understand that she would be embarrassed if anyone else found out, don't you? Her being a cop and all. She'd never live it down."

After Jordan had left, Rafe pondered how to handle letting Dawn know that a fellow police officer was on to the fact that she had a security detail assigned to protect her. He was still mulling it over when he pulled into his own driveway. Hitting the remote control for the garage door, he eased his car inside and parked. Then he got out of the car and hit the button to close the garage door before opening the connecting door into the house. Taking his coat off and hanging it up in the hall closet, he wandered back into the kitchen to make himself a whiskey and soda. Carrying his drink back into the living room, he settled down into his recliner with a sigh of satisfaction. He knew from experience that he needed a little winding-down time before he went up to bed. Otherwise, he'd just toss and turn and get more and more frustrated as sleep eluded him. His Uncle Nick had been the same way. More times than he could count, they'd sat right here in this living room, winding down together after a day on the job.

That practice had ended when he'd met and married Cynthia, however. He'd moved into her apartment after the wedding. That had lasted for a few months, while they went house hunting. After months of searching for just the right place, they'd finally found what they wanted – a split-level, three bedroom house in a brand new development. And they'd been happy there. At first. Until Cynthia decided that she didn't like being married to a cop. Then the quarrels had started, the endless nagging. Why couldn't he get a different job? One with more regular hours, so that they could spend more time together. One that wouldn't constantly screw up their vacation plans. One that would pay better. He could go back to school at night, get into law school. Once he'd graduated and passed the bar, he could open his own practice. With her training as a legal secretary, she could handle the office side of things. It would be the perfect arrangement.

No matter how many times he'd told her that he didn't want to leave his job, that he was a cop and wanted to stay a cop, she wouldn't let it alone. Once Cynthia got an idea in her head, not even a stick of dynamite would dislodge it. She wanted to be married to a lawyer. Since Rafe wouldn't oblige her, she'd found someone else – one of the partners at the law firm where she worked, an older man who'd fallen head over heels in love with her. When she had informed Rafe that she wanted a divorce, he'd agreed without much of a fight. Anything to end the constant nagging. He'd moved out, gotten a place of his own, a tiny efficiency apartment not far from work. But then Nick had gotten sick, and he'd moved back into his uncle's house so that he could help out as much as possible. After Nick's death, he'd inherited the house, so he'd simply decided to stay.

Nick's death had hit him hard, and he knew that Dawn had been similarly affected. Even now, two years after Nick had passed, sometimes he still couldn't believe that his uncle was gone. He wondered how Nick would have handled the cases they were working on right now, how he would have proceeded.

In the morning, he decided, he and Dawn would go over the case files together with a fine-tooth comb. They'd find the link. They had to.

Rafe left for work early the next morning and had breakfast at Fredo's. Not just for the good food, but also with another purpose in mind. There were a couple of guys he needed to have a word with, and he expected them momentarily. Sure enough, a few minutes later, they walked in. Their real names were Hal and Morgan, but Dawn, a fan of Dr. Seuss, always referred to them as *Thing One* and *Thing Two*.

They saw him sitting there and were about to pass him with a nod when he said, "Gentlemen. A word with you?"

He stood up and led the way into the private dining room. One of the reasons Sloan had invested in and expanded the restaurant was for purely practical reasons: the office above the private dining room gave the security team assigned to Dawn a convenient place to watch police headquarters while Dawn was inside. By watching from the office window, they could easily determine when Dawn left the building and pick up her tail again. At first, Dawn had deliberately given them the slip, but after her conversation with Maeve, she simply ignored the two of them and let them go about their job.

Entering the private dining room, Rafe pulled out a chair at the table, sat down, and without preamble said: "You got spotted."

The two exchanged a glance, and then Hal asked, "Who?"

"One of the patrol officers who generally goes home by the same route as Detective Cimarron. You were too obvious, and he got suspicious, called in the plates, figured out you were Lewellen Security. Fortunately, he decided to come to me with the information before taking it any further. I explained the situation to him, and he's promised to keep it quiet."

"Will he keep his promise?"

"Yeah. He wants to make detective. The last thing he needs is to piss off two Homicide detectives by embarrassing them. He's too smart for that. Better for him to keep his mouth shut. That way he'll have two friends up the ladder who owe him one."

"Have you notified Detective Cimarron?"

"Not yet. I'll have to, though – eventually."

Hal looked at his partner and said, "We'll have to notify Mr. Lewellen."

"Is that absolutely necessary?" Morgan replied.

"If you want to keep your job, it is. I've worked for Sloan Lewellen longer than you have. The best way to get yourself fired is by trying to hide something from him."

He held his partner's eyes for a moment, then turned back to Rafe. "It won't happen again."

Morgan obviously wasn't happy. "How are you going to promise that? We don't keep her in sight, and something happens to her, Mr.

Lewellen won't just fire us – he'll have our heads. It's different when she's on the job – she's usually with him" - he nodded in Rafe's direction - "but when she's on her way home at night, she's all alone. And don't tell me that being a cop is enough to protect her. Out of all the professions, cops have one of the highest mortality rates. We were hired to protect her. We can't do it with our hands tied behind our backs."

"He's right about one thing. If someone is going to target Detective Cimarron, they're more likely to do it when she's alone, on her way to or from work. And we can't assist her if we aren't close by," Hal commented to Rafe.

"I've been thinking about that," Rafe replied. "Maybe I can convince her to install a Sergeant in the Trunk."

Morgan looked puzzled, but Hal, who had been a cop for twenty years before going into the private sector, understood the lingo immediately. "A GPS tracking device? That would help. We'd know where she was without having to keep her in sight. We could get in front of her more often than not. That would mix things up a little. You actually think you can convince her to let us put a tracking device in her car?"

"Once I let her know that another cop has spotted you, she might be more open to the suggestion. The last thing she wants is for anyone to know that she has a private security detail following her."

Hal nodded. "Let us know what she decides. In the meantime, we'll do our best to be discreet. However, protecting the subject's life is our main priority – not her reputation."

"Understood." Rafe finished his coffee and set his cup down. "I'll be in touch."

Dawn took the news that Jordan had spotted the Lewellen Security team assigned to her more philosophically than Rafe had expected. With a shrug of her shoulders, she said, "Someone was bound to catch on sooner or later; I told Sloan that. At least it was someone you're sure can be trusted to keep his mouth shut. And I've got enough on my mind right now to spend too much time thinking about it. Take a look at this." Tapping her finger on a photograph of the campsite in the Crystal Rogar case, she placed it side by side with a photo that Walsh had taken of the evidence he'd found at the place where Will Preisinger had gone over the cliff. "You see it?"

At first he didn't, but then he got it. "The beer bottles. It's the same brand at both scenes."

"Yeah, and it's not the most common brand, either. I looked it up. It's produced at a small, local brewery in Black Line, Vermont."

"Never heard of it before."

"Neither had I. It's not sold nationally. I checked. So do you buy that it's just a coincidence that bottles of Black Line beer happened to turn up at two different crime scenes in states as far away as Alaska and Colorado?"

Rafe grinned. "Nope. No way."

Dawn grinned back at him. "Now we get to the good part. Do you know where our first possible victim, Alissa Gordena, was raised?"

"I bet I can hazard a guess. Black Line, Vermont?"

"Right on your first guess."

Rafe thought about it for a minute, then said, "I'll have to update the lieutenant. She's at home today, so I'll have to get ahold of her on her cell."

"Shit." It was the first word that Lieutenant Westbrooke uttered after Rafe outlined the latest developments in the case. "I was hoping that you were wrong. I'll have to inform Chief Wirthing. It will be up to him as to whether or not to call in the Feds. How would you feel about that?"

"Not thrilled," he admitted. "At the same time, though, the more people we have on the case, the better chance we have of finding Lee."

"It's Sunday. Chief probably won't make a decision until tomorrow. In the meantime, what's your plan, Sergeant?"

"Follow up on the first victim – Alissa Gordena. If she really was the first victim, and not just the first one we found, there's the possibility that she had some sort of personal relationship with the perp. We'd like to fly up and interview her mother personally, then check out the plant that manufactures Black Line beer."

"Fly to Vermont? Not sure the budget can handle that."

"There's a Lewellen Air flight leaving shortly that's heading in that general area of the country. Cimarron can make arrangements for the two of us to be on it, which means that we can fly up and back at no expense to the department. The only expense would be for a rental car."

"Okay - I think that the budget can handle that. Go ahead and make the arrangements, and update me as often as possible on this one, Rafe."

"You got it, LT." As he disconnected, he caught Dawn's eye. "She's letting the Chief know the latest."

"You think he'll want to call in the Bureau?"

Rafe shrugged. "Not sure. In the meantime, we keep working the case. You get ahold of Ty?"

Dawn nodded. "He's already on his way to Nyetimber. By the time we get there, he'll be fueled up and ready to take off."

"Great. Onward and upward, partner. Next stop: Black Line, Vermont."

Dawn adjusted herself more comfortably in her seat on the private jet Ty had elected to fly on their trip to the East and looked over at Rafe, who was seated across from her. "You want something to eat or drink? There's plenty of stuff on board; Ty made sure it was stocked up before we left."

"I'm okay for now. Maybe later." They were the only passengers on the plane. Although he hadn't filled the lieutenant in on all the details, Rafe was aware that this wasn't a regular Lewellen Air flight; Ty was actually flying to Trenton, New Jersey, in order to visit an old friend, and he was making a little detour to drop them off in Vermont before continuing on to his ultimate destination. Dawn's Satphone rang just then. Rafe listened to her side of the conversation and saw the corners of her mouth lift slightly. When she ended the call, he lifted his eyebrows inquiringly. "You look like a cat who's just heard that a bunch of cage-free canaries are moving into her house. What's up?"

"Prentiss just told me that he and Noritaki struck gold on the second canvass of the neighborhood surrounding the park where Cullen's body was found. They spoke to one of the residents who wasn't at home when we did the first canvass. He lives right across from one of the entrances to the park. When they showed him Cullen's picture and asked him about the night of the murder, he recalled seeing Cullen enter the park with another man at about 10:00 p.m. And he's positively identified the other man as Jago Bolt."

"Nice. That will help when we get J.B. into the box. If Cullen's mother is involved, he'll be more likely to flip on her, try to deal for a lesser sentence."

"Yeah. I don't think that we'll ever get connect her with the death of Gwen's dad, though. Officer Taylor said that what probably caused the accident was a leak in the power steering. When they reconstructed the accident, it looked like her dad was rounding a sharp turn when the power steering went out. He swung the wheel too hard as a result, over-corrected, and went off the road into the trees. They found a puncture in one of the hoses that had caused the fluid to leak, but it looked like it could have occurred naturally. And since it was an older car, it didn't have an indicator light to warn him that there was a problem."

Rafe nodded thoughtfully. "And he wouldn't have spotted any fluid on the garage floor, because according to Cullen's letter, Monieque washed off and hosed down the garage floor every day that week. And without any other evidence pointing to foul play, there's not nearly enough to charge her. Any good defense attorney would have the case thrown out within an hour. But if we can connect her to Cullen's death, prove that his suspicions were correct, it might be enough for Ellanor Torrense to get an exhumation order for Cullen's father. If poison is found when they do the autopsy, it'll be hard for Monieque to wiggle out of that one."

They were both silent for a minute or two, then Dawn said, "I'd like to do some more research on the Preisinger case. I can use my phone to link up and look for any other missing person reports or incidents that seem to fit. There are more out there than the ones we turned up, Rafe. I can feel it."

"Yeah, I think you're right about that." Pulling out his tablet, he said, "While you do that, I'll get caught up on some of the reports and other paperwork. Might as well make the best use of our time."

By the time the jet touched down in Burlington, Rafe had waded through a considerable amount of paperwork, but Dawn had had no luck in finding additional cases that had possible connections to the Preisinger case. Philosophically, she put her phone aside, said goodbye to her husband, and got off the plane with Rafe. Since they had arranged for the rental car in advance, they were soon seated in it and on their way to the home of Alissa Gordena's mother in the small town of Black Line, Vermont.

Miranda Gordena looked like she hadn't slept in years, Dawn thought. She had been extremely cooperative, though, inviting them in right away and offering them coffee. They had the Vermont State Police to thank for that. The detective who had handled the Gordena case had been unable to join them, due to a bad bout of the flu, but he had cleared the way for them with Mrs. Gordena. Dawn and Rafe had accepted her offer of coffee more to put the poor woman at ease than for any other reason. Deep lines of worry marred her face, and her hands moved nervously as she spoke. Making coffee seemed to steady her, however, and she answered all of their questions eagerly. Anything, she'd said, to help find out what had happened to her daughter.

They chatted at first, trying to get a feel for Alissa, for the family, for the time period leading up to the point when Alissa and her boyfriend had gone missing. Nothing out of the ordinary had happened, Miranda insisted. Alissa had been her normal, happy self. No, they hadn't noticed anyone paying any unusual attention to her.

"What about boyfriends, Mrs. Gordena?" Dawn asked.

The tired eyes became dewy as Alissa's mother fought back the tears. "Lissa was very popular. Always. Even in grade school, she always had a boyfriend." She paused for a minute, took a sip of tea. "Let's see. There was Paul, of course. He took Lissa to her eighth grade dance. After that, it was Jamie. Then Drake, then Kirk. Last couple of years of high school, though, she went out pretty steadily with Mel Eamont. She only broke up with him when she went to college. After she met Breckon. Breckon Petteril. The one who..."

She grabbed a tissue, wiped her eyes. Cleared her throat.

Dawn gave her a moment to compose herself, then asked, "What about artists, Mrs. Gordena? Any of the guys in her life have an artistic bent?"

"Oh, dear, not that I know of. I mean, Mel Eamont's main passion in life was basketball. He played all the way through high school. He's in graduate school now, studying to be a lawyer. I ran into his mother just last week. She's been very kind to me, since I lost Lissa. So naturally I asked her about Mel."

"And the others?"

"Jamie moved away. That must have been three years ago now. Last I heard, Drake and Kirk were at some college in Florida, majoring in girls and surfing. Paul stayed closer to home. He got a degree in computer science and started his own business, which is doing quite well, I understand. No, I wouldn't describe anyone that Lissa ever went out with as an artist."

She had been back in the past for a while, remembering Alissa in grade school, in high school. But now reality intruded on her pleasant memories. She said wistfully, "The first few years after it happened, I always hoped. Maybe they'd run away together or something. Even though there was no reason for them to. But then, when they found Breckon's remains last summer... I knew she was gone."

Her voice broke again, and this time she couldn't hold back the tears. Dawn reached out and took Mrs. Gordena's hand, silently offering comfort. Miranda looked deep into Dawn's eyes for a moment. Then she murmured, "You know, don't you? You know what it's like to lose someone you love."

Dawn inclined her head, and that was enough. Miranda clasped her hand even more tightly and said, "Detective, what happened to my Lissa? Why have you and Sergeant Melbourne come here all the way from Colorado to ask me about her?"

Dawn exchanged a look with Rafe. Then she responded, "Mrs. Gordena, what we tell you can't be repeated to the press."

Miranda's eyes flashed. "Bunch of vultures!" she exclaimed. "Especially after they found Breckon. 'Mrs. Gordena'," she mimicked, "'How do you *feel*?' Mother of God! How did they think I felt? The body of my daughter's boyfriend had just been found. Didn't they know how painful that was for me? It was the death of all my hopes. They kept after me even when I refused to talk to them, hoping to parade my grief all over the news. No, you can rest assured that anything you tell me won't find its way into the press."

"Okay, then." Dawn took a deep breath. "Mrs. Gordena, there's a chance that a connection exists between your daughter's disappearance and a case that Sergeant Melbourne and I are currently investigating in Colorado."

It took Miranda only a moment to grasp the implications of what Dawn had said.

"You don't think it was an accident. You think my daughter –and Breckon– were killed," she said flatly.

"We can't tell you much more, Mrs. Gordena, because the investigation is still ongoing. But that possibility exists, certainly."

Miranda groped for and clasped Dawn's hand again. "Find him! Find whoever took my Lissa away from me! Promise me you'll find him!"

Dawn thought of Naomi Preisinger, sitting at her son's bedside in Mountpelier.

"We'll find him, Mrs. Gordena. Whatever it takes, however long it takes, we'll find him."

Rafe was quiet as he got into the driver's side of the car they had rented in Burlington, but Dawn knew that he wasn't pleased with the assurances she had made to Alissa's mother.

"Rafe? She needed that. She needed to know that we care about what happened to Alissa."

Rafe didn't look at her as he turned the key in the ignition and concentrated on pulling away from the curb in front of the Gordena residence. "You may not be able to keep your promise to her, Dawn. It's early days yet. We don't even know for sure that the two cases are connected. And it isn't our case."

"I know, I know. Maybe I shouldn't have said anything. But I have a feeling, Rafe. A feeling that we're about to bust this thing wide open." She broke off as her cell phone signaled her and took a moment to look at the incoming text. "It's Ty."

"Is he back from Trenton already?"

"No, but he's leaving shortly. It won't take him long. It's a short flight."

Something in her tone made Rafe say, "Problem?"

Dawn replied, "No – there's no problem. It's just – Ty texted that he needs a favor. He didn't go into the details, but he wants us to 'play along' when we get back to the plane."

"Does this have something to do with that old friend he was planning to meet?"

"I'm not sure. He's been close-mouthed about Brody, but I've been getting a feeling lately that something is wrong. I guess we'll find out when we get back to Burlington."

It was a good thing, Ty reflected, that he had some buddies who were currently stationed nearby at McGuire Air Force Base. Getting an unconscious friend who topped out at 6'7 and weighed 230 pounds into the cabin of the six-passenger jet he'd flown east from Colorado was definitely not a one-man job. With his buddies' help, however, he had achieved the task, and was now airborne and back on his way to pick up Dawn and Rafe in Vermont.

He wondered what Dawn would make of Brody. Though Ty had told her about his friend, and she had some inclination about the deep bond that existed between them, she had never met Brody. His latest assignment for the shadow agency he worked for had required him to work deep undercover for an extended period of time. Ty himself had not even heard from Brody for almost a year until he'd received a phone call a few days ago. Though Brody hadn't said much, Ty knew him well enough to sense that something was wrong. Very wrong. Under the circumstances, he'd decided that it would be a good idea to drop in for an unannounced visit. What he'd discovered during his visit had confirmed his suspicions that all was not well with his friend. So he'd arranged for Brody to take a little vacation. An impromptu little jaunt to Colorado. And if Tyrell Lewellen had anything to say about it, the next stop on Brody's vacation itinerary would involve a trip to Mountpelier General Hospital.

Dawn and Rafe were already on the ground and waiting when he touched down in Burlington. When they climbed aboard and saw the unconscious man strapped into one of the passenger seats, Dawn barely even raised an eyebrow.

"Brody?" she said.

"Yeah. He told me that he needed a change of scenery, so I suggested that he come and visit us in Colorado for a while. He's really looking forward to it."

A snore from Brody punctuated Ty's last comment.

"Yep. I can see that."

Rafe had kept quiet during this exchange, but a grin as wide as the Grand Canyon split his face. He wisely didn't say anything, but strapped himself into his own seat. Dawn, however, moved forward and strapped herself into the co-pilot's seat next to Ty.

"It looks like it's going to be a mighty interesting visit," she said.

Ty just grinned.

When they arrived at the duplex, with the help of Rafe and the men from the Lewellen Security detail who were assigned to Ty that day, they managed to get Brody inside and down the steps to the guest room off the recreation area on the ground floor. It was easier to carry him down than up, they reasoned. Besides that, the couch down there would provide Ty with a comfortable place to spend the night, since he really, really needed to be close at hand when Brody woke up in the morning. Simply to convey a few minor pieces of information to his friend, of course - like where he was, for example, and just how it had come about that he had gone to sleep in New Jersey and ended up as a temporary resident of the beautiful state of Colorado. After he'd explained everything sufficiently, Ty figured it would probably be a good idea to relocate to another area of the house for a while – just to give the big guy some time to think it over. And if he could pull off a speedy enough exit, he might just get away with only a few bumps and bruises...

Once Brody was bestowed in the guest room, Ty felt that he'd earned a reward for his efforts, so he determined that spending some time kicking back and watching sports on his big screen TV was in order. Walking over to the refrigerator behind the bar, he pulled out a beer and settled himself into his favorite leather recliner. He heard Traitor padding down the steps and watched as she flopped herself down at his feet, panting and looking up at him pleadingly.

"You already had your treat today. Mrs. T. always gives you one after dinner. What makes you think you're going to get another one out of me?"

"The fact that you are putty in her hands might have something to do with it. She knows that sooner or later, you always give in," Dawn commented. Ty had filled her in a little on the plane, so she knew why he had decided to spirit Brody out of New Jersey and bring him home with them. Once she'd understood the circumstances, she made no demur, but simply said, "You're a good friend, Ty."

She made no move to sit down and join him, so he asked, "Want a beer?"

Dawn shook her head. That didn't surprise him, as Dawn tended to go for wine or cocktails rather than beer. But her eyes took on an intent look as she gazed at him sitting relaxed in his chair, sipping from his bottle of beer.

"Did you and Rafe accomplish what you set out to do today?" Ty asked.

She nodded absently, then wandered over to the refrigerator, looked in briefly, and commented, "They're all the same brand."

"What?"

"The beer bottles. You have about three dozen in there. And they're all the same brand."

"Sure. It's my favorite."

"So if you were going on a camping trip, you'd just get a cooler and pull out as many as you thought you needed for the trip," she said thoughtfully. "You wouldn't even need to stop at a store."

Ty looked at her thoughtfully. "What's this all about, Dawn?"

A frown creased Dawn's brow. Technically, she shouldn't talk to Ty about an ongoing investigation, but this was different. He already knew far more about the case than the average civilian did. And she knew she could trust him not to disclose any of the details of the investigation.

"I think he's from Vermont."

"The guy you're after? Why?"

"We found three other cases we think are tied to ours. At two of the scenes, one in Alaska and the one here in Colorado, some beer bottles were found. Same brand. Black Line."

Ty frowned. "Never heard of it."

"Neither had I. Turns out that it's bottled by a brewery in the town where one of the victims lived. Rafe and I stopped by and visited it on our way back to Burlington. It's a small outfit, Ty, with a limited production each year. Turns out that it's sold primarily in Vermont and a couple of its neighboring states. They don't have the capacity to branch out any farther than that."

"It does sound like it's unlikely to be a coincidence," Ty said thoughtfully. "But you never know. Brand loyalty is a funny thing. It's not outside the realm of possibility that two guys, one from Alaska and one from Colorado, visited up there and liked the beer so much that they brought back a stash of it. Or it could have been a gift from a friend."

"A friend," Dawn mused. Then she got to her feet. "I have to talk to Carl Brassner again."

"Who's Carl Brassner?"

"Will Preisinger's roommate."

She could have spoken to him on the phone, but Dawn felt she got better information when she could talk to a witness face-to-face. She texted Rafe on the way over to Will and Carl's apartment, letting him know that she was following up on her latest hunch. He didn't text her back right away, so she went up to the apartment alone.

She had let Carl know that she was coming in advance, so she was not surprised when he opened the door right away. "Detective Cimarron? What's this all about?"

Dawn walked right over to the refrigerator and gestured toward it. "Mind if I take a look inside?"

"Uh, well..."

"If you have anything in there that you technically shouldn't at your age, I'm not going to make an issue out of it. I just need to confirm a hunch."

"Okay – go ahead."

When she opened the door of the refrigerator and looked in, Dawn immediately spotted the beer bottles. Taking one out, she looked at the label. Not Black Line, she observed with satisfaction. Turning to Carl, she questioned, "Yours?"

"Uh, no – that's Will's. I don't really care for beer. I'm more into... " His voice trailed off when he recalled just who it was he was speaking to.

Dawn looked at the label again and said thoughtfully, "This is a lager. That's a dark beer, right?"

"Yeah, Will's kind of a snob about beer. He only drinks lagers. He says that the other types are crap – not real beer."

"But none of these types of bottles were found at the campsite."

"No - Will is kind of funny about that. He doesn't believe in drinking when he goes camping. Says it's foolish. You have to keep your wits about you any time you're out in the woods, he always says. Never know what you might run into."

Dawn thought for a moment and said, "Neither you nor Will is old enough to legally buy beer."

Carl stared down at his feet as he replied, "Some of Will's friends are old enough."

Dawn put the bottle back in the refrigerator and shut the door. "Thank you, Carl. You've been a big help."

"Really? You think this might help you to find out who tried to kill Will and took his girl?"

"Maybe. Only time will tell, though. What's the latest news on Will's condition?"

Carl shrugged. "Not much change, unfortunately. I was going to stay at the hospital tonight, but Will's mom told me to go home and get some sleep."

Dawn paused as she reached the door. Here was someone else who was trying to be a good friend. "Mrs. Preisinger gave you some good advice, Carl. Take care of yourself. You'll be in better shape to help support Will and his mother that way." She reached out and gripped his hand for a moment, then made her way out of the apartment and down to her car.

In response to the text she had sent him earlier, Rafe called Dawn when she was on her way back home. He listened intently when she told him what she had discovered.

"It's interesting, but not conclusive," he commented. "For all we know, Lee could have brought the beer."

"Possibly, but I don't think so. Speaking as a woman, if I were going on a camping date with a guy and volunteered to bring the beer, I would have been careful to find out his favorite brand before I got it. I buy the guy some beer and it turns out he doesn't even like it, I'm not going to win any points with him. And the beer bottles were empty, remember? No way Lee drank all of them by herself. Plus, there's the beer that was poured out behind the rock. Will's the one who sat there. He's the one who poured it out, because it's not the kind that he likes. Black Line isn't a lager."

"You're starting to make a hell of a lot of sense, partner. But we're going to need more than this in order to break the case, Dawn. None of this is bringing us any closer to finding Lee."

"We're getting closer, Rafe. I can feel it my gut. We're almost there."

"I hope so. Hey, speaking of almost there, I just got word from Florida. Jago Bolt will be on his way back tomorrow. His flight gets in at 10:48 a.m."

"So with any luck, we'll be able to talk to him sometime tomorrow afternoon."

"Right you are. I have to say that I'm looking forward to hearing what old J.B. has to say for himself. Should be mighty interesting. But for right now, I'm about ready to shut it all off for a while and take a break. See you in the morning, Dawn."

Ty was still downstairs when she returned home, so she decided to take the time to update her notes and review everything they had on the case, from start to finish. She'd lost track of the time when she heard a noise behind her and looked over her shoulder to see Ty standing in the doorway.

"Hey," she said. "What time is it?"

Ty consulted his watch. "Just after midnight. You about ready to call it a night?"

Dawn looked at the stacks of papers on the table. "I might as well. I'm just spinning my wheels here. I'm still wide awake, but I don't seem to be getting anywhere."

"So put it away for the night and let it gel for a while. You may not feel tired, but your mind obviously needs a rest."

"Yeah, I guess so." She saw something in his face that had her saying, "What?"

"You really don't remember, do you?"

"Remember what?"

"As of," he glanced at his watch, "six minutes ago, it's your birthday, Dawn."

"Oh," she said blankly. "You're right. I hadn't even given it a thought."

"I did, and there's some champagne, strawberries and melted chocolate with your name on it waiting for you. Why don't you go upstairs while I get everything together and bring it up?"

"Okay. You know, you may be the prince of all husbands, Ty. Most of my married friends have told me that when it comes to birthdays, their significant others are hard-pressed even to recall the date, if asked."

"Yeah, well, you know how it is with us high-handed busybodies. We just can't help ourselves. It's built into our natures, I guess...and there goes the eye-roll again." He shook his head. "Can't be good for you, Dawn. Just can't be."

Since he was about to ply her with champagne and strawberries, she figured that maybe she should just let that one go, so she shrugged her shoulders and headed for the stairs. On his way back to the kitchen, Ty called over his shoulder, "Dawn? Change into that black thing I like so much, would you?"

She couldn't help it. "Okay. But I'm afraid I might be a little sleepier than I thought. All that eye-rolling takes a lot of energy, you know."

It was nice to get in the last line, for a change.

Once she was in her bedroom, she grabbed the "black thing" and decided to take a quick shower. Afterward, she smoothed lotion on, picked the nightdress up, and fingered it appreciatively. Suspended by criss-cross straps across the shoulders, the shimmering gown swooped into a dramatic V in the front and plunged deep in the back. Folds of diaphanous fabric gathered beneath the bust and fell from the waist into an elegant train of silk and scalloped lace. As she slipped it over her head, the whisper-soft material caressed her as it flowed over her body like water.

The only light that greeted her when she walked back into her bedroom was firelight. Ty was sitting on one of the chairs in front of the fireplace. On a table next to him, a green bottle peeked out of the top of an ice bucket, and the promised bowl of strawberries and pot of chocolate sat next to it. A box tied up with a fancy ribbon lay there as well. As she sank down into the chair on the opposite side of the fireplace, Ty handed her a flute of champagne.

"Happy birthday, Dawn."

Striving for a light tone, she said, "We should have a toast." She raised her glass, clinked it with his, and said simply, "To us."

"I'll drink to that."

Dawn always marveled at the way in which good champagne could taste both sweet and dry at the same time. It slipped over her tongue, refreshing and bubbly and just a little intoxicating. She looked across at Ty, smiling a little.

"Aren't you going to open your present?"

Dawn picked up the box and said, "It's so pretty. It's almost a shame to open it." She carefully slid the gold bow and ribbon off and opened the teal blue box.

"Oh....." Rubies and diamonds winked at her, fire in their very depths. "They're so beautiful..."

"Here, let me help you try them on."

She rose from the chair so that he could more easily fasten the necklace around her neck. When he had finished with that, he moved around so that he was facing her again while she put on the matching earrings. Clad in the shimmering black gown, her long dark hair streaming down her back, the glittering diamonds and rubies dangling from her ears and resting on her décolletage reflecting the glow of the firelight, she took Ty's breath away. He swallowed convulsively and managed to say, "You look like some sort of princess, Dawn."

"I feel like a princess. You make me feel that way. No one's ever made me that way before. Not in twenty-eight years."

"Twenty-eight years ago today," he said slowly, "I was six years old. I didn't know it then, but you know what? The day you were born was the best day of my life."

She was touched that he'd actually made the effort to put it into words, for she knew that expressing his deepest feelings did not come easily to him. Closing the space between them, she put her arms around him and touched her lips to his. She had meant it to be just a light thank-you type kiss, but it swirled and deepened and turned into something much more urgent.

The chocolate and strawberries would just have to wait for a while, she thought. Or maybe not...

Chapter 6

Lee finished eating the sandwich and chips that Michael had brought her and set the plate aside. At least he didn't plan on starving her; he'd been feeding her regularly. It had taken a couple of days, but she'd recovered totally from the effects of the drug, and she felt strong and healthy once again. And she'd learned more about his demented motive for abducting her.

She had within herself a remnant of an obscure Norse goddess named Vanadis. At least, that was what Michael believed. And if Michael believed it, Lee was going to play along. If he thought she accepted the role he had assigned to her, he was more likely to let her live for a while longer, she reasoned.

Right after that first encounter on the day she'd awakened – and God knew when that was – she'd lost track of the days - he'd given her some hot soup and coffee, and she'd eaten it meekly, pretending to accept her situation. Anything to placate him and lull him into believing that she bought into his whacked-out fantasy. In the meantime, she needed some sort of advantage. With the thought in mind that knowledge is power, she turned to face him and requested, "Tell me more about Vanadis, Michael."

Maya Shilltoe stumbled into the kitchen blearily on Monday morning, intent on only one thing: coffee. The party at Drew's house had lasted all weekend, and she had only made it home and crawled into bed during the wee hours of the morning. If Dr. Heronn didn't adhere to such a strict attendance policy, she would have been tempted to cut her eight o'clock economics class at the University and sleep in this morning. However, she'd already missed two classes this semester, and if she missed another one, Dr. Heronn would drop her a full letter grade. She couldn't afford that.

Coffee in hand, she wandered into her roommate's room and frowned. No sign of Lee. For a minute she was worried, but then she remembered that the salon was closed on Mondays. Lee must've grabbed the opportunity to spend some extra time with Will, she decided.

Moving into the living room, she flopped down on the couch and turned on the television. Better check on the weather before deciding what to wear today, she thought. You never knew what Mother Nature was going to throw at you during this time of year.

First she had to sit through a few commercials; then the newscaster blathered on about a protest at some chemical plant somewhere. Who cared? She leaned back and closed her eyes, only half paying attention, waiting for the weather to come on. Suddenly, she sat bolt upright, listening incredulously. The newscaster was saying, "Still no change in the condition of Will Preisinger, the young man who fell from a cliff on Saturday and barely escaped with his life. Sources at Mountpelier General tell us that he is still in a coma, and doctors are unsure if he will make a complete recovery. With us here now is Mitch Louvain, a well-known rock climber and outdoors man, who will give us some tips on avoiding such accidents and staying safe when camping in rough terrain..."

Maya didn't wait to hear the rest. She got up frantically and grabbed her cell phone. Punching in Lee's number, she waited impatiently for her roommate to pick up the phone. When there was no response from Lee, she tried texting: *Where r u? I just heard the news. r u ok?*

Still no response. Maya waited for a few minutes, then made a decision. Running back into her bedroom and throwing on some clothes, she grabbed her keys and headed out the door. Jumping into her car, she drove purposefully toward Mountpelier General Hospital.

When she sat down at the breakfast table, Dawn picked up the birthday cards that were lying on her plate and went through them, carefully making no comment about the black eye and other sundry bruises that were beginning to form on the left side of Ty's face.

"Have a good night?" she said blandly.

"Wonderful. You?"

"Even more than wonderful. In fact, I can't think of a superlative expressive enough to do it justice. But after you left to go check on Brody and spend the rest of the night downstairs, I went back to sleep and had a weird dream. You remember my old friend Desiree? She and her husband named their first kid Bonaparte. Well, now they're expecting another kid, and in my dream, Desiree told me they were going to name him Nebuchadnezzar. Why would anyone inflict a name like Bonaparte or Nebuchadnezzar on a child, Ty?"

Tyrell shrugged. "Beats me."

"It looks like someone did."

"Did what?"

"Beat you."

"Oh, this." Ty fingered the bruises gingerly. "Let's just say that Brody was a little...disoriented when he woke up and found himself two thousand miles away and in a different state this morning."

"I hope that Brody doesn't get disoriented too often."

"Oh, no. Just when he gets taken off guard, that's all. It doesn't happen very often. Brody getting taken off guard, I mean."

"Do I get to meet him this morning? Is he coming up to join us for breakfast?"

"No, he was feeling out of sorts this morning, and he wanted to make himself more presentable first. Make a good first impression, you know?"

Dawn walked over to the refrigerator and poured herself a glass of orange juice. "He's your friend, Ty. I don't care what kind of first impression he makes. He's always welcome here. Make sure he knows that."

"I will. Hey, listen – I talked to Mom this morning. She may stop over later."

"What time?"

"Actually, any minute now."

Dawn shook her head regretfully. "I'll probably miss her, then. I have to go into work as soon as I get showered and dressed. Give her my love, though. Tell her if we get this case wrapped up soon, I'd love to go shopping, spend a little time with her before she heads back to New Orleans. Do you know how long she plans to be in town?"

"I think she plans on staying for at least a week. I'll tell her what you said. She really enjoys spending time with you, Dawn."

"The feeling is mutual." Dawn bent down and kissed him hard on the mouth. "Tell your friend Brody to stop messing with that face. It's not under warranty any more, and I'd have a hard time replacing it."

Ty watched her as she passed through the connecting door into the other part of the house. Pouring another cup of coffee into a king-size mug, he carefully negotiated the staircase that led to the ground floor. Brody was still lying where he had left him, half on and half off the couch. His eyes were closed, but that didn't mean anything, as Ty knew very well. Brody always slept with one eye open, and he had the reflexes of a cat. Ty didn't relish the thought of having another go-around this morning. He stayed out of reach of those massive arms as he set the mug cautiously on the coffee table.

"What's that?" Brody growled.

"I brought you some coffee. Peace offering."

"You damned near kidnapped me, flew me two thousand miles away across the country, and you think that a mug of coffee is good enough for a peace offering?"

"Like I tried to tell you earlier, I didn't kidnap you. I merely invited you to come out for a visit, and you agreed that it sounded like a good idea. See? Nothing to get mad about."

Brody reached out, grabbed the coffee cup, and took a gulp. "I don't remember agreeing to anything. And even if I did, it doesn't mean anything, because I wouldn't have agreed if I hadn't been shit-faced drunk."

"Yeah, well, whose fault is that?"

"Yours, and you damned well know it. You showed up at my door with a couple of bottles of fifty-year-old single malt scotch. How was I supposed to resist that? Stuff must cost more per ounce than gold."

Ty assumed an expression of extreme innocence and responded in an aggrieved tone, "I hadn't seen my best friend in over a year. You think I was going to show up on his doorstep empty-handed?"

Brody just gave him the evil eye. "You're the most conniving son of a bitch I've ever met, Tyrell Lewellen. So you can forget about the innocent act. I'm on to you, remember?"

"Yeah, I never could fool you, Brody. Like when you came to visit me when I was in the hospital after the accident. You weren't fooled by me at all when I tried to put a brave face on everything. Told you to go along home. I was fine: I didn't need anyone. Especially not my best friend."

The scowl on Brody's face would have scared a great white shark out of his wits. "That was different," he muttered.

"How so?"

The coffee mug smashed as it hit the wall across the room. "Because they didn't tell you they might have to cut half of your leg off, that's why!"

There was a pregnant pause while the two just glared at each other. It was soon broken, however, as they heard a voice from the top of the stairs. "Ty? Are you down there?"

Brody knew that voice. Speechless, he watched Ty move to the foot of the stairs and call out, "Yeah, Mom, I'm here. Come on down."

Brody ran a hand through his hair, looked down and saw that the jeans and t shirt he wore were presentable enough, and scrambled to his feet. Leaning against the couch, bracing himself on his good leg, he saw Maeve Lewellen crossing the room toward him.

"Brody! My dear boy, how wonderful to see you again!"

No one else in the world could get away with addressing Brody like that. A second later, Maeve's arms were around his waist, embracing him warmly. Stepping back, she examined him in the way that only a mother could. Then she said, "Ty tells me you're in town to get a second opinion from an orthopedic surgeon. Something about a leg injury? My dear, how wise of you to come. You should *never* rely on just one opinion where surgery is concerned. Now, you just sit yourself down again and make yourself comfortable. I know just the man you should consult. He and his wife are two of my oldest and dearest friends. I'll give them a call, and we'll see if he can get you in for an appointment this very afternoon."

Turning to her son, she said, "Tyrell! Why isn't there something to eat or drink around here for your guest? Didn't I teach you any manners at all?"

"Uh, right, Mom. I'll take care of it right away."

As he watched Ty beat a strategic retreat back up to the kitchen, Brody reflected that *conniving* didn't even begin to describe Tyrell Lewellen. The man was a freakin' tactical genius.

Dawn hurried into the hospital, making her way toward intensive care at top speed. She had been on the road for barely five minutes when she'd gotten the call from Rafe. Will Preisinger's mother had contacted him with some encouraging news: A girl had come into the hospital to check on Will, informing Naomi that she was a friend of Will's girlfriend. At last, someone who actually knew something about Lee!

She spotted Naomi in the waiting room. Beside her sat a girl who looked to be about nineteen or twenty, a petite brunette who was perched on the edge of her seat, foot tapping the floor nervously. Springing up as Dawn entered the room, she said, "Are you the police? I came as soon as I heard about Will. I figured that Lee would be here too, but no one seems to know where she is! What's happening? Oh my God, where's Lee?"

Dawn pulled out her ID and showed it to the girl. "In answer to your first question, I'm Detective Dawn Cimarron. And this," she added as Rafe entered the room, "is my partner, Sergeant Rafe Melbourne. And your name is?"

"Maya Shilltoe. Lee's my roommate. And my friend."

"Okay. Maya, can you tell me Lee's full name and address?"

"Leanne Zarafin. But she goes by Lee. We live in the Wharfe Apartments, right off campus. The address is 150 Franklin Avenue. Apartment 4B."

"What about her parents? We'll have to get in touch with them."

"Her father died a couple of years ago. Colon cancer. Lee was pretty broken up about it. Her mother's name is Vivian Zarafin. She still lives here in Mountpelier."

"You know how we can get in touch with her?"

"I have her number, but contacting Vivian won't do you any good. It's Monday morning. She's probably been on a bender all weekend. You'll have to wait for her to dry out before you'll get anything that even resembles a sensible answer out of her. Besides, she's the last person who would know where Lee is. Lee hasn't spoken to her mother in months."

Maya paused for a minute, picked up a bottle of water from the table in front of her, and sipped. Then she continued, "When her dad was alive, her mother wasn't too bad, but after he died, Vivian went completely out of control. That's why Lee moved out as soon as she graduated from high school last May. She just couldn't take it anymore."

"Her mother is still the next of kin. We'll need her contact information."

"Hang on - I've got her phone number right here." Maya pulled out her cell phone and rattled off the number from her contact list.

"Thank you, Maya. Now, what about your living situation? Do you have any other roommates?"

"No, it's just the two of us. At first I was going to live by myself. I like my privacy, and my dad is paying the bills, so I can afford it. But then Lee needed a place to stay. She's one of the few people I could actually stand the thought of living with, so I let her move in. She helps out with the rent, the utilities, things like that. I told her she didn't have to, on account of my dad's taking care of everything, but she insisted. Lee's like that."

"Okay. Maya, how old is Lee? What about her date of birth?"

"Well, let me think... Her birthday is December twenty-first. She's eighteen, almost nineteen."

"How long have you known Lee?"

"About four years now. We were freshmen in high school. I was new in town, and Lee took me under her wing." Maya smiled reminiscently. "I was a little shy back then."

"What about a physical description, Maya? We have a photograph of Lee with Will, but it's in black and white and it isn't full length. Can you give me her approximate height and weight?"

"Height? She's taller than I am – maybe about 5'8 or 5'9? And she watches her weight. She tries to stay between 124-127 pounds."

"Hair and eye color?"

"She has blonde hair. Her eyes are blue."

"Okay. Now, when did you last see Lee?"

"On Thursday. She was all excited. She was going camping for the weekend with Will."

"Can you tell me what she was wearing?"

"Well, she had on these skinny black boot-cut jeans that made her legs look like a mile long and a sort of fuchsia-colored tank top. She was wearing black boots and her black leather coat. I told her that she was crazy, dressing like that for a camping trip at this time of year, but she just laughed. She had other clothes in her bag – more practical things, you know? But it wasn't just a camping trip; it was a date. She said that she wasn't planning on staying in those particular clothes very long, and Will would keep her warm."

"How long had she been seeing Will?"

"Just for a few months. They met in late July or early August – I can't remember which. Lee got a flat tire on her way home from work. She doesn't have a road service like Triple A or anything, and she couldn't afford to call a tow truck. So she was really grateful when Will pulled up and offered to change the tire for her. She asked him to come back here afterward, made him something to eat to sort of thank him, you know? And he asked her out for a date. They clicked right away, and they've been together ever since."

"What about prior relationships? Ex-boyfriends?"

"Well, there was Jason. Jason Lostuck. She went out with him all through our senior year at high school, until she caught him cheating on her right after graduation. She ended it then."

"How did he take it? Was he upset?"

"Oh, no. He just shrugged it off. In fact, he's still seeing the other girl. Last I heard, they were engaged."

"What about before that, Maya? Did she date anyone else in high school? And what about the time between breaking up with Jason and getting together with Will?"

"Let me think. She went with Chad Colnie for a while. Before that, it was Dorian Hotler. But she wasn't serious about either of them."

"Maya, my next question may sound a little strange, but trust me, it's important. Can you tell me if Lee had a favorite kind of beer that she liked to drink?"

"Beer? Not really. If we're at a party, she'll pretty much drink whatever they have. She's not choosy. But she does have a limit. Two beers. No more. You can't get her to drink any more for love or money. Probably has something to do with her mother."

"Thank you. Now, Maya – has Lee been worried about anything, lately? Like someone hanging around who didn't seem to belong, who made her uncomfortable?"

"You mean like a stalker or something?"

Dawn nodded.

"No, nothing like that. It's pretty much been business as usual. I go to class, Lee goes to work at Martine's Beauty Stop. That's a day spa and salon down on 21st Street. Lee's a hair stylist. She does nails, too, and she's really good at it. She did mine just before she left to go camping with Will." Maya looked down at her hands, studying fingernails painted a deep blue and studded with tiny gold beads that marched down the center of each nail. "What else can I tell you? I like to party on the weekends, but Lee hasn't gone along with me that much for the last couple of months. She likes to spend all of her free time with Will, and he's just not into that."

Maya dragged her gaze away from her nails and focused her dark brown eyes on Dawn. "I'm just rambling on. I can't seem to think straight. It's all so confusing, so unbelievable. And why are you asking me all these questions? I thought Lee had an accident or got lost or something. What's going on?"

"We're not sure, Maya, so we have to explore every possibility. And it would help if you would allow us to look around your apartment. We'd like to take a look at Lee's computer, look at her Facebook page, see if she kept a journal or something that would help us out. She may have noted something in there that might help us. And we might want to take her hairbrush or toothbrush with us. Would you have any objection to that?"

Maya's eyes grew even wider and rounder than before. She was no fool. She understood the significance of the request for the hairbrush and toothbrush.

"You think Lee is dead. You want that stuff for DNA," she said flatly.

"We're not sure of anything, Maya. We just need to follow the protocols for situations like this."

Maya fumbled in her pockets, produced a key ring, and pulled one of the keys off.

"Here's my key. My bedroom's the one on the left. Lee's is on the right. There's a toothbrush holder in the bathroom. Lee's is the green one. Mine is pink. Take whatever you need. Anything to help find Lee." She paused for a moment, then added, "The password to her computer – she has it written down, in case she forgets. It's on a bookmark in the volume of poetry she keeps on the nightstand next to her bed. She doesn't have a Facebook page. Lee's very protective of her privacy. I can't imagine that she keeps a journal, either. Same reason."

Dawn reached out and took the key. "Thank you for all of your help, Maya. We'll see that the key is returned to you as soon as we are finished. In the meantime, would you leave us your contact information? And what are your plans for today?"

"I'll give you my cell phone number. I've got classes from ten until four, but I'm not budging from this spot until I find out what's happened to Lee. She's my best friend. That's more important than keeping my grades up. Besides, she'd want me to stay with Will." Maya reached out and took Naomi Preisinger's hand. "If you find anything out, you'll know where to find me."

No one was answering the phone at the Zarafin house. Vivian's cell phone was going straight to voice mail as well, so Dawn and Rafe dispatched two patrol officers to drive over to the house and see if they could contact Lee's mother in person. However, there was no sign of Vivian Zarafin. Her car was not in the driveway, and inquiries among the neighbors yielded no results. The only thing to do was have the officers check back periodically and wait for her to show up.

The hospital wasn't that far from Maya and Lee's apartment, so they decided to stop there next. Using the key that Maya had provided, they let themselves into the apartment. They found themselves in a fairly spacious living/dining area, with a galley-style kitchen off to the left.

"I'll take this room and the kitchen," Rafe said. "Why don't you start on Lee's room?"

The bedroom on the right contained a single bed with a nightstand next to it against the right-hand wall. On the left side stood a small desk, with an old-fashioned desktop computer on it. Neatly made, the comforter on the bed was decorated with a geometric pattern in dark pink and dull gold, surrounded by a wide border in cocoa brown. A dust ruffle of pink and cocoa stripes flowed down from the box springs to the floor below. Pillows in a variety of shapes were carefully arranged against the headboard.

Walking over to the far side of the bed, Dawn found the volume of poetry, an illustrated copy of William Blake's *Songs of Innocence and Experience*. The bookmark fell out as she picked the book up. She put the book back on the nightstand and retrieved the bookmark from the floor. The computer password was written on it as promised. Dawn crossed the room to the desk and placed the bookmark next to the computer. On a dresser against the other wall, she spotted a hairbrush. Crossing over to that side of the room, she lifted it with a gloved hand and carefully sealed it in an evidence bag. Then she moved into the bathroom and did the same with the green toothbrush from the toothbrush holder. Returning to the bedroom, she sat down at the desk, booted up the computer, and began skimming through the files.

"Find anything interesting?" Rafe asked as he entered the room.

She shook her head without bothering to turn around. "Not much. Projects and papers, obviously from when she was still in high school. Some saved searches on financial aid and scholarship opportunities for college. A budget planner, her resume, some cover letters to go along with it. A list of consignment, thrift and resale stores in the area. Let me click on her pictures file next."

Rafe leaned over her shoulder to look as she scrolled through the pictures that Lee had downloaded. "Not that many. Mostly of her and Maya or her and Will. One or two of her with an older man – probably her father. None of her with anyone who looks like she could be the mother."

Dawn nodded. A clearer picture of the missing girl was forming in her head. "She wasn't extravagant. She had her budget planned out and lived well within her means. She'd made a break from her family and was trying to build a new life for herself. No college yet, but she's making inquiries, planning for the future."

Dawn moved away from the computer and checked the dresser, the closet. She fished a few receipts out of the wastepaper basket. "She has some nice clothes, but not new ones. Looks like she got most of her stuff from consignment and resale shops. Good way to look like a million bucks without spending a lot of money. Wasn't too proud to wear second-hand clothes. Smart and practical."

"Keeps her space tidy as well," Rafe remarked. "I glanced into Maya's room after I finished in the living room and kitchen. Place looks like a hurricane hit it."

Dawn nodded and returned to sit down at the desk again. She scrolled through the pictures again, stopping at one of Lee by herself, sitting on a railing, laughing, her hair blowing in the wind. Something about the girl was tugging at the strings of her heart. She pushed the feelings down ruthlessly. Too much emotion had no place in an investigation of this sort. She needed to remain cool and professional. Deliberately, she closed the picture file and shut down the computer. Rising from the chair, she took one long last look around, trying to see if there was anything they had missed.

"We done here?" Rafe asked. When she nodded, he said, "Let's get out of here then. We're due to talk to Lee's employer next."

The salon where Lee worked was closed that day, but the owner, Martine Rothay, had agreed to come in and meet with them once she had learned that Lee was missing.

She must have been watching for them, for the door of the salon flew open even before they reached it. Martine, a tall forty-something woman, had a rather square face, dominated by huge, heavily made up dark eyes framed by bronze hair cut into a stylish angled bob. She invited them in, offered them coffee, and sank into a chair in the waiting area of the salon. In answer to their questions, she said, "I haven't seen Lee since she left here after her shift on Wednesday night. She asked me about two weeks ago if she could take a couple of vacation days, and I was happy to oblige. Girl hasn't taken a day off since she started working here. Not a single sick day. You know, she got her license at the age of seventeen by enrolling in a Vo-tech program when she was still in high school, and she started working for me part-time even before she graduated. She's really good, and the customers all like her, so I was happy to offer her a full-time job when she graduated. Employees like that girl are worth their weight in gold. And Lee – she's special."

Martine reached down absently to straighten a pile of magazines before she continued. "She's crazy about that new boyfriend of hers - Will. They haven't been going out that long – just a few months – but she seems really happy. And so excited about going camping with him this weekend. Me? I'd rather pack up and go somewhere warm than go camping in Colorado in the fall, but Lee thought it would be romantic. And she said they could keep each other warm."

Dawn took the lead in questioning Martine, asking her basically the same questions that they had asked Lee's roommate. But Martine did not have much information to add. Lee had seemed perfectly normal when she had last seen her. And no, she hadn't noticed anyone unfamiliar around who was paying undue attention to Lee.

After they had left Martine Rothay, Dawn and Rafe spent the rest of the morning canvassing the local real estate offices. Armed with Barbara's sketch, they made the rounds. Finally, after hours of pounding the pavement, they caught a break. One of the agents, a man named Trevor Stoss, thought he recognized the man in the sketch.

"It was a few weeks ago," he said. "This guy who looks a lot like the man in the sketch comes around looking for a house to rent. He was really specific about what he wanted, and the only one I had that matched his requirements was a house that had just come on the market. At first he seemed pleased. It was a small, two-bedroom place, with an attached garage and a finished basement. But then he said that the garage was too small and that the basement wasn't nice enough. Well, the garage was described as being a two-car deal, but they would have to be pretty small cars. It's really more of a one and one half car garage, you see? Bigger than a single, but not quite big enough to really be described as a two-car garage. And the basement? He wanted one with a bathroom down there, and then he complained that there wasn't enough light. It's a basement, right? It's underground. What was he expecting? A sun room?"

"Did you see him again after that?" Rafe inquired.

"No, he didn't come back. Guess he found what he wanted through some other agency."

"Do you remember his name?"

"Can't say as I do. He was a walk-in, so I never wrote it down in my appointment book."

"What about an address?"

"Never got that far. If he'd wanted the house, I would have had him fill out all the forms, but just an inquiry? No. Clients looking for a house to rent want to start right away. Make them stop and fill out a bunch of forms first, they could decide to walk away, find somebody else."

"What about a phone number?"

"He didn't leave one. I pressed him for it, but he said no, he'd be in touch with me."

"What about his car? Do you remember what kind of car he was driving?"

"Let me think. It was a truck, actually, not a car. A full-size pick-up truck. American-made, not foreign. Maybe a Chevy Silvarado or a Dodge Ram?"

"Color?"

"Nothing flashy. Kind a beige color, I think."

"Older, newer?"

"Didn't look brand new. Looked like it had some miles on it. Look, I really wasn't paying much attention to his ride, okay?"

"Okay. What about the guy himself? Anything else strike you about him?"

Trevor Stoss pushed his glasses back up on his nose and considered. "He didn't say much. Pleasant enough, but not talkative."

"Any unusual quirks or habits?"

"Not that I recall. Look, I have an appointment in a few minutes. I need to get going."

"Okay. Here's my card. Call me if you remember anything else."

As Stoss hurried away, Rafe turned to Dawn. "He wanted a large, two car garage."

Dawn nodded. "And a basement with a bathroom and a lot of light. Because he's an artist? Why not just convert one of the upstairs rooms into a studio?"

"Easier to turn a basement into a prison. And if he needs a prison..."

Dawn finished it for him: "There's a chance that Lee is still alive."

Chapter 7

Michael had hardly been able to contain himself when the girl had asked him to tell her more about Vanadis. None of the others had understood the way this one did. They had cried and argued and pleaded, refusing to acknowledge the truth. But this incarnation of his goddess – she had some glimmer of understanding. He'd been working on a sketch right then, but he'd laid it aside for the time being and responded to her question eagerly.

"Vanadis is the Norse goddess of snow and ice. I'm descended from the Norse, the Vikings, on my father's side, you see. But I wasn't really interested in my Viking heritage until Vanadis started appearing to me. Since then, however, I've spent a lot of time researching the ancient Norse religion. Do you know anything about it?"

Lee considered her words carefully before replying, "Not really. What I know about the Vikings comes from what I've seen in the movies or on television. Most of the time, what they show are Vikings on their ships, spending their time sailing around, invading foreign lands, raiding and pillaging."

She was afraid that she might have offended him by mentioning raiding and pillaging, but Michael just nodded at her. "I know - most people think that Vikings were just marauders, but that's a complete stereotype. Only a small percentage of them went raiding. Most of them were farmers or traders in their native Scandinavia. And they were a sophisticated, deeply spiritual people."

He frowned, then continued, "The books about the ancient Norse religion – they've got it all wrong. Most of them claim that Vanadis was just another name for Freyja. But Vanadis was actually an entirely different goddess. There was never any connection between her and Freyja."

"Why did they get it wrong, Michael? The ones who wrote the books?"

"There just aren't that many references to Vanadis. The so-called experts – they assumed she was another manifestation of Freyja. But they're wrong. You see, she told me so, herself."

A sharp finger of dread jabbed Lee in the stomach. He was even crazier, more out of touch with reality than she had originally thought. But she kept her expression bland and her tone neutral as she encouraged him to continue talking.

"She told you so? When?"

Michael picked up the sketch again and continued working on it as he answered, "When I was ten. I was on a hunting trip with my father and my brother. Somehow I got separated from them. I got lost, and I nearly died. But then she appeared to me – Vanadis. She was just a shadow, that first time. A glimmer, barely an outline. But her voice was strong and clear. She gave me the strength to get up and keep going. With her help, I found my way back to the campsite, the tent. Vanadis saved my life. Since then, I've devoted my life to her. And in return, she explained everything to me."

Lee took a deep breath so that she could keep her voice steady as she replied, "What did she explain, Michael?"

"About my forefathers. How they were priests, dedicated to her worship. And she explained to me why her image was so faint when she first appeared to me. You see, Loki was responsible. He was her antithesis, an evil god of maleficence and fire. And he was jealous of her, jealous of her goodness, her beauty, and her great power. So he set his wolf Fenrir upon her, and the beast tore her into pieces. She couldn't die, though – she's immortal. Her spirit endured. But it's been fragmented, scattered about inside mortals all over the face of the earth."

Michael's face lit up with a beatific smile. "After she was sure that I understood fully, Vanadis gave me a mission. She told me how to find the scattered pieces of her spirit and reunite them. I've managed to identify several over the last few years. Since then, every time she appears to me, her image is less shadowy. It's growing stronger, more substantial. And when our work here together is done, she'll be even stronger still."

As Dawn and Rafe left the office of Trevor Stoss, Rafe's cell phone rang. He picked up the call, listened intently, and then replied, "Okay. We're on our way." Turning to Dawn, he said, "Jago Bolt is back in town and already has himself a lawyer. They're waiting for us at headquarters."

Surprised, Dawn responded, "He had a public defender assigned to him already?"

Rafe shook his head. "Private attorney. Which means that Mr. Bolt has a nice stash of cash set aside somewhere. Now where do you suppose someone like J.B. acquired the kind of money to do that?"

"Oh, I don't know. But - just a guess, mind you - Monieque Torrense, perhaps?"

"Oddly enough, the same idea had occurred to me. Come on, partner. Let's go have a little chat with good old J.B."

"Is the D.A.'s office sending someone down to observe?"

"Yeah. Bob Toravo will be on hand. Just in case someone wants to play *Let's Make a Deal*."

When they entered the interview room at headquarters, J.B. and his attorney were already waiting for them. After Rafe went through the usual routine for the record, the attorney, Moss Calavon, opened by saying, "The charges against my client are ridiculous. Mr. Bolt was a good friend of the victim and had no motive to kill him. In addition, he was on a flight to Florida when the murder occurred. I demand that the charges against my client be dropped immediately."

Rafe leaned back in his chair and answered in an amused tone of voice, "You know, Calavon, one thing I've always admired about you is your chutzpah. With the evidence we've got against your client, he's going down for Murder One."

Moss Calavon shook his head. "No way. The fingerprint on the murder weapon is meaningless. According to my client, his knife was stolen from him a few weeks prior to the crime. Given those circumstances, it's no wonder that his fingerprint was found on it. You've no proof that puts the blade in his hand on the night that Cullen Torrense was killed."

"Your client file a police report when his knife was stolen?" When Calavon made no response, Rafe said, "Thought not. With a witness who saw J.B. enter the park with Cullen shortly before the murder and your client's fingerprint on the knife, you willing to try to sell your bullshit story to a jury? Because all that's going to get your client is a needle in his arm."

"There's no way the DA is going for Murder One. You can't prove premeditation."

"Oh, I think we can. Especially after the warrant we've filed for Monieque Torrense's bank records comes through. Did you know that she recently inquired about who gets Cullen's trust fund in the event that he died before he reached the age of 21? Or that she paid for your client's little vacation to Florida, which conveniently got him out of town just a few short hours after Cullen Torrense met his unfortunate end? And I'll bet we find that she made a large withdrawal from her account shortly before the murder."

Switching his attention from the attorney, Rafe looked J.B. directly in the eyes. "We've already gotten a warrant to look into your finances, J.B. What do you think we're going to find when we look for bank accounts in your name?"

Before his lawyer could stop him, J.B. sneered and replied smugly, "You won't find anything."

"No? What about safety deposit boxes, then?"

At the expression on J.B.'s face, Attorney Calavon interrupted to say, "Pause the record. I need a few moments to confer with my client in private."

"Be my guest." After complying with the attorney's request to pause the record, Rafe motioned to Dawn, and the two of them strolled out of the interview room nonchalantly, where they found ADA Toravo waiting for them in the corridor.

"I know Calavon," Toravo said. "Like you say, he has chutzpah. He'll start off by trying to deal for Criminally Negligent Homicide, with the minimum one-year sentence. After you've stopped laughing, offer Second Degree Murder, and make it clear we'll be expecting J.B. to do the full twenty-four year sentence for a class 2 felony. Then it will be his turn to laugh, because he knows that there's no way we'll get a conviction on Monieque Torrense without J.B.'s testimony. He'll then try for a charge of Manslaughter, again with the minimum sentence. Tell him we're not going to settle for less than Murder Two, but in exchange for his testimony against Monieque, we'll take it down to a class 3 felony, with J.B. serving the max. Calavon will make one more attempt to deal it down to Manslaughter, but I'm not going there. The most Bolt would have to serve would be six years, and I'm not letting a cold-blooded murderer get away with that."

"You sure he'll take the deal?"

"With the alternative being Murder One and the death penalty? Yeah, with the evidence you've dug up, he'll take the deal."

The door swung open behind them, and they saw Attorney Calavon in the doorway. "Gentlemen, we're ready to resume the interview."

After they had gone back on the record, the negotiations followed the pattern that ADA Toravo had predicted. Once the deal had been struck, Calavon looked at his client and said, "Go ahead, J.B. Tell them everything."

J.B. shrugged his shoulders, and in an attempt at bravado, said, "It's no big deal. Cullen's mom invited me over to her house one day last week. She offered me a few drinks and asked me if I'd heard from Cullen lately. I told her the truth – that since Cullen got out of his last stint in rehab, he'd been avoiding me. Made me mad, too, because Cullen and I go way back. I thought we were friends, and now he's treating me as if I was a pile of garbage. Like he's too good for me or something, now that he's gotten clean. I thought Mrs. Torrense would get mad when I said that, but instead she sympathized with me. Told me Cullen had changed, and he hadn't been treating her with the respect she deserved either. In fact, maybe she'd be better off without him. Then she looked at me and said that she'd heard that I was a pretty dangerous character. Well, I had to agree with her on that. And then she got all skeptical on me. 'Oh, come on,' she said. 'How dangerous could you be? I'll bet you haven't done anything all that bad. Like you haven't killed anyone or anything like that.' I told her not to be too sure about that. When I told her that, she kind of nodded and asked me if I'd like to make some money. Well, of course I did. Then she told me that she'd pay me $20,000 to get rid of Cullen for her."

"Do you remember the exact date that this conversation took place, J.B.?"

"I think it was the Thursday before I... before it all went down. Yeah, it was that Thursday, the week before. I remember because I'd just gotten back that day from a trip to Black Hawk. Thought I'd try my hand at the casinos. Didn't have much luck, though."

"Okay. So what happened after Mrs. Torrense offered you the $20,000?"

"Well, I told her that it was a lot of money, but I wasn't sure I wanted to do it, what with Cullen being a friend and all. But then she reminded me about how he was treating me lately, and by the time she was done, I was mad enough to agree to off Cullen for her."

"How did you manage the money arrangements?"

"Well, I told her I wanted some up front. So she gave me a thousand that night, and promised me the rest when it was done."

"She paid you in cash?"

"Yeah. I wouldn't have accepted anything else. After she gave me the thousand, she told me it would be a good idea for me to get out of town for a while after it was done, and she offered to send me to Florida for a little vacation. I jumped on that offer, of course. I'd never been to Florida before. Anyway, we agreed on the date, and I told her I'd come right over to her house after Cullen was taken care of for the rest of the money."

"If Cullen was avoiding you, how did you get him to agree to meet with you?"

"I texted him that I wanted to make a change, get clean like he'd done. I wanted to find out more about that rehab place he'd been in, see if it would work for me. Cullen texted me back and agreed to meet with me to talk it over."

Dawn spoke up then. "Why did you stab Cullen, J.B.? Why didn't you just make it look like a drug overdose?"

"Yeah – me and Cullen's mom talked about that. It was supposed to be the way it went down. I had some stuff with me that was real high grade. Hadn't been cut at all, so it wouldn't have taken much to be lethal. I thought that there was no way that Cullen could resist it when I offered him some of the really good shit. But he did. Said if I wanted to go on being a loser, that was my choice, but he had different plans for his life. Well, when he called me a loser, I sort of snapped. I pulled out my knife and stuck him so quick that he didn't even have a chance to react. He just fell down, gasped and choked a few times, and that was that. He was dead. So I left him there and went over to his mom's house to get paid."

"She just handed the rest of the money over? She didn't ask for any proof?"

"She asked me to take a picture of the body as proof."

"I see. Did you use your cell phone to take the picture?"

"Yeah, but I deleted it right after I showed it to her. Then she gave me the rest of the money, and I left. I went right home, packed up, and headed for the airport."

"Was Mrs. Torrense upset when she found out that Cullen refused to take the drugs and you had to use another means to dispose of him?"

A look of sly cunning crossed J.B.'s face. "I was thinking she might get upset if she found that out. She was pretty set on the fact that it had to look like a drug overdose. So I took a picture that just showed his face and his shoulders, you know? She never saw the blood or the knife."

After they'd concluded the interview and the attorneys were putting the final touches on the plea agreement, Dawn and Rafe headed back up to the bullpen to update the case file and work on their reports. They also called the lab and asked them to bump the analysis of J.B.'s cell phone up to top priority.

"Dumb-ass didn't even realize that the picture could be retrieved, even if he deleted it," Rafe commented. "I'll bet when he heard about the picture, that's when Calavon decided to fold his cards and go for a deal. Knew that we'd already gotten a warrant and would go over the cell phone with a fine tooth comb. We'd have found the photograph eventually, and there was no way around that one."

After they'd completed the necessary paperwork, they checked on the status of the warrant for Monieque Torrense's bank records and were pleased to find that it had been granted. The forensic accounting squad was already on the job, following the money from that end. Meanwhile, they had also dispatched a team to get the cash from the safety deposit box that J.B. had rented. Once they had it, they could dust the bills for fingerprints. Since Monieque had once worked part time at a day care center, her fingerprints were on file. With any luck, they might find a print or two on the money.

The next step was to make some inquiries in Monieque Torrense's neighborhood, see if anyone had seen J.B. at her house on either of the dates in question. Dawn suggested that they start with Mrs. Lillipinner, the neighbor who had witnessed Cullen's last meeting with his mother.

On the way over to the section of town where Monieque Torrense lived, Rafe commented, "You know, I've seen a lot, but it made my blood run cold when J.B. told us that Monieque asked for a picture of her son's body as proof that he was dead."

"Yeah, I had the same reaction," Dawn agreed. "Like Ellanor Torrense said, you'd think that Cullen of all people would have been safe from her. But she's a narcissist, Rafe. They go through cycles of idealization and devaluation when it comes to relationships. Once Cullen grew up, stopped providing her with the kind of uncritical adoration that she craved, and became a source of disappointment to her, he lost most of his value in her eyes. In addition to that, like most narcissists, it's all about power for her. Cullen had slipped out from under her control, and she couldn't stand that. From there, it was just a step further for her to figure that she deserved better than that and scheme to find a way to turn the whole situation around to her benefit. It's not very common, mothers killing their own children, but it's happened before. Remember that woman in South Carolina who drowned her two kids because her boyfriend told her that the kids were an obstacle to their future relationship?"

"I remember. There was also a case in Colorado Springs not too long ago where a mother set the house on fire with her three kids inside for the insurance money. Turns out that the dad was in on it, too. I guess Monieque Torrense was cut from the same cloth."

Abruptly changing the subject, he said, "What's going on with Ty's friend? Any news about that?"

Dawn nodded. "Ty sent me a text this morning to let me know that Maeve persuaded Brody to see a specialist about his leg. Knowing Maeve, I'll bet she's already scheduled an appointment and has him on his way to the doctor's office. I'd better take a moment to check for an update and let Ty know that I'll probably be working late tonight. If everything breaks just right, we might be able to haul Monieque Torrense in for a session in the box before the end of the day. Now that's something I'm looking forward to."

As soon as Ty pulled the car back into the garage and opened his door, Traitor jumped into his lap, barking excitedly and licking his face enthusiastically.

"That dog's useless as a watchdog," Brody commented from the back seat. "She's never seen me before, but she treated me like a long-lost friend when she came downstairs this morning."

"That's because she was hoping you'd give her a treat. I keep some down there in a cupboard over the bar. She doesn't look upon strangers as threats – only as brand new potential sources of treats. Besides, she doesn't need to be a watchdog. I've already got two of them."

Brody grunted as he got out of the back, and Ty, giving Traitor a final pat and setting her down on her own four feet, walked around and helped his mother out of the front passenger side. Brody had spotted the security detail following them at once. He hadn't commented, but Ty had known the moment Brody had made them. He'd talked to Brody right after the kidnapping, just before Brody had left the country, so it was no surprise to his friend that he had a security detail following him. Knowing Brody, he was probably critiquing their performance on the way to and from the doctor's office.

Brody thrust his bad leg, now enclosed in a soft cast, out of the car first, followed by his good leg. He took a pair of crutches from the seat beside him and used them to keep all the weight off his right leg as he maneuvered his way into the house. After what the doctor had told him, he wasn't taking any chances.

Maeve was holding the door open for him, and he thanked her as he entered the house and made his way down the steps. When he reached the bottom, he crossed over to the couch. Depositing the crutches on the floor beside him, he sank down onto the couch with a sigh of relief.

Ty had followed him down and strolled over to the refrigerator behind the bar. Pulling out two cold ones, he popped the tops and walked over to the couch, offering one to Brody before seating himself in the adjacent recliner.

"You want a snack or something?"

Brody shook his head. "Not right now. Isn't your mom coming down?"

"She said she had to make a phone call, so she went over into Dawn's study. After that, she's going to find Mrs. T. and talk to her about dinner. She said something about asking my cousin Lotti over to join us."

"Isn't she the one who's taking care of your little sister?"

"Yeah. She just got out of a bad marriage and needed a job, so Dad hired her to be sort of a nanny for Echo." And that, Ty thought, was enough said about Sloan Lewellen. While he himself had maintained a good relationship with both of his parents after their divorce, the same couldn't be said about Brody. When he'd found out that Sloan was splitting from Maeve and marrying someone young enough to be his daughter, Brody had called Maeve and offered to kick the living shit out of Sloan. His mother had declined the offer, but Ty knew that his friend had still not let go of the resentment he felt toward Sloan.

To change the subject, he gestured toward Brody's leg. "Doctor Gellraien pulled a few strings to get you into surgery on Thursday. After you're out of the hospital, you can come back here to recuperate. I have a home gym back there" – he inclined his head to the left – "where you can do all the physical therapy you need."

"What about your wife? How's she going to feel about having a long-term house guest, one who she's never even met before?"

"Dawn and I already talked about that. She says that you're always welcome here."

"She could change her mind. What if she decides that she doesn't like me?"

"Well, she will like you. What's not to like? And if she doesn't, she can always avoid you by staying over on the D-side."

"The D-side?"

Taking a last satisfying pull from the bottle, Ty finished his beer, stood, and three-pointed it into a strategically placed recycle bin. Then he turned back to answer Brody's question.

"The D-side stands for Dawn's side. It may look like one house from the outside, but ours is actually two houses – a sort of duplex."

"Why do you need two houses?"

Ty wandered over to the pool table and began pushing the multicolored balls around idly. "It's like this. I'm crazy about Dawn. We're crazy about each other, in fact. But after we got married, we discovered that we weren't so crazy about living together."

He picked up a stick, racked the balls, positioned the cue ball, and broke. As the balls scattered across the table, he continued, "Just one example – the house we lived in right after we got married had a nice, spacious home office. We set it up so we could both use it – desks, chairs, computers, everything we needed; but Dawn never used it. She was always using the dining room table as a desk. And sometimes the paperwork overflowed onto the kitchen table. It drove me crazy. Meanwhile, I hired Mrs. T. as a sort of cook/housekeeper without talking to Dawn about it first. That drove *her* crazy. And there were other things too."

Since one of the balls had landed in a pocket on his first break, Ty settled in for a game of Fifteen in a Row. He aimed for the four ball, connected, and watched with satisfaction as it slid smoothly into the pocket. "Anyway, we decided to get some professional help. Couples counseling, that sort of thing. After we talked everything out, we realized that we wanted to live together, but that we each needed our own space. So we built this house. My mother helped us out with some of the design and the decorating, and on the original plans for the house, she labeled one side the 'D-side', and the other the 'T-side'. And the names stuck."

"She let your mom help with the decorating?"

Trust Brody to zero in on that, Ty thought. "Yeah. She and Mom hit it off right away. Dawn had never done much decorating before, and since my mother's an interior decorator, she offered to help. They actually had a lot of fun together, choosing the stuff for each side of the house."

"What about you? Didn't you get a say?"

Ty managed to shrug as he knocked another ball into the pocket. "I don't care that much about colors and furniture and things like that. Mom knows my tastes, so she'd bring me a sketch and I'd say, 'Fine, Mom,' and that was that. Except down here. I picked out everything down here personally." He paused his game to look approvingly around his domain before concentrating on sinking the nine ball.

"What about the other side?"

Damn. The nine ball spiraled along the top of the pocket and then spun out again. End of game. He put the cue stick away and walked to the far wall. Leaned against it and grinned like a small boy. "Let me show you," he said. He pushed a button on the wall, and it began to retract, revealing the rest of the basement.

Brody lifted his eyebrows and whistled with appreciation. "Holy shit, Lew. You've got yourself a freaking sports bar down here."

Ty smiled as his friend used the nickname he had acquired in the Air Force. He crossed over to the other side, waving his hands at his creation. "Dawn wanted her own exercise equipment upstairs next to her bedroom, and she doesn't watch much television, so she gave me a free hand down here. On both sides."

Brody had no doubt of that. The right hand wall on the other side of the basement had a huge flat screen TV mounted on it, surrounded by at least six more smaller TV's. A long bar ran down the length of that wall with at least a dozen bar stools facing the TV's. He could see some classic arcade games against the far wall, as well as a ping pong table, an air hockey table, and a Foosball table. Against the rear wall, a basketball hoop had been set up, and he caught a glimpse of a putting green as well.

"Soon as you recuperate from your surgery, we'll throw a party. Invite Vin and Sam, Ozzie, Barney, Ash, Hank, Sully – everyone. We'll have the biggest blow-out the state has ever seen."

Brody's lips curved into something that was almost one of his rare smiles. "You've got it all figured out, haven't you, Lew?"

Ty flopped down into the chair next to him again. "We'll get Mom to handle the food part of it. Remember the Super Bowl party she organized for us a couple of years back? This one will be even better."

Brody took another sip of his beer, which he was nursing along. "What about Dawn?"

"She won't have a problem with anything. Like I said, she and Mom are tight."

"If they get along so well, why isn't she here, while your mother is visiting?"

"She's working on a big case right now. College kid got pushed over a cliff, and his girlfriend was apparently abducted. Dawn's been working night and day to find the girl. Mom understands. Once the case is closed, Dawn will be around a lot more, and they'll spend some time together. But as long as there's a chance that the girl is still alive? Dawn will pretty much come home to sleep and maybe have breakfast. That's it."

"And you're okay with that?"

Ty shrugged. "She's a cop. I knew that when I married her. The hours go with the job. Besides, if it weren't for the fact that she's a cop – I don't think I'd be sitting here right now. Those guys, the ones who kidnapped me? They never had any intention of letting me go once the ransom was paid. They'd have killed me. I'm alive today only because of Dawn. She put her own life on the line to get me out of there. In fact, it was touch and go there for the both of us for a while. But we pulled through, together. That's not something I'm ever likely to forget."

Maeve disconnected the call, picked up her glass of wine, and stared into its depths thoughtfully. She'd talked to Mrs. Tilner and told her to take the night off. She, Maeve, would take care of dinner.

Ribs, she'd decided. Both Ty and Brody loved them. Provolone sticks, some wings, and pepperoni-stuffed zucchini for appetizers.

Man-food for her son and his friend. A loaf of crusty bread, a big Caesar salad, baked potatoes, some green beans almondine, and strawberry shortcake for dessert would round off the menu nicely. She'd decided on some Chicken Marsala as well, in case Lotti didn't care for ribs.

William, the manager of one of her favorite restaurants, had been delighted to hear from her again. He'd have everything delivered to her son's address in plenty of time for dinner, he'd assured her. So nice doing business with Mrs. Lewellen again.

She'd called Sloan next to arrange for some time off for Lotti. Sloan had been accommodating, which, to be fair, was what she'd expected. Next, she'd talked to Lotti herself and cajoled her into accepting the dinner invitation, no easy task. But she'd prevailed in the end, and Lotti would be arriving within the next hour or so.

Satisfied with her efforts so far, Maeve took a sip of wine and considered Brody's situation. Dr. Gellraien had, with Brody's permission, consulted with his original doctor in New Jersey. It had turned out that the first doctor had only been covering himself from any chance of a medical malpractice suit when he'd mentioned the possibility of amputation to Brody. Full disclosure of all possible consequences of the surgery, no matter how unlikely, was necessary. The odds that complications might arise that required amputating the leg were actually quite small. Brody had studied the numbers and decided that he could live with the percentages, so the surgery had been scheduled for Thursday. Paul Gellraien had had to pull some strings and shift his own schedule around a little to accommodate Brody, but that's what friends were for. He had certainly come through for Maeve.

She glanced around the study, remembering how much she and Dawn had enjoyed furnishing and decorating it together. The sage green walls harmonized neatly with the elegant coffered ceiling, done in a light buttery color and accented in white. The couch she sat on faced a fireplace, with floor-to-ceiling bookshelves on either side. They'd gone with neutrals for the couch and the matching chairs on either side of it, a soft, creamy eggshell color. More bookshelves lined two of the other walls in the room, and a large plant sat in one corner. They'd added a few touches of aqua, chocolate brown, and burgundy to the room as accents, and the final result was soothing, tranquil, calming. A necessity for Dawn, she thought, to have a place like this to retreat to at the end of a hectic day.

She'd liked Dawn right from the first, but she would have welcomed her into the family no matter what her personal feelings were, given that she owed her son's life to Dawn. Maeve's warmth had broken through Dawn's natural reserve very quickly, and the two of them had become fast friends. She'd always wanted a daughter, and now Dawn had stepped into that role.

A yawn escaped her. She looked at her watch and decided that she had plenty of time for a nap before Lotti arrived. Stretching out on the couch, she pulled one of the sofa pillows under her head. As she drifted off to sleep, she thought how nice it would be to spend some time with Dawn once she had closed the case she was working on. Maeve only hoped it would be sooner rather than later. Eventually, she had to go back to New Orleans...

Lotti finished applying lipstick and studied the results. The new shade that her friend Bree had insisted she try complemented her ash-brown hair and gray eyes. She reached for the blush and applied some to her cheeks, then brushed on mascara and eyeshadow. When she was done, she stared back at the woman facing her in the mirror. She knew that her birth certificate recorded that she was twenty-six years old. Right now, however, she felt about sixty. She wandered over to the window and stared at the well-manicured lawn below.

For the first ten years of her life, this house had been like a second home to her. Her father had been Sloan's first cousin, and the two of them were as close as brothers. After her father's death, however, everything had changed. Her mother had remarried, and they'd moved away. Her stepfather, Jerry, was an attorney who specialized in international law. Over the next few years, they'd moved around constantly. First, a year in Japan, then a couple in China. After that, they'd spent time in Germany, the United Kingdom, France, Italy, and the Netherlands. The constant travel had taken its toll on the marriage, though, and her mother had divorced Jerry shortly before Lotti's eighteenth birthday. Her mother had fallen in love with France during the time they had spent there, however, and had decided to relocate and make France her home. Lotti herself, meanwhile, had elected to come home to the U.S. to attend college. She'd only managed to visit with Sloan and his family a couple of times in all of those years.

She'd met Riley at the beginning of her junior year in college. He'd seemed so perfect at first. He was senior, just a year away from graduation, and he'd been so attentive, so loving, so caring. The epitome of romance. He'd showered her with gifts, written poetry to her, convinced her that she was the center of his universe.

After he had graduated from college, he'd taken her on a month-long trip to Hawaii. To celebrate, he'd said. She'd been intoxicated, madly in love with him. Originally, they'd planned to wait until she graduated the following year to get married, but he'd persuaded her to change her mind. Why wait? He'd get a job close by the University, he'd said, and she could spend her senior year as a married woman just as easily as a single one.

By the time they'd returned from Hawaii, they were married. And then it had begun. Scarcely a week later, he had informed her that his father had offered him a job as a vice president in the family company. Its headquarters were located in Riley's hometown of Plantain, a medium-size city in southwest Illinois.

"No problem," she'd said. "I'll just transfer to one of the local colleges and finish out my senior year there."

He'd been delighted with her response and had offered to do all the paperwork for her, pay the tuition, everything. After some research, she'd decided to transfer to Merrimac, a small private college located in the heart of the business district in Plantain. Riley's office was not far away, which was extremely convenient. Maybe they could have lunch together on a regular basis.

When she'd walked onto campus the first day, however, she was stunned. Although Riley had assured her that he had taken care of everything for her, there was no record that she was enrolled in the college. No tuition had ever been paid.

She'd been furious. She'd marched into the front door of their home like an avenging fury and confronted him.

He'd been so busy, he said. What with moving and starting the new job – he'd just forgotten about it.

"That's no excuse!" she'd shouted. "I was counting on you!"

He had responded by backhanding her. Afterward, he had stared at his hand as if it didn't belong to him, seemingly stunned.

His voice full of contrition, he'd said, "I can't believe I did that. I'm so sorry, sweetheart. I don't know what came over me. It'll never happen again."

He'd taken her into his arms, embraced her, soothed the hurt away. He'd bought her roses, dozens of them, and expensive jewelry to "make up for it." She could enroll during the winter term, he'd told her. It was all probably for the best, he'd continued. Taking a semester off would give her time to adjust to her new home, her new life.

But when the winter term had come, he'd found another excuse for putting off her return to college. When she'd protested, he'd given her a black eye. And that pattern had continued throughout their marriage.

Why did I put up with it for so long? she wondered. Even as the thought crossed her mind, she knew the answer. Pride. Pride and shame and that insidious type of brainwashing that the experts called Battered Woman Syndrome.

The violence had escalated as the years went by, but she hadn't made any attempt to leave him. He'd told her that he'd kill her if she even thought about it. One day about a year previously, however, everything had changed. Riley had beaten her so badly that her entire body seemed to be one large bruise. He'd forbidden her to leave the house while he was at work that day, but something had snapped in her. She'd wandered around the neighborhood, dazed, confused, until a man working outside in his yard had noticed her. He was an older man, gnarled and grizzled, and she'd never met him before.

"Lady, somebody really did a job on you. You look like you could use a friend."

She hadn't even known how to respond. When he'd started to call the police, however, she'd begged him not to.

"He'll kill me," she'd said.

Jim, as she discovered later was his name, had pondered that for a minute.

"What about your parents?"

She shook her head. "My dad's dead. And I can't tell my mother – she'd be so disappointed in me."

"Aunts? Uncles? Cousins?"

She'd answered slowly, "Sloan. Sloan Lewellen. He's my cousin."

"Tell me your name, and give me his number."

She'd told him her name and recited the number without even having to think about it. She'd called it so many times during her childhood that she still had it memorized.

Jim had called the house and gotten through to Sloan, who fortunately had been working from home that day.

"Sloan Lewellen? My name's Jim Telfee. I'm calling from Plantain, Illinois, and I've got a lady here in my house who's scared to death and looks like she's been beaten within an inch of her life. Her name is Charlotte Nordgram, and she says she's your cousin." He paused for a moment and said, "Just a minute."

He'd handed her the phone, and she'd said tentatively, "Hello?"

"Lotti?"

At the sound of his voice, something broke inside her. All she'd been able to do was whisper, "Sloan?" And then she'd started sobbing. Jim had taken the phone back and gotten her a drink of water. After she'd calmed down enough, she got back on the phone.

"Lotti, listen to me. Jim's going to take you to the airport. Just get in his car and go with him. I'll be there in two hours to pick you up. Don't worry about anything. I'm on my way, honey."

Sloan had been as good as his word. The private plane had landed as scheduled, and Sloan had bounded off the plane and enfolded her in a bear hug. He'd shaken hands with Jim, expressed his thanks, and said he'd be in touch. Then he'd hustled Lotti aboard the plane, where she'd gotten another reassuring hug from her cousin Ty.

A few hours later, Sloan had ushered her in his front door. *"You're home now, Lotti. You're safe."* The words that Sloan had spoken as they'd entered the house had become a mantra to her, a secret talisman to drive away all the demons of her past.

She'd been alarmed when Sloan had announced his intention the next day of flying back to Plantain, confronting Riley, and arranging for Lotti's things to be sent to her. She'd begged him not to; Riley was too dangerous.

"Don't you worry, Lotti," Sloan had answered grimly. "By the time Ty and I are through with him, it's Riley Nordgram who's going to be afraid."

Whatever Sloan and Ty had said and done must have had the desired effect, for she'd never been troubled by Riley again. The divorce had been handled by Sloan's attorneys and was granted in record time. By then, she'd settled into her new job as a sort of nanny for Echo. The external bruises had faded. But the internal scars from those years with Riley had never entirely healed.

Sighing, she picked up her handbag and headed out the door, down the stairs. She still had trouble going out, even though Sloan had arranged for her to be protected by his own security company. But

Maeve had been insistent. And, as many others had discovered before her, it was almost impossible to say *no* to Maeve.

When Lotti rang the doorbell at Ty and Dawn's house, Mrs. Tilner answered and showed her back to the kitchen on the left. There Maeve greeted her with a hug and a kiss.

"So glad that you could make it, Lotti. You're saving me from being the only female at this little dinner party. Dawn is hung up at work on a big case right now, so she won't be able to make it home in time."

Turning to Mrs. Tilner, Maeve smiled and said, "I thought you were going out on the town, taking advantage of having some free time tonight, Mrs. T."

"I'm leaving in a little while. A friend of mine is coming to pick me up. I'm just waiting for her to get here. Thanks for giving me the night off, Mrs. Lewellen."

At the sound of a horn outside, Mrs. Tilner said, "That'll be her now. You coming over for breakfast in the morning? I can make you some blueberry pancakes. I remember how much you like them."

"No, I think I'll have breakfast at my hotel tomorrow. But thanks anyway, Mrs. T."

After Mrs. Tilner had left, Maeve turned and beamed at Lotti. "I've ordered dinner in from Quinerius. It should arrive any minute now. We're going to eat downstairs, save Ty's friend Brody from walking up the stairs. You've never met Brody, have you?"

Dawn and Rafe walked down Mrs. Lillipinner's sidewalk and noted that the car they had spotted earlier parked across the street in front of Monieque Torrense's house was still there. Mrs. Lillipinner, who had insisted that they call her Josie, informed them that the car belonged to Monieque's new boyfriend. Apparently, he and his son had been coming over every evening since Cullen's death. She'd gone on and on about how Monieque seemed to be absolutely devoted to the boy. Dawn had run the plates and discovered that the car belonged to a man named Martin Dellpeaur. And he wasn't the only one that Josie had observed visiting Monieque in the last few weeks. She'd also seen Cullen's friend J.B. there on several occasions. When pressed, she had been able to recall the dates as well.

"Ah, the policeman's best friend – a nosy neighbor with an excellent memory. Let's knock on a few more doors and see if anyone else noticed Mr. Bolt around the neighborhood recently."

At Rafe's suggestion, Dawn frowned for a minute. "I was hoping we'd be able to get her in for questioning tonight, but you're right. Let's talk to the other neighbors first and wait until the morning to question her. If we try it tonight, the boyfriend is apt to want to go along with her, or he might insist that she call a lawyer. That's the last thing we want."

"Agreed. We'll finish our canvass of the neighborhood first. Bring her in tomorrow, hopefully catch her when she's alone and off-guard." Seeing Dawn frown, Rafe asked, "What's wrong?"

"Nothing's wrong, exactly. I'm happy with how the Torrense case is progressing. But we seem to have come to a stand-still on the Zarafin case, Rafe."

"I understand how you feel. But we have to run with this case while it's hot. And if we can get Monieque Torrense wrapped up tomorrow morning, we'll be able to get back to the Zarafin case in the afternoon. For one thing, we've got that interview with Tamara Norti's parents all set up. They might be able to give us something. After we speak to them, we'll pound the pavement and talk with every real estate agent in Mountpelier if we have to. If Trevor Stoss saw him, surely someone else did. And maybe the next guy we talk to will have the guy's name written down in his damn appointment book. That's the kind of break we need, something that will give us a lead on who the guy is and where he's keeping Lee. And perhaps we'll get lucky and find her alive, Dawn. But I wouldn't count on it. It's been three days now. All the odds are against it."

Chapter 8

Lee sat on the edge of her narrow cot and looked around her basement prison, considering her surroundings. She had to figure out a way to escape. If she didn't, she was as good as dead. The last conversation she'd had with Michael had only reinforced what she'd already guessed. He had no intentions of allowing her to leave this place alive.

After he'd finished his demented tale about his encounter with a Norse goddess no one had believed in for a thousand years, he had finished his sketch. Then he had gone upstairs to prepare dinner for both of them. After dinner, he had sat down at his easel, prepared his palette, and started working on an oil painting, apparently using the sketch as a model. When she'd asked him what the subject was, he'd responded that it was a painting of her, of course. Not as she appeared to be on the outside; no – he was painting a portrait of her as she really was.

He'd worked on the canvas only for a short time before saying that he was finished for the day. Then, bidding her goodnight and switching the light off, he'd gone upstairs once again.

When he'd returned the next morning, she had tried to engage him in conversation once again. He had chatted with her for a little while, informing her that it was the upcoming winter festival that had drawn him to Mountpelier. He loved to walk around and look at the ice sculptures; it made him feel closer to Vanadis. In fact, he had bought himself some tools and had begun trying his hand at ice sculpting himself. After that, however, he had not been inclined to talk. He said that when he worked on an oil painting, he did his best work in total silence. So she had kept quiet, which had pleased him so much that he had left the dim light at the foot of the stairs burning for her *that evening when she had begged him not to leave her in the dark for another night.*

She'd tested the shackle around her ankle over and over, trying to find some give in it, some way she could slip it off. But it was no use – the shackle was too tight. She thought about trying to pick the lock, but she didn't have access to anything that she could use as a tool, and she didn't know the first thing about picking locks, anyway. For a while, she'd almost lost hope, but then a scene from Will's favorite movie, the one that he insisted was the best film ever made, popped into her head. The main character – she couldn't remember his name, but Tim Robbins had played him - had used a small rock hammer to chip an escape route through the crumbling walls of his prison cell. Scooting back to the far side of the cot, she examined the cinder block wall in which the staple holding the chain was imbedded. The cinder block wasn't exactly crumbling, but if she had some kind of tool, maybe she could loosen enough around the staple to break the chain free...

Dinner the night before had been a success, Maeve decided as she ate the grapefruit that she'd ordered from room service for breakfast. Lotti had been at ease around Ty, whom she had always looked up to as a sort of older brother, and Brody had exerted himself enough to be civil, if not precisely charming. The ribs had been a hit, and after dinner, Ty and Brody had wandered over to play some of Ty's arcade games while she and Lotti had chatted.

After she finished her grapefruit, Maeve crossed over to the desk in her hotel room and opened her laptop. She needed to Skype with her best friend, Daphne Bartelli. When she connected with Daphne, her friend wasted no time, but got right to the point.

"I can't believe you didn't call me last night. Did you tell Sloan we went to Greece with Julian Notler?"

"Yes, I did."

"How did he take it? Was he jealous?"

"He didn't seem too happy about it."

"Good! What's your next move?"

"I don't have one. I'm not even thinking about Sloan right now. I spent the whole day yesterday getting Ty's friend, Brody, to consent to some necessary surgery. It wasn't easy, trust me."

"Brody's the one who saved Ty's life back when Ty was with Pararescue, right?"

"Yes. I don't know all the details, but I do know that I owe Brody my son's life. And he has no other family, so we've sort of adopted him into ours. Although I'm going to have to keep him away from Sloan while he's here. He's never forgiven Sloan for the divorce."

"Now there's a good man. Like to meet him some time. Didn't you tell me that he offered to kick Sloan's ass for you?"

"Right after the divorce, yes."

"He big enough to do it?"

"Definitely, but I don't want him hurting Sloan. I told him so."

"See, that's your problem. You're still in love with Sloan Lewellen. After the way he treated you, you should hate his guts."

"I did for a while. Then it sort of cooled off."

"That bitch Renea still in the picture?"

"No. According to Lotti, Renea doesn't even make an effort to see her own daughter, let alone Sloan."

"That's good news."

"Daphne?"

"What?"

"He offered me a job."

"A job? What kind of job?"

"He wants me to decorate the new wing he added onto the back of the house. Lotti says that he built it for him and Renea, but after she moved out, he stripped it bare. He didn't move back into our old room, either. Instead, he remodeled the East Wing to include a sort of nursery for Echo and moved into a suite of rooms across the hall from the nursery."

"Are you actually considering taking the job?"

"I told him that I'd have to think about it, but I'm inclined to say *yes*. Think about it, Daphne. I'll be paid to do what I used to do for free. And I'll be able to wipe out every trace of Renea from the house as well."

"Not every trace, Maeve."

Maeve hesitated for a minute before responding. "I don't hold anything against a tiny baby, Daphne. She's the one innocent person in all of this."

They chatted for a few more minutes; then Maeve explained that she had to get going and signed off. But she never admitted to Daphne that her friend was right. She was still in love with Sloan Lewellen. She could barely remember a time when she hadn't been. And she wasn't sure that she would ever be able to forgive him.

When Ty came down for breakfast the next morning, he immediately saw the note on the table: *Breakfast downstairs today*. He made his way down the steps and turned the corner. Brody was stretched out on the couch, polishing off what looked like a mountain of blueberry pancakes. He was surprised to see that Dawn, who was rarely down before him, was perched on a nearby chair, finishing up a slice of her usual toast with peanut butter and chatting with Brody. Pleased to discover that his wife and his best friend had finally met and seemed to be getting along just fine, he looked for the nearest source of food, which he spied on the counter in the bar area, where Mrs. Tilner had apparently set up a sort of buffet.

"Morning, all."

Dawn arose and greeted him with a good morning kiss as he crossed to peek under the covers of the warming pans on the buffet.

"You'd better score yourself some blueberry pancakes before they're all gone, Ty," Dawn said. "And guard Mrs. T. with your life. Brody is talking about stealing her away from you."

Ty shot a warning glance at Brody. "Take Mrs. T. away from me and die, Brody. She's mine." And then he spied Traitor, cosied up beside Brody, making no move to greet Ty with her usual ecstatic welcome. "You trying to take my dog away from me too?"

Before Brody could say anything, Dawn spoke up in his defense. "It's not Brody's fault, Ty. I told you that Traitor deserves her name. Somehow or other, she's guessed what's in store for her today, and she's zeroed in on Brody as a potential source of protection."

"How could she have figured it out? We haven't said anything in front of her. I even made the appointment while she was outside chasing squirrels."

Dawn shrugged. "I don't know. She seems to have sixth sense about some things. I've got to run. Have fun today when you take her to the V-E-T."

As Dawn proceeded up the stairs, Ty filled a plate with a generous portion of blueberry pancakes. He sat down opposite Brody and gave Traitor the beady eye. "Brody's not going to be able to save you. Face it like a soldier, girl – there's a trip to Doctor Dog in your near future."

Traitor responded by refusing to look at him and tucking her nose behind Brody's back. Brody gave her a sympathetic pat, forked up another serving of pancakes, and said, "When's the appointment?"

"We have some time yet. It's not scheduled until ten o'clock."

"What about the flight that's bringing my bag in?"

"It took off about an hour ago. By the time the pilot gets to New Jersey, picks up the bag, and gets back, it'll be about one this afternoon."

"I can't believe that you forgot the bag in the first place."

"Well, if I had known that being parted from it for a day or two would give you a bad case of separation anxiety, I wouldn't have. I'll know better the next time."

"There better not *be* a next time. You even *think* about trying a stunt like that again, there'll have to be *two* surgeries on Thursday – and the first one will be to remove my foot from your asshole."

"I look forward to you being healthy enough to try it. But even when you're one hundred percent, Brody, I'm still quicker than you are. And I'm twice as sneaky."

"You're not quicker than I am. If you were, you wouldn't be sporting a black eye right now, would you?"

"Yeah, well, I've got news for you, pal. I let you get a few licks in, figured I owed it to you to let you take a shot at me. But if I ever really wanted to elude you, you'd never get near me. I've got planes and jets and helicopters, remember? Once I'm in one of those babies, you'd have a hard time catching me. Unless you've learned how to fly some time in the last year?"

"No, but I'd find a way to get you. Count on it."

"You're forgetting about the sneaky part. Even you have to admit that I have the edge there."

"So get your sneaky ass moving. I don't want to hang around here all day. I'll go with you to see" - he glanced down at Traitor – "Doctor Dog, and then we can go to the airport." Brody smiled evilly. "Once I have my bag again, you won't be able to get to one of your planes fast enough, fly-boy. I'll have about a dozen different ways of slowing you down."

"Just remember – someone's got to take you to the hospital on Thursday."

"I'll get your mother to do it."

"She won't. Not if you've just kicked my ass, that is."

"That's low, even for you – hiding behind your mother."

"Yeah, yeah – whatever it takes. Like I said: Don't ever underestimate the sneaky factor."

It was the sound of snoring that woke Vivian Zarafin up that morning. That and the army with iron-shod boots that was marching through her head. She stumbled out of bed and made it to the bathroom, holding onto the sink to keep herself upright. For a minute she thought she might be sick, but the feeling passed.

She had been a fool, a weak fool, to let Buzz talk her into spending the last few days with him. She knew him for what he was, a lying, cheating louse, yet she still hadn't been able to resist the temptation to go to him when he had called her on Friday night. The days had passed by quickly in a drunken haze of booze and sex. For a time she had felt wonderful, but - as always - it didn't last. Now she felt even more empty and lonely than ever.

Turning the taps on, she sluiced her face with water. Feeling marginally better, she returned to the bedroom and found her clothes. Getting dressed only took a minute or two, and then she was grabbing her purse and heading out the front door. She was surprised to discover that though the sun was shining overhead, the temperature had dropped considerably, and there was about half an inch of snow on the ground. Her car was in the driveway, but she realized that she'd have to clear it off before she did anything else. She quickly opened the driver's side door, tossed her purse into the passenger's seat, and grabbed her ice scraper. Once she'd cleared off the windshield, she got in the driver's seat and fished her key chain out of her purse. She tried to put the key into the ignition, but her hands were shaking so badly that it took her a couple of attempts before she managed it. She hesitated a moment, but then she reached back into her purse for the flask that she always carried. *Just one drink*, she thought. One drink would steady her, and then she'd be able to make it home.

When Monieque Torrense opened the door to her house in answer to their knock, Dawn let Rafe do all the talking. Rafe informed Monieque almost apologetically that they were holding Jago Bolt for her son's murder, and mentioned that J.B. was making what Rafe considered to be some wild and frankly unbelievable claims. Would Monieque mind coming down to the station for questioning, just to clear up some things for them?

When Jago Bolt's name was first mentioned, Dawn caught just a flicker of alarm cross the other woman's face, but she'd covered it up quickly. She had expressed surprise that J.B. was being held for the murder; after all, he was her son's friend. But she made no objection to coming down to headquarters with them. If they would just give her a few minutes to get ready, she'd follow them down in her own car.

At headquarters, Rafe steered her into the interview room, where Monieque eased herself into a seat. She was a rather plump woman of about average height, but she had managed to minimize the extra pounds she carried on her frame by choosing expensive and stylish clothes that flattered her curvy figure and drew the eye up to her main assets, which included wide, china-blue eyes set in a smooth baby face, a flawless complexion, a straight little nose, and a lush, full mouth. Her blonde hair, which Dawn suspected came straight from a bottle rather than from Mother Nature, was perfectly coiffed in an attractive bob and swept back from her carefully made-up face.

Once Monieque had settled herself into her chair, Rafe said, "Mrs. Torrense, protocol requires me to give the Miranda warning to anyone we bring in for questioning. Would that be okay with you? Just to take care of the formalities, you know?"

"Oh! It never occurred to me that you would have to read me my rights. But I suppose if you have to…"

"Yes, ma'am, we do. I'll just do it right now, get it over with, okay?"

"Well, I guess if you have to do it, it's not a problem for me. Go ahead."

"Okay. I'm going to go on the record now, just to make sure we do everything according to the proper procedure." After he'd started the record and read the Miranda warning, Rafe said, "Now, do you understand your rights, Mrs. Torrense?"

"Yes." Fluttering her eyelids, she added, "and please call me Monieque."

"All right, Monieque. Now, you're aware that we've arrested a young man named Jago Bolt on suspicion of the murder of your son, Cullen Torrense, aren't you?"

"Yes, you told me that when you came to my house. I'm totally shocked to hear that he had anything to do with Cullen's death. They were friends, you see. I just can't believe that he would ever do anything to hurt my son."

"So you are acquainted with Jago Bolt, Monieque?"

"Oh, yes – but we've always called him J.B., not Jago. He's been in and out of the house ever since Cullen started high school. That's when they met. They didn't know each other before, because they attended different grade schools."

"Can you tell me the last time you saw Jago Bolt?"

"Oh, dear me – not for ages now. There was no reason for him to come over once Cullen had moved out of the house."

"And that would be how long ago?"

"Well, let's see – a few months, at least."

"Now, I know that this is going to come as a shock to you, Monieque, but when he was questioned about the murder, Mr. Bolt made a rather startling claim. To be blunt, he implicated you in your son's death. In fact, he claimed that you paid him to kill Cullen."

"*What*? Are you serious?"

"I'm afraid so, Monieque. I know that it sounds fantastic, but that's what he said."

"That's crazy! Cullen was my only son. He was more precious to me than anything else in the world. Surely you didn't believe J.B., did you?"

"Well, Monieque, when someone makes a claim like that, we have to follow up on it, no matter what our personal beliefs might be."

Dabbing her eyes, she responded brokenly, "It's wicked! It's just plain evil of him to say such a thing. Why would he make such a horrible accusation?"

Dawn got into the conversation then, saying in a hard tone of voice, "Oh, please. You can cut the act. And it hasn't been months since you last saw J.B. We have witnesses that saw the two of you together last week."

"How dare you speak to me like that? Have you no feeling, no compassion for a grieving mother?"

"Hold on now," Rafe said. "Let's all calm down. Detective Cimarron, I'm feeling the need for some refreshment. Why don't you get us some coffee?" Turning to Monieque, he said, "What about you, Monieque? Coffee okay with you?"

Glaring at Dawn, she said, "If you have something cold, that would be better. Maybe some iced tea?"

"I think we can handle that, don't you, Detective Cimarron?"

Dawn just shrugged her shoulders and left the room.

"Sorry about that, Monieque. She hasn't been a detective for very long. I'm still sort of teaching her the ropes. I'm afraid she hasn't had much experience in interviewing people."

"Well, I hope that she catches on quickly, or she isn't going to have much success. Her attitude leaves a lot to be desired."

"Well, she did have a point, though. I mean, some of your neighbors did see you and J.B. together fairly recently. Perhaps you'd forgotten?"

"Wait a minute, let me think. Oh! – you're right. J.B. did come over a couple of times during the last few weeks. I'd forgotten about it. The first time he came over to ask for Cullen's new address, and the second time to pick up a jacket he'd forgotten to take with him the week before. It was so insignificant, it just slipped my mind."

Dawn reentered the room just then, a cup of coffee in one hand and a glass of iced tea in the other. She made no comment as she placed them on the table and resumed her seat. Rafe politely handed the glass of tea to Monieque before picking up his coffee and taking a sip. *Now comes the tricky part*, he thought.

Right on cue, Dawn snapped, "Did you ask her about the money yet?"

Monieque nearly choked on her tea. "Money? What money?"

Dawn replied, "J.B. had almost twenty thousand dollars stashed away in a safety deposit box, Monieque. And guess what? You withdrew that exact amount from your bank account just a few days before the murder. And your fingerprints were found on some of the bills."

Rafe looked at her reproachfully. "Now, Cimarron, I'm sure that there's some reasonable explanation for that. Isn't there, Monieque?"

She burst into tears, then. Sobbing, she blurted out, "He was blackmailing me!"

"Wait a minute – Bolt is a blackmailer? That's why you gave him the money?"

Rafe's soothing tone of voice had the desired effect. Monieque stopped sobbing and said, "Yes! That's why I said I hadn't seen him recently! I didn't want anyone to know!"

"Okay, Monieque – calm down. What was J.B. blackmailing you about?"

"I can't tell you!"

"Well, I'm afraid that if you don't, some people may be inclined to believe his story. Don't you think you'd better come clean, tell us what really happened? You don't want anyone to think that you actually paid him that money to kill Cullen, do you?"

"No, no!"

"Then you'd be better off if you tell us the whole story, Monieque."

"Do you promise you won't tell anybody?"

"I can't promise that. But I'm sure that whatever it is can't really be that bad."

He waited for a moment, saying nothing else. Finally, she took a deep breath and said, "Okay, I'll tell you. He - J.B. - had evidence that I was having an affair."

Rafe said in a puzzled tone of voice, "He was blackmailing you about that? I don't understand. Why would you pay him not to tell anyone, if that's all there was to it?"

"The man I'm having an affair with – he's married!"

"Fooling around with a married man, huh? Shame, shame, Monieque," Dawn said mockingly.

"Shut up! And it's Mrs. Torrense to you!" Turning her shoulder to Dawn, Monieque looked into Rafe's eyes and said soulfully, "I know it's wrong, but we couldn't help it. We love each other!"

"But I'm still not clear why having an affair made you the target of a blackmailer. I mean, you're a widow, right? You have no spouse who'd get upset about it. Why didn't he go after the man you're involved with? Seems to me he'd be the more logical choice."

"Oh, he's not very well-to-do. That's why J.B. came after me instead."

"I see. Can you tell me his name? The man you're seeing, that is."

"Uh... His first name is Joe. And frankly, I don't think it's any of your business what his last name is, so I'm not going to tell you. I don't want to make any trouble for him. His wife might find out."

"No problem. We don't need his last name at the present time. Now, where did you and Joe meet?"

"In the park. The one near my house. I met him when I was walking there one day."

"You go walking in the park on a regular basis?"

"Oh, yes. I like to keep in shape."

"And on one of these walks you met Joe. When was that, precisely?"

"Back in August, I think."

"Did you start seeing him right away?"

"Not right away, no. I mean, it made me uncomfortable at first, the fact that he was a married man. We just sort of started talking to each other, and then one day he asked me to go for coffee with him. It wasn't long after that we realized we were in love. And then, we kind of got carried away. We've been seeing each other ever since."

"Okay. Now, when did J.B. first approach you with his blackmail scheme?"

"About a week ago. I was flabbergasted. At first, I told him that I wasn't paying a cent, but later I realized that I just couldn't bear for everything to come out, so I agreed."

"In that case, here's something that's puzzling me. Why didn't you just deny it – the fact that you and Joe were having an affair? Did J.B. have some sort of proof?"

"Yes, yes! He'd taken pictures of the two of us together."

Rafe frowned. "It still seems to me that you could have come up with an innocent explanation for why the two of you were together, explained the whole thing away."

"No, we couldn't. You see, the pictures were...of an intimate nature."

Rafe raised his eyebrows. "Now, that's a different story. Where did J.B. take these pictures? At your house?"

"No – Joe and I were at a hotel."

"At a hotel? How did J.B. pull that off?"

"I don't know! He wouldn't tell me. I about died when he showed me those pictures!"

"How did he take them? On his cell phone?"

"Yes. He showed them to me that first night he came by."

"Did he hold the cell phone while he showed them to you, or did he give it to you to hold?"

"Wait a minute – I think that he gave the cell phone to me, but I'm not positive."

Rafe turned to Dawn and said, "See? I told you there was a reasonable explanation for why her fingerprints were found on the cell phone."

There was a knock on the door just then. Rafe went over to see who it was. After a brief conversation with the person at the door, who stayed just out of sight, Rafe turned back and said, "Excuse me for a few minutes. There's something I have to attend to."

After Rafe left, Monieque studiously ignored Dawn, until the latter said, "You want to know what I don't understand, Monieque? We've already checked J.B.'s cell phone, and we didn't find any scandalous pictures of you and your lover on it. Care to explain that?"

"I'm afraid that should be obvious, even to you. J.B. must have deleted them."

"Uh-uh. No good. Even if pictures are deleted, they're still in the phone's memory, and our techs can retrieve them."

"Then J.B. must have used another phone that day. Maybe one of those throwaway ones. I don't know! And I don't want to talk to you anymore!"

"Suit yourself," Dawn said comfortably. Then she added, "Here's a thought: If J.B. used a different phone, then how come your prints are on the one in the lab downstairs?"

"You're obviously too stupid to understand. I refuse to listen to your nonsense any longer." She looked up with relief when Rafe came back into the room.

"Sergeant Melbourne, I'm tired. I don't want to answer any more questions. I want to go home."

"Sure, Monieque. We'll only be another minute or two. Just a couple more things. There's something I don't get. According to your neighbor, Mrs. Lillipinner, the man you've been seeing over the past few months is named Martin, not Joe. And he's not married; he's a widower with a young son." Shaking his head sadly, Rafe went on, "I'm afraid that it just doesn't fit with your story."

Before she'd had time to assimilate Rafe's comments, Dawn asked, "And Monieque? If you're such a devoted mother, why haven't you done anything about making funeral arrangements for your son? According to our information, the only person who's made inquiries regarding the final disposition of Cullen's body is his aunt, a woman named Ellanor Torrense – not you."

Whirling on Dawn, Monieque cried, "I couldn't deal with it! I've been almost paralyzed with grief! I loved my son, and I'm too broken to handle things like that right now! My son meant the world to me. Don't you get that?"

"No, and Cullen didn't either – at least not according to his stepsister."

"Gwen Mallinder? That little bitch hates me! She'd do anything to hurt me. You can't believe a word she says!"

"But we don't have to take her word for it. You see, Cullen wrote everything down. He put it all in a letter and mailed it to Gwen just before he went off to meet J.B. in the park. Want to hear what he says?" Taking the letter out of a folder that lay on the table, she read what Cullen had had to say about his suspicions concerning his mother.

"It's all lies! That letter must be a forgery! I loved my son! Ask anyone who ever saw us together! No one will believe that I had anything to do with his death!"

"Oh, I think they will, Monieque. Especially after they learn that within days after being notified about her son's death, his mother, who claims to be so grief stricken that she can't even handle making funeral arrangements for him, began initiating legal proceedings that will enable her to claim a large sum of money that Cullen's father left to him in a trust fund."

Monieque jumped up out of her chair. "I'm not staying here one more minute. I'm getting a lawyer, and I'm going to sue you for defamation of character!"

"Sit down, Monieque. You're not going anywhere."

"You can't keep me here!"

"Oh, but I'm afraid we can. We can hold you for twenty-four hours just on suspicion." As Monieque lifted a hand threateningly, Dawn added, "Hitting me won't help you, Monieque. All it will do is get you charged with assaulting a police officer. You really want to go there?"

Turning to Rafe, Monieque appealed, "Sergeant Melbourne, if I have to stay here, I want a lawyer. And I don't want that person," she said, pointing at Dawn, "present during any questioning. I refuse to answer any more questions as long as that individual is in this room."

"Let the record show that Mrs. Torrense has invoked her right to be represented by an attorney. End interview for the present time," said Rafe. Making a note of the time, he rose from his chair and said, "We'll have to leave you alone for a little bit, Monieque. We need to make arrangements for you to contact a lawyer."

"Fine. I've had about enough of you – both of you!"

When they joined him in Observation, the huge grin on ADA Toravo's face revealed teeth so perfectly white that it was a wonder it didn't blind them.

"Man, it was a treat watching the two of you work her. You had her eating out of your hand, Rafe!" Pointing his index finger at Dawn, he added, "and that's the first chance I've had to watch you be the bad cop. You were downright nasty to her, D.C. Didn't know you had it in you. Usually you two play it the other way around."

"We decided before going in that I'd be the good cop this time," Rafe said. "From what we've learned about her, we guessed that she's more comfortable with men, more hostile toward women. We figured that if she thought I sympathized with her, she'd be more likely to open up to me. She has a lot of confidence in herself when it comes to manipulating men."

"Yeah. She thought you believed every word of her bullshit story, right up to the end. And D.C.? She really, really wanted to hurt you. In fact, if looks could kill, you'd be lying dead on the floor right now."

"I know. I'm all broken up about it, too."

"Well, now that the two of you have gotten the ball rolling, it's time for me to run with it. I'll take it from here, see that she gets her attorney. And whoever she gets to represent her is not going to be happy. You shot her credibility to pieces by catching her in so many lies. Hell, even a low-life like J.B. is going to look good by comparison. And that's good news for our side. We'll let her talk things over with her lawyer. In the meantime, we'll get a warrant for her arrest. We'll have her arrested, charged, and booked in no time at all."

"You going for Murder One?" Rafe inquired.

"A mother who cold-bloodedly hired a hit man to knock off her only son so that she could get her hands on his trust fund? You bet we're going for Murder One. It will be a pleasure to toss Monieque Torrense into prison for the rest of her miserable life, or better yet, put her narcissistic ass on Death Row."

"Can't argue with that. We'll see you later, Bob. We've got another hot case that we need to move up to the front burner."

"The Zarafin case? I heard about that one. Any news?"

Rafe shook his head. "No. We've got some leads we need to follow up on, though. In fact, in about an hour, we have a Skype interview set up with the parents of another possible victim, this one up in Michigan. Maybe they can give us something we can follow up on, help us to find the girl. For her sake, I just hope it's not too late."

Chapter 9

She needed a tool. If she went to the extreme length that the chain allowed her, she could just glimpse a tool chest – one of those standing ones like her dad's – at the far end of the room. But it might as well have been on the moon, for all the good it did her. No way was she ever going to be able to reach it. She turned her gaze from that direction and focused her attention on the items that were closer to her reach. At first her heart sank, because she could see nothing but Michael's painting and sketching supplies, which were of no use to her. But then she spied something else; some sort of funny-looking tool lying amid a bunch of empty paint tubes and rags on a shelf next to Michael's easel. It looked like a combination between an ice pick and a chisel. She recalled his comment that he'd begun trying his hand at ice sculpting, and wondered if that was one of the tools he used. In any case, it was ideal for chipping away at cinder block. If only she could figure out a way of reaching it. Chained as she was, she couldn't get anywhere near enough to touch it, even with her fingertips. But maybe she could figure out a way of bringing it to her... Moving into the powder room, she looked at the basic toiletries that Michael had provided. Her gaze passed over and dismissed most of the items: the hand towels and wash cloth, the roll of toilet tissue, the cake of soap, the toothbrush and tube of toothpaste. But the hairbrushes: maybe she could make use of those. There were two of them, a round brush with soft, natural bristles, and a vent brush with widely spaced bristles made of a hard plastic. Thoughtfully picking up the latter and considering it for a moment, she carried it over to the bed and set it down on the floor. Stripping the sheet off the bed, she twisted it until it resembled a long rope. Then she knotted each end, wrapped one end around the handle of the brush three times, and tied another knot to secure it to the sheet. Keeping one end of the sheet in her left hand, she used her right hand to toss the improvised rope and grappling hook toward the shelf. Not long enough. She pulled her rope back in and extended it by twisting and knotting the pillowcase onto the end of the sheet. Tried again. Still not long enough. Bracing herself, she shrugged off the thin blanket she was wearing around her shoulders, twisted and knotted it as well, and secured it to the pillowcase. She tested each knot to make sure that it was tight enough, because if any part of this jury-rigged contrivance came loose, she might not be able to retrieve it. Taking the hairbrush in one hand, she flung it once again toward the tool shelf, whipping her body and snapping the rope at the same time. The hairbrush hit the wall near the shelf and fell to the floor. She pulled it back and repeated the process. This time the brush hit the shelf itself. Once more she reeled her line back in. Judging the distance carefully, she made another cast. Bull's-eye! The brush landed directly on the shelf, nestled in the folds of the painting rag that swaddled the tool she so desperately needed. Carefully, she tugged on the line, praying the brush would be heavy enough to dislodge the item that she sought. She almost let out a cheer as the stiff bristles of the hairbrush caught on the chisel-like tool. She tugged on her rope again, and had to stifle another cheer as, with a thud, both hairbrush and chisel fell to the floor. Now, all she had to do was make another cast and get the hairbrush into the right position so that she could use it to drag the precious tool across the room and into her waiting hands...

The state trooper who had investigated the case of their missing daughter had persuaded Tamara Norti's parents to come down to the station, so that he could be present with them during their Skype interview with the detectives from the Mountpelier police. He identified himself as Sergeant Joel Chernet; then he introduced Dawn and Rafe to Mr. and Mrs. Norti.

The first thing that Dawn noticed about Elizabeth and Elliot Norti was that they had the same look of exhausted resignation about them that Miranda Gordena had had. Elizabeth did most of the talking. Her husband held her hand tightly, but did not seem inclined to talk, at least not in the beginning.

Dawn asked most of the questions: open-ended questions at first, taking them through the last few days before Tamara had gone hiking with her boyfriend in the Porcupine Mountains one day and had never come back.

"Everything was just normal," Elizabeth Norti insisted. "Tamara commuted to her classes at the local community college here on weekdays. She was home for dinner most nights. She'd been going with her boyfriend, Blake, since they were both in eighth grade. She didn't have a boyfriend before then; we wouldn't permit it."

Elizabeth took a deep breath before continuing, "That Saturday, the day they left to go hiking, it was unusually warm for that time of year. Normally the mountains are pretty inaccessible from the late fall until mid-spring – it's not uncommon for there to be ninety inches of snow or more up there from November through April. But that day, it was in the high fifties. Both Tamara and Blake loved to go hiking. They left early in the morning and promised to be home by five o'clock. We were going to have dinner together. I'd made lasagna – it was Tamara's favorite."

She faltered for a minute, then resumed her account. "When they didn't get back by five, we weren't worried at first. Tamara was always running a little late. Blake was much more punctual, though. So when they weren't home by five thirty, I called Tamara's cell phone. When she didn't answer, we tried Blake's cell. When he didn't answer either – that's when we began to get worried. So we called the park rangers and told them we were worried about Tamara and Blake. We knew where they liked to park their car, so one of the rangers went to look for it, to see if it was still there. It was."

Elizabeth took another ragged breath before going on. "It was getting dark by that time, so the park rangers knew that something was seriously wrong. No one in his right mind would hike in those mountains after dark, not at that time of the year. And the temperature was supposed to drop below freezing that night. The rangers started a systematic search, but they couldn't do much that night, in the dark... We didn't sleep at all that night. All I could think was, 'Please let them be safe, please let them be together, please don't let my baby freeze to death'."

Her husband clutched Elizabeth's hand convulsively, then took up the story himself when it became apparent that his wife was unable to continue.

"The rangers and some volunteer search teams looked for them all through the next day, but there was no sign of either Tamara or Blake.

Then, on Monday, we got the call. They had found Blake, dead, at the foot of a cliff. But there was no sign of Tamara. For a few more days, we still hoped. But then there was a big storm. The temperature dropped below freezing, and twenty inches of snow fell in one night. No one could have survived that. We had to face facts: our baby was gone."

Dawn said gently, "I'm sorry for your loss, Mr. and Mrs. Norti. I wonder if you could tell me if Tamara was concerned about anything just before she went on that trip. Did she mention anyone who might have taken an unusual interest in her, made her feel uncomfortable?"

"No, not that I know of." Elliot looked at his wife, who also shook her head negatively.

"Dad?"

Elliot Norti turned his head and spoke to someone off-screen. "What is it, Katelyn?"

Dawn couldn't make out what the other person said, but then a third face appeared on the screen.

"Detective Cimarron, this is our younger daughter, Katelyn. She remembers something. It might be important; it might not. Anyway, she insists on telling you." He turned to his daughter. "Go ahead, Kate."

Katelyn Norti, who looked to be about fifteen, did not look much like her sister. Her brown hair was a short spiky cap, she wore what looked like dozens of tiny studs in each ear, and her lips had been painted a goth-like black. Only her eyes were similar – they were the same deep blue as Tamara's.

"There was this guy," Katelyn began.

"When, Katelyn? Can you tell me when and where?"

"About a week before it all happened. We were in the park. Tamara and I, Blake and his friend Dave. I was a lot younger than the others, but Tamara was really good about letting me tag along, as long as it was something casual, like hanging around in the park. The guys were throwing a Frisbee around, and Tamara and I went to watch this artist guy."

Dawn felt a prickle at the back of her neck. "Artist guy?" she inquired.

"Yeah. A bunch of people were crowded around him, and he was doing sketches of different girls in the crowd. For free. He said that he just needed the practice, so he wasn't charging anything. I thought that was strange. I mean, nobody does anything for free these days, you know? Anyway, after we'd watched him do about three or four of these sketches, he glanced around and saw Tamara in the crowd. He smiled at her and asked her if she wanted to be next. She was all excited about it, so we went up right next to him. He had a stool for her to sit on, so she sat down and he started working on her portrait. The thing was – it took him a really long time. He was finished with the others in just a few minutes, but he spent almost half an hour on Tamara. He was chatting with her the whole time, too. At first I thought he was hitting on her, but once she told him that she had a boyfriend, he sort of backed off. He just asked her really general questions after that, like what were her favorite hobbies and stuff. And she told him how much she enjoyed hiking, that she and Blake went hiking together a lot. Well, Tamara's sketch was taking such a long time that a lot of people in the crowd got bored and began to drift away. And when he was done, he said that was the last one he was going to do that day, and he started to pack up. I was a little miffed because he didn't want to do my portrait, but I got over it. Tamara and I just went back over to Blake and Dave. They'd finished playing with the Frisbee, so we went off to one of the vendors and got some hot dogs. And while I was putting some ketchup on my hot dog, I happened to look over to where the artist was, and he was staring at Tamara. When he saw that I had noticed, he waved at me and walked away. I don't know if any of this helps, but you asked if anyone was taking an unhealthy interest in Tamara. I'm not certain if I'd call his interest unhealthy, but he sure paid more attention to her than he did to any of the others who sat for him that day. And when I caught him looking at Tamara while we were at the hot dog stand – there was just something about the way he was looking at her that struck me as odd. But Blake and Dave were with us, and the guy had gone away, so I didn't think much about it again, until now."

"Did he ever tell you his name, Katelyn?"

"No. We never asked. He was just the artist guy."

"What about the portrait? Did he give it to Tamara when he was finished?"

"Yeah. It was really good."

"What about a signature? Did he sign it?"

"I'm not sure. I could look, though. We never cleared out Tamara's stuff. If I look in her room, I'm pretty sure I could find it. I don't think she would have thrown it away. Like I said, it was really good. Guy had talent."

"Okay, Katelyn. You've been very helpful. But now I need to speak to Sergeant Chernet again."

When Sergeant Chernet's broad face appeared on the screen, Dawn asked, "If I send you a sketch one our witnesses here collaborated on, would you be able to put together a photo line-up and see if Katelyn can identify him as 'the artist guy'?"

Chernet nodded slowly. "I can do that. I'll also go back to the house with the Norti family and conduct the search personally. That way, everything will be official, and the proper chain of evidence will be maintained. If we find it, I'll shoot you a copy right away, Detective."

"Thank you, Sergeant. We'd appreciate that."

"You know, when you first contacted us, I thought that you were just blowing smoke – trying to make a big case out of a simple missing person's investigation. I don't mind telling you now that, after looking at the latest information you sent us and listening to what Katelyn had to say, I'm inclined to believe that you're on to something. Better than even odds that the two cases are connected after all. So you'll be getting all the cooperation you need from us. Just wanted to let you know that."

"Again, we appreciate your cooperation. I'll keep you updated on things as they are unfolding here. But I'd like to ask you to keep it out of the press, if you could. We think that there's a fair chance that our missing girl, Leanne Zarafin, might still be alive. Any of this gets out and the perp realizes that we're looking for him, her chances for survival might be negatively impacted."

"I understand. There will be no leaks to the press from our end. You have my word on that. I'll get that photo line-up ready as soon as you send us the sketch of your suspect. After Katelyn has a chance to look at it, I'll let you know if she recognizes the guy. Then I'll follow the Norti family home and begin the search for that portrait of Tamara. I'll be in touch."

When Ty pulled up to offices of Lewellen Air after the appointment at the Vet's, Traitor, who had been glued to Brody's side all morning, bounded out the door as soon as Brody opened it and whined at Ty's feet until he picked her up.

"Oh, so now I'm your best buddy again, huh? You ought to be ashamed of yourself. Sticking to Brody as long as you thought he could be of any use to you, and then dropping him like a hot potato once you realized he wasn't going to be able to save you from the vet." Since she was already comfortably ensconced in Ty's arms, Traitor took no offense at his tone. She contented herself with licking his face enthusiastically.

Brody had maneuvered himself out of the car by that time and joined them. He looked around, noting the offices and hangars and other buildings that made up Lewellen Air.

"When's that flight coming in?"

"It should be here in a few minutes. Unless it got held up or something. Or maybe the pilot made an error and is going in the opposite direction. You know – like "Wrong Way" Corrigan. Started out for Long Beach in California, ended up in Ireland. It can happen to pilots, you know. Something screws up their navigational instruments, and they go hundreds, even thousands of miles off course. It's even more likely to happen to pilots when someone has been threatening to kick their boss's ass."

"You even think about trying something like that, and there's no place you could run where I won't find you. Even your mother won't be able to save you then, hot shot."

"No, but my wife the cop might."

As Brody rolled his eyes at that one, Ty continued, "But it's not going to come to that. Here she comes now." He nodded toward the bright silver streak in the sky that was making its final approach as it prepared to land. A minute later, the landing gear deployed, and the jet set down smoothly on the runway. As it came to a halt, Ty sauntered over toward the pilot's side of the plane, with Brody close behind him on his crutches.

After taking the time to inform Ellanor Torrense and Gwen Mallinder about Monieque's arrest for Cullen's murder, Dawn and Rafe left headquarters and hit the real estate offices again. As they walked out of what seemed like the millionth office they had visited that day, Dawn's phone rang. She answered it automatically.

"Cimarron."

"D.C.?"

She would have recognized Detective Ralph Sokoto's voice even if his name hadn't already flashed up on caller ID. "What's up, Sok?"

"Eddleston and Garrone just brought in Vivian Zarafin, Leanne Zarafin's mother. They were swinging back toward her house when they noticed a car being driven erratically, so they pulled it over. Turns out it was our girl, and impaired is too mild a word to describe her condition. Anyway, they brought her downtown, got her some coffee, tried to sober her up. And this is the weird part, D.C. As soon as they brought the subject of her daughter up, started telling her that Leanne may have been kidnapped, she started shaking and screaming hysterically. She said that she always knew this day would come. But it's what she said next that floored all of us. She says that *she's* the one who kidnapped Lee!"

"Are you screwing with me, Sok?"

"Uh-uh. Gospel truth, D.C."

"She sober now?"

"Yeah, like I said, Eddleston and Garrone gave her some time to sober up before they started questioning her. Then, after she dropped her bombshell, they had her take another breathalyzer test. She's just under the legal limit."

"Okay. Sit tight and keep a lid on this. Sergeant Melbourne and I will be right there."

She disconnected and told Rafe what Sokoto had just informed her. He pursed his lips in a soundless whistle and said, "This case just keeps throwing curve balls at us. All right, let's go and find out what motivated Vivian Zarafin to cop to kidnapping her own daughter. Personally, I think it's a waste of time, though. Either she's drunk or she's crazy, because all of the evidence, including what Will said before he lost consciousness, points to abduction by a stranger, and a male at that."

Dawn made no response and maintained her silence in the car on the way back to headquarters. After glancing at her profile a couple of times, Rafe said, "You okay, Dawn?"

"I'm fine. Why do you ask?"

"You seem a little off, that's all. Noticed it first when we talked to Alissa Gordena's mother. You all right with handling this particular case?"

"If you're asking if it's affecting me emotionally, the answer is 'yes'. There's something about this one, about that girl, Lee, that's getting to me. But I'm okay, Rafe. It's not affecting me nearly as much as the Bidasoa case did. And that case hit home far more than this one does. I handled that one, and I'll handle this one as well. Don't worry about me."

The Bidasoa case had involved the stabbing death of a father and his teenage son. Rafe had been concerned then that certain similarities between the murders and the tragedy that had befallen her own family would compromise Dawn's ability to work the case, but she'd shaken it off and had done a superb job. So if she said she was able to deal with this one, he'd take her word for it.

When they got back to headquarters, they headed straight for the sector where the interview rooms were located and met up with Ralph Sokoto, who was standing outside the door to Interview Room A. Through the window on the door, they could see Vivian Zarafin perched on the edge of her chair at the table, nervously sipping at a cup of coffee.

With a jerk of his head at Vivian, Rafe asked, "She been read her rights?"

Sokoto shrugged his shoulders and replied, "Yeah – we Mirandized her already. Everything is on record. She refused a lawyer, and then she clammed up. And here's the really weird part: she says she isn't saying another word until she has a chance to explain everything to you, D.C."

"She mentioned me by name? She give any reason for that?"

"Nope. Just seems to think that you're the only one who'll understand. Maybe she saw you on television after the Lewellen kidnapping case. There was a lot of press about that one. Especially after the two of you ended up getting married. Maybe it appealed to the romantic in her. Who knows? Anyway, she's all yours now. Meanwhile, I need to contact the lieutenant. She asked me to notify her when you got here so that she can come down and observe."

"She actually told you in so many words that she kidnapped Lee?" Dawn asked.

"Yeah. We were trying to break it gently to her. Told her that we were afraid that we had some bad news for her, that it looked like her daughter may have been kidnapped, when she blurted it out."

"Did she ask for any of the details about the circumstances surrounding Lee's disappearance?"

"No, like I said, she started shaking and sobbing hysterically as soon as we mentioned the word 'kidnapped'." She's barely spoken a word since, except to say she wanted to talk to you. If you ask me, the woman's nuts."

Vivian Zarafin glanced up sharply as Dawn entered the room with Rafe, a peculiar combination of expectancy and apprehension flitting across her face. Dawn took a seat in a chair opposite Vivian, who sat facing the one-way mirror behind which Lieutenant Westbrooke would be observing the interview. After updating the record with the information that she and Sergeant Melbourne had entered the interview room and noting the date and time, Dawn said, "Mrs. Zarafin, I understand that you have been notified of your rights and have declined representation by an attorney at this time. Is that correct?"

"Yes. I don't need a lawyer. I just need to talk to you. To explain..." her voice trailed off, and she glanced over at Rafe, who had remained standing by the door.

Seeing her look of hesitation, Dawn said, "This is my partner, Sergeant Melbourne. Would it be okay if he stays in here with us?"

"Why does he have to be here?"

"He doesn't. I'll ask him to leave if it would make you more comfortable. But we normally work as a team. That's why he's here."

After taking a long look at Rafe, Vivian turned back to Dawn and said slowly, "I guess it's all right. As long as he doesn't interrupt. I've got something to say to you."

"I understand. Thank you for allowing Sergeant Melbourne to remain. Now, I understand that you told Officers Eddleston and Garrone that you know something about the kidnapping of your daughter, Leanne."

Vivian replied, "I'm sorry. But she was already dead. You have to understand that she was already dead. There was nothing I could do to help her."

Dawn allowed herself only a fleeting moment of sorrow before she responded, "So you're saying that Leanne is dead?"

Vivian shook her head impatiently. "No, no – not Leanne. The mother."

"The mother?"

"Yes – the birth mother. She'd broken her neck in the fall. There was nothing I could do for her. So I picked Leanne up and took her away. You have to realize that I never thought of it as kidnapping. I just wanted to take care of her, that's all."

Careful not to let any confusion show on her face and feeling her way carefully, Dawn said, "I see. What did you do next?"

Instead of answering the question, Vivian met Dawn's eyes and then looked away, saying with a touch of defiance, "You were only twelve years old, and Leanne was just a baby. There was no way that a twelve-year-old could have taken care of a baby. And she needed a mother. She needed me."

A cold hand reached in and squeezed Dawn's heart. Her head was pounding and she had the sensation that she was suffocating; she couldn't breathe. But she knew. Despite the evidence, despite the nightmares - in her heart, she had always known.

Ignoring her physical symptoms, Dawn willed herself to go on, calling upon all her training to keep her voice steady. "You said that Leanne was just a baby. So this all happened a long time ago, correct?"

"Yes. Sixteen years ago. That's when I found her. That's when she came to me. And I knew – she was meant to be mine. So I took her home and gave her a new name. Leanne. Leanne Zarafin."

The room was starting to whirl around, and Rafe started toward her, but she waved him back.

"Vivian, for the record, this baby you found - what was her original name? Her name before you took her, I mean."

Vivian's voice was so low that it was barely audible: "Marina. Marina Cimarron. But you already knew that, of course." She looked up, met Dawn's eyes. "I was a really good mother to her. I promise you that."

Dawn answered mechanically, "I'm sure you were, Vivian. Now that you've talked with me, would you mind filling in the details for Sergeant Melbourne? I need a little time by myself. Just to take things in, you know? It's been kind of a shock."

Vivian reached out and took Dawn's hand. Even though her flesh crawled at the woman's touch, Dawn didn't snatch her hand away.

"Of course. I'm so glad you understand. I was afraid that you might not. Take all the time you need."

Dawn nodded, rose from her chair, and walked out the door. Just as she expected, the Lieutenant was standing outside, about to enter.

Lieutenant Westbrooke took one look at her and said, "Sokoto - go back in and take Detective Cimarron's place in interview." As Sokoto reentered the interview room, the lieutenant did not say a word; she just turned and led the way to her office. When they got there, she said, more gently than was customary for her, "Sit down, Detective."

Dawn collapsed into a seat and waited while Lieutenant Westbrooke got her a glass of water.

"Drink."

She obeyed like an automaton. The lieutenant, looking at her thoughtfully, said softly, "What's your husband's number, Dawn?"

Even the lieutenant's rare use of her first name hardly registered. She answered mechanically, and as if from a great distance, heard the lieutenant's side of her conversation with Ty. No, Detective Cimarron was not hurt. She'd just had some shocking news, and it would probably be better if her husband were by her side. She'd fill him in on the details when he got there.

As Lieutenant Westbrooke disconnected, Dawn roused herself to say, "DNA. Do you have a kit?"

"I can get one. Hold on." The lieutenant made a quick call, then hung up and turned back to Dawn.

"We took her hair brush and toothbrush from the apartment, Lieutenant. They'll be able to get DNA from one or the other..."

"I'll take care of it, Detective."

"They never found her body. The others, yes – but not my sister's. Not Marina's. Did you know that?"

"Yes. I made it a point to familiarize myself with the case when you came into the unit." She paused as if to say something else when one of the patrol officers came in with a kit. She handed it to Dawn, who took out a swab and ran it over the inside of her cheek. Capping it and taking all the proper precautions to make sure there was no contamination, she handed it back to the lieutenant.

"I'll tell them to put a rush on it, Detective. With any luck, we should get the results back in a few days."

"Thanks, LT." She broke off as Ty entered the room. He came right to her, and she tried to rise, but he took one look at her and pushed her gently back into her chair. He held onto her hand as Lieutenant Westbrooke quickly filled him in on what was going on.

When she had finished, Ty said, "I wonder if I might have a little private time with my wife, Lieutenant?"

As the lieutenant stood up and began to move toward the door, Dawn said, "LT? Marina's middle name – it's *Lee*. My mother always called her by both names – Marina Lee. Sometimes my sister had trouble saying the Marina part, so there were times she'd sort of slur over it and refer to herself simply as 'Lee'. I'd forgotten that until just now. I've never thought of her as anything but *Marina* in all these years."

"I'll inform Sergeant Melbourne of that fact, Detective. Why don't you take some time and search your memory further? See if there's anything else you remember that could help."

After the lieutenant had left, Ty knelt in front of her and ran his hands up and down Dawn's arms gently.

She said numbly, "I'm off the case. It's Marina – and I'm off the case."

"Did the lieutenant say so?"

"She didn't have to. We both know the rules. Personal involvement compromises objectivity, and it creates loopholes for the defense to slide through when a case comes to trial. I can't be involved. And it's killing me."

He didn't know what else to do, so he kept rubbing his hands up and down her arms. He sucked wide at the comforting bit, and he knew it. Thanks to counseling, he'd improved some over the last year or so, but he still wasn't very good at it. He didn't know what she needed. His tendency in situations like this was to crack a joke in order to relieve some of the tension, but he knew his wife. She'd probably sock him.

"Dawn? Baby?" He was uncomfortable with endearments and therefore rarely used them, but it must have been the right thing to say, because some of the blankness went out of her gaze, and she actually looked at him. "Would it be okay if I called Mom and Dad, let them know what's going on? They'd want to be here for you."

She blinked a little and responded, "Yeah – you probably should."

He pulled out his cell to make the call just as Rafe entered the room. One look at Rafe's eyes and he said, "Uh – I'll just step out for a minute."

Rafe pulled a chair up across from her so that his knees were almost touching hers. He said quietly, "We've finished the interview. She gave us permission to search her house, Dawn. She says she kept the clothes that the baby was wearing the day she found her."

When Dawn didn't respond, he continued, "The lieutenant called Captain Penrose, asked him to take over as primary on this aspect of the case, take care of conducting the search. He's the one who worked the original case with Nick in the first place, remember? He may be riding a desk now, but he's still a damn good detective. He'll know exactly what to look for. And he still has pictures of Marina from the original case file. We'll do an age progression, compare the result with pictures of Lee. Fingerprints too. There were some lifted from the nursery during the original investigation that were tiny, obviously Marina's. We'll dust Lee's bedroom at the apartment, see if we get a match."

Dawn's head felt like it weighed about a hundred pounds, but she managed to nod it. Then she said, "None of this is going to get us any closer to finding her, Rafe."

"I know. That's why I didn't object when the lieutenant suggested that Captain Penrose take the lead on that aspect of the case instead of working it myself. We'll keep pounding away at it, D.C. Sooner or later, we're bound to get a break. And when the word starts spreading that the missing girl is a relative of one of our own – the cops are going to start pouring in. We'll have all the help we need."

"Dawn?"

She turned at the sound of Ty's voice. "Mom and Dad are on the way. They're going to meet us across the street at Fredo's."

He held out a hand to her wordlessly, and she arose from her chair and took it. Holding on tightly, she said, "Rafe? Find her. Please find her."

Rafe swallowed a lump in his throat as he replied, "We will, Dawn. We will."

As Dawn walked out of the room with Ty, Rafe felt a growing sense of dread. His gut told him that they would eventually find the girl now known as Lee. But alive or dead? That was the question.

Chapter 10

She could have wept with relief when she finally snagged the tool again. It felt like she had been trying for hours, but it was probably only a few minutes. Slowly and carefully, Lee dragged it toward her. When she was finally able to grasp it, she felt a wave of exultation. It was her own personal Holy Grail, about to provide her salvation. Before she attempted to use it, however, she quickly unknotted her makeshift rope and remade the bed, just in case Michael decided to come down and pay her a visit. Then she grasped the chisel and took it over to the far side of the cot. With a grim tenaciousness she hadn't even known she possessed, she carefully began chipping away at the cinder block around the staple that secured the chain to the wall.

When they entered the private dining room at Fredo's, Ty's parents were already there. Maeve said nothing, but just walked over, put her arms around Dawn, and held her tight. To Ty's astonishment, Dawn's shoulders started to shake, and he realized that she was crying. He shifted from foot to foot uncomfortably, wondering if he should stay put or go to her. But then Maeve raised her head and caught his eye, signaling him to leave the room. Relieved, he and Sloan walked out the door and stood uncertainly in the hallway outside.

Ty leaned against the wall and blew out a breath. "Dad? I've never seen Dawn cry before. I mean never, not once in all the time we've been together. I don't know what to do."

Sloan considered for a minute, then said, "For right now, leave it up to your mother. When we go back in, take your cue from her. She understands how uncomfortable you are and what Dawn needs right now."

"Okay, okay. Man, I never thought that anything would ever upset Dawn enough for her to cry about it. I've seen her scared after having a nightmare, but she generally handles it just fine, calms down pretty quickly. All she needs from me is a little comforting, a little soothing. And she usually handles any other kind of stress by exploding, letting off some steam. I know how to handle that. But tears? This is a first for me."

Sloan didn't reply, but just leaned against the wall with him companionably.

A few minutes later, Maeve came to the door. "Ty? She's doing better now. Go and order some tea for us."

As Maeve disappeared back into the room, Ty breathed a sigh of relief. Concrete action – something he could actually *do*. Now, that he could handle.

When the servers appeared with the tea service, he and Sloan reentered the room with them. Dawn was sitting on the sofa. Her eyes were red and swollen, but she seemed to have recovered some of her usual composure. He sat down next to her and took her hand, gave it a squeeze.

Dawn returned the pressure and said, "I'm okay now. I need to call Aunt Mattie and Uncle Pete, let them know what's happening."

"I could take care of that for you. If you want me to."

At Dawn's nod of assent, he pulled his cell phone out, got up, and went back into the hallway once more.

Maeve, meanwhile, had poured out a cup of tea and offered it to her daughter-in-law. Dawn sipped the hot, fragrant tea and let its calming influence relax her jangled nerves. The crying jag had shocked her almost as much as it had Ty.

Maeve studied Dawn carefully as she sipped her own tea. The color had come back into Dawn's cheeks, and her hands were steady as she lifted the tea cup to her lips. Good.

Ty eased back into the room and sat down again next to Dawn. "I told Pete and Mattie what's going on. Mattie wants to know if you want her to be here. I told her I'd have you call her back, let her know." He absently accepted the cup of tea that Maeve proffered to him. "Mattie's pretty shocked. She asked me how you were doing, how you were handling everything. I told her you had a rough time with it at first, but Mom was with you, and you seemed to be handling it better now." He took a sip of tea, then asked, "What's next, Dawn? What else can I do for you?"

"I'm not sure. I'm not even thinking straight. After all these years, finally news of Marina. But still, I'm not sure whether she's alive or dead."

"Actually, I'm a little confused by how that's possible," Maeve confessed. "You see, I thought that your sister died years ago, along with the rest of your family." She reached over and put a hand over one of Dawn's. "You don't have to talk about it if you don't want to. But sometimes, talking it out helps."

Dawn put her teacup down slowly and nodded. "Maybe you're right." She collected her thoughts, and then said, "You know that my mother was holding Marina when it all happened, don't you?"

"To tell you the truth, I'm a little fuzzy about the details. It was sixteen years ago, wasn't it? At the time, my mother was ill, in the hospital. She was still living in New Orleans then, and I'd flown out to be with her. So I have only the vaguest memories of the news stories."

Dawn hesitated briefly before responding, "I need to go over it all anyway, get it fresh in my mind. If it's all true, I'll have to be interviewed again, as a witness. So I'll start from the beginning...

"We lived in Denver for the first few years after I was born. My mother worked as a legal secretary in a law office. My dad was a financial manager for some big company there – I don't remember which one. Then, when I was about four, my dad's cousin died and left him his entire estate, including the ranch. It wasn't a working ranch any longer – Dad's cousin had sold off all but thirty acres of the land and most of the stock. He'd kept only some chickens and a few horses. But that still left the main house, the bunkhouse, a couple of barns, and some other outbuildings.

"My dad was fed up with the business world. His job paid well, but the high stress, the long hours, the politics – he'd decided that it wasn't for him any longer. He wanted a simpler lifestyle, and so did my mother. She wanted to stop working and spend more time at home with my brother, Josiah, and me. With the money that Dad had inherited from his cousin and with what he and my mother had saved up, they had enough to quit their jobs and move out to the ranch house. My dad was a woodworker, and he could make marvelous hand-crafted furniture. He set up a workshop in one of the barns and started his own business. After a couple of years, it really started to pay off. Mom was able to stay at home, and she decided to home-school Josiah and me, since the ranch was so far away from the nearest school.

"Marina was born on the ranch. I thought that she was the most beautiful creature that I'd ever seen. She was Mom's baby, but I was her big sister, so in a way, she was my baby too..."

Dawn paused for a minute to take another sip of tea, then continued, "On the day that it happened... my dad and I went out hunting. It was wild turkey season. I didn't particularly like to hunt, but I enjoyed spending time with my father, so I went along whenever possible. He didn't take us with him when he was hunting big game, but he always took Josiah and me along with him when he went turkey hunting. But that day, Josiah didn't come with us. He was eleven, and he was always getting into some kind of trouble. He was grounded for some reason – I don't remember why - and part of the punishment was that he didn't get to go hunting with us. So Dad and I set off alone..."

She closed her eyes for a minute, conjuring up in her mind a picture of the way it had been, that last time they had been together as a family. Her mother holding Marina, clad in the pink sundress and white sweater she and Mom had made together for the baby. Josiah sitting at the table, eating breakfast nonchalantly, pretending that he didn't care that they were going hunting without him. Dad standing next to her, doing a last minute check to see that he had everything that they needed for the day. And she herself, a skinny twelve-year-old, dancing with impatience, wanting only to be gone...

She gave herself a mental shake, opened her eyes, and went on with her story: "We didn't have much luck that day. And then my father tripped over a rock that was buried in the ground under some leaves and sprained his ankle. So we started back home. Dad kept his hand on my shoulder and used the shotgun he was carrying as a sort of crutch, and we'd almost made it back when we heard a lot of noise coming from the vicinity of the house. It was just over the next hill, and when we got to the top, we saw them, the boys on the motorcycles. Mom was down there in the meadow beside the house, with Marina in her arms. The boys on the motorcycles had surrounded them, and kept circling them, swerving right toward her, forcing her back toward the edge at the end of the meadow. There's a sharp drop-off in that spot. It's not that far down, maybe twenty feet, but it's sheer and steep."

She took another breath and prepared to force herself to go on. At some point, Ty's hand had found hers again, and he was gripping it tightly.

"I'm not exactly sure of the sequence of the next events. It all happened so fast. Josiah burst out of the house with a can of pepper spray. He ran over and tried to get them with it, but they were too fast for him. One of them dodged him and got behind him, swatting the can out of his hands and knocking him flat. Meanwhile, Dad had brought his shotgun up. He couldn't fire it at them, because they were too close together. He might have hit Mom or the baby or Josiah, who'd recovered quickly and was already back up on his feet again. So he fired a warning shot in the air. That distracted the one who'd knocked Josiah down, and he stopped for a moment to look in our direction."

She picked up her teacup again and took a sip, scowling for a minute as she realized that the tea had gone cold. Maeve picked up another cup, poured out some fresh tea from the pot, and silently handed it to Dawn, who took it and sipped at it gratefully. After a minute or two, she took up the story again.

"Josiah took after my dad, so he was big and strong for his age. He launched himself into the one who had stopped and knocked him off the motorcycle. They were rolling around on the ground together. Then he – the other guy – managed to get on top of Josiah, and I saw him raise his hand straight up in the air for a minute. He had a knife…"

Her hand was shaking in Ty's now. He said softly, "Dawn, you don't have to go on. Don't force yourself to."

Dawn shook her head. "I need to," she said simply. Taking another cleansing breath, she picked up where she had left off. "Dad was racing down the hill as quickly as he could on his injured ankle, and I started to follow him. When he realized that I was behind him, he turned around and shouted, 'No, Dawn! Run! Hide!' So I turned around and ran back up the hill and into the woods. I never saw any of my family alive again."

She rose shakily to her feet. "Excuse me for a minute. I need to use the ladies' room." As Maeve rose to go with her, Dawn shook her head, so Maeve sank back into her seat. She turned to Tyrell. "If she doesn't come back in a few minutes, I'll go check on her. She just needs a little time alone now."

"Okay. Should I do anything? What can I do?"

"Tell us the rest of the story. It'll save her from telling it when she comes back."

Ty got out of his chair and prowled around restlessly as he took up the tale. "Her memory isn't very clear about what happened next. She remembers hiding in the woods, but she's not sure how long she was there. The police found motorcycle tracks all over the place, and she remembers hearing the sounds of engines, so apparently they tried to find her, get rid of the only witness. But after a while, she remembers only silence. She was afraid to move, but she finally got up the courage to leave her hiding place and go for help. She knew where the nearest ranger station was, and she made her way there. Pete Nevo was on duty, and he called the police. Both Nick and Rafe Melbourne came in, and Rafe got some of the story out of her – enough to send them over to check out the Cimarron ranch."

He ceased his prowling and sat down again heavily. "They found her father and Josiah lying in the meadow, dead. They were both riddled with knife wounds. Her father had apparently used the butt of the shotgun as a club, because the police found blood on it that didn't match any member of the Cimarron family. Her mother was found lying in a stream that ran along the foot of the drop-off. She didn't drown, though. She'd broken her neck in the fall. But there was no sign of Marina. They searched for her for days, but the only thing they ever found was the white sweater she had been wearing that day. It was pretty torn up, and when the police tested it, they found traces of saliva on it. Not human, though. The saliva came from a bear."

Tears trickled from Maeve's eyes as she said, "So all this time she was afraid that...?"

Ty nodded. "Yeah. She still has nightmares about it."

"How old was she at the time?"

"Which one? Dawn, or the baby?"

"Both, I guess."

"Dawn was twelve. Marina was about two and a half at the time."

"What happened next?"

"They asked Dawn who her closest relative was, and she gave them Mattie's name. Mattie filed for custody immediately. She and Dawn's mother were step-sisters, not actual blood sisters, you know. However, they were really close, and since Dawn's parents had specified Mattie as the guardian of their minor children in the event of their deaths, the court had no problem awarding custody of Dawn to her. Pete stopped in to check on Dawn periodically, and that's how he and Mattie met. After they got married, they bought a small house in the same neighborhood where Nick and Rafe Melbourne lived. The five of them bonded over the years and formed their own sort of family. Then, after Peter retired, he and Mattie moved out to the ranch. Dawn didn't want to sell it, and she needed someone on the premises to take care of it."

"The police caught them, didn't they? The ones who killed Dawn's family?"

"Yes, and that's a whole other story..."

He broke off as Dawn came back into the room.

Miranda Gordena walked slowly down the street. Since the police from Colorado had visited her, she'd been trying to get out more, get some exercise. But she was badly out of shape. She stopped for a minute at the corner only a block away from home, trying to get her breath. Looking around, she caught sight of the Makella place and sighed, remembering how beautiful its gardens had once looked. *Elena Makella must be turning in her grave*, she thought. When Elena had been alive, the house had been pristine, the yard a showplace. After her death, her husband and her older son had not wanted to keep up with the gardens, so the flowers had been torn out and the entire yard reseeded with grass. Her younger son, Vaughn, had begged his father not to do it. But he had been only ten years old at the time, and his pleas to maintain the gardens the way his mother had left them had fallen upon deaf ears. She could still hear Justin Makella explaining to his son that he would have to hire a gardener to keep up with everything, and he couldn't afford that. And maybe he couldn't have – not then. Later on, though, the family's financial picture had changed dramatically, when Justin had struck it rich by marketing some cutting-edge computer program that he had invented. How tragic that he and Briden, Vaughn's older brother, had had so little time to enjoy their new-found fortune. It was only a couple of years later that they had both lost their lives in some sort of accident while they were on a hunting trip. She had thought for a while that Vaughn might use some of his inheritance to plant the gardens once again, but it had never happened. Vaughn just wasn't there often enough nowadays for it to matter, she guessed. She'd seen him only a few times over the last few years, and then only during the summertime. He apparently avoided the cold Vermont winters and spent them elsewhere. And who could blame him? With another sigh, Miranda started walking again, progressing steadily toward home.

Vaughn Makella – she thought. He'd always had such a crush on Alissa.... Suddenly she stopped dead in her tracks again. A question that Detective Cimarron had asked about her daughter came back to her: *Any of the guys in her life have an artistic bent?*

Miranda picked up her pace. By the time she reached her front door, she was practically running. Rooting in a drawer, she found the card Detective Cimarron had left with her where she had tossed it. Grabbing her phone, she began to punch the numbers in.

When Miranda Gordena's name popped up on her Caller-ID shortly after she had rejoined Ty and her in-laws in the dining room, Dawn answered the call automatically. She listened intently to what Miranda had to say. She then told Miranda that she needed to notify her partner, who would call her right back.

After she disconnected, Ty asked, "Something to do with the investigation?"

"It was Miranda Gordena, the mother of another suspected victim. She gave me a lead. A name."

Sloan, who had been silent all this time, asked, "What can we do to help?"

Dawn pondered only for a second or two before replying, "I'll be violating all sorts of rules by revealing the details of an ongoing investigation to you, but I don't care about that right now. Marina – Lee's time is running out. I can feel it in my bones. We need more information, and we need it fast."

"Give me the name. I'll get you the information."

Dawn considered her options for a moment, then said slowly, "Vaughn Makella. He grew up in Black Line, Vermont."

Sloan noted the name down and nodded. "I'll have a detailed report for you as soon as possible."

"Thanks. In the meantime, I have to go back across the street, notify Rafe. I promised Mrs. Gordena that I'd have him call her right back."

As soon as he caught sight of them, Rafe cut across the bullpen to meet them.

"How you holding up, D.C.?" he asked.

"As well as can be expected. You need to call Miranda Gordena. She remembered something, and it might be important."

Rafe wasted no time, but punched the number in on his desk phone as soon as Dawn gave it to him.

"Mrs. Gordena? This is Sergeant Melbourne."

"Thank you for calling me, Sergeant. I started to tell Detective Cimarron, but she said I needed to talk to you. About Vaughn Makella."

"You think he might have had something to do with Alissa's disappearance?"

"I'm not sure, but after I got to thinking about everything you and Detective Cimarron said, I remembered..."

"Just start at the beginning, Mrs. Gordena. Tell me about Vaughn Makella."

"He was a neighbor of ours. Still is, technically, but I haven't seen much of him in years. He and his family lived right down the street from us. His parents were Justin and Elena Makella."

"Were?"

"Yes. Elena died many years ago. Vaughn would have been about ten. Brain aneurysm. So young, too. I thought that Vaughn was going to die from grief. He and Elena were so close..."

"Why do you think Vaughn may be connected to what happened to Alissa?"

"Well, for one thing, you asked if any of Alissa's boyfriends were artists. Vaughn was never one of Alissa's boyfriends, but he had a terrible crush on her, and he was quite a good artist. He used to ask her to sit for him sometimes. You know, as a model. I still have some of the sketches and paintings he did of her. He did fine work."

"You said that the fact that he was an artist was one reason that made you decide to call. Were there other reasons?"

"Well, I never knew all the details, but when he was about sixteen, Vaughn apparently had some sort of nervous breakdown. He was actually hospitalized for over a year. However, when he returned home, he seemed back to normal again. I wouldn't even have given it a thought if you hadn't mentioned the artist angle."

"You said you hadn't seen him around much in recent years. He doesn't still live down the street?"

"Not exactly. You see, he inherited the house when his father and brother died, but he doesn't come around very often. He can live anywhere he wants, though. His father, Justin Makella, was quite well off. In his will, Justin left everything to be divided equally between his two sons. But since Briden, the brother, died in the same accident as their father did, Vaughn inherited everything. And that's the thing, Sergeant Melbourne. That's another reason I decided to call. Justin and Briden disappeared while they were on a camping trip. Their bodies weren't found for several months. They were found at the foot of a cliff, just like Alissa's boyfriend, Breckon Petteril."

Rafe wrote the name down on a slip of paper and handed it to Noritaki, who immediately sat down at a computer to do a search on Vaughn Makella. Then he asked, "Mrs. Gordena, do you know where Vaughn Makella is right now?"

"No. I understand that he travels a great deal. I don't know where, but he has an aunt, Lauretta Hurnel. She might know."

"Can you give me his aunt's full name, address, and telephone number?"

"Yes, but it may not do you much good. He visits her every once in a while, but he doesn't keep in any kind of regular touch. It worries Lauretta, because she never knows exactly where he is or how to reach him."

"Not even on his cell phone?"

"He doesn't have a permanent one – just the throwaway kind. He uses one for a little while, then he gets rid of it and buys another one. He never tells anyone the number, either. He's a little paranoid about cell phones and computers." She paused for a minute. "In fact, Vaughn's a little paranoid about a lot of things."

Rafe's cell phone signaled an incoming text just then. Holding his desk phone with one hand, he pulled out his cell with the other. It was from Kara, one of the secretaries he was friendly with upstairs, and contained only five words: *He's on the way down!*

Rafe swore under his breath and held the cell phone up so that Dawn could see the message.

Dawn nodded and mouthed, "I'll be across the street." Then she and Ty turned and departed.

Good thing, too, as the door burst open shortly afterward and the Minotaur, Captain Wesley Collander, strode in with his usual self-important strut. He didn't deign to speak to Rafe or even look at him, but crossed over directly to the lieutenant's office, slamming the door behind him. Moe looked up as he strode in, leaned forward, and placed both hands on her desk.

"You need to take Melbourne off the case."

Moe leaned back in her chair and looked him steadily in the eye. "What case are you talking about, Captain?"

"You know damned well what case I'm talking about. The missing girl, the one who may be Marina Cimarron."

News had traveled fast, Moe thought. "Why would I take Sergeant Melbourne off as primary on the case?"

"Don't play dumb with me, Westbrooke. He's got a personal involvement in the case."

"I don't see it that way. The only person who has a personal involvement in this case is Detective Cimarron, who very properly removed herself from the investigation as soon as she realized that the missing girl might be a family member."

"Melbourne and Cimarron are close. Too close. He's like a member of her family. His objectivity is compromised."

"I disagree."

"I don't care if you disagree! I'm telling you to take Melbourne off the case!"

Moe stood up slowly and looked Collander directly in the eye. "This is my department, Captain. If you disagree with how I am running it, you are free to make a complaint by using the proper channels. For now, however," she moved around the desk and opened the door, "I have complete confidence in Sergeant Melbourne and in how he is handling this case."

Collander's face was so red that Moe thought he might be going to have a stroke. He stormed out of her office, saying over his shoulder, "You haven't heard the last of this, Westbrooke."

As Ethan Bardner sat in Ada Mainyre's living room sipping tea, he realized that he had struck the mother lode of information on Vaughn Makella. Less an hour ago, he'd been sitting in his office working on another case when his boss at Vespasian Investigations in Burlington had walked in and told him to drop everything else, jump into his car, and get to the nearby town of Black Line immediately. Once he got there, he was to squeeze out of its inhabitants as much information as possible about one Vaughn Makella. Time was of the essence, and expense was no object. The client was willing to pay a fat bonus on top of the regular fee for the information, but he wanted it in a hurry.

Ethan had been chosen out of all the detectives in the large private investigation firm because he was a Vermont native, and in the state of Vermont, that mattered. His first stop at the home of Vaughn Makella's aunt, however, had netted him no results at first. Lauretta Hurnel was not in residence at the moment, her elderly neighbor had informed him. She had left a week ago to visit some friends down in Florida. Ethan had whipped his hat off, called her ma'am about every other word, and admired the flowers in her garden. She'd invited him over for a closer look, and in the ensuing conversation, discovered that they had several mutual acquaintances in his home town of Burlington. After that, finessing an invitation to tea had been easy.

She'd feigned reluctance to talk about her dear friend Lauretta's nephew at first, but soon her desire to gossip won out against any scruples she might have had. Yes, she was acquainted with Vaughn. She'd known him all her life...

"He was such a dear little boy, the apple of his mother's eye. Briden, her older boy, wasn't at all affectionate, but Vaughn – what a sweetheart! He was always ready with a hug and a kiss, and so sensitive! So artistic! So imaginative! Elena, his mother, was overjoyed that Vaughn shared some of her own interests, like art and literature and poetry. She loved her husband and her older boy, but they were more into football and baseball and outdoor stuff like hunting and camping. In fact, if you can believe it, her husband tried to stop Elena from developing Vaughn's artistic gifts and talents. Said she was making a sissy out of the boy – can you imagine that?"

Actually, Ethan could imagine it very easily, but he said nothing; instead, he just raised his eyebrows in silent encouragement for Ada to continue.

Ada reached for one of the shortbread cookies that she had set out on the table and bit into it appreciatively. After she had consumed the cookie, she continued, "Vaughn was inconsolable when his mother died. I never saw a boy grieve so. Of course, Lauretta tried to step in and give him some of the mothering that he needed. But Justin, - his father" -she rolled her eyes -"was hell-bent on what he called 'weaning Vaughn away from too much feminine influence' and 'making a man of him'. Vaughn was only ten when his mother passed away, you know. Instead of giving him time to grieve, though, what do you suppose his father did? He forced that little boy to go on a camping trip with him and Briden only a week after the funeral! He knew that Vaughn hated camping, but he didn't care one bit about what Vaughn wanted. He said that camping with him and Briden would help Vaughn, keep him occupied, help him work through his grief."

Ada shook her head sadly and picked up the teapot. "Would you care for another cup, Ethan?"

He hated the stuff, but he was willing to drink a gallon of it in order to prolong the tea party and keep her talking, so he put an enthusiastic smile upon his face and said, "Yes, please, Mrs. Mainyre. If it's not too much trouble?"

"Trouble? Not at all. I can't remember the last time I had a young man over for tea. It makes me feel young again. Now, where was I?"

"You were talking about a camping trip they went on after Vaughn's mother died."

"Oh, yes. Do you know, Vaughn nearly died on that trip? His father and brother were so wrapped up with their precious hunting that they lost track of Vaughn. He got separated from them and was lost, all alone, for almost forty-eight hours! They had search parties out looking for him, but somehow he managed to find his way back all by himself. He just wandered into the camp again two days later. And do you know what his father did? He blamed Vaughn for the whole thing! Said that Vaughn should have been more careful. A ten-year-old being blamed by the negligent father who didn't take proper care of him! Lauretta heard the whole story when she went over to stay at the house to help nurse Vaughn after he contracted bronchitis shortly after they got home. Well, it was no surprise that he got sick. It was a lucky thing that he didn't die of exposure, because it was really cold, the whole time that Vaughn was lost."

"Must have been hard on his aunt," Ethan commented.

"Oh dear, yes," Ada agreed. "Lauretta always said that Vaughn was never the same after that. So when he had that trouble – well, she was kind of expecting something like that to happen. But I'm not supposed to talk about that."

Instead of pushing too hard and trying to pry the information about Vaughn Makella's "trouble" out of her, Ethan reached for another cookie. "These are wonderful, Mrs. Mainyre. Did you make them yourself?"

"I'm afraid not. I used to cook and bake quite a lot, but as I've gotten older, I've had to rely more and more on store-bought things. I got those from Rorhich's, the local bakery. Selma Rorhich may be the biggest gossip in town, but her shortbread cookies are almost as good as my own. Selma kept trying to pry the story about Vaughn's troubles out of me, but I didn't say a word to her. If I had, it would have been all over town!"

"I can see that you're one who can be trusted to keep a confidence, Mrs. Mainyre," Ethan said mendaciously. "No wonder Mrs. Hurnel confides in you."

Beaming at him, Ada poured out another cup of tea. "Well, it wasn't easy to keep what she told me confidential," she said. "Especially after Maudie Burtenn blabbed about the fact that Justin Makella had had Vaughn institutionalized..."

Keeping any trace of curiosity out of his voice, Ethan said, "Well, Maudie Burtenn never was able to keep a secret."

Ada latched onto that comment like a sucker fish. "Oh, are you acquainted with Maudie, then?"

Mentally crossing his fingers behind his back, Ethan nodded casually and took another sip of tea.

"Well, if you already heard about it from Maudie, I suppose it can't hurt to explain to you about how it all happened. Fingering the beads she wore around her neck, Ada resumed her story. "Like I said, Vaughn was always imaginative. He was always pretending he was somebody else. Most children do, you know. They pretend that they're Batman or Superman or some other hero. So when Vaughn started telling everyone that he was Michelangelo, nobody thought twice about it – they thought he was just pretending. His mother was Italian, after all, and she had instilled in him a great regard for the artists of the Italian Renaissance. But then he started insisting that his family call him by that name and refused to answer to anything else. That's when they began to realize that he wasn't just imagining things; he actually thought that he was the reincarnation of Michelangelo! And that wasn't all," she paused to insert another shortbread cookie into her mouth, "he also went about telling people that on his father's side, he was descended from ancient Viking priests, and that he had visions of some Viking goddess whom he called *Vanadis*. At that point, his father decided that enough was enough. He took Vaughn to a psychiatrist. When Vaughn refused to cooperate, his father had the boy committed to a mental institution."

"How old was he then?"

"Oh dear, let me think. I guess he would have been about sixteen by then. At first he wasn't allowed to have any visitors, but that changed after about six months or so. Once he was allowed visitors, Lauretta used to drive up there and spend time with him every chance she got. Good thing too. Neither his father nor his brother ever went to visit him in all the time he was there – not once!"

"And it wasn't that far away, was it?"

"No, no – it only takes about an hour to get to The Brieuc Center."

"And he was better when he came back home, wasn't he? That's what I understood."

Ada nodded her head vigorously. "According to Lauretta, the doctors figured out what was wrong with Vaughn and used a combination of medication and therapy to treat the problem. When he came home about a year later, he was his old self again. Perfectly normal. He finished high school and enrolled in college. Of course, his father wouldn't let him study art, which is what Vaughn wanted to do, so he enrolled in a business program instead. It bored him out of his skull, but he was desperate to please his father, so he stuck it out. He still kept up with his art, though - but just as a hobby. At least until the accident happened..."

"How old was Vaughn when he lost his father and his brother?"

"It was during his first semester of his sophomore year. They went on a camping trip and never came back. Poor Vaughn. He just couldn't accept the fact that they were gone. Even after they found the bodies the next summer, he still wouldn't believe it. Lauretta had to arrange for the funeral and internment, because Vaughn was still in denial. He refused to attend either service, which sure shocked some of the busybodies around here. And even after his father's executor had done all the necessary paperwork to have the will probated and the estate settled, Vaughn wouldn't touch his inheritance. He didn't spend a penny of it – not for years. His father had set up a trust fund for his college education, so he used that to finish college – but he switched his major to art, which was what he had wanted to study in the first place. But the rest of the money? He wanted no part of it.

"That went on for a couple of years, until finally Lauretta insisted that he get some grief counseling. It must have done him a world of good, because he finally started listening to Lauretta when she told him that his father would have wanted him to use the money to enjoy life. He went on a tour of Europe, visited all of the great museums, studied all of the Old Masters. Lauretta was a little concerned when he went to Italy, kind of afraid that some of that "Michelangelo" nonsense would start up again, but when he came home she realized that she had been worried about nothing. Vaughn was fine, and he's been fine ever since."

"Has he been around here recently?"

"Not since the summer. We'd had a terrible storm that knocked out the power for several days. Vaughn came as soon as Lauretta called him and told him about the power outage. He was terribly concerned, and he was very angry at Holden Owenroe as well."

"Oh? Why was that?"

"Well, Holden is his next-door neighbor, and Vaughn pays him to look after his house when he's out of town. Vaughn has one of those gas-powered emergency generators over at his house, and he made it clear to Holden that he was to start it up immediately any time Vaughn was out of town and the power went off. But when he came home that time, he blew up when he discovered that the power had been off at his house for almost twelve hours before Holden came over and turned on the emergency generator."

"Why did Holden wait so long?"

"Oh, it wasn't Holden's fault! Just before the power went off, Holden's wife fell and broke her ankle. Holden had to rush her to the emergency room, and then he had to wait with her for hours before anyone treated her. And Vaughn didn't need to be so harsh with him, regardless. I mean, what's the big deal? The house was unoccupied at the time. I don't understand why Vaughn got so upset just because the power went off for a few hours."

"Maybe he has a refrigerated wine cellar or something."

"Maybe you're right," Ada said doubtfully. Then she looked at the clock, and when she noticed the time, she put her teacup down sharply. "Oh, dear me! I'd lost track of the time. I'm sorry, Ethan. I have to get ready and leave for choir practice at the church in a few minutes."

Ethan put his own teacup down and rose smoothly. "Thank you for inviting me to tea, Mrs. Mainyre." With a splendid disregard for the truth, he added, "I can't remember when I've had such a good time."

As he bid her goodbye at the front door and walked across the street to his car, he was mentally rubbing his hands in anticipation. That fat bonus for speedy results was practically in his pocket already.

They had cut him out of the loop. That's all Wes Collander could think about as he paced across his brand new office. The promotion from Lieutenant to Captain and the raise that had gone along with it were meaningless to him, as long as his new position left him out in the cold. The chain of command now bypassed him, and he wasn't used to that. And after years of being the Chief's powerful right hand, it wasn't sitting well with him. The fact that Moe Westbrooke, whom he'd known since she was a green, wet-behind-the-ears rookie, could dismiss him with impunity galled him. But he knew a way to fix her wagon, and Rafe Melbourne's too. Punching a number into his cell phone, he said to the person who picked up on the other end, "Meet me at the usual place. Ten minutes."

Maeve insisted that Dawn eat something when she and Ty returned to the private dining room at Fredo's, so she forced some soup and a sandwich down. After she finished, however, she pushed back from the table abruptly.

"I can't stand sitting still and doing nothing. I need to find a work space somewhere close so that I can continue working on the rental property angle. Even if I'm duplicating some of what Rafe and his team are doing, at least I'd feel like I was accomplishing something."

"There's an office you can use upstairs," Sloan said cautiously.

"Yeah, I figured you had a space up there where your minions can hang out and twiddle their thumbs while I'm hard at work across the street."

Sloan shrugged and waved a hand toward the door. "Come on. I'll take you up." He led the way out the door and up the stairs. At the top, he paused for a moment before a door that had a nameplate on it reading *Aemilian Consulting*.

When she noticed the name plate, Dawn said, "I can't believe that you actually put a fake nameplate on the door to hide the fact that this is really a hang-out for a couple of clowns from Lewellen Security. Don't you think that that's taking it a little too far?"

"It's not a fake," Sloan replied absently. "If you look it up, you'll see that Aemilian Consulting is a branch of Vetranio Enterprises, which is a division of the Erkina Corporation, which is a subsidiary of The Lewellen Group. See? Everything aboveboard and legal."

Dawn stood stock-still for a moment. "I hadn't thought about that."

"Thought about what?"

"That you can set up a company that's four or five steps removed from its parent organization so that unless you dig deep down, you could miss the connection between them." Dawn took a deep breath and then let it out slowly. "We've been looking for single men matching our perp's general description who have rented a house in this area over the past month. But what if he's not actually doing the renting? What if he just scoped out the properties and then rented the one he wanted under a corporate name instead?"

Sloan produced a key card and opened the door to the office. Hal and Morgan sprang up immediately as he entered. After telling them to go downstairs for a while, he picked up the conversation where Dawn had left off. "He might not even be renting, Dawn. The real estate market in certain areas around Mountpelier is really hot right now. You can buy a piece of property and then turn it around and sell it at a profit in a relatively short period of time." As a speculative expression crossed Dawn's face, he added, "If you want to look for corporate properties that have been acquired recently, I could probably help you with it."

Dawn considered, then nodded. "Okay. I'll concentrate on rentals. If you could handle the corporate ownership side, it'd be a big help."

"I can give a hand as well," Ty said. As Dawn and his father turned to stare at him simultaneously, he added defensively, "Hey, I might not like doing it, but I know my way around a computer, and I've done my share of research. Had to, before an op., when I was in the Air Force."

"The more people we have working on this, the better," Sloan said. He pondered for a minute, then added, "You know, Lotti's helped me on more than one occasion when I've been working from home. If she were here to assist, I could work twice as fast."

Dawn thought it over. "What about the baby?"

"I could watch her."

All three of them turned toward her in astonishment at Maeve's suggestion.

A little amused at the joint reaction, Maeve said, "What's the matter? Do you all think I can't handle taking care of a baby?"

Sloan swallowed hard before answering. "Uh... Are you sure you don't mind, Maeve? You don't have to. Fredo's wife, Rosa, has a sister who is generally available to come over and help out any time Lotti needs some time off."

Maeve shrugged. "In case you've forgotten, I like babies. Besides, since I'm not very good at doing research on a computer, and Lotti is, if I watch the baby while she helps out, it'll make me feel like I'm contributing something to this operation."

"Uh... okay, if you're sure about this."

Maeve shrugged her shoulders. "No problem."

There was a slight pause, and then Dawn filled it by saying, "Okay. Fill Lotti in and ask her if she's willing to help. As long as..." Dawn hesitated for a moment, not sure how to proceed.

Sloan understood immediately. "Don't worry. Lotti can be trusted to keep everything in confidence. She's very discreet. In fact," he added with an attempt at humor, "clams could take lessons from her when it comes to keeping one's mouth shut."

"All right. Give Lotti a call, and let's get started."

"I need to go downstairs for a minute or two and update Brody, let him know what's going on," Ty interjected.

"Brody's here?"

"Yeah, he was with me at Nyetimber when I got the lieutenant's call, and he insisted on coming along. Didn't want to intrude, though, so he's hanging out down in the bar."

He was taking them all to the cleaners. Hopping around on his one good leg, Brody was still beating the pants off all of his opponents at the pool table. A pile of money lay on one corner of the table, but when Ty signaled him from the doorway, Brody grinned and pocketed it before putting his cue away, grabbing his crutches, and making his way across the bar to the door. Ty led the way back to the private dining room, where he let Brody in on what was going on with Dawn.

After Ty had finished, Brody said, "Anything I can do?"

Knowing Brody's aversion for drone work in general and research in particular, Ty responded, "Uh... not right now. Maybe later. I'll let you know."

"How's your mom handling everything?"

"Pretty well. My cousin Lotti is coming over, and Mom's going to watch Echo while Lotti helps Dad with some of the research."

Brody scowled and said ominously, "You mean he actually had the balls to ask your mom to baby-sit?"

"No, no – it wasn't like that at all. Mom offered to do it – out of the blue. Shocked the hell out of all of us."

Brody digested this information and then said, "I'll give your mom a hand." When he saw Ty's expression of disbelief, he growled, "What's your problem?"

Ty said hastily, "No problem. No problem at all. I just can't picture you helping to baby-sit, that's all."

Brody responded, "I like kids. As long as they're not too little. I'm not real comfortable around infants, but once they're able to walk around and do something other than eat and sleep and poop, kids are kind of fun. Just make sure that your cousin brings a lot of toys with her."

"I'll send her a text. If she doesn't bring enough, we can always go and raid a toy store later."

Rafe picked up the phone immediately when he saw that it was Sergeant Chernet calling back from Michigan. He had sent a photograph of Vaughn Makella and asked Chernet to have Katelyn Norti take a look at it. Skipping any preambles, he said, "This is Melbourne. What have you got, Sergeant?"

"That photograph you sent us – the one of Vaughn Makella? Katelyn Norti has positively identified him as 'the artist guy' who did a portrait of her sister Tamara a couple of weeks before she disappeared. I'm sure you've also noted the resemblance between Makella's photograph and the sketch your witness from the coffee shop came up with of the guy who was watching your missing girl and her boyfriend from across the street when they exited the sporting goods store."

"Yeah, we noticed it. What about that sketch the guy did of Tamara? Did Katelyn or her parents locate it?"

"They're still looking. I'll let you know if they find it." Sergeant Chernet paused for a minute and said, "You've got the death penalty there in Colorado, don't you?"

Rafe answered in the affirmative and then hung up, understanding what Chernet was intimating. Michigan had been the first state in the country to do away with the death penalty, abolishing it in 1846. As badly as Chernet wanted to get the guy responsible for taking the life of Tamara Norti, he wouldn't urge the local DA to push for extradition if the State of Colorado could make a capital case against the killer and get the death penalty. With that, Rafe was in total agreement.

Dawn wrinkled her forehead and frowned in frustration as she continued with the tedious task of searching rental and property records. The sound of Sloan's cell phone ringing distracted her for a moment, and she looked over to where he was working at another desk, Lotti beside him. At the expression on his face, she felt a stab of hope. *Please let it be a lead of some kind. Something, anything*, she thought.

Sloan was finishing up his conversation. "Okay. Thanks for getting me the results so fast. Just a reminder: don't email the written report. Fax it to the number I sent you instead." He hung up and turned to face Dawn. Ty rolled his chair over so that he was close beside her.

"That was the private detective I hired to dig up information on Vaughn Makella," Sloan said. "I think he's onto something that could help."

After Sloan had summarized Ethan Bardner's report for her, Dawn said slowly, "We need to get this information to Rafe."

"Agreed. But I want to do it in such a way that no one can trace your involvement with it, Dawn. I don't want you to jeopardize your career."

Dawn smiled wanly. "My career is way down on my priority list right now. I'll do anything, including tossing my career in the toilet, to get Marina back."

"What about this?" They both turned to Ty as he spoke. "Your agent's still there in Vermont, right?" When his father nodded, Ty continued, "Have him get one of those throwaway cell phones and call the information in anonymously. Rafe and his team are making inquiries about Vaughn Makella as well, right? So have your agent say that he heard that the police in Mountpelier are looking for the dope on Makella. He doesn't want to get involved, but he does want to be a responsible citizen and tell them what he knows. That way, when they trace the call, the only information they'll be able to get is the cell phone's number and the location of the cell tower it originated from. The agent can then toss the cell phone, and no one will be any wiser regarding who the information came from."

Dawn's own cell rang just then. She glanced at it, put it on speaker, and picked up immediately. "Rafe? Can you tell us anything?"

"I can't give you the details, but the suspect that Miranda Gordena gave us looks promising. What I really called you about was to tell you that I heard back on the fingerprints from Captain Penrose. He was able to compare the fingerprints from three sources: the ones taken from your home during the original investigation, the ones from Lee's apartment, and some from the bedroom Lee used in Vivian Zarafin's home. They're a match, Dawn. Leanne Zarafin and Marina Cimarron are definitely one and the same."

Chapter 11

When she heard the sound of Michael's footsteps treading down the stairs, Lee was ready. Once she'd gotten loose, she'd immediately gone over to the tool chest, hoping to find something inside that she could use as a weapon. But the chest had been locked, and she'd broken her chisel when she'd tried to force it open. Just then, she'd heard Michael unlocking the door to the basement, so she'd decided to implement plan B. Taking the pillow and settling it behind her, she used it to conceal the place where she'd pried the staple out of the wall. Then she sat on the edge of the cot, arranged the blanket to hide the links of the chain in her lap, propped her elbows on her knees, and put her head in her hands. When Michael rounded the corner and saw her, he stopped abruptly.

"Is something wrong?"

She lifted her head up slowly. "I don't know. I don't feel well. My head hurts, and my body aches. I think I might have a fever. Do you have a thermometer?"

Michael looked dumbfounded. Shifting his weight uncomfortably from one foot to the other, he replied, "Uh... No, I don't have a thermometer."

"What about some ibuprofen or aspirin?"

"No, I don't have those either. But I have some medication I can give you that will relax you and put you to sleep. You won't be bothered by the pain then."

Something about the way he said it made the hairs stand up on the back of her neck. Lifting her head up from her hands, she took a good look at him. There was a look in his eyes that she hadn't seen there before, and she didn't think it boded well for her. So she pasted *a brave smile on her face and said, "Thanks. Maybe I'll take some if it gets any worse. Before I try that, however, I'd like to try putting a cold wash cloth on my forehead. Maybe that will help." She started to rise, then faltered and sank back down on the cot.*

Moving toward her, Michael said hurriedly, "Here, let me get it for you." As he turned his back to go into the powder room, Lee struck with the swiftness of a rattlesnake. Leaping onto his back, she whipped out the chain and wrapped it as tightly as she could around his neck.

Rafe set his phone down and stared at it thoughtfully. After he'd given Dawn the news about the fingerprints, she'd told him about her insight regarding the idea of looking for corporate as well as individual renters or property owners. Then she had made an oblique reference to anonymous phone calls; how they were usually the bane of a police detective's existence, but some of them – a very small proportion – were gold, and shouldn't be ignored. Before she hung up, she'd expressed the hope that the investigation into the suspect's background in Vermont was going well and urged him not to ignore any leads, no matter how doubtful the source might be. Then she had disconnected abruptly.

He knew his partner, and he knew Tyrell and Sloan Lewellen. No way they were sitting across the street wringing their hands and doing nothing. And if they'd found something? Dawn would choose an indirect way of getting the information to him, rather than reveal that she had been breaking protocol, involving civilians, and investigating on her own.

He walked over to the team assigned to digging up as much background data as possible on Vaughn Makella. Asking for an update from the members of the team, which included Ralph Sokoto and Officer Jordan, he was informed about the anonymous phone call from Vermont. He read the notes they handed him concerning the information that the anonymous source had given them. After he had finished reading the notes, Rafe directed the team members to try to trace that call and verify the source; then he made his way back to his own desk, sat down again, and looked up a different number on his computer. Punching in the number on his phone, he waited for someone to pick up on the other end. Identifying himself, he asked to speak to one of the therapists at The Brieuc Center, the private psychiatric hospital where, according to the anonymous caller, Vaughn Makella had been confined at the age of sixteen.

"I'm sorry, Sergeant Melbourne, but I can't give you any data on whether someone called Vaughn Makella was ever a patient here. You must know that doctor/patient confidentiality is sacrosanct and cannot be violated."

Taking a deep breath, Rafe decided that playing dumb was the best way to finesse some useful information out of the therapist that the receptionist had connected him with, Dr. Fiddich.

"I respect your position, Doctor, but I thought you were allowed to break confidentiality if you discover that the patient poses a danger to himself or to others."

"That's true only if the patient himself indicates to the therapist that he is seriously considering suicide, or if he makes a credible and serious threat to severely injure someone else. I can't break my patient's right to confidentiality just because the police have a hunch that he might be a person of interest to them in an ongoing case."

"So you were Vaughn's therapist?"

Annoyed when he realized that he'd almost given himself away by referring to Vaughn as 'my patient', Dr. Fiddich snapped, "I can neither confirm nor deny that. It's none of your business which of our therapists have treated any particular patient. And I haven't even confirmed that anyone named Vaughn Makella was a patient here."

Injecting a soothing note into his voice, Rafe repeated, "I understand and respect your position, Doctor. But if you learned that one of your patients was a danger to himself or to others, you'd be concerned, wouldn't you? You'd want to do whatever you legally could in order to safeguard your patient and those he is interacting with, wouldn't you?"

Dr. Fiddich answered cautiously, "The key word here is *legally*. As I just indicated to you, there isn't anything I can legally do to help you in this situation."

"But you're an expert, Doctor – right? You could give me an opinion if I outlined a hypothetical case, couldn't you? As long as we're speaking hypothetically, there's not a problem, right?"

There was a pause on the other end before Dr. Fiddich responded, "I can listen to your hypothetical case, but I can't promise you that I will be able to comment on it. You're treading on some very blurry legal ground here, Sergeant Melbourne."

"Okay – you don't have to respond at all if you're uncomfortable. Just listen, okay? Just hear me out."

There was another pause; then Dr. Fiddich replied, "Go ahead."

"Well, let's say that there was this kid who was having some problems. He was delusional, having hallucinations, so his family had him committed to a reputable psychiatric hospital for treatment. Now this hospital was one of the best, so they were able to diagnose the problem and find the right medication to treat the patient. After a while, this hypothetical patient was able to return home and live a fairly normal life again. He had a very responsible father who made sure that he took his medication, so everything was fine. Until a few years later, when the father was killed in a tragic accident. The kid had a hard time dealing with it, and without supervision, he didn't keep up with his medication. So he became delusional again, started hallucinating once more. First of all, he deluded himself into believing that he was the reincarnation of a famous artist. Let's pick one at random, shall we? A famous one like – I don't know – DaVinci or Michelangelo maybe. On top of that, he started hallucinating and convinced himself that he was having conversations with some of the gods or goddesses in Norse mythology. You know, like Odin or Thor or Freyja – or perhaps a more obscure one like Vanadis..." Rafe let his voice trail off at this point and waited expectantly for a response.

There was a long moment of silence on the other end of the line; then Dr. Fiddich said, "I'm sorry, Sergeant Melbourne, but I cannot comment on your hypothetical scenario. I bid you good day." He hung up abruptly, and Rafe hit the *end* button on his phone with a grunt of satisfaction. The doctor had done the ethical thing and had protected his patient's confidentiality. But he'd given Rafe what he needed. That silence had spoken volumes. And by telling Rafe that he could not comment even on a hypothetical premise, Dr. Fiddich had unintentionally confirmed that Rafe's scenario was uncomfortably close to the truth.

Now that he had something to indicate that they should take the information the anonymous caller from Vermont had provided seriously, he needed to update Lieutenant Westbrooke. Afterward, he needed to brief his team and have them be on the lookout for anything in the case that had a connection to Norse mythology or to the famous

Renaissance artist Michelangelo. Then he needed to call New Jersey and inform the detectives in charge of the Gordena case that Vaughn Makella freaked out any time the power went off in his unoccupied house. Getting a search warrant for that house might be a really good idea.

Maeve sat back and sipped at a glass of white wine, watching the scene being played out before her with a good deal of amusement. Brody was sitting on the floor a little distance away and slowly rolling a ball across to Echo, who was stationed close to Maeve's feet. When the ball reached her, the baby chortled with glee, picked it up, and batted it at Brody, who fell back and pretended to be hurt as the ball smacked into his chest.

"Ouch! Hey, kid, have some mercy. You're killing me here."

In response, Echo scrambled to her feet and toddled over to him, wresting the ball out of his hands and proceeding to bounce it off Brody's head.

Brody took it for a while, but then he tossed the ball aside, got a hold of Echo, and lifted her up, pretending to drop her and then catching her at the last minute. Echo pulled herself up and grabbed a double handful of Brody's hair, tugging at it enthusiastically.

"Hey, careful with the hair, kid." When Echo cheerfully ignored him and began winding his hair around her little fingers, Brody sighed and said mournfully, "I hate to break this to you, kid, but you're just as bad as your half-brother. And even he's never stooped to hair-pulling." He freed his hair from her clutches, tossed it back over his shoulders, and turned her away from him, facing Maeve. But then he took a deep breath, and a look of comical dismay crossed his face.

"Uh-oh."

"Is something wrong?" Maeve asked.

"Uh - no, but something over here sure smells, and I don't think it's me."

Amused, Maeve crossed over and plucked Echo from his arms. After getting a whiff of the odor emanating from the baby, Maeve said, "You're right. This baby definitely needs to be changed. Hand me that bag over there, would you, please?"

As Brody complied, he commented, "Maybe I'd better wait outside or something."

Maeve, who had located the changing pad and a clean diaper, responded in an absent tone of voice. "Go ahead and wait outside, if you need to. After all, this is a life-threatening situation here. Probably one of the most dangerous you've ever had to face in your entire career."

Brody, who had been gathering himself up to make a quick exit, said slowly, "Well, I guess if you put it that way..." He settled himself back down again, but kept his eyes averted.

After what seemed like an eternity, Maeve said, "There now! All nice and clean and fresh again, Echo!" Then to Brody, "You can look over this way now. The world is once again safe from poopy diapers."

Looking over cautiously, Brody responded, "Where is it?"

Maeve pointed to a thin green plastic bag. "In there. It just needs to go into the garbage can."

"Not the one in here, right?"

Maeve rolled her eyes, scooped up Echo with one arm, picked up the plastic bag with the other, and left the room momentarily. When she returned, she resumed her seat and pulled a round plastic ring out of the bag of toys that Lotti had left with them before she went upstairs to help Sloan. Echo grasped it and shoved it into her mouth, sucking on it contentedly.

Brody, meanwhile, heaved himself up from the floor and made his way over to the chair next to Maeve's. After watching Echo for a minute or two, he said, "You really don't mind it? Watching the baby, I mean."

Maeve picked up her wine glass again and toyed with it. She thought about pretending to misunderstand Brody's comment, but then decided to meet the subject head-on. "If Renea were still in the picture, it would be different. But she's gone, and I don't have it in me to hold the fact that Echo shares some DNA with a person I can't stand against such an innocent child." She met Brody's questioning gaze levelly. "I can't deny, however, that the fact that Echo doesn't resemble Renea at all helps."

"What does she look like?"

"Who? Renea?"

At Brody's nod, Maeve said, "I'd forgotten that you've never actually seen her." Clearing her throat, Maeve continued slowly, "She has red hair and green eyes. She's quite beautiful, actually."

"I don't care how beautiful she is – she could never hold a candle to you. Nobody can. And Sloan Lewellen is a fool."

Maeve took Brody's hand and gave it a quick squeeze before releasing it and replying gently, "Don't think that I don't appreciate your championing me, Brody, but as I told you when it all happened originally, Renea wasn't the only problem between Sloan and me. And Sloan never so much as went out on a date with her until I filed for divorce."

"*You* filed for divorce?"

"Yes. I had been away for months, setting up my business in New Orleans. Sloan came down to visit me one weekend and we had a big fight about it. He ended up giving me an ultimatum: either I return with him to Colorado, or he would file for a legal separation. When I refused to go back with him, that's just what he did. I was so angry that I countered by filing for divorce. So, you see, it's not all Sloan's fault."

Unwilling to let Sloan off the hook that easily, Brody responded, "I don't know about that. He should have tried to work things out with you. Instead, he started seeing someone else. You never did that."

Maeve shrugged. "No, but there were other issues between us – private issues that I have no intention of discussing – so don't be so quick to judge Sloan. It takes two to make a marriage, Brody. Sometimes it takes two to make a divorce as well. Which is not to say that I wasn't hurt and shocked when Sloan married Renea so quickly after the divorce. I cut off all communication with him for months. If Ty hadn't had that accident not long after it all happened, we might never have started speaking to each other again. It was only then that we decided we had to try to get along with each other – for Ty's sake. The last thing he needed was for his parents to be sniping at one another over his hospital bed. And then when he was kidnapped... but I don't want to think about that. Suffice it to say that by the time Sloan realized he'd made a mistake and divorced Renea, I was ready to try to be friends again, at least."

"Still, the fact that he and Renea had a baby together..."

Maeve held up a hand, and Brody's voice trailed off. "Sloan has full custody, and the baby doesn't remind me of Renea at all. In fact, the first time I saw a picture of Echo, I was struck by her resemblance to Sloan's mother, Veronique. She was a lovely person. I like to think that Echo will grow up to be just like her. So trust me when I say that interacting with Echo is not at all painful for me, Brody."

Echo pulled the teething ring out of her mouth just then and threw it across the room.

"Wow, what an arm, kid!" Picking up the ball they had been playing with earlier and twirling it on his finger, Brody said, "Ready for another game?"

After he'd met with the lieutenant, briefed his team, and spoken with the police in New Jersey, Rafe was just about to get back to work on the real estate angle when his cell phone rang. Since the caller ID showed that Naomi Preisinger was trying to reach him, Rafe picked up the call. "Mrs. Preisinger? This is Sergeant Melbourne. How's Will doing?"

"That's what I'm calling about, Sergeant! Will just regained consciousness. He wants to talk to you as soon as possible."

"I'm on my way." Grabbing his jacket, Rafe told Sokoto, who was acting as his second-in-command on the team, where he was going. Then he raced out the door.

Rafe caught a brief glimpse of Carl Brassner and Maya Shilltoe in the waiting area, but he didn't stop to talk to them. A harried-looking nurse was exiting Will's room as Rafe walked toward it. When he entered the room, he discovered Naomi Preisinger engaged in a heated conversation with her son.

"Will, you were downright rude to that nurse. And you can't refuse your medication!"

"I know my rights! They can't give me drugs without my consent, and I am refusing my consent! I don't want any more of that shit until after I've talked to the cops; it makes me all dopey and confused."

"But Will..." A look of relief crossed Naomi Preisinger's face as she caught sight of Rafe. "Sergeant Melbourne. Thank God." Turning back to her son, she said, "Will, this is Sergeant Melbourne, from the police. He's the one in charge of your case."

Will looked Rafe over with eyes that were pain-filled, but shrewd and alert. He said to his mother, "Mom, I love you, but I need you to leave now, just for a few minutes. I need to talk to the Sergeant alone."

After Naomi had left, Will said, "The first thing I asked when I woke up was 'Where's Lee?' And you know what my mom said? She said that Lee's fine. She claimed that Lee has been here the whole time, but she left just a little while ago to go home and get some rest. And you know what? Mom's lying. I can always tell. So before I answer any of your questions, I want an answer, and I want the truth. Where's Lee? Is she dead?"

Rafe made sure he looked the young man right in the eye as he replied, "We don't know where Lee is, Will. She's missing. We're looking for her, and as far as we know, she's still alive."

Will closed his eyes briefly. When he opened them again, he said, "Go ahead and ask me your questions. I'll tell you everything I can."

After Will had filled Rafe in on his confrontation with the man who called himself Michael, Rafe said, "Okay, Will. Now, I have some pictures here that I'd like you to look at. Tell me if any of them looks like the guy."

Will went through the pictures quickly; then he pointed to the one of Vaughn Makella. "That's him. His hair is shorter in this picture, and it's a different color, but that's Michael."

As Rafe put the pictures away, Will asked, "Do you know him? Do you know where he took Lee?"

Rafe answered carefully, "We think we know his real name. And we're following up some leads that we hope will lead us to the place where he could be holding Lee."

"You think she's dead, don't you?"

"I won't lie to you, Will. When someone is the victim of an abduction by a stranger, if we don't get them back within the first twenty-four hours, the chances for survival diminish significantly. However, there are some elements in this case that have led us to believe that Lee still has a chance."

"I should have protected her better. I should never have let her go near that creep."

"It's not your fault, Will. From what you said, the guy seemed harmless. Only a mind reader could have guessed that the beer was drugged. And despite being drugged, you fought back, you survived. In fact, if you hadn't let the park ranger who found you know what had happened, we wouldn't have known even to start looking for Lee."

There was a knock on the door, and Naomi Preisinger entered hard upon it. "Time's up. I want you to take your medication now, Will Preisinger. And I don't want any lip about it."

"He told me about Lee, Mom. You shouldn't have lied to me."

"No, I shouldn't have. All I was thinking was that you were in enough pain already, and I wanted to spare you any additional grief."

Tears sprang into her eyes as she said contritely, "I'm sorry. I won't lie to you again."

Nerves were stretched so tight in the offices of Aemilian Consulting that Ty thought something was bound to snap at any minute. Dawn was restless, her foot beating an endless rhythm on the floor as she concentrated intensely on the screen of her computer, all the while downing cup after cup of coffee in an effort to keep herself sharp and alert. Lotti was working at a computer on the other side of the room, tapping a pencil nervously on the surface of her workstation with one hand while using the other to scroll through the endless data she was reviewing on the screen. Even Sloan, usually impervious to nerves, kept running his hand through his hair, which Ty knew he did only on the rare occasions he was suffering from some sort of anxiety.

"Dawn? I think I might have something."

Springing out of her chair so quickly that it went flying across the room, Dawn sped over to Lotti's workstation. Ty's cousin was pointing to a particular name on the screen: Valhalla-Buonarroti Industries. "Isn't *Valhalla* the name of the home of the gods in Norse mythology?"

Excitement was coursing through Dawn's veins like quicksilver. "Yes. This has got to be it! I have to call Rafe." She started to reach for her cell phone, but Sloan shook his head and put his hand on her arm, arresting the movement.

"Dawn, wait. You don't want to ruin your career by betraying that you are working the case after officially withdrawing from it."

She turned on him furiously. "Take your hand off my arm! I'm calling Rafe, and I don't give a damn if anyone finds out that this information came from me. We have to get moving on this *now!*"

"Agreed, but there's a better way. Let me make the call. I'll be the concerned father-in-law, just checking to see if there's any news. Rafe is smart enough to make sure that no one on his end of the conversation gets wind of the fact that I communicated this piece of information to him at the same time."

It took Dawn only seconds to think it over. "Okay. We'll do it your way."

When Rafe returned to headquarters, he was surprised to find that the bullpen was nearly deserted. Hearing noises from the break room, he strolled over and glanced inside. Almost the whole unit was inside, watching the television grimly. To his dismay, he realized that the newscaster was talking about the case, and had somehow gathered more details than had been approved for release. He'd caught just the tail end of the segment, however, so when it was over, he asked, "How much did they reveal, Sok?"

"Just about everything," Sokoto replied disgustedly. "Lee's name, the fact that she's been abducted, the possibility that she might be Marina Cimarron – shit, they even knew that Will was out of the coma and was being interviewed by the police. How the hell did they find out, Sarge? I'll swear it didn't come from any of us."

Rafe had his suspicions, and Wesley Collander figured prominently in them as a suspect, but he merely said, "How's the Lieutenant handling it?"

"She's scheduled a press conference in an hour. Says she's going to try to do damage control, but good luck with that."

"Well, we can't do anything about it now. Anything else develop while I was at the hospital?"

"We heard back from Sergeant Chernet in Michigan. Katelyn Norti found the portrait that Vaughn Makella painted of her sister Tamara. It's signed *Michael,* and there's a little angel flying over the signature."

Rafe nodded. "Michelangelo. It's all starting to come together." He briefed Sokoto on his interview with Will Preisinger. Then he said thoughtfully, "We know who the son-of-a-bitch is. But where is he? What..." He broke off as his phone signaled an incoming call. After looking at the caller ID, he said, "It's Sloan Lewellen. Probably wants to know what the hell is going on. I'll have to take this, Sok."

Sokoto nodded absently and wandered over to where Prentiss and Noritaki were working on the real estate angle. He heard Rafe greet Sloan and give him the usual bullshit about working the case, pursuing all available leads, etc. Not even with someone as powerful and influential as Sloan Lewellen could they discuss the details of an ongoing case – even one that affected him so personally.

After Rafe disconnected the call, he walked over to where the three of them were gathered and said, "Look, we've already figured that he'd want some place off the beaten track. And from the information that our anonymous caller gave us, the whole thing started when he was lost on a camping trip in the mountains when he was a kid. That's when he started hallucinating and obsessing about that goddess person – Vanadis. Maybe he feels closer to her, more connected to her, when he's in parkland or wilderness areas, somewhere in or near the mountains." Pulling up a map on the computer, he studied it for a moment and then said, "He wouldn't want to be too far from civilization, so let's concentrate on rural areas that are within an hour of the spot he liked to hang out in – the shopping district where the coffee shop and the sporting goods store are located. That gives us four areas to search: Yellow Ridge, Mount Eyrie, Kerner's Knob, and Traynor's Fork." Looking around, he said, "Prentiss, you take Yellow Ridge; Noritaki – Mount Eyrie. Sokoto, you look at Kerner's Knob, and I'll take Traynor's Fork."

Rafe decided to wait about five minutes, just so it wouldn't look too suspicious. Then he said, "Wait a minute... I might have found something." As Sokoto looked over his shoulder, Rafe tapped the computer screen. "It's a house located on a few acres in Traynor's Fork. It's owned by a company called Valhalla-Buonarroti Industries. Isn't the name *Valhalla* connected somehow with Norse Mythology?"

"Yeah. That's where the gods lived – Thor and Odin and the rest of them. Let me look up *Buonarroti*." Sokoto punched the information in on his computer. "Bingo! Here's the Michelangelo connection. The artist's full name was Michelangelo di Lodovico *Buonarroti* Simoni. You find anything else on this company?"

"I'm checking... whoa, here we go: Valhalla-Buonarroti Industries is a subsidiary of Baldr Enterprises, which is a limited liability corporation whose sole member is one Vaughn Makella." Rafe pushed back his chair. "I have to update the lieutenant, get her to push Judge Portentia for a warrant. In the meantime, call and see if either of our helicopters is available, Sok. We need to get out to Traynor's Fork as quickly as possible."

But Sokoto was shaking his head. "No good, Rafe. There was a big pile-up on the Interstate about an hour ago. From what I've heard, more than a dozen vehicles were involved, and there are multiple injuries. Both helicopters were called out to the scene."

"Okay – then call the Civil Air Patrol, Sok. Given the circumstances, I'll bet that they can put a helicopter at our disposal within minutes. We'll take a team and fly out there. That way, as soon as the lieutenant notifies us that the warrant has come through, we'll be on the spot, ready and waiting."

Dawn paced the floor impatiently. "It's been almost fifteen minutes since you gave Rafe the information about the house in Traynor's Fork, Sloan."

"I'd tell you to be patient, Dawn, but I think you'd just haul off and hit me."

Dawn sat down at one of the desks. "You're probably right." She looked hopefully over at Ty as his cell phone rang. After a monosyllabic conversation, Ty disconnected.

"That was Sokoto. The Civil Air Patrol has been asked to provide transportation for an upcoming operation by the Mountpelier Police. I've had Jack and my search and rescue team waiting on standby with our fastest helicopter. They can be there in eight minutes."

"I'm not sitting here and waiting. Maybe I can't be part of Rafe's team, but I need to be there."

"I figured that, so I've got another helicopter ready and waiting on top of the Lewellen Building. It will take us about six minutes to get over there, board, and be ready to follow when we see Rafe and his team take off. I've been checking out the topography, and there's an open spot not far from the house where I can set down. We'll be close enough to observe, but not so close that we'll be in the way of the operation."

"I'm going with you."

Ty turned at the sound of Brody's voice and lifted an eyebrow. "You gonna be able to keep up on those crutches?"

"Even on crutches, I'll leave you behind in the dust, hot shot."

Ty shrugged. "It's fine with me, as long as Dawn's okay with it."

"At this point, I don't care if Lucifer himself wants to go along with us. Let's move!"

Ty had parked his car directly in front of the building, so the three of them jumped in. Ty floored the gas pedal and sped toward the Lewellen Building with a fine disregard for the posted speed limits.

On the way there, Dawn asked Brody curiously, "What brought you upstairs at just the crucial moment?"

"Lotti came downstairs to check on Echo. When I asked her what was going on upstairs, she said that you might have just had a big break, so I decided to go up and check it out."

That was all the time they had for conversation before the car pulled up in front of the Lewellen Building.

As Ty reached down to open his door, Brody picked up the bag sitting beside him on the back seat of the car. Tossing it to Ty, he said, "Take that for me. It might come in handy." Ty hooked it over his arm and caught up with Dawn, who was already racing toward the doors of the building. Brody followed close behind them.

Sloan must have called ahead and cleared the way for them, for one of his employees was waiting for them at the front door. With a brief greeting to Ty, he led the way to one of the elevators and entered the code to open it. As the door opened with a soft hiss, the three of them scrambled inside, where Ty hit the button for the roof, sending the elevator smoothly upwards. When it stopped, the trio raced to the waiting helicopter, Dawn noticing with a corner of her mind that Brody hadn't been kidding when he said that he would be able to keep up. He maneuvered himself on his crutches faster than many uninjured people she knew could have managed on two good legs. Within minutes they had boarded, and Ty took off in pursuit of the other helicopter, which had just lifted off from police headquarters and was heading in the direction of Traynor's Fork.

Chapter 12

Gasping and shaking with fury, Michael tried to pry Lee's hands loose and unwind the chain from around his neck. Lee fought to hold on, amazed at his strength. She hadn't expected him to react so quickly; she'd counted on him being so shocked that he would be still for a second or two so that she could implement the second part of her plan. She'd stuck one of his smaller paint brushes into her hair, thinking that she could hold the chain with one hand, grab the brush with the other, and wind it into the chain, using it to tighten the improvised garrote enough to incapacitate her adversary. But she hadn't been granted that second or two of grace. She needed both hands to hold on and repel Michael's efforts to get loose.

He gave up trying to pry the chain loose and tried a new tactic, flinging himself violently backward against the wall. Lee's head spun as it smashed into the hard surface, but she held on doggedly. Again and again Michael repeated the maneuver, slamming her against the wall. She maintained as long as she could, but after he turned sideways and her shoulder hit the wall with brutal impact, her arm and hand went numb. Losing her grip on the chain, she fell to the floor.

Michael unwound the chain from his neck and dove toward her as she gathered herself up to a sitting position. She had just enough time before he landed on her to swing one of her legs up and land a solid kick in his groin. As he doubled over with pain, Lee gathered the chain up, pushed herself to her feet, and made a break for the stairs. Praying that he had left the door at the top unlocked, she raced up the steps. The sound of footsteps pounding behind her alerted her to the fact that Michael was up and moving as well. Reaching the top, she grabbed the handle of the door and nearly wept with relief as it turned easily. Shoving the door open, she dove through the doorway. Quick as a cat, she rolled over and lashed out with her legs, felt the entire house shudder as she kicked the door shut. Then she was on her feet again, desperately reaching for and turning the key in the deadbolt.

The pounding began from the other side of the door, and she felt the house shudder again from the force of the blows. For a moment she was frozen with fear, afraid that the door might give way and he would be upon her before she had time to gather her wits and still the frantic beating of her heart. But the door was solid, and the stout lock was holding. She forced herself to move away and look about her. She was in the kitchen area of the house. Running to the counter, she began pulling out drawers until she found what she was looking for. A fierce smile crossed her face as she grasped the long-handled butcher's knife in her hand. She had a weapon. Now she needed to find her way out of here. Racing to the front door, she unlocked it and looked outside. A sidewalk in front of her led to a driveway, with a large attached garage on the left. All around, however, nothing but snow-covered trees met her gaze. The icy wind trailing across her bare arms reminded her that she needed two things: warmer clothing and transportation of some sort. Moving into the adjacent living room, she spied her long black coat folded over the back of an easy chair, her boots placed neatly beside it. Grabbing the coat, she thrust an arm through one sleeve; then, transferring her knife from one hand to the other and letting the chain drop to the floor, she shrugged her other arm in. With the chain still shackled around her right ankle, there was no hope she could pull a boot over it, so she decided to abandon the boots.

One part of her mind had registered that the pounding on the cellar door had stopped. For a moment she entertained the hope that he had just given up trying to force the door. Back in the kitchen, however, her heart sank. The pounding started once again, and to her horror, she watched as the wood around the deadbolt splintered, and the edge of a hatchet appeared. Apparently, Michael had not had any trouble accessing his tool chest.

She thought about waiting on the side of the door and thrusting the butcher's knife into him when he broke through, but gave up that plan when she spotted the car keys hanging neatly from a peg on the wall next to the sink. Grabbing them, she sprinted to the door on the far side of the kitchen. Opening the door, she found herself, as she had hoped, in the garage. Two vehicles stood there: a pick-up truck, and a *much larger type of truck that she couldn't identify. When she pressed the "unlock" button on the key, she heard the locks on the pick-up truck disengage. Pulling the door open, she scrambled up into the driver's seat, yanking the chain up after her and depositing it on the floor. Dropping the knife on the seat beside her, she jammed the keys into the ignition with one hand and was in the process of tugging the door closed with the other when she saw a blur of movement out of the corner of her eye and felt a violent tug on her hair. Screaming with fear and rage, she groped wildly for the butcher's knife...*

As Ty set the helicopter down in a field only yards away from the house, just seconds after the one carrying Rafe and his team had landed practically in the front yard, Dawn trained her binoculars on the house. Rafe and Sokoto moved into position at the front door, while Prentiss and Noritaki raced around to the back. She saw Rafe pound on the door, and when no one answered, step back and kick the door in. When the minutes ticked by and she saw no one exiting the house, she could stand it no longer.

"I'm moving closer." She jumped to the ground and started running toward the house, Ty just behind her. At the perimeter, she watched as the door on the attached garage swung open. She caught sight of a large beige pick-up truck and saw that Rafe and his team were gathered in there, looking at something on the ground beside the driver's side door. She ran up the driveway, but as soon as he saw her, Rafe came out of the garage and caught her arm.

"What's going on? What have you found?" she asked impatiently.

He didn't bother to tell her that she shouldn't be there; they both knew it, just as they knew that it would take a court order plus a small army to get her out of there. So he didn't waste his breath arguing with her or attempting to get her to leave. "There's nobody here, Dawn. We found evidence that someone was being held in the basement, but there's no one there now. It looks like he had two vehicles in the garage, and one of them is missing." He paused for a minute, then said, "There's a small puddle of blood on the floor of the garage."

"How fresh? Is it congealed or hardened yet?"

"Pretty fresh. It's just beginning to congeal. I think we just missed them, Dawn. Sokoto is in touch with the DMV, having them run a search on any vehicles rented to Valhalla-Buonarroti Industries. With any luck, he hasn't had time to get too far away. We'll find them, Dawn."

Sokoto joined them just then. "Got it! It's a reefer truck, a ten footer, white." He rattled off the license plate number.

"Okay. Here's what we're going to do. Prentiss and Noritaki will stay here, secure the scene, wait for the patrol units and the crime scene techs. The rest of us will look for the truck. There are roads going south and east out of here, but nothing to the north or west. Sokoto, you and I will go in the first chopper, start looking along the southern route." He turned to look at Ty. "You can take the area to the east. If you spot the truck, contact us immediately. Let us take him down if at all possible. It'll be cleaner that way."

Ty stopped for a moment to talk to the members of his search and rescue team who were aboard the other helicopter, and two of the paramedics on the team quickly descended and transferred to the other chopper.

Just before Ty got the bird into the air, Dawn said to him, "You know what a reefer truck is, or do I have to look it up on my cell?"

Ty hesitated just for a minute before he replied, "A reefer truck is a refrigerated truck, Dawn."

Michael took one hand off the wheel to check the bandage on his shoulder. The bleeding seemed to have stopped at least. He still couldn't believe that she had tried to kill him. When he'd caught up with her just as she got into the driver's seat of his pick-up truck, she'd whirled and struck at him with a butcher's knife. Fortunately, he'd still been holding the lathing hammer he'd used to chop through the door to the basement and free himself. He'd gotten it up in time to deflect the blow, which had been aimed for his heart, so the butcher's knife had turned aside and caught him in the shoulder instead. He'd grabbed her with his good arm and pulled her out of the truck, backhanding her with the hammer side of the tool. If he'd hit her dead-on or lashed out with the hatchet side of the tool, the blow would probably have killed her, but she twisted aside at the last minute, and the hammer had caught her on the side of the head instead, stunning her momentarily. He hadn't taken any chances then. Grabbing some duct tape from a nearby shelf in the garage, he'd trussed her up, binding first her hands, then her feet. When she'd recovered enough from the blow to begin struggling against the bonds and started screaming at him to let her go, he'd put a piece of duct tape over her mouth as well. Then he'd picked her up and tossed her into the back of the reefer truck before seeing to the wound on his shoulder. He was relieved to see that it was not as deep as he had feared, so he'd cleaned it thoroughly and put some antiseptic on it before placing a sterile gauze pad over it, winding some bandages around his chest and shoulder, and securing everything with some white medical tape. Then he'd returned to the garage and headed out.

Once he'd seen the newscast, he'd known that he couldn't stick with his original plan and take her back home with him, as he had with the others. Since the boyfriend had come out of his coma and told the police about the attack, they now knew that they had an abduction on their hands, not just a lost girl. And the boyfriend had seen him, could identify him. He'd already determined that he was going to have to finish up early this time, leave the girl behind, and put as much distance between himself and the state of Colorado as he possibly could.

Earlier, when he had gone down to the basement and she'd told him she was sick, it had seemed like the perfect opportunity. He'd planned to dissolve enough of the sleeping medication in a glass of water to render her unconscious. Afterward, he would place her in the back of the reefer truck. In the freezing cold of its interior, hypothermia would quickly set in, causing her to fall gradually into a stupor. She would slip away as easily and as painlessly as possible. Then he would take her to the mountains and set the remnant of the goddess free from the girl's mortal body.

Well, the first part of his plan may have gone awry, but he could still go through with the second part. Even though he was furiously angry with her, he would still leave her in the icy embrace of the mountains. He owed the part of her that housed the goddess that.

"There it is!" Brody shouted.

Dawn and Ty had seen it too, and Ty immediately contacted the other chopper, letting them know the location where they had spotted the reefer truck. Just then, the driver must have realized that the helicopter was in pursuit, because he began to accelerate, barreling along the narrow country road at a dangerous rate of speed. Ty didn't have to be a mind reader to know what his wife was thinking: if the truck continued to gain speed, it would crash, and there was no guarantee that either of the occupants would survive.

With that in mind, Ty took the helicopter down until it hovered right above the truck. Just as he expected, the driver reacted by slowing down, looking out the windows and checking his mirrors, trying to determine just how close the chopper was. As soon as the truck began to decelerate, Ty took the helicopter up again, then dropped down so that he was hovering just in front of the truck, matching its pace and speed. Once again, the driver, thinking that he might crash and disoriented by the sight of the helicopter whirling in front of him, decreased his speed. Ty took the chopper up again. Choosing his spot carefully, this time he set the helicopter down on the roadway, at a little distance in front of the truck. With no way around the obstacle, and obviously fearful of crashing, the driver slammed on the brakes and brought his vehicle to a complete stop.

Dawn wasn't taking any chances by waiting for the other helicopter to arrive. Descending from the chopper and drawing her weapon, she shouted, "Police! Don't move a muscle! Keep your hands on the steering wheel where I can see them!"

Ignoring her commands, the driver ducked down and rolled across the front seat. Flinging open the passenger-side door, he dropped down, hit the ground, and began running up the hill on the opposite side of the roadway.

Dawn reached the truck. Tearing open the door on the driver's side, she swept the interior with her weapon. Finding it empty, she raced along the side until she was almost to the rear of the truck. Standing with her back against the side of the truck, she paused a minute, then darted a quick glance around the truck. Nothing. She couldn't expose herself for more than a second, however - for all she knew, her adversary could be armed. The whole time, she was aware of the fact that Ty had exited the helicopter shortly after she had and was shadowing her. She was also aware that Brody had opened the side door of the helicopter, but she hadn't seen him descend.

When Ty reached her, he said, "Give Brody a minute. He'll have the situation contained shortly."

Just then, she saw something fly out of the helicopter in the direction that the suspect had taken. A second later, she heard a scream and a thud. Then she heard Brody's voice: "Go ahead. The suspect is down. I'll make sure he stays that way."

Without giving further thought to the method Brody had used to bring down the suspect, Dawn began moving around to the back of the truck, just as the second helicopter arrived on the scene and landed. Rafe was bounding out of the chopper almost before it touched the ground, and he was by her side in a matter of seconds. "Let me do it, Dawn," Rafe said urgently.

It took all of her professionalism, but Dawn nodded and stepped aside. Pulling open the rear door, Rafe leaped up into the back of the truck. Immediately, he shouted, "She's here! Get the paramedics!" Bending down, he scooped up the figure that was lying on the floor of the truck and carried her to the door, handing her down to the paramedics, who had wasted no time in scrambling out of the helicopter. Placing her on a gurney, they swiftly took her vitals and began administering treatment.

Dawn stood by, her eyes fastened on Lee's face as the paramedics worked on the unconscious girl. She was only dimly aware that Ty stood beside her, a hand on her arm for both comfort and support. She didn't even spare a thought for what was going on regarding the suspect; she had seen Ralph Sokoto head up the hill in the direction where she had last seen the man she assumed was Vaughn Makella, and she was content to let Sokoto handle that situation. Sirens sounded in the distance, and she soon registered the fact that additional police units had arrived on the scene, but still she did not look away. Presently, however, she became aware that someone was standing on her other side, and she recognized Captain Penrose's voice when he said,

"Marina Cimarron. After all these years. Who'd have thought it? Even Nick was pessimistic in the end, and he held out hope longer than anyone else did. Except for you, D.C. I have to admit; I thought you were just being stubborn and unrealistic when you refused to believe that she was gone. Wouldn't even have her declared dead when the time came. I've never been happier to admit that I was wrong."

"She's coming around!"

At the paramedic's words, Dawn moved forward and grasped the arm rail of the gurney.

"*Marina*," she whispered. Then in a louder voice, she said, "*Lee*."

The girl had been facing away from her, but at the sound of Dawn's voice, she turned her head – and stared at Dawn out of their father's blue eyes.

Maybe it was the fact that she was the only other woman present, or maybe on some level, blood recognized blood, for Lee immediately reached out and grasped Dawn's hand, holding it tightly.

"Who are you?" she asked in a shaky voice.

Eyes filling with tears that she refused to allow to fall, Dawn squeezed her sister's hand and said simply, "Dawn – I'm Dawn." She paused for a moment and then added, "I'm a detective with the Mountpelier Police." Indicating Rafe, she said, "This is my partner, Sergeant Rafe Melbourne. Whenever you feel able, he'd like to talk to you, take your statement. But right now, there are a couple of people we need to call, let them know you're safe. They're waiting for you at the hospital: Will Preisinger and Maya Shilltoe." She didn't mention Vivian Zarafin. If Lee asked for her, she'd let Rafe handle it, but she wasn't about to bring the woman's name up.

At the mention of Will's name, Lee's face lit up with a combination of confusion and hope.

"Will's alive? But he went over the cliff! I saw him fall; I thought sure he was dead."

Rafe took over smoothly. "Will managed to grab and hold onto a rock shelf long enough to break his fall. He was injured - pretty badly, in fact; but he's on the road to recovery now. How would you like me to call him so that you can talk to him yourself?"

"Yes, yes – call him right away! I need to talk to him, hear his voice for myself!"

Rafe put a call through to Will, who had been moved out of intensive care to a regular room. Smiling broadly, Rafe said, "Will? I've got some news for you – good news. We've found Lee. She's alive and well, and she's right here, waiting to talk to you." Handing the phone to Lee, Rafe turned aside and drew Dawn, Ty, and Captain Penrose a little to one side.

Ralph Sokoto, meanwhile, had headed up the hill toward Brody and the man he assumed was Vaughn Makella. From the helicopter, he'd watched helplessly as Makella exited the reefer truck and sped up the hill, inwardly cursing at the thought that the suspect might actually get away before the copter landed and they could apprehend him. Then he had seen a giant figure move to the side door of the chopper already on the ground, whirling a bolo over his head and flinging it expertly toward the fleeing suspect. The bolo had caught the fleeing man neatly around the knees, halting him in his tracks. He had flailed his arms around wildly, trying to stay on his feet, but to no avail. As the suspect pitched forward, Sokoto saw the giant grab a pair of crutches, and more quickly than he would have believed possible for a man so impaired, move up toward the man on the hill, who had managed to sit up and was struggling to unwind the bolo from around his legs. He didn't succeed, however, for just then the giant had reached the suspect, and Sokoto saw him appear to stumble on his crutches and fall, landing directly on top of the man on the ground.

"Who the hell is that?" he'd shouted to Rafe.

"Friend of Tyrell Lewellen's. Name's Brody. Some sort of government agent, I think. Don't know what branch."

There was no time for anything else, for the chopper set down just then, and Rafe had leaped out the door and sped toward the reefer truck. Sokoto sprang out right after him, heading toward the duo on the hill.

When he reached them, he saw that Brody was lying sideways across the trunk of the other man, his huge bulk effectively pinning the other down. One crutch lay to the side. The other was still in Brody's hand, however, and was resting across the suspect's throat.

Brody waited until Sokoto was standing directly over them; then he deadpanned, "I've fallen, and I can't get up."

Sokoto had to suppress a grin upon hearing the classic line coming from the lips of someone as massive as Brody. Carefully keeping his face and his tone bland, he responded, "I'll give you a hand up in a minute. I have to check on the suspect first. Is he conscious?"

"Yeah, but he's not very talkative. I'm afraid that the place where the crutch landed might have something to do with that. I was just attempting to get up and sort of move it when you arrived."

Brody's tone was innocence itself, and Sokoto answered in kind. "Yeah, it's unfortunate that you happened to land the way you did. Must be uncomfortable for the guy. Why don't you hand that crutch to me? I'll take over from here."

Brody obliged, lifting the crutch from the other man's throat and handing it over to Sokoto, who placed it carefully on the ground near the other crutch, well within Brody's reach. Crouching down and taking out his handcuffs, Sokoto said, "How about trying to roll off him now?" Brody scooted aside and Sokoto quickly flipped the suspect over, pulled his arms together behind his back, and fastened the handcuffs securely around his wrists.

Eddleston and Garrone arrived just then and assisted Sokoto in getting the prisoner to his feet. Brody rolled over onto his side, got up on his good knee, and reached for his crutches while Sokoto was listing the charges and advising the suspect of his rights.

"Vaughn Makella, you're under arrest on suspicion of assault and battery, attempted murder, unlawful detention, and kidnapping. You have the right to remain silent. Anything you say can and will be used against you in a court of law. You have the right to speak to an attorney, and to have an attorney present during any questioning. If you cannot afford a lawyer, one will be provided for you at government expense. Do you understand?"

Vaughn Makella just sneered at him and responded scornfully, "My name is Michelangelo, and I don't answer to anyone but the goddess. I don't need anybody's help except hers. She'll take care of me."

"Great. I just hope this goddess of yours is a member of the Bar with a license to practice law in the state of Colorado. Oh, and by the way, it would also help if she has a good background in criminal law and lots of trial experience. Otherwise, I just can't see her being of much use to you."

Makella did not rise to the bait, but kept his mouth shut and refused to utter another word. Brody, who had gotten to his feet in the meantime, followed the officers down the hill toward the waiting paramedics, who had finished with Lee and loaded her aboard the rescue helicopter.

After the paramedics had checked on Makella's condition, Ty said, "He in urgent need of medical care?"

"No. He actually did a good job of treating the wound on his shoulder. The bleeding has stopped, and he's in no immediate danger."

"Then he's not setting foot in either of my birds. Turning to Sokoto, he said, "You can take him back in one of the black and whites. I don't want him anywhere near the victim or my wife."

Sokoto nodded. "Agreed." He took Makella by one arm, and with Eddleston on the other side, walked the suspect over and hustled him into one of the waiting police cars. Ty watched as the vehicle pulled away, then turned to Rafe. "You going back in one of the other cars?"

"No. Sokoto and I talked it over while the paramedics were doing their thing. He's going to take Makella through the booking process and try to get a statement out of him. I'm going in the helicopter with Lee.

We'll get her to the hospital, and then I want to take her statement as soon as possible. What about Dawn?"

Ty looked over at the helicopter he had piloted in, which Dawn had re-boarded after the paramedics had gotten Lee safely aboard the other. "I'm not sure what she wants to do next. We'll talk it over when we get back to the city."

Captain Penrose stepped forward at that point. "If she's up to it, I'd like Detective Cimarron to come in to headquarters before she heads to the hospital. There's an item we retrieved from the search of Vivian Zarafin's house that I need her to identify, if possible."

Ty shrugged and jerked his head toward the helicopter where Dawn was waiting. "Go ahead and ask. It's up to her."

As Captain Penrose went over to talk to Dawn, Ty said to Rafe, "You'd better get moving. They're waiting to take off." He paused for a minute, then added, "Take care of my sister-in-law."

"Count on it. In the meantime, you take care of my partner. See you later."

Rafe turned and walked to the waiting helicopter, which took off as soon as he boarded. Ty watched it rise smoothly into the air and begin its flight back to Mountpelier. He was still watching it when Captain Penrose returned and addressed him.

"D.C. is agreeable to returning to headquarters and seeing if she can identify what we found at the Zarafin residence. As soon as you're ready, then, we can head back to town and get the process started. I'd like to ride along with you in the helicopter, if you don't mind. It'll save time."

In answer, Ty simply nodded and proceeded back to the chopper. While Penrose climbed in via the side door, he crossed to the other side and got into the pilot's seat. A glance at Dawn told him she was in no mood to talk, so he merely took her hand in his and held it for a moment. Then he got the bird into the air once more.

At the hospital, Rafe waited as patiently as he could while Lee was taken through the admitting process, had her head injury checked out, and had her overall condition evaluated. At one point there was a scream, and he saw Maya Shilltoe push her way past a nurse who had tried to block her way into the cubicle Lee had been assigned in the emergency room. Rushing to Lee's side, she threw her arms around her, sobbing the whole time.

After Lee had assured her friend that she was okay, the nurse firmly escorted Maya out. Then they got the news that the doctor wanted to keep Lee overnight for observation. Before she allowed them to take her to her own room, however, Lee had insisted on visiting Will in his. At first, the medical personnel had balked, but when Lee had threatened to get up and walk out, they had capitulated and permitted her a brief visit with Will in his room. Rafe had waited with Naomi Preisinger just outside the room, trying to give them a little privacy. After Lee had spent just a few minutes with Will, the nurse in charge had insisted on taking Lee to her own room. Detective Noritaki joined them at that point, as Rafe had requested, and after Lee had been settled into her own room, Rafe was finally able to take her statement.

He took her through the entire story, beginning with the afternoon that she and Will had left to go on their camping trip, up to the moment she had lost consciousness in the back of the reefer truck. She faltered then and said hesitantly, "I'm surprised that my mother isn't here. Didn't anyone notify her?"

Rafe exchanged a glance with Noritaki before saying, "About that, Lee. There's something I have to tell you." As gently as he could, he told her the truth about herself and about Vivian Zarafin.

When he had finished, Lee was silent for a minute or two. Then she said slowly, "So you're saying that my real name is Marina Cimarron, and that the detective who was there when I woke up – the one who said her name was Dawn – is my sister? Are you sure?"

"As sure as we can be without the DNA results, which we're expecting in a day or two. However, there's really no question in any of our minds. Vivian Zarafin herself admitted the truth about your identity, and we have fingerprint evidence substantiating her assertion."

"What will happen to her? My moth.... I mean Vivian."

"That's up to the DA's office. I'm not sure how they'll proceed."

"What about my sister? Can I see her?"

Rafe was a little surprised that she had accepted the news about who she really was so easily, but he was relieved as well. It would make it a lot easier on Dawn when she was informed that her sister had accepted the truth and wanted to see her. So he said, "Now that I've taken your statement, you can see her as soon as you want to. She had to remove herself from the case officially when it came out that she had a personal relationship with you, but she's followed all of the developments since then as closely as possible, and when we got the lead on where Makella was holding you, she made sure that she was on the scene and as involved as protocol allowed. If you'd like, I'll contact her immediately, tell her that you'd like to see her. She's over at headquarters right now, looking over some evidence removed from the Zarafin house with Captain Penrose, the lead detective on the case."

He paused for a minute, then added, "I know for a fact that she'll want to see you as soon as possible. You know, the rest of us had given up hope that we'd ever find you alive, but not Dawn. She had her doubts from time to time, but in her heart she always believed that you were out there somewhere, and that she'd find you again. She never had you declared dead, even after all these years."

"Truly?"

"Yeah. Take my word for it: She's been waiting for this moment for sixteen years."

At headquarters, Captain Penrose allowed Dawn to review the items that had been taken from the Zarafin house. Indicating a stack of journals, he said, "She wrote it all down, D.C. Everything, from the moment it all began. Vivian was camping with her husband about a mile away, and she decided to go wading in the stream nearby. When she heard the sound of a child crying, she immediately made her way toward the sound. She found Marina at the edge of the stream, sitting on the bank and sobbing. She picked the baby up and went to check on your mother, only to discover that she was dead. It was then that the idea came to her to just take the baby away with her. She waded back up the stream to where the motor home she and her husband were traveling in was parked, with Marina in her arms. No wonder the search dogs were unable to get the scent."

"What about Marina's sweater? Why did she remove it?"

"She looked puzzled when we asked her that. According to her, Marina wasn't wearing a sweater when she found her. I guess that Marina had pulled it off before Vivian found her. In any case, she never noticed it. When she got back to the camper with the baby, her husband said that they had to notify the police at once. But Vivian refused to consider it. She'd been trying to have a child for years, without success, and she'd gotten it into her head that since she was the one who found Marina, she had the right to keep her. When her husband wouldn't go along with her at first, she got hysterical and threatened to commit suicide. He gave in after that, thinking that he'd give her a little time to think it over before trying to talk some sense into her.

"They weren't from around here; they were from New Mexico, and they had come to Colorado for a vacation. So when he couldn't persuade Vivian to give up the baby, the husband, whose name was Laurence, just started driving toward home. They were out of the area long before the first responders arrived on the scene. And on the way back to New Mexico, Laurence started considering all the ramifications of the situation. Apparently, he was desperately in love with Vivian, and her inability to have children had had a terrible effect on her. She was severely depressed, and it got even worse when they were turned down after they tried to adopt."

Captain Penrose waited to see if Dawn had any questions, but when she said nothing, he proceeded, "When they got near their home, they checked into a motel and started looking at the news, trying to find out any information about a missing child from Colorado. Well, as you know, it was a big story at the time. The fact that the rest of your family was killed and that you were the only survivor was well-known. As the days went by and the search for Marina was called off, Vivian began to think about how they could pull it off – keep the baby without any repercussions. She pointed out to her husband that they were already in trouble because they hadn't called the police immediately, as they should have. They'd crossed state lines too, so there was a possibility that they could be charged with kidnapping. Gradually, she brought him around to her way of thinking. The baby's parents were both dead, so why shouldn't they step in and raise her?"

"How did Marina handle all of that?" Dawn interjected. "I can't believe that she would have just meekly gone along with a couple of strangers."

"Well, according to the journal, Marina was inconsolable at first. Wouldn't stop crying. And she got really upset when Vivian started to call her by the new name she'd originally chosen – Anna. Marina kept insisting that her name was 'M'rena Lee'. So Vivian compromised and decided to call her Leanne." He paused for a moment, then said gently, "Kids that young – it doesn't take long for them to forget. Within a relatively short period of time, she had adjusted to the situation and accepted that Vivian and Laurence Zarafin were her parents."

"What about documents? They would have needed to produce a birth certificate when she started school," Dawn pointed out.

"Now, the way they handled that was really clever. Had a little bit of luck, too. Turns out that Laurence came from a small town just a few hours from where he and Vivian were living at the time. He knew that an old friend of his worked in the Bureau of Vital Statistics there. He went up to the old hometown one Friday and met the guy at the office. Took him out for a few drinks. Then Laurence told the other guy that he'd left his jacket back at the office. The other guy let them both back in after hours, when everyone else had gone home. Then Laurence produced a flask and persuaded his old friend to have a few more drinks. He slipped the friend a Mickey, and when the guy passed out, he searched for and found where they kept the blank birth certificates. It was a small town, and sixteen years ago they were still doing everything by hand. They didn't start recording births electronically on the computer until almost five years later. So Laurence made out the birth certificate, forged his friend's signature, and used his notary seal to make it all official. He then made a copy, which he inserted into the proper file, and waited for his friend to wake up. When his friend had recuperated enough to walk, Laurence helped him home and put him to bed. Then he drove back to his own house with what looked like a perfectly genuine birth certificate."

Penrose paused for a moment. Taking a sip of water, he continued, "Well, they couldn't show up at their own residence claiming that Vivian had just given birth to a two-and-a-half year old baby. So Vivian rented a car and took Marina with her to a little town she'd once visited in California, while Laurence went home and put their house on the market. He told the neighbors that they had spent only a few days vacationing in Colorado before deciding to spend some time in California, and that they had liked it so much that they had decided to relocate there. He was self-employed, and she wasn't working at all, so it was easier for them than for most couples. After he put their house on the market, Laurence drove back to California and rejoined Vivian. He then stayed in California and watched Marina for a few days while Vivian went back to New Mexico to arrange the details of the move. She told the neighbors that they had discovered that it would be cheaper for them to buy new furniture than to pay a moving company to move their existing stuff, so she held a moving sale and disposed of just about everything except for their clothes and a few other personal belongings.

"They found a house they liked in California and settled down there for a few years, but Marina kept coming down with all sorts of childhood ailments, and Vivian decided that they needed to move back here to Mountpelier. Her husband tried to convince her that it was a crazy idea, but she insisted. She'd gotten it into her head that Marina was like a plant that had been uprooted from its native environment and would thrive better in the area where she'd been born. She pointed out that plenty of time had passed, and there was no reason for anyone to make a connection between their six-year-old daughter and a child who had gone missing years before - one who was presumed to be dead. So Laurence gave in. They moved back here, and Marina's health improved, so they stayed. And the rest is history."

Dawn took it all in for a minute; then she said, "Rafe told me that Vivian kept the dress Marina was wearing the day she disappeared. I'd like to see it next."

Captain Penrose reached into an evidence box and pulled out an item carefully marked and wrapped in protective plastic. A tiny, bright pink sundress.

"Now, we need to go on the record for this, D.C."

Dawn nodded and waited while he turned on the recorder and went through the proper procedure for interviewing a witness. After he noted the date, the time, and the identities of those present, he began formally, "Detective Cimarron, can you identify this object?"

Dawn felt a shiver travel down her spine as she reached out, her hand hovering just over the dress. The years rolled away, and she was twelve again, watching her mother as she worked on the sewing machine in the corner of the living room at the ranch house. It still stood there, untouched now for sixteen years.

Dawn nodded. "Yes, I can identify it. This is the pink sundress my sister Marina was wearing on the day that she disappeared."

"Are you sure about this?"

"Positive. My mother..." She paused for a second or two, swallowing hard and struggling to maintain her composure. Missing only a beat, she continued, "My mother made the dress herself. We actually chose the material for it together. And if you look closely at the inside of the back yoke of the dress, you'll see that the initials *VC* have been embroidered on the seam. Those initials stand for Vana Cimarron. My mother always marked the clothes she made that way."

Penrose opened his mouth to ask another question, but broke off as Lieutenant Westbrooke entered the room. With a fake scowl, he said,

"You planning on bumping me off this case and taking it over yourself, Moe?"

She retorted in kind, "Fat chance, old man. You're not palming all this extra work off on me. You started this, you and Nick Melbourne. Now you can damn well finish it."

Turning to Dawn, she said, "How are you holding up, Detective?"

Dawn met her gaze steadily and replied, "I'm fine, Lieutenant."

"Good. I just heard from your partner. He's finished taking your sister's statement and told her the truth about who she really is. She's asking for you now, Cimarron. So get your ass over to the hospital. That's an order."

Dawn arose with alacrity. "I'm on my way, LT."

She walked toward the door, but then stopped and looked back over her shoulder as Captain Penrose called out to her, "D.C.? When things settle down a little, meet me over at Fredo's some afternoon. I'll buy you a drink. You did good work on this one, you and Rafe. All of us should get together and celebrate. And we'll make a toast to Nick, too. He trained you, the both of you, so this is his victory as much as anyone else's. Let's lift a glass or two in his memory. Wherever he is right now, I'll bet there's a grin as wide as the Colorado River on his face, now that you have Marina back again. Hell, he might even be doing cartwheels up in heaven, for all we know."

Swallowing a lump in her throat, she responded, "Thanks, Captain. I'd like that."

Passing through the door into the hallway, she looked around for Ty, who had promised to wait for her. Spying him seated on one of the hard benches at the end of the hall, she made her way toward him. He had his cell phone out and was occupying himself by playing some sort of game on it. When he caught sight of her, however, he shoved his cell back into his pocket and rose immediately. Searching her face with a keen eye, he said, "How did it go?"

"All right. He gave me some information about how Marina ended up with the Zarafins, and he had me identify a little dress that they found in Vivian Zarafin's house. It was the one Marina was wearing when she disappeared."

"Okay. So what's next?"

"I need to get over to the hospital. Rafe told Marina - Lee - everything, and she's asking for me."

"C'mon, then. I'll drive you over."

"You don't have to. I can get over there on my own."

This time it was Ty who rolled his eyes. "Right, like I'm going to let you go through this on your own. Not happening, Dawn."

"Fine. Okay. Let's get moving, then."

She didn't say much on the way to the hospital, and Ty didn't press her for details. But as they approached the hospital entrance, he said, "Shit."

Dawn, who had shut her eyes momentarily, opened them and said, "What?" But she didn't need an explanation. Standing outside the hospital entrance was a veritable army of reporters. And the last thing she felt like doing was battling her way through them.

She turned to Ty, but didn't bother to say anything, as she could practically see the wheels turning in his head. Content that he would come up with a plan for avoiding the press, she leaned back as he gunned the car past the entrance and sped away before anyone could even think about following. A few blocks down the road, he entered a parking garage and pulled into an empty slot. The security detail assigned to him that day pulled smoothly into the slot beside him. Getting out, Ty opened the door to the back seat of the other car and motioned Dawn inside. As he got in beside her, he told the driver, "Back to the hospital. There's a back entrance with a gated private parking lot that only doctors connected to the hospital are allowed to use. Take us there."

The driver nodded, but said skeptically, "How do you plan on us getting past the gate?"

"Dad sits on the board, and The Lewellen Group has a part-ownership in this particular hospital. We've done it before. Just pull up, tell them that you're Lewellen Security, and hand them my ID. They'll let us through."

Ty pulled his driver's license out of his pocket and handed it to the driver, who grunted, pulled out of the parking space, and made his way to the exit of the garage. Ty ducked down out of sight, and Dawn followed suit. It was not a long trip back to the hospital, and accessing the hospital by way of the private back lot worked out according to plan. They both sat up again as soon as they passed the gate, and exited as soon as the car pulled up to the entrance. Once they were inside, Ty led the way to a bank of elevators. Pushing the *Up* button, he asked Dawn, "What floor?"

Dawn said blankly, "I forgot to ask. Give me a minute and I'll text Rafe."

Ty waited patiently, and then just as the elevator doors opened, she said, "Fifth floor. Room 5421."

It seemed to Dawn that it took them forever, but it was actually less than a minute later when they arrived at the fifth floor and began walking down the hall toward Room 5421. When they got to it, Dawn paused for a moment just outside the door.

"You want me to go in with you?"

Dawn considered, then shook her head. "Not this first time. I think I need to talk to her alone."

"Okay. We passed a waiting area on the way here. I'll wait for you there."

The door stood halfway open, so Dawn gave it a little tap and then entered the room. Rafe and Maya Shilltoe were sitting in the chairs on either side of the bed, but they both stood up immediately when they saw Dawn. She saw Maya bend down and whisper something into Lee's ear and Lee shake her head in response. Maya gave her a quick kiss on the cheek and said, "I'm going down to check out the vending machines and get a little snack. I'll be back soon, Lee." She didn't stop to talk, but just nodded at Rafe and Dawn as she left the room.

Rafe, meanwhile, glanced from her to Lee and said, "I'll leave the two of you alone for a while, let you get reacquainted."

As he passed by Dawn, he gave her arm an encouraging squeeze. Once he had left, Dawn slowly made her way to the side of the bed.

"Hi," she said.

There was an awkward pause while she waited for Marina – no, *Lee*, she reminded herself – to respond.

Lee was feeling the awkwardness of the situation as well, so she blurted out the first thing that came to her mind. "We don't look very much alike." Then she flushed and said, "Sorry. That didn't come out quite like I meant it."

Swallowing the lump that was threatening to choke her up, Dawn replied, "That's okay. And you're right. At first glance, we don't look much alike at all. You have Dad's coloring, and I take more after Mom. Dad was blond-haired and blue-eyed, just like you. I got Mom's dark hair and brown eyes. But there is a resemblance. If you look carefully, you'll see it in the shape of our faces and around the nose and the mouth."

After considering her for a minute, Lee said, "I guess you're right." She was silent for a minute, and then asked hesitantly, "Do you have a picture of them? Our parents, I mean."

"Not with me, no. But I have plenty at home. I can bring some with me tomorrow."

"Sergeant Melbourne said that we had a brother, too."

"Yes – Josiah. I have a family portrait of all of us together. It's sitting on the nightstand next to my bed. I'll bring it with me tomorrow as well."

"I'd like that," Lee said. And then she added wistfully, "When I was growing up, I always wanted a sister."

Dawn reached out and grasped Lee's hand. Giving it a squeeze, she said, "You've always had a sister, Lee. You just didn't always *know* that you had one."

When Dawn entered the waiting room, she was surprised to find Maeve and Sloan sitting there with Ty. They all stood up when she walked in, and Maeve immediately came forward. Placing a gentle hand on Dawn's arm, she inquired, "How did it go?"

"Pretty well, actually," Dawn replied. She looked around and then inquired, "Did Rafe go back to the station?"

"Yes. He said that he had a mountain of paperwork to do before he could call it a night. So everything went well with your sister?"

Dawn nodded. "She asked me a little bit about the family, and I told her about all of you and about Aunt Mattie and Uncle Pete. She said she'd like to meet everybody, but not quite yet. She's still getting used to the idea that she's not who she thought she was for all those years. It's not as hard on her as I thought it would be, though I suspect it would be a lot more difficult if Laurence Zarafin were still alive and facing charges along with Vivian. It turns out that she was much closer to him than to her. She and Vivian have had a rocky relationship for years. Apparently, Vivian was extremely possessive of Lee while she was growing up. That, along with her drinking problem, drove a wedge between them. Can't say that I'm sorry about that, by the way."

"What about her physical health?"

"She's in pretty good shape, actually. She sustained a blow to the head when she fought with Makella while attempting to escape. Though it bled a lot, the doctors don't think that she has a concussion, but they're keeping her overnight just to be sure. She has a few other bumps and bruises from when she hit the floor of the garage and from when Makella tossed her into the back of the truck, but nothing else major. Up until her escape attempt, Makella apparently didn't hurt her at all, which is good news. It'll make the recovery process a lot easier."

"Are you staying with her tonight?"

Dawn shook her head. "No. Her friend Maya came back, and she promised to stay with Lee unless the nurses kick her out. I decided that Lee's had enough for one day, so I told her that I needed to get going and promised to come back first thing in the morning. She said she'd like that, so I said goodnight and left." Looking at her watch, Dawn exclaimed, "I had no idea it was so late. I guess that we should all head for home." When she saw Ty exchanging looks with his parents, she said, "What do you know that I don't?"

"There are reporters in our neighborhood, on the street outside our house, Dawn."

"There are? We live in a gated community, damn it! How did they get in?"

"At a guess, some of them must have friends or acquaintances in the neighborhood and used them to get past the guard at the gate. And as long as they stay on the street and don't set foot on our property, we'd have trouble making them leave, Dawn. Freedom of the press and all of that, you know."

"Okay, so what's the plan? Do we check into a hotel?"

"That's what I suggested at first," Maeve interjected. "I thought it would be best if you just came back to the hotel with me. But when I called over there to see about getting you a suite close to mine, the man at the desk said that there are reporters camped out there as well. So Sloan came up with another idea. He suggested that we all go back to his house, stay with him for a few days. I think it's a good plan, myself."

Dawn looked at Ty. "What do you think?"

He shrugged. "I'm fine with going over to Dad's, but it's up to you, Dawn."

A slow smile spread across her face. "I'd love to see any reporter try to get past Sloan's security. Okay, let's do it. But what about Brody?"

"I already talked to Brody," Maeve said. "He's fine with the idea."

"Sounds like a plan, then." Turning to Sloan, she said, "Thanks. Staying with you for a couple of days will sure save us a lot of unwanted attention."

Ty moved forward and put an arm around Dawn's waist. "Let's move out then." To his father, he said, "I'll tell the guys who brought Dawn and me in to swing over and pick up Brody. He went back to Fredo's while Dawn and I were at headquarters. Then Dawn and I can ride back with you and Mom, if that's okay with you, Dad."

"Sure. There's plenty of room. We came in the limo."

Dawn was happy to hear that. Behind the blacked-out windows of the limo, they would all be safe from prying eyes. Then she had a thought. "What about Marina? Lee, I mean. I wouldn't put it past some reporter to sneak up here and try to get an interview with her."

"Good point. Now that Rafe has gone, I wouldn't put it past them either," Ty affirmed.

"I could station a couple of Lewellen Security guards outside the door," Sloan suggested. "Tell them to check with Lee before allowing anyone into the room."

It only took a few seconds for Dawn to weigh the idea in her mind. "All right. Let me run it by her first, see if she's okay with it. Be right back."

She returned within minutes. "Lee's okay with the idea. She hadn't thought about the fact that reporters might try to get in and bother her. She was a little floored at the thought of having her own private security team, and she was also afraid of imposing at first, but I managed to talk her around. She said to tell you that she accepts your offer with thanks, Sloan, and she'd like to meet you tomorrow and thank you personally, if you're not too busy."

"I'll make the time. She's family now, Dawn."

Dawn was touched and found it difficult to speak, so she merely took his hand for a moment. Then she turned to Ty and said, "Come on. Let's blow this joint." She and Ty led the way, with Maeve and Sloan following.

The limo was waiting for them at the door, and they climbed into the back quickly. Ty paused for a moment to speak briefly to the team who had driven him and Dawn to the hospital; then he got in as well. The limo pulled away from the curb smoothly, and they were on their way.

The drive to Sloan's house took about half an hour, so Dawn leaned back against the cushions and closed her eyes. *Just for a minute*, she thought. *Just for a minute...*

When she opened her eyes again, she was surprised to find herself at her father-in-law's front door. Turning to Ty, she looked a question at him. He shrugged in response and said, "You were out for the whole trip here, Dawn. Come on, let's get out and get you up to bed."

He held out his hand and helped her out of the limo and through the front door, where Sloan and Maeve were waiting for them. She presumed that Brody must have arrived ahead of them and already gone to his room, as he was nowhere in sight. Pausing briefly to hug and kiss her father and mother-in-law goodnight, she followed Ty up the stairs to a suite on the second floor. She passed through the sitting room with barely a glance and proceeded directly into the bedroom beyond. Tossing her jacket onto a chair beside the bed and carefully placing her weapon on top of it, she was surprised to see some of her own toiletries set out on a vanity nearby.

Seeing her bewilderment, Ty said, "I called Mrs. T. right after Mom and Dad and I first started discussing spending the night here, asked her to pack some things for both of us. After you gave the okay, I called and arranged for everything to be sent over here while you were talking over Dad's offer to provide some security guards for Lee."

"Oh. Good idea. I never even thought about what we were going to do about stuff for tonight and tomorrow morning." She walked over to the closet to check out the clothes Mrs. Tilner had provided, wandered into the bathroom to inspect things in there, and came back into the bedroom to examine the contents of the dresser. The fatigue she had experienced earlier in the limo seemed to have vanished, and she continued to prowl about the room restlessly. Ty stood in the doorway, watching patiently and waiting. He made a mental note to call Nolan and Sylvia Drizedale in the morning, schedule an appointment with them. Dawn was going to need to talk about this, and experience had taught him that the best place for her to do that was in a counseling session. But his wife wasn't going to wait for a counseling appointment to blow off some steam. He knew all the signs and symptoms. She had contained her emotions pretty well since her initial crying jag at Fredo's, but now an explosion was imminent.

He didn't have to wait long. Whirling around and facing him, Dawn said sharply, "Do you know what that Zarafin bitch had the nerve to say,

Ty? She said that she was a *good mother* to Lee. I'd like to go over there right now and shake her, make her face the truth. After I'd bashed her face in a couple of times, I'd say to her, 'You were never her mother! Her mother's name is Vana Cimarron! You had no right to her!'"

Ty crossed over to her and caught her arms, tried to draw her close. But she resisted, pounding on his chest while she continued her rant.

"Captain Penrose told me that she'd watched all the newscasts, read all of the articles about the case. She knew why the search for Marina was called off, what the police believed had happened to her, but she still didn't come forward and do the right thing. She tortured us - Aunt Mattie and me and everybody else who cared about Marina. Sixteen years, Ty! She let us go on believing the worst for sixteen years!"

She kept it up for a little while longer, but eventually stopped pounding and dropped her hands to her sides, the rage she felt apparently expended somewhat. He put his arms around her and stroked her back, but said nothing. Eventually she lifted her head and scrubbed her hands over her face. Pulling out of his arms, she crossed over to the nightstand by the side of the bed, where a pitcher of water and a couple of glasses stood. She poured out a glass of water and gulped some down. Then she took a deep breath and said, "I pounded on you again, took it all out on you. I'm sorry."

"Yeah, and it's a great big deal, too. What with me being so delicate and all. But if you want to make it up to me, feel free."

Dawn's head snapped up as she looked him right in the eye. "Feel free? Are you kidding? You *let* me pound all over you. You could have stopped me at any time, and we both know it. You're not getting make-up sex over something so trivial."

Good, Ty thought. *That distracted her*. He put his most innocent face on, the one he knew she could see right through, and said in a wounded tone, "You pounded on me. You just admitted it. Shouldn't you have to do something to make up for it?"

She slammed the glass down, walked over to the dresser and drew back her foot to kick it before remembering that she was a guest in someone else's house. Spinning around, she said, "I can't believe that you're thinking about sex at a time like this."

"Why not? You just found your sister after sixteen years. I'd say that calls for a celebration. And what better way to celebrate than with sex?"

Exasperated, Dawn said, "Don't you ever think about anything else?"

"Of course I do. Let's see, there's sports, jet planes, helicopters, fast cars, food, television, and beer. See? Lots of other stuff up in the old noggin besides sex. But you can't blame a guy if sex gets top billing."

Stalking over to the vanity and picking up the hairbrush, she ran it through her hair a couple of times, then winged it across the room in his direction, but not directly at him, Ty noted. It passed a good two inches to his right. Sighing, he walked over to the bed and flopped down on his back. Lacing his fingers behind his head, he said speculatively, "Looks like you're all wound up and just full of vim and vigor tonight, Dawn. If you want to get a good night's sleep, you could go outside and take a brisk walk around the grounds before turning in for the night. But if you'd rather stay here, I think I could come up with a more creative and satisfying way for both of us to wind down."

At that one, Dawn choked and tried to stifle something between a gasp and a giggle. Taking that as a sign of encouragement, Ty picked up a pillow from the bed and hurled it at her. She caught it easily.

"You want to start a pillow fight? Fine." She flew across the room, leaped onto the bed, and began pummeling him mercilessly. He took it for a while, then wrested the pillow from her and tossed it aside. Pulling her down on her back beside him, he linked hands with her. She didn't resist, but simply lay there quietly beside him, staring up at the ceiling. He gave it a minute or two, then said, "Feeling better now?"

"Yeah."

"Tired enough to turn in and get a good night's sleep?"

"No."

He waited another minute, then said, "Offer's still open, if you're interested."

She turned her head to look at him. "You know what I'm going to do first thing in the morning? I'm going to go on the Internet, find a website that defines the word *incorrigible*, and paste your picture right next to it."

"Yeah, that's what they all say."

"There'd better not be any 'all' about it, buster. Just you and me."

"Always and forever, Dawn. That's what we promised, remember?"

"I remember." *Ah, what the hell*, she thought. Maybe he was right. Turning her head so that she was facing him, she said, "We need to be clear about a few things. First of all, you're about as delicate as ... as ..."

Frustrated, she said, "What did I compare you to the last time we had this conversation?"

"I've never claimed to be delicate before. The last time, I said that you hurt my sensitive feelings. And you responded that I was about as sensitive as a rhinoceros."

"Okay, so I can't use that one again. I'm going to have to think of another one. Something with a really, really, hard head and a thick hide." She furrowed her brow in concentration.

"Elephant?" Ty suggested. "Wild boar? Hippopotamus?"

"Hippopotamus. Yeah, that's a good one. You're about as delicate as a hippopotamus, Tyrell Lewellen. Second," she continued, "this is not make-up sex. It's a celebration. You got that?"

"Oh, absolutely, Dawn."

"Third..."

"There's more?"

"You bet. Third... Oh, crap – I forgot what I was going to say."

"It'll come back to you," he said in a comforting tone of voice. She decided that whatever the third thing was, it could wait. It was time for action, not words. So she rolled over on top of him, fitted her mouth to his, kissed him with all the heat that was welling up inside of her. And then it was just the two of them. *Always and forever*, she thought, just before she lost the power to think coherently at all.

Chapter 13

As he walked up the sidewalk to Vaughn Makella's house in the wee hours of the morning, Sergeant Joel Chernet was met half-way by a man whom he recognized as his counterpart in the Vermont State Police, Sergeant Marcus Oppenwall.

"Chernet?" After a brief nod from the other, he said, "I'm Oppenwall." Inclining his head toward the house, he said, "From the photographs you sent us, we're pretty certain that one of them is yours."

"How many total? You didn't mention it when we talked earlier."

"Five. We've already positively ID'd one of them – Alissa Gordena. We're fairly certain that another is Crystal Rogar. If you can identify a third, that'll leave us only two more to go."

"Thanks for letting me come in and check out the scene in person. The Michigan State Police appreciates the cooperation."

Oppenwall shrugged. "Coroner's been here and the crime scene techs have finished processing the scene, but they haven't taken them away yet. So you might as well come on in." Oppenwall led the way into the house and proceeded downstairs to the basement. Crossing to the back wall, he indicated a large door. "We found them in there. According to the records, Makella had it installed six years ago."

He slid the door open, and Chernet found himself inside a large, walk-in freezer, of the type he had previously seen only in commercial properties like grocery stores and food production plants. There were built-in shelves lining the walls. And five of the shelves were occupied. Slowly making his way across the floor, he scanned the bodies laid out on the first two. Shaking his head, he shifted his glance to the third. Blowing out a breath and running a hand over his brow, he approached the figure that lay on the third shelf, staring down at it for a long minute.

"That your girl?"

Chernet nodded and said, "That's her. Tamara Norti. I've known for a long time now that there wasn't a ghost of a chance of finding her alive, but I never imagined I'd find her like this."

He bent down to examine her more closely. She was lying flat on her back, with her arms crossed over her chest. She was still wearing the clothes she'd had on when she disappeared, and from what Chernet could make out from her frozen features, she looked peaceful enough. So there was a chance, at least, that the sick bastard who had taken her hadn't tortured or assaulted her before he had robbed her of her life. A small comfort, perhaps, but at least it was something that he could offer to her family.

Straightening up, he asked, "Was the coroner able to determine anything about the cause of death? Beyond the obvious, I mean."

Oppenwall shook his head. "Not yet. He'll have to get the bodies back to the lab first, thaw them out. He'll be able to tell us more after he does the autopsies." Looking around and indicating the empty shelves, he added, "If he hadn't been caught, that girl in Colorado would've ended up on one of those shelves next. And who knows how many others? Looking up at Chernet, who topped him by a good six inches, Oppenwall inquired, "Has he said anything yet to the Colorado cops?"

"Not yet. When I talked to Rafe Melbourne last night, he said that Makella's psychiatrist had heard about the arrest on the news and had immediately gotten in touch with them, insisting that if he had gone off his medication, Makella wasn't competent enough to make a decision about getting legal representation. He demanded that they get Makella an attorney and arrange for a psychiatric evaluation before they question him. Given Makella's history of mental problems, the District Attorney's office decided to do just that. No point in getting a confession out of him only to have a judge throw it out on the grounds that he wasn't competent."

"What about the victim? Was she in good enough shape to be interviewed?"

"Yeah. Melbourne didn't go into the particulars, but he said that the girl was able to give them a full and detailed statement, enough to hopefully put Makella away for a long, long time."

"And Sergeant Melbourne's partner? Is it true that the victim's turned out to be some sort of long-lost relative, or is that just a rumor that the press is trying to turn into their usual media circus?"

"It's no rumor; it's been confirmed. Turns out that the victim, Leanne Zarafin, really is Detective Cimarron's sister, who went missing sixteen years ago. It's almost enough to make me believe in that karma shit. Anyway, Melbourne says that the press has pounced on the story like a bunch of hungry jackals on the scent of fresh meat, so Cimarron has holed up at her father-in-law's place. He's some sort of business magnate, lives in a mansion on a private estate surrounded by really high walls and patrolled by his own private security company. Must be nice, having a place like that to retreat to whenever you want to escape from an army of asshole reporters."

It was still dark out when Lee awoke. She yawned for a minute, then sat up and swung out of bed. Moving to the window, she pulled the drapes aside and looked out. The sky was lightening in the east, promising that dawn would be breaking any minute. She thought about going back to bed, but rejected that idea. There was no way she would be able to get back to sleep, not until she'd seen Will again, at least. She'd slipped downstairs last night after Maya had left and spent some time with him. They'd talked for a while, and he'd been astonished when she told him what she'd found out about her past, how she'd just met her sister. Then a nurse had come in to do something to Will's leg, and she'd had to leave. They had not had nearly enough time together, she thought.

Grabbing the robe and slippers that Maya had run home to get for her, she crossed to the door. The two security guards standing there had introduced themselves to her last night as Frank and Steve. When they saw her, they both smiled, and Frank said, "Good morning, Lee. How are you feeling today?"

"Better, thanks. Uh – I'm going to run downstairs for a few minutes to check on Will, see how he's doing. If my friend Maya shows up while I'm out, would you let her know where I've gone?"

"Sure thing. I'll just walk down with you. Steve here can keep an eye out for your friend."

He fell into step beside her as she walked down the corridor to the elevator. They rode down to the third floor together, and soon she was outside the door to Will's room.

"I'm just going to peek in on him. If he's asleep, I won't disturb him, but if he's awake, I'll probably be staying for a while."

"Okay. I'll wait for you out here."

Will's eyes were closed when she tip-toed in, but he opened them immediately when she approached the bed.

"Hi," he said huskily.

"Hi. How are you feeling today?"

"Well, yesterday I felt like a truck ran over me, and today I just feel like crap, so I suppose that's an improvement. You?"

"Just a little headache, that's all. They're talking about releasing me later today. I guess I got off easier than you did."

"I'm not so sure about that. Come here." In a surprise move, he tugged on her hand and pulled her into the bed with him.

"Will! I can't be in bed with you in the hospital! I'm pretty sure it's against all sorts of rules!"

"Screw the rules. Seriously, what are they going to do to us if they catch us? Drug me and push me over a cliff? Abduct you and chain you to a wall? Oh, wait a minute: been there, done that. So let the hospital staff do their worst."

"Well, I guess if you put it that way..." She was silent for a moment, then she said, "I've got something to confess to you, Will...I think I'm in love with you."

"Well, that's a problem."

Whatever she had expected, it wasn't that. Insulted, she tried to get out of the bed, but Will held her tight and said, "Ask me why it's a problem."

"Okay, I'll bite. Why is it a problem that I think I'm in love with you?"

"It's a problem because you only *think* you are, when I'm damn sure that I'm in love with you."

When Ty strolled into the family dining room for breakfast, he discovered that Sloan, Maeve, Brody, Lotti, and Echo had all arrived before him. The only thing surprising about that situation was that Brody was peacefully occupying the same room with Sloan Lewellen. Ty made another mental note to himself, this time to check the news and see if hell had frozen over. Given how the big guy felt about his dad, he'd been hesitant the night before when his mother had proposed extending the invitation of spending the night at Sloan's house to Brody. However, Maeve must have said something, somehow persuaded him to soften his attitude toward Sloan a little. Which was a good thing, Ty mused. It wasn't easy on a guy when he knew that one of his best friend's fondest wishes was to kick his father's ass.

"Morning, everyone." Passing by Echo in her highchair on his way to where breakfast was laid out on the sideboard, he ran his hand over her silky hair. She looked up at him and grinned, gurgling something unintelligible while stuffing a handful of some sort of weird looking mini-toast into her mouth.

After he'd gotten himself some coffee, filled his plate, and taken a seat at the table next to Brody, Maeve asked, "How's Dawn this morning, Ty?"

"Fine. She's up and dressed, but she needed to make some calls before coming down. She's already talked to her Aunt Mattie and to Lee this morning, and now she's on the phone with Rafe." He stopped for a moment to take a sip of coffee and eat a couple of strips of bacon. "Man, that's good. Anyway, we're going to the hospital right after breakfast to check on Lee, find out what her plans are after she's discharged."

He broke off as his wife appeared at the door of the dining room.

"Good morning, Dawn," Maeve said. "Did you sleep well?"

"God, yes. Better than I have in years." Making her way to the sideboard, Dawn provided herself with some coffee and toast and then moved to the table and took a seat across from Ty.

After she'd had a chance to drink some of her coffee and take a few bites of her toast, Sloan said, "Ty was just telling us that the first thing on your agenda this morning is to go to the hospital to see your sister. I thought I'd come along with you, if that's okay."

Dawn nodded. "Fine with me. I was hoping that Maeve could come along as well. Then I could introduce Lee to both of you at the same time."

"As long as you don't think it will be too overwhelming for her, Dawn," said Maeve.

"I don't think it will be. She seems to be amazingly resilient. That's one thing that hasn't changed. She was like that even when she was a baby. Nothing much seemed to faze her for long." She finished off her toast and then frowned. "The bad news is that Chief Wirthing is holding a press conference this morning about both cases and has asked me to be present, say a few words. I'm not real happy about it, but what the Chief wants, the Chief gets."

"How are you planning on handling it?" Sloan inquired.

Dawn shrugged. "The Chief is going to give a statement that sounds like a big deal, but really only confirms some of the details that the press has already dug out on its own. Then I'm going to tell them that I visited my sister in the hospital last night; yes, she is doing well, and yes, it was a joyful reunion. When they ask me how I feel, I'm going to resist the temptation to point out what a stupid question that is, and reply that I am ecstatic that my sister has been found alive and well after all these years. When they ask me about Vivian Zarafin, I'm going to give them the line about how I can't make any comment about an ongoing case. Then I'm going to tell them that Lee and I need some time to get re-acquainted and ask them to cut us a break and allow us to deal with the personal aspects of this case in the privacy of our family. If they ask if and when Lee is going to make a statement, I'll tell them that Lee doesn't want to talk to anyone but friends and family right now, and to please respect that. Then I'm going to smile and politely refuse to answer any more questions."

"That's good, that's good, Dawn." Sloan hesitated for a minute before inquiring, "Mind if I make a suggestion?" When she inclined her head in assent, he said, "Consider satisfying the worst of public curiosity by having a picture taken of you and Lee together at the hospital and releasing it to the media. Once they have that, they might be more inclined to leave you alone for a while. Just a thought."

Dawn thought it over for a minute. "You may be right. I'll talk it over with Lee, see how she feels about it. In the meantime, what about you and Maeve, Sloan? You two are going to be pestered for comments and information almost as much as we are."

Sloan glanced over at Maeve, who gave him a nod. "We've been talking about that. If it's okay with you, we're going to release a statement saying that we are rejoicing with our daughter-in-law now that she has found her sister and that we look forward to welcoming Lee into the family. Then we're also going to make a plea of our own for privacy. And if you do decide to release a picture, it might be a good idea to let us handle that as well. That way, it reinforces that this is a family matter, quite apart from your role as a member of the Mountpelier Police Force. What do you think?"

Dawn turned and said, "Ty?"

"I like it. Dad's right; the public needs to see that we're handling this as a family, and that you and Lee are part of that family. It'll give the plea for privacy a little more impact, a little more punch."

"Okay, then. If Lee agrees, that's what we'll do." Drinking the last of her coffee and placing her napkin beside her plate, Dawn pushed back from the table and got to her feet. To Lotti and Brody, she said apologetically, "I just realized that I've barely said a word to either of you. I'm sorry; I didn't mean to be rude."

Lotti smiled and said, "Don't worry about it, Dawn. If anyone has an excuse to be a little preoccupied and skip the social niceties right now, it's you. Go and see your sister. I'll look forward to meeting her, when she's ready to be introduced to the rest of the family."

Brody added, "Uh – same thing. What she said."

"We're good, then." Turning to Ty, she said, "Ready?"

"Yep. Mom and Dad?"

"Just let me run upstairs for a minute or two and get a few things. I'll meet you outside," Maeve said.

"Thank God that when your mother says she'll only be a minute or two, she means it literally," Sloan commented. He led the way to the door and into the waiting limo. Maeve joined them almost immediately, and Sloan signaled the driver to head out.

.

When they reached the hospital, they used the back entrance again and went straight up to Lee's room. Dawn introduced her sister to Ty and his parents, and Lee thanked Sloan profusely for the security guards he had provided. After that, it didn't take Sloan long to persuade Lee to join the rest of the family at his house. Seeing that Lee was comfortable with her family, Dawn felt better when she had to excuse herself in order to attend the press conference at headquarters. After promising to rejoin the others at Sloan's house as soon as she could, she went on her way to the station, where the press conference went pretty much as planned. When it was over, she went upstairs with Rafe, who had also been present at the press conference, with the intention of finishing the reports on both the Torrense and Makella cases. As they walked into the bullpen, the first person they saw was Ralph Sokoto. When he caught sight of Dawn and Rafe, Sokoto immediately dived off his chair and plopped down on the floor.

"I've fallen, and I can't get up," he moaned, in a good imitation of Brody's performance when Sokoto had found him lying prone on top of Vaughn Makella.

A universal groan went up from everyone else in the bullpen. "For God's sake, give it a rest, Sok," Prentiss said. Turning to Dawn and Rafe, he explained, "He's been doing that all morning. Every time we turn around, there he is on the floor again, repeating that same line."

"I can't help it, Prentiss. You should have been there. Finding our suspect down, with a seven foot giant on crutches lying on top of him, that was pretty good. But when he cracked that line, it was priceless. What a parody!"

"I'm so glad to hear that your work schedule allows you to give amateur theatrical performances while you are on the job, Detective Sokoto. Since you seem to have so much extra time on your hands, perhaps I'm not keeping you busy enough?" Lieutenant Westbrooke said from the doorway of her office.

Knowing his lieutenant, Sokoto replied, "Uh, well, LT, you'll be happy to know that you just caught my final command performance of the day. My shoulder will be firmly applied to the detective wheel from here on in."

"I'm glad to hear it." Turning to Dawn, she said, "Cimarron? In my office." Once they were both inside and seated in her office, Moe said, "I wish I'd thought to record him on my cell phone before I encouraged him to cut it out. It really was kind of funny." On a more serious note, she asked, "How's your sister today, Detective?"

"Much better, Lieutenant. They're releasing her from the hospital shortly, and she's going to stay with us at my father-in-law's house for a while."

"Good. Have you been informed about the developments regarding the suspect's house in Vermont?"

"Yes, my partner updated me when I spoke to him on the phone first thing this morning. He told me about Alissa Gordena, Crystal Rogar, and Tamara Norti. What about the other two girls they found? Have they identified them?"

Lieutenant Westbrooke shook her head. "No – not yet. It may take some time for them to do so. Meanwhile, Vaughn Makella has been arraigned on the charges relating to your sister and Will Preisinger. Everything else is on hold now, pending the outcome of the psychiatric examination. He may get off, you know. In his case, the insanity defense might just work. How are you going to deal with it if that happens?"

Dawn replied, "If he truly is insane, I don't really care if he goes to prison. I'd be just as happy to see him confined to a mental institution.

But I will do everything in my power to see to it that he is never released. Even if in the future they claim he's cured, he should never be allowed to walk the streets again as a free man. I don't particularly want to see him suffer; I just want to make sure that he doesn't ever get a chance to hurt anyone else, ever again. In the meantime, as soon as I finish up the paperwork and attend the arraignment for Monieque Torrense, I'm putting in for a few days off, LT. I've got sixteen years worth of catching up to do with my sister."

"Good idea. Speaking of the Torrense case, we just heard from Monieque Torrense's sister-in-law. Now there's a woman who doesn't waste any time. Right after she was informed about the arrest yesterday, she petitioned to have her brother's body exhumed. Apparently, she has some clout in her hometown. That, coupled with Cullen's letter and the fact that Monieque has been charged with her son's murder, was enough to have a judge grant her petition. They exhumed the body last night, and Ellanor Torrense paid top dollar for a private autopsy to be done right away. Results just came in. Arsenic. Poor guy was loaded with it."

"How did the doctors at the hospital miss it?"

"Monieque and Cullen's father were away visiting friends in her hometown at the time, remember? It turns out that the primary care physician on the case was Monieque's godfather. He apparently doted on her, was putty in her hands. You can bet that the bitch planned it that way, waited to administer the killing dose of arsenic while they were away from home and her husband was under her godfather's care, just to head off any chance of an autopsy. Apparently, the doctor did initially want to have one done, because Cullen's father was so young and died so suddenly. But Monieque pitched a fit at the very suggestion. She reminded her godfather that her husband had suffered from pancreatitis for years, and it was obviously the cause of death. Told him she couldn't bear the thought of having him cut open, begged him not to request an autopsy. In the end, he gave in and signed the death certificate. And then she was home free. Or so she thought. But now that arsenic has been found, I wouldn't be surprised to find that there'll be some additional charges leveled against Monieque shortly."

"What about the charges against Vivian Zarafin? Has the DA decided what he's going to do yet?"

"He has. Kidnapping. Second degree, Class 4."

"And the Feds?"

"No decision from them yet. I don't know if they'll go through with pressing charges. They may take into account the fact that there was no ransom demand and that there doesn't appear to have been any physical or sexual abuse in this particular case. We'll have to sit tight, let them interview your sister, see what they decide. It's early days still on that one, Cimarron. Have you thought about how it might affect your sister, having the woman whom she regarded as her mother for sixteen years be charged with kidnapping?"

"I'm not sure how she'll handle it. I do know that the two of them were not particularly close, especially during the last few years, since Laurence Zarafin died. So I'm hoping that it won't affect her too adversely. When it comes to the case against Vivian, though, I'm going to let Rafe handle communicating the details to Lee. It's better if I keep out of it entirely."

"Agreed. Well, if you want to file those reports before it's time for you to leave for Monieque Torrense's arraignment, you'd better get started, Cimarron. Dismissed."

Dawn had just exited the courtroom after the conclusion of the arraignment for Monieque Torrense when she heard someone call, "Detective Cimarron!" Thinking that it was a reporter calling her name, Dawn kept walking toward the elevator that would take her to the ground floor of the courthouse. She'd fended off a ton of reporters already, smiling and repeating "No comment" until she thought they'd finally given up on trying to get her to add to the statement she'd made at the press conference earlier. She was in no mood to tangle with any more reporters. Now that she'd had the satisfaction of seeing Monieque Torrense indicted on murder charges, she just wanted to get back to Sloan's house and join the others. Aunt Mattie and Uncle Pete were on their way, and she wanted to be there to introduce them to Lee.

"Detective Cimarron!" she heard again. Annoyed, she turned around to face the pesky reporter who wouldn't give up. But her expression changed when she saw that it was Gwen Mallinder who was hurrying down the hallway toward her.

"Thanks for stopping," Gwen said. "I just wanted to thank you."

Given the girl's attitude during their previous encounters, that was the last thing Dawn had expected. Gwen must have read her expression, because she flushed and said, "I guess you're surprised. I haven't been very nice to you, have I?"

Recovering, Dawn said smoothly, "Being nice is overrated. But courtesy? That's something you won't get far in life without, Gwen."

"Yeah, that's what Cullen's Aunt Ellanor says. You should have heard her on the phone, persuading that judge to grant the exhumation order. She was really persistent, but she managed to stay polite the whole time. I've got to learn how to do that. You've heard the news, haven't you? About Cullen's dad?"

"Yes, I was informed about that development this morning."

"I'm glad that she'll go down for that as well as for killing Cullen. But I'm pissed off about my own father. According to everyone I've spoken to, there's not enough evidence to charge her with killing my dad. Even though everybody knows she did it. Ellanor told me to wait and get the trial transcripts and then file a civil suit for wrongful death against Monieque. She said that in a civil case there doesn't need to be guilt without a possible doubt, like in a criminal case – only a preponderance of evidence. And if Monieque's found guilty of killing Cullen and his dad just to get her hands on their money, it would add weight to the case. But it's not enough! I want that monster to suffer, to go down for killing my dad too! I hate her so much that I have trouble sleeping at night. I can't seem to think about anything else."

Pausing for a minute to compose herself, she went on, "I heard about you – about how your sister was kidnapped, about how the rest of your family was killed. How did you deal with it?"

Dawn took a moment to consider how much she wanted to reveal to this girl. Finally, she decided to tell her the complete truth.

"After my parents and my brother were killed, all I could think about was getting revenge on the boys who did it. I used to fantasize about different ways to torture them, make them hurt as much as I did."

Gwen looked startled. "You did? You actually thought about torturing them?"

Dawn nodded. "I was so full of hate, wanting revenge so bad that I could practically taste it."

"Do you still feel that way?"

Dawn met Gwen's eyes and said, "No. My aunt arranged for me to get some counseling on a regular basis, and the counselor convinced me that those boys had done enough damage to my family. If I had given way and acted on my desire for revenge, or even allowed the thought of it to continue to obsess me, I would be helping them to destroy the happiness of the only member of my family who had survived – me. I learned that I had to let it go, turn the page, and get on with my life. They were sent to prison, and that had to be enough."

Gwen responded, "I don't know if that will be enough for me. But I'll think about what you said." She shifted from one foot to the other and looked down at the floor uncomfortably, and Dawn thought that she had finished what she wanted to say. But then Gwen looked up again, met Dawn's eyes, and said, "You know, all those years, I thought of Cullen as an aggressor. It turns out, though, that Cullen was a victim too. When he was a kid, he was just a victim in waiting. It must have shocked the hell out of him when his mother turned on him. He may have been a little monster when he was younger, but he didn't spoil himself, and he didn't deserve to die like that. I want justice for him, now that I realize that it takes a monster to create a monster. You can't let the monsters get away with it. You have to fight them. If I let go of my anger, it would be like giving up the fight."

Dawn replied, "Be careful. There's an old saying that goes something like this:

'He who fights with monsters must take care lest he thereby become a monster. And if you gaze for long into an abyss, the abyss gazes also into you'." She watched and waited, giving Gwen some time to reflect on what she had said, then added gently, "Be careful that your anger against Monieque doesn't become an abyss of hatred that you can't climb out of again, Gwen. That's the last thing your father would want."

"I'll have to think about that. You're right about one thing, though – my dad would want me to be happy."

"You know, there are support groups out there for family members of murder victims. I could give you some information on them, if you like."

"Uh... sure. Okay. Maybe it would help." The elevator arrived just then, and they stepped inside and rode it down together. As they were getting off on the ground floor, Gwen asked, "Is that why you became a cop? Because of what happened to your family?"

"Yes. I doubt if I would have even considered it as a career if I hadn't lost my family the way I did."

"But you found your sister, right? Does that help?"

"It does. But now, like you, I have to deal with my feelings toward the person who took her and kept her from me all those years. You're not the only one struggling with the desire for revenge, Gwen."

"How are you dealing with it?"

"The same way I eventually learned to deal with the loss of the rest of my family. Let the justice system take care of it, and move on."

"Oh... You know, that quote you talked about earlier – the one about monsters? I think I've heard it before, on TV or something. Who said it?"

"Nietzsche. I don't agree with most of his philosophy, but he did come up with a couple of winners. Here's another good one: '*If it doesn't kill you, it will make you stronger.*' What happened to your father didn't kill you, Gwen. You can use it to grow stronger, turn yourself into a person he would be proud of."

"Yeah. I guess you're right." Gwen pulled out her cell phone and checked the time. "I have to get going. Ellanor flew back to Arizona last night in order to deal with the arrangements for the autopsy, but she's due back shortly, and I told her I'd meet her flight at the airport, tell her about the arraignment."

"Give her my regards. Good-bye, Gwen."

"Good-bye." Then, with a fierce smile, "See you at the trial, Detective."

"See you then." As Gwen hurried off toward the exit, Ty strolled up beside her.

"All finished?"

"Yeah. You get mobbed by reporters outside?"

"Oh, I had to dodge a few of them, but it was no big deal." Taking her arm, he said, "C'mon, let's get out of here."

On their way to the exit, she asked, "How's Lee?"

"Fine, fine. We've got her all settled in, and Mom and Dad are taking good care of her."

"What about Aunt Mattie and Uncle Pete?"

"On their way. We should make it back just about the same time they're due to arrive."

She reached down and linked her hand with his in a rare public display of affection. He was surprised, but said nothing. Still holding onto his hand, Dawn walked with Ty out to the waiting limo. As she'd told the lieutenant, she and her sister had sixteen years worth of catching up to do.

Chapter 14

Ty swung himself out of the pool, shook the water off, grabbed a towel, and dried off. Slinging the towel around his neck, he walked up the stairs to the balcony at the far end of the pool house and joined his father, who was standing at the railing that overlooked the pool deck. Looking down, he regarded the scene appreciatively. His mother had designed the pool area years previously, and she had outdone herself on it. The pool was shaped like a large figure eight and bisected in the middle by a bridge in the shape of a skewed polyomino. It was kept fresh by the constant inflow of water from the waterfall at the far end of the pool. Strategically placed around it were pink and white hibiscus, as well as aeonium rosettes in blue, green, pink, and purple. Cape primroses also bloomed there, along with aloe, agave, and yucca amid a riot of ferns – Boston and maidenhair, lemon button and staghorn. Since it was cold outside, the retractable roof of the pool house was closed, but plenty of light shone in from the windows all around.

Below, still in the pool, Dawn and Lee were hanging onto the edge of the pool, talking to Maeve, who was seated on a chair close by. Not far away, Lotti and Rafe were talking and laughing, all the while keeping an eye on Echo, who was splashing in a baby pool that had been set up for her on the side of the pool deck. On a reclining deck chair, Will Prcisinger was talking with Brody, who was standing with his back against the wall, supported by his crutches. Brody had been fortunate enough to come through his surgery the previous Thursday without any complications and had been released from the hospital on Saturday, the same day that Will had finally been pronounced recovered enough to leave the hospital.

That had been yesterday. Now they were all gathered together, at Maeve's insistence, having a belated birthday celebration for Dawn. Aunt Mattie and Uncle Pete had left shortly after Dawn had cut the cake and opened her presents earlier in the day, but the rest of them had adjourned to the pool house to continue the party.

As Ty watched, Dawn and Lee emerged from the pool together, Dawn clad in a two-piece electric blue bathing suit and Lee in a white bikini. Lee went over to talk with Will, but Dawn, after exchanging a few words with Maeve and wrapping a sarong around her waist, strolled up the stairs to join Ty and Sloan.

With one accord, they made their way to the bar at the far end of the balcony, where Sloan immediately began assembling the ingredients for a pitcher of martinis. Soon they were all seated at the big round table in the bar, sipping at their drinks. Maeve, now wearing a cover-up over her swim suit, presently came up to join them. Seeing her shiver a little, Sloan said, "You cold? I could get a fire going, if you like."

"Oh, a fire would be lovely," Maeve replied.

As Sloan worked on getting the fire started in the fireplace, Maeve looked at the pitcher of martinis and wrinkled her nose.

Sloan noticed her expression and grinned. "Still don't like martinis, huh?"

"No, and I don't think that I'll ever acquire a taste for them. Make me something a little less medicinal, would you, Sloan? You know what I like."

"Right. One Tequila Sunrise, coming right up."

Seeing how comfortably they were interacting with each other, Dawn reflected on what a change the last week had made in their relationship. When she and Ty had first gotten together, his parents had spoken to each other only when necessary, and with a sort of chilly politeness. Now, you'd never even guess that they were divorced.

Another sign of the healing in their relationship had occurred at the luncheon, when Dawn had opened one of her presents and found a ruby ring and bracelet inside that matched the necklace and earrings that Ty had given her. The card attached to the present had read, *'To Dawn, with love from Maeve and Sloan.'* They had never gone together on a present for her before. So there was plenty of food for thought there. She wondered what the future held for Sloan and Maeve Lewellen.

Rafe came up the steps and joined them just then. Glancing down at the pool area and noticing the empty baby pool, Sloan said, "Where did Lotti and Echo go?"

"Echo decided she'd had enough, so Lotti took her in to give her a bath and change her. She said that they'll be back in a few minutes."

After he'd had time to take a few sips of the martini that Sloan had poured for him, Dawn asked Rafe, "What were you and Lotti talking about? You seemed to be having a good laugh."

Rafe shrugged his shoulders and replied, "We discovered that we both spent some time in Catholic schools. We were comparing experiences and trading war stories. Then she asked me about the class I taught last summer – the self-defense class for women. Apparently, Sloan mentioned it to her. She's thinking of signing up for the next one I teach."

"Sounds like a good idea," Dawn commented. She was about to draw some more details out of him, but her attention was distracted by the arrival of Lee, who'd come up to obtain refreshments for Brody and Will so that they wouldn't have to negotiate the steps. After she'd delivered a martini to Brody and a soft drink to Will, Lee climbed back up the steps and leaned against the railing, laughing and talking to the two of them. Presently, Lotti returned with Echo, who was now clad in a pair of jean overalls with a matching red plaid skirt. As soon as she saw Maeve, Echo started squirming in Lotti's arms, stretching her arms out toward Maeve, who reached up and took her from Lotti, settling the baby on her lap. Echo curled up contentedly and amused herself by sucking on a set of plastic rings that Lotti had brought with her.

Looking at the two of them, Dawn thought about mothers. She watched as Maeve chatted with Ty, saw the love and pride in her eyes as she gazed at her son, all the while tenderly holding another child – this one not her own. She thought of Vivian Zarafin, whose obsessive desire to be a mother had led her to resort to kidnapping, and of Monieque Torrcnse, who had first idolized but then ultimately destroyed her own son. And finally she nudged open another inch the door in her mind behind which the memories of her own mother dwelt – memories too long closed off.

A pat on her knee drew her out of her introspection. Echo had escaped from the protective circle of Maeve's arms and toddled over to Dawn, arms raised in the universal baby signal for "up".

Dawn looked down at Echo, then over at Lee, remembering another tow-haired child, once lost, but now restored to her, vibrant and alive and happy. And then, just as if she had done it a thousand times before, she reached down, secured a firm grip on the baby, and swung her high up into the air.

The End

www.ingramcontent.com/pod-product-compliance
Lightning Source LLC
Chambersburg PA
CBHW031949240626
47153CB00003B/922